RAID OF THE

WOLVES

DONOVAN COOK

First paperback edition November 2021

Cover design by Rafael Andres

ISBN 978-1-8383008-2-1 (paperback)
ISBN 978-1-8383008-3-8 (eBook)

www.donovancook.net

For my Grandparents

CONTENTS

CHAPTER 1

"Odin, please don't let them get me," Halvard pleaded as he hid behind the old oak tree, gasping for air. "I should have listened to my wife. Why didn't I listen to her?" He fought the urge to peek around the tree, afraid they might see him. "But he promised so much plunder and fame. How could I say no to that?"

A twig snapped behind him, the sound of it echoing around the trees. Halvard held his breath. They were closer than he realised. He thought he had lost them, but they had found his scent again. "Please, Odin, I beg you. Don't let them get me," he whispered. Halvard had to move. He had to run, otherwise, he would never get away from them. But he had been running for so long already and could not shake them. They were unrelenting. A pack of hungry wolves unwilling to give up the chase. Halvard sensed the movement nearby, heard the soft growl on the breeze. He pushed himself off the tree and ran as fast as his legs would take him. Halvard heard them calling to each other as they gave chase. "Thor, protect me." He tried a different god. Perhaps the god of thunder would listen to him. They were getting closer. Halvard felt them snapping at his heels as he pushed himself through the forest, the low-lying branches slapping his face. He tried not to look over his shoulder, knowing it would do him no good. In the end, he could not resist the urge any longer. He needed to know how close they were. Halvard glanced back and saw his pursuers hot on his heels, but did not see the root sticking out of the ground. Pain shot through his jarred shoulder as Halvard landed hard on the forest floor. Before he could get up, the leader of the pack jumped on his back. Halvard wanted to send another prayer to the gods as the pack leader growled in his ear, but knew there was no point. The gods had abandoned him.

"Nowhere left to run," a deep voice growled. Strong hands lifted him up and threw him against a tree. Halvard winced at the pain in his shoulder as he saw his pursuers clearly for the first time. There were seven of them, all wearing brynjas and with weapons at their sides. All of them ready to kill him.

Standing in front of him was a tall man with broad shoulders, his light-coloured hair tied up in a knot behind his head. His beard, the same colour as his hair, had a long thick braid in the middle. His arms were covered in golden rings and a fine-looking sword sat on his hip. On either side of him stood two warriors who were complete opposites. One short enough to be a dwarf, the other tall enough to be a giant. The dwarf had a squat frame with thick limbs and a neck wider than his head. The sides of his head were shaved and covered in tattoos. A thick bushy beard and moustache sat under a large round nose surrounded by many scars. Even in the shade of the trees, Halvard saw the violence in his eyes. The giant had a slim, muscular frame with long, sinewy arms, his long hair the colour of watered-down blood. Like their leader, both men's arms were covered in arm rings.

"Just keep Ulf away from this one. They die too fast when he talks to them." The short man nodded to his right. Halvard looked at the young warrior glaring at him while panting like a caged beast. His long light-coloured hair was tied behind his head, revealing three scar lines which ran down the right side of his face, from his eye to his mouth. Halvard wondered what had caused those scars.

"If they told me what I wanted to know, then they wouldn't die so fast," the young warrior responded, his soft voice laced with hatred.

"If you gave them a chance, then perhaps they would tell you something," another shot back, sneering at the scarred warrior. The two men faced each other, the tension between them silencing the surrounding forest. Halvard thought of trying to slip away while their attention was not on him, but then he spotted the tall warrior smiling at him. He let go of the breath he was holding as his shoulders sagged.

The leader of the group knelt down and looked Halvard in the eyes. "I will not lie to you, you will die today." Halvard's face dropped, but the warrior held up a finger as if there was still some good news for him, smiling as he did so. "But you get to choose how you die—like a coward or like a man."

Halvard opened his mouth to speak, but no words came out. He did not know how to respond.

"Perhaps he can't speak," one of the pack said. This one was the second tallest of them, but unlike the tall slim warrior, he was round. Halvard wondered how he had kept up with the rest of them. The fat warrior gave an apologetic glance towards the young warrior with the scarred face.

"No, he can talk. You could hear him praying to Odin when he thought he had escaped us," another said. This one was the same height and weight of most men who spent years fighting in the shield wall and had the same face as the fat one.

"Odin must be busy then, or not care about this worm," the dwarf responded cruelly. The leader was still kneeling in front of him, his grey eyes never leaving Halvard's.

"So, what's it going to be?"

"We are wasting our time with this!" The young warrior pulled his sax-knife from his belt and stomped towards Halvard, the snarl on his face sending a shiver down Halvard's spine.

Their leader held a hand up to stop him, but he was now close enough for Halvard to see his eyes. As dangerous as a deadly sea storm, there was only death in them. They were grey like that of their leader, only his was more like grey of a sword blade, whereas their leader had a darker grey. The young warrior's face twisted in a scowl, the scars on the side making Halvard feel a fear he had never felt before.

"I can only hold him back so long. He is keen to find your *king*," their leader said to him, his voice calm.

"M… my king?"

"Griml," the young warrior sneered the name.

Halvard's eyes darted to the other warriors in the group. They were all watching him. "He is not my king."

"You fought for him, no?" Their leader scratched below his ear.

"Yes, but I only wanted to go on the raid. I did not want to fight in that battle."

"But you still did."

"Enough of this! Where is Griml?" the young warrior shouted in frustration. He made to take a step towards Halvard, but again, their leader held a hand up to stop him.

"My friend here wants to find Griml, so do I, as a matter of fact." The leader's face darkened as if he just remembered something.

"Why? You won the battle. He has no army left," Halvard protested, not understanding why these men had been hunting him.

"Because he took everything from me!" the scarred warrior screamed, charging at Halvard. This time, their leader did nothing to stop him. The young warrior grabbed Halvard by his tunic, almost lifting him off the ground. His red face contorted, making the scars look even worse, but it was his eyes that made Halvard wince. Before the knife got near Halvard's throat, two of the warrior's companions grabbed him and dragged him away. The young warrior struggled as he tried to free himself from their grip, hissing and spitting at Halvard.

"The boy your leader sacrificed before the battle was like a brother to him," their leader explained. "So you can understand why he is a bit angry."

A bit? Halvard thought. "You've been hunting me and my friends for days because of a mute?" Halvard was confused by this.

Their leader did not answer, but a dangerous wolf grin replaced the smile on his face. "Where is he?" His tone now matching his face.

"I... I don't know?" The others took a step closer, while the scarred warrior was pacing behind them. The surrounding trees were quiet, as if all life had fled the impending danger. "I… I heard he went north." Halvard suddenly wanted to help them.

"North?" the tallest warrior asked. "Not towards his ships?"

"Probably had no one to crew them," the fat one suggested.

Their leader thought for a while. "There was another with him, the one who brought him the young boy?"

"Why do you want to know about him?"

"He is—" the dwarf started, but stopped when their leader glared at him.

Halvard remembered the young boy who had walked into their camp, looking all smug as he led the mute before him at sword point. "T… they split up after the battle."

"Split up? Why?" their leader growled.

"I… I don't know. Ove told me they argued and then Griml pushed the boy away."

"Who is Ove?"

"He is my wife's brother, a small man with a shaved head."

"Was." The dwarf smiled. Halvard's shoulders sagged.

"Did this Ove tell you which way this boy went?" Their leader leaned in closer, his wolf eyes searching inside Halvard's head for the answer.

Halvard shook his head, trying to push himself away from those eyes, but the tree behind him would not budge. Their leader stared at him for a few heartbeats before he seemed satisfied.

"Well, Odin knows I'm a man of my word. You answered our questions–"

"You believe him?" the young warrior asked before he could finish.

"I do." The look on his face showed he was not going to argue over it.

"So now what?" the one who didn't like the young warrior asked.

"Well, he answered our questions, so he gets to die like a man, like I promised." Their leader smiled.

Halvard had to choke down the tears which threatened to erupt after hearing that. He had hoped that by answering the questions, they might let him live.

"You invaded my father's land. Burnt our farms and killed our people. You really think I was just going to let you go?" Their leader read Halvard's mind. "But I can give you a chance. I think that is only fair after your co-operation." He smiled when the light appeared in Halvard's eyes.

"Just kill him and finish this, Snorri. It's getting late," the fat one complained, rubbing his stomach.

But his leader raised a hand and responded, "No, Drumbr, he answered our questions. I'm a man of my word. He gets to die like a man, but he also has a chance to live."

Halvard saw the smiles on the faces of the men around him and knew what was going to happen now. It was something that he had done before himself and knew the odds were against him. But it still gave him a chance. He just hoped the Norns gave him that chance. "I have to fight one of you."

Snorri nodded with a wolf grin on his face.

"Who am I fighting?" Halvard got to his feet. No one made a move to stop him. He tested his shoulder. It still hurt, but he didn't think it would hinder him.

"You get to choose which one of us you want to fight," Snorri said, his hands on his waist.

"I have no weapon or shield." Halvard looked at the warriors in front of him. They all had shields on their backs and Halvard was surprised they had kept up with him for days, running with all that extra weight on them. But most notable of all was the fact that they were all experienced fighters. He knew from the arm rings they wore, the scars on their arms and faces, even from their confident looks. Halvard tried not to let that bother him. He was an experienced warrior himself and had fought in many battles in his life. He should have been confident. But he wasn't.

"You can use this one." The fat warrior threw him a sword he had been carrying on his back.

Halvard caught the sword and recognised it. It had belonged to one man from his village who had travelled with him. It meant another wife who would never see her husband again.

"You can use my shield." The one who looked like the fat warrior rolled the shield towards Halvard, who nodded his thanks.

"So, which one is it going to be?" their leader asked. He took a step back, so he was in line with his men, making them all look like thralls lined up in a market square.

Halvard studied them all, trying to find the opponent he had the best chance of beating. He wasn't going to fight the fat one. One misstep and he would be carved in half by the enormous axe on his back. Their leader looked too dangerous, and he had heard what the scarred warrior had done in the battle. If he could cut his way through a group of men so easily, then Halvard would never stand a chance against him. The tallest one had a long reach, leaving Halvard at a disadvantage. The other two were not as tall as their leader and the scarred warrior, but both were taller than Halvard. That left the short one. Halvard studied him carefully. He was short and stocky, like a barrel of ale. Like the others, he was an experienced fighter, but Halvard felt like he would have the advantage of reach. All Halvard had to do was stop him from getting too close. That was how he could defeat the short warrior and, gods willing, make it back to his wife alive. "I'll fight the short one."

"He called you short," the one who didn't like the young warrior said, an amused smile on his face.

"At least he didn't call me a dwarf," the short one responded, stepping forward.

"He is thinking it, though. You can see it in his eyes," the tall one said.

"Aye, they all think it." The small one smiled a dangerous smile.

"Take off your brynja, Thorbjorn. Let's make the fight fair," Snorri, their leader, said.

The dwarf looked like he was about to argue, but then shrugged and took off his belt. He handed it to one of his companions and took off his brynja.

Halvard's jaw dropped. He would never have done that. He would want all the advantages he could have. Looking at their leader again, Halvard asked, "If I defeat your man, you swear you will let me live?"

Snorri smiled, while the others laughed. The young warrior only glared at him. "If you defeat Thorbjorn, then as Odin is my witness, I will let you live."

Halvard did not like the way Snorri said that, but there was nothing he could do about it. If he refused to fight, they would just kill him. He shrugged and picked up the shield, finding comfort in its weight.

The short one, Thorbjorn, stepped forward, having taken off his brynja and now, like Halvard, only wore a sweat-stained tunic to protect his body.

The forest suddenly came alive with the sounds of birds screaming from the trees, like hungry spectators, as the two men circled each other, both crouched behind their shields. A large raven landed on a branch above them, announcing itself with a loud cry. Odin was watching.

Halvard attacked, not wanting to give the short warrior a chance to settle. He stabbed high with his sword, hoping to force Thorbjorn behind his shield. It was an old trick his father had taught him. Thorbjorn fell for it and lifted his shield to block the strike. Halvard kicked the shield a moment after his sword struck, hoping to send the dwarf flying onto his back so he could stab him in the chest. But that didn't happen. Instead, Thorbjorn squatted behind his shield and used his stocky frame to absorb the kick. Halvard bounced back and could do nothing as Thorbjorn shoved him, but fall onto his back. Instinctively, he raised his shield to his chest, but no attack came.

Halvard opened his eyes and saw the short warrior standing there, smiling at him. He got back to his feet and attacked again, this time slicing at Thorbjorn's stomach. The short warrior jumped back and stabbed with his own sword. Halvard just brought his shield up to block the blow. He took a step back. Rushing at the short warrior was not doing him any good. He had to think of something else. Halvard glanced at the raven, its beady stare seeming to mock him. Gritting his teeth, Halvard attacked again. He stabbed at Thorbjorn's chest, but the short warrior twisted out of the way, at the same time cutting at Halvard's leg. The warrior's companions cheered, but Halvard felt no pain. He thought the cut had missed until he felt the warm liquid running down his leg. Thorbjorn smiled at him, which frustrated Halvard even more. He glanced at the other men, wondering if he had made a mistake by choosing to fight the short warrior. Suddenly, all of them seemed unbeatable. Backing off, Halvard hid behind his shield as he thought about running again. He dismissed the thought as his leg stung. The cut would not let him get far, and at least this way, he could still get into Valhalla.

"What are you waiting for? Ragnarök?" Thorbjorn taunted him. "Come, I'll make this easy for you." Thorbjorn threw his shield to one side. Now he only had his sword. None of his companions said anything, the only reaction being the eye roll from their leader.

Halvard looked at the raven sitting on the branch above them. It had gone quiet now as it watched and waited. Its beady eyes locked on him. *Die like a coward or die like a man.* No one had ever called Halvard a coward before. He roared as he attacked, but Thorbjorn dodged the blow and Halvard received a shallow cut in his side for his effort. He tried not to think about it as he turned on his heels with a backhanded slice, which Thorbjorn ducked underneath and gave Halvard another shallow cut on his leg. Halvard stabbed, aiming at Thorbjorn's chest, but Thorbjorn deflected the blow as Halvard hoped he would. He immediately punched his shield, catching Thorbjorn on the shoulder and sending him falling backwards. Before Halvard could take advantage of this, Thorbjorn quickly rolled back to his feet.

"Not bad." He smiled an unworried smile as he shook the life back into his arm.

Halvard was getting angry now. He felt humiliated by this dwarfish man who was just taunting him. Mocking him in front of the gods. Halvard glanced at the raven, briefly wondering what Odin must be thinking about this fight. He screamed as he charged again, pulling his arm back for a swing which would take Thorbjorn's head off if it landed. But it never did. Thorbjorn spread his legs wide and ducked under the swing, at the same time shifting to his left. The momentum of Halvard's swing took him further than he wanted to be and before he could do anything about it, Thorbjorn rammed his sword into his side. Halvard grunted as the blade grated on his ribs before slipping into his chest, the pain freezing him in place.

"Hold onto your sword," Thorbjorn said as he pulled his out, his voice gentle.

Halvard collapsed, gripping his sword tightly as the world around him went dark. The last thing he heard was Thorbjorn.

"One day we'll share a drink in Valhalla."

"You took your time." Snorri watched Thorbjorn clean the blood from Bloodthirst, his sword.

"Had to make the most of it. Ulf usually kills them before we can get this far." Thorbjorn sheathed Bloodthirst, smiling at Ulf. But Ulf wasn't listening. Instead, he watched as the raven flew away.

"Really beginning to hate those birds," Brak said as his brother collected the sword Halvard had used.

"Aye, one of them seems to be following Ulf around," Oddi, the tall warrior, responded while swatting a fly away.

"Mother says that Odin is watching Ulf, that's why one of his ravens is always following him." Snorri was also watching the raven now.

"She would know," Thorbjorn said.

"So we know nothing new," Ulf finally said after the raven disappeared from view. The others laughed, realising Ulf had not heard what they had said. "What?"

"Nothing," Snorri said. It felt good to laugh after the weeks they've had.

"Ulf's right, though. He told us the same as the others, Griml went somewhere north, alone." Asbjorn glanced at Ulf, the same way he always did when he mentioned Griml's name. Ulf knew there was an accusation in there somewhere. There always was. *Makes a change from him blaming me for the deaths of my family.*

He turned his attention to Snorri now, who had gone serious as he stared at the body of Halvard. Other ravens had arrived and were hopping from one branch to the next while screaming at Snorri.

"Griml is from the north, or at least that's what the skald, Gudrun, told us," Oddi said after realising that Snorri wasn't going to respond.

"That's if you believe his tale." Thorbjorn pulled his brynja over his head, flinching as a beard hair got trapped in one of the rings.

"It's not hard to believe that a man who happily sacrificed Vidar just to anger Ulf would kill his jarl and slaughter the entire village."

"All over a bloody woman, more trouble than they are worth." Thorbjorn spat to the side to emphasise his point.

"You think he's gone back there?" Brak Drumbr, the brother of Brak, asked. Drumbr meant large, a nickname he got because of his size. Both men were named after their father and his father before him.

"No," Snorri shook his head slowly, "from what Gudrun told us, all the jarls in the north want him dead and their king has banished him for life."

"Then why go north?" Ulf asked.

"Only the Norns know that." That was Snorri's response when he didn't know something and wanted to end that conversation. "Where are we?" Most of them shrugged. They had lost track running down the remnants of Griml's army.

Oddi looked around, stroking his beard. "I think we are in the lands of Jarl Arnfinni,"

Thorbjorn sucked in his breath, "And he would be very upset if we killed people on his land without stopping by his hall and explaining ourselves."

"I'd rather face an ice giant than go to his hall, but Thorbjorn is right. And besides, with the state Thorgilsstad is in now, we can't afford to upset the second most powerful jarl in Vestfold," Snorri responded, his face dark.

"Who is Jarl Arnfinni?" Ulf saw the sneer on Snorri's face.

"You'll see." Drumbr patted him on the shoulder as they walked off.

"How is your father?" Jarl Arnfinni stared at them down the length of his nose from his seat. The jarl took a drink from his drinking horn, richly decorated with a gold rim and legs made to look like dragon heads. They had not received a warm welcome from the jarl when they arrived late in the afternoon. But the jarl respected the laws of hospitality and had invited them into his hall for a meagre meal and poor ale. From the way the jarl smacked his lips after his drink, and the mischievous grin on his face, it was easy to guess that what he was drinking was a lot better than what they had.

Inside the hall, the air was dank and smelt of rushes that had not been cleaned out for a long time. The fire in the hearth had been given only enough wood to provide some light, but not to do much else. Ulf scanned the hall, taking in the weapons and shields which hung on the walls. Most of them looked older than Ulf and all of them covered in dust. The shield which hung above the jarl caught Ulf's eye. Painted on it was a black, snarling wolf, the symbol of Thorgilsstad. Only half the benches were filled, mostly by grey beards and bald heads, but what surprised Ulf the most was that there were no women in the hall.

"My father is fine. He sends his regards," Snorri responded, his voice cut like mid-winter ice on exposed skin.

Jarl Arnfinni raised an eyebrow as he licked the grease off his ring-covered fingers. Unlike the thin vegetable stew they were given, the jarl was enjoying some slices of meat. "Does he now?"

Snorri did not respond. Ulf's hand moved to where his sword would have been — surprised at how naked he felt without Ormstunga by his side. The sword had belonged to his family for generations, and Ulf only recently got her back after Griml took her. She had a golden hilt with a half circle pommel, with an image of Jörmungandr circling the valknut. The dark red wooden grip led to a thick golden crossguard decorated with two intertwining serpents. On her blade, the sword's name engraved in runes, with serpents on either side. All of it a testament to her origins. According to legend, Tyr had the sword made from a piece of Jörmungandr's tongue which Ulf's ancestor had sliced off. The sword had come from a dark place which meant it was bad luck to draw her blade in direct sunlight. A message engraved on the serpents on the crossguard warned her wielder of this.

"I heard about the battle at The Giant's Toe. They say you won a glorious victory for your father," the jarl continued when he saw Snorri wasn't going to respond.

"It was my father's victory, he was there as well." Snorri glanced at Ulf, the look saying more than words could.

"In body, yes, but they said that when the time came to charge, your father froze like a spring in the middle of winter. You had to call the charge after one of your men stormed their army on his own. Possessed by Tyr, so they say." Arnfinni ran his eyes over Snorri's men, trying to work out who it could have been.

The hall went silent at that moment, so silent Ulf heard the snapping sound of the wood as it was being devoured by the flames in the hearth and the grinding of Snorri's teeth. Snorri's hirdmen looked like they were about to erupt from their seats, but a signal from Snorri kept them in place.

"You were not there, Jarl Arnfinni," Snorri said through grit teeth. "It was an unusual situation." Snorri gripped the bench he was sitting on, his knuckles white, like he was trying to keep himself in place.

Jarl Arnfinni smiled an unfriendly smile. "So I've been told. Odin knows what I would do if my blood betrayed me like that." The jarl enjoyed getting under Snorri's skin. "Speaking of which, how is my daughter?"

"Daughter?" Ulf said out loud, the sudden change in conversation catching him off guard. Snorri glanced at him.

"Jarl Arnfinni is Gunnhildr's father." Oddi whispered to him. Ulf studied the jarl's face for the first time. Not easy in the dark light of the hall. He saw the pudgy face, his shaved head and long red beard, and a pig-like nose. Ulf was surprised he had not seen it before.

"Your daughter is doing well, jarl."

"Can't even say her name, can you?" the jarl sneered at Snorri. The hall was silent again. Ulf realised that nobody was eating or drinking, as all eyes were on the exchange between the jarl and Snorri.

"So Jarl Arnfinni is an ally of Jarl Thorgils?" Ulf kept his voice low in the silence.

"Aye," Thorbjorn grimaced as he took a sip from his ale. "Thor bugger me, but I'm sure his men pissed in this ale."

Oddi smiled at Thorbjorn before explaining to Ulf, "They are now, but that wasn't always so. Thorgils and Arnfinni loved raiding each other's lands, constantly trying to outdo each other. But King Halfdan was not happy about it. They were, and still are, his two most powerful jarls and he needed them to unite instead of fighting each other. As luck would have it, Arnfinni had an unmarried daughter—"

"Odin only knows who would want to marry that pig-faced bitch," Thorbjorn interrupted.

"—who was a few years younger than Snorri." Oddi ignored Thorbjorn. "Neither jarl was happy about it, but they couldn't go against the king."

"But Arnfinni still seems really upset by this." Ulf looked at the jarl, who was sitting in his decorated seat. He was now talking to one of his men, occasionally glancing at Snorri. Ulf did not like the look of the jarl.

"He's just jealous because Thorgils gained more from it," Thorbjorn responded, looking at his ale and trying to work out if he really wanted another drink. The only person not bothered by the poor ale was Drumbr, who was happily guzzling it down.

Oddi saw the confused look on Ulf's face. "Thorgils' raiding has been more successful than Arnfinni's. Most of Arnfinni's wealth had come from raiding Thorgils' land, and when the king stopped that, he lost out. He is also unhappy with the fact that Snorri's first-born son was named after Thorgils and not him."

"And he knows my father is weak at the moment and is probably working out how to take advantage of that." Ulf had not noticed that Snorri had been listening to their conversation.

Jarl Arnfinni attracted their attention with a loud burp, and the smile on his face showed he was going to enjoy what was about to happen. "Thorvald passed through here, not so long ago."

Snorri had to restrain himself from jumping to his feet, and Ulf saw the bulging neck muscles. "What did the shit want?" Snorri growled. Ulf eyed the men around the hall. They were enjoying this, and a few seemed to hope that Snorri would attack their jarl. Perhaps that was the plan. Snorri was well known for being as easy to provoke as a beehive.

"Come now, Snorri. That's not a nice thing to say." The jarl smiled with a shrug. Ulf saw him wink at an old warrior sat next to him.

"He betrayed my father." Snorri was panting, his face as red as the flames in the hearth.

The jarl saw this and smiled. "Yes, it can't have been easy for your father." Snorri bared his teeth, but otherwise did not respond to this. "You lost a lot of men in that battle, did you not?"

"Thorgilsstad still has enough men to defend her, Jarl Arnfinni." Oddi answered the question before Snorri could say something dangerous.

"Ah, if it isn't the son of Jarl Amund." Arnfinni looked at Oddi like he had just seen him for the first time. The tension in the hall was as thick as the smoke from the fire. "I didn't see you there in the shadow of your cousin."

"Most men in Norway would disappear in my cousin's shadow," Oddi responded with a smile. If the remark offended him, he did not show it, but Ulf knew that Snorri and Oddi were as close as brothers.

"Perhaps that was the problem with Thorvald. Perhaps he was tired of being in Snorri's shadow and sought a way to get out of it."

Snorri shot to his feet, unable to hold himself any longer. He leaned forward, resting his knuckles on the table. "You don't come to my father's aid when he requests it, and then you give shelter to that treacherous worm. Loki has shown more loyalty to the gods than what you have shown to my father!"

The jarl smiled as he signalled for his men to calm down. They did not like the way Snorri spoke to their jarl. Again, Ulf glanced at the door, where their weapons were stored. "First, that battle had nothing to do with me, so why would I send my men? Second, as Odin is my witness, I did not know that Thorvald had betrayed your father. Not when he arrived anyway." Arnfinni smiled. It felt like he was goading Snorri, and Ulf struggled to understand why. "But come now, sit down and let us enjoy the rest of the night."

Snorri took a deep breath and sat down. "Do not drink another drop of this piss," he said under his breath. He also gave a signal to the Brak brothers, which Ulf did not understand.

They passed the rest of the night in grim silence. The jarl had decided there was no more to gain from provoking Snorri and spent the rest of the evening talking to those around him and drinking. Ulf lost himself in his thoughts and did not notice when the Brak brothers left the hall.

"Where are the brothers?" Ulf asked when he saw they were not there anymore.

"You'll find out soon enough," Oddi said to him, his face giving nothing away.

A while later, Ulf was woken up by a gentle hand on his shoulder. He had not realised that he had fallen asleep and felt sheepish. All around him, Arnfinni and his men were snoring, some of them still sat on their benches.

"Come," Snorri whispered to him. Only then did Ulf see that none of the others were in the hall. He followed Snorri as they crept out.

The others were waiting for them outside the hall. Brak handed Ulf his weapons, Ormstunga and Olaf's axe. It had belonged to his uncle Olaf, who had been killed by Griml. Ulf stroked the names of his family he had carved onto the haft. He always felt comforted by this, as if their spirits were imbued in the axe. It also reminded him of the oath he had made to Odin the summer before.

"Is it done?" Snorri asked Asbjorn, who arrived from the back of the hall.

Asbjorn nodded. "They won't be getting out that way."

"Good, now this door. And quietly." Snorri pointed to the main entrance of the hall. Ulf saw the bodies of the men who guarded it heaped to one side. The work of the brothers, he guessed.

"You sure this is a good idea?" he asked Snorri, finally understanding what was about to happen when he saw Oddi and Drumbr return with enough torches for everyone.

"Not really." Snorri smiled his wolf smile. "But Arnfinni is planning on attacking Thorgilsstad. Odin knows I can't let that happen."

"For once I agree with Ulf," Thorbjorn said, surprising everyone. "You know Halfdan will not be happy if you kill one of his favourite jarls."

"Relax, he won't know it was us." Snorri smiled and patted Thorbjorn on the shoulder. "Now let's get this done." He took two torches from Drumbr and handed one to Ulf.

The main door of the hall was barred shut, and the men spread themselves around the hall. At Snorri's signal, they threw the torches onto the roof. Ulf watched as his torch arched through the air and landed on the dry thatch. It was early spring and there had been no rain for a few weeks now. The fire caught quickly and raced along the roof; the flames leaping into the air almost as if in joy. Oddi and the brothers ran to the back door to make sure no one escaped from there, while the rest of them stood in front of the main door, weapons ready. Ulf looked around the village, taking in the few ill-maintained longhouses.

"Why is no one stopping us?"

Snorri glanced at the houses, unconcerned. "Most of them are empty or filled with old women. Arnfinni can't afford to feed all his men, so he sends them away when he doesn't need them."

Soon, the entire roof was aflame, and the fire started spreading to the dry timber post of the walls. Ulf stood there, mesmerised by the flames as his mind drifted back to the funeral of Hulda, the thrall he had been sleeping with and who had been killed by Thorvald. He heard the song sung by Lady Ingibjorg, Snorri's mother, but knew there was no one around him singing it. The powerful notes of the song sent a shiver down his spine, which he could not hide.

"Beautiful, isn't it," Snorri said. Ulf could only nod. "Like a giant offering to the gods."

The roar of the fire, like that of a giant beast, almost drowned out the screaming from inside the hall as someone started banging on the door.

"Well, they're awake now," Thorbjorn commented. "Guess they'll think twice before insulting you and your father again."

Asbjorn smiled at the comment, but the others just watched the hall burning in grim fascination. The screaming inside was getting louder now, and the banging on the door more frantic. Ulf guessed the flames had spread to the inside of the hall. The heat was so intense that it forced all of them to take a step back. They shielded themselves with their weapons as if they were facing Surtr, the fiery giant from Muspelheim. Ulf thought he heard the gods laughing in the roar of the flames and wondered what they would think of this.

The gods love chaos, Ingibjorg's voice whispered in his ears.

The entire hall was on fire, the flames greedily eating through the wood and thatch as the screams inside changed. Sweat stung Ulf's eyes, and when he glanced at his friends, he saw Thorbjorn wiping his face with his hand. But none of them moved further away and so Ulf remained where he was. There was a loud groaning noise as the roof collapsed inward, and the screaming stopped. The only sound now were the flames as they consumed the remains of the hall. All eyes were on Snorri as he stared at what was now nothing more than a huge funeral pit. The brothers and Oddi returned from the back of the hall, the three of them wearing big smiles on their sweat-drenched faces. Snorri sheathed his sword, satisfied that no one had survived. He spat in the hall's direction before turning around and walking away.

CHAPTER 2

The raven flew ahead of them as they walked into Thorgilsstad, guiding them home after their journey. Its cry rang out as it landed on the roof of the hall, telling the people of Thorgilsstad that the son of their jarl had returned.

"You'd think we lost the battle," Thorbjorn commented, shielding his eyes from the glare of the sun. It was early spring and even though the warm weather had chased the cold of the winter away, it could not do the same for Ulf as he walked with his friends, barely uttering a word — his gaze fixed on the floor and shoulders slumped. They had spent the months after the battle at The Giant's Toe chasing down the remnants of Griml's army, those who stayed to prey on the bændr. For Snorri and his hirdmen, it wasn't just about protecting the farms. They were hunting for Griml. A man the size of a mountain who had disappeared and no matter how many they had questioned, no one knew where he had gone. Not even Jól had given them time to relax. Ulf was tired and frustrated, but he wanted to find

Griml, so he had endured the cold winter months and the many nights sleeping in the open.

"Aye, we might have won, but the cost was more than this village was prepared to pay," Oddi responded, with a quick glance towards Snorri. "Especially the jarl." Snorri's only response was his curled lip.

"Not just the jarl." Drumbr glanced at Ulf.

"He feels like he is to blame for what happened," Oddi said.

"He is," Asbjorn sneered, glaring at Ulf's back and ignoring the stares from his friends.

Ulf wasn't paying attention to them as he walked ahead of his friends; he just wanted to lie down and do nothing. Ulf didn't care what Asbjorn thought, only about the death of his friend and the pain he had brought to this village. Looking up as they approached the hall, he saw the raven staring at him, its mouth half open as if it wanted to say something to him. "Why are you still here? Hasn't Odin had enough chaos yet?"

"You think all this is because of Odin?" Ulf heard the child-like voice, almost dropping his shield as he thought the raven had answered him, but then realised it was Snorri's eldest, standing behind him.

"Hello, Thorgils." The boy had his mother's nose, which reminded Ulf of Jarl Arnfinni and the burning hall. Ulf shivered as he remembered the screams and wondered if he would ever forget that noise.

"Are you back for good, or will you leave again soon, like last time?" Thorgils asked, staring at Ulf, his eyes wide as always. Especially after Snorri had told the boy of how Ulf had killed a giant bear and saved his father's life. The only truth in that story was that Ulf had killed a bear. The rest was Snorri embellishing the tale.

"I think we'll be here a while, but it's not for us to decide," Ulf responded, glancing at the raven. It was still sitting on top of the hall, its head tilted to the side, listening to the conversation. *Probably so it can report it back to Odin.*

Young Thorgils looked at Ulf for a while, as if considering his words. Finally, he said, "My father always says that we do not control our own fate, but the Norns do. They are the ones who decide what our destiny will be." The boy frowned, trying to understand the words he had just spoken.

"Yes, he does." Ulf looked at Snorri, who was watching their conversation. His customary cheerful smile gone, another victim of the battle at The Giant's Toe. Snorri had never carried the weight of his fate. That the Norns controlled it freed him of its responsibilities. Ulf now wondered if Snorri still felt the same.

"My grandfather is still ill." Young Thorgils' voice snapped him out of his trance.

"I'm sure he will be better soon," Ulf said unconvincingly.

"Grandfather's been like this ever since the battle," young Thorgils continued, as if he didn't hear Ulf. He chewed on his bottom lip. "The other boys say that my grandfather is like this because of what happened."

Ulf looked at the raven again, its head still tilted. Jarl Thorgils had not been seen outside of his longhouse since the battle, and only Ingibjorg and Snorri could go in.

"Don't you have other things to do than harass the great Bear-Slayer, son?" Snorri saved him from having to respond.

"I'm on my way to meet Ebbe. He's been training me on how to fight with a sword." The boy beamed as he showed off his wooden sword.

"Make sure you listen to everything he says," Snorri said, smiling at his son. Young Thorgils seemed to be the only thing that still brought some joy to Snorri over the winter. Snorri ruffled his son's hair before sending him away. "Soon he'll be old enough to stand in a shield wall."

"If he's anything like his father, then he'll bring Norway to her knees," Ulf responded, clapping his friend on the back. He glanced at the raven and walked into the hall. Inside, the air was chilly. Ulf closed his eyes as he breathed in the earthy aroma mixed with the smoke from the hearth fire. Like most men who had no wives or family farms nearby, Ulf slept in the hall. He walked to his chest and was about to open it when he saw Lady Ingibjorg sat on Thorgils' seat. That was another change from the battle. With Thorgils in his current state and Snorri spending weeks hunting down Griml's army, Lady Ingibjorg became the temporary ruler of Thorgilsstad.

"Welcome back, Ulf."

"Lady Ingibjorg." He still felt uneasy around her. But she was one of the few who did not hold Ulf responsible for what had happened, instead insisting that Ulf was merely a part of Odin's game.

"You look tired." She rested her chin on her hand, her green eyes searching his soul. Some believed her to be a witch, able to speak to the gods and see the future.

Ulf nodded. "We had a long night." He took off his belt with his weapons and placed them in his chest. The sun was reaching the end of its daily journey and soon the hall would be filled with men and women. Although the mood would be as dark as the night sky.

"So I've heard." Her words send a shiver down his spine. *Did she know about the hall burning?*

"The ravens?" Ulf asked her. Lady Ingibjorg gave him a coy smile instead of responding as Snorri walked into the hall with his hirdmen behind him. His smile quickly faded when he saw his mother scowling at him.

"Snorri, what have you done?" Her voice took on the tone of a mother chiding a disobedient child.

Snorri shrugged. "Nothing, mother. It's good to see you as well."

"Don't do that. If I were you, I'd not go home for a while."

Snorri raised his eyebrows, surprised by this. "You know?"

"Of course I know! By Frigg, how can you be so stupid!"

"Told you," Thorbjorn said. Snorri looked at him before shaking his head.

"I had no choice; he was planning to attack us." Snorri shrugged, staring at the thralls, who scurried away.

Ingibjorg sat down again and straightened her dress before leaning back. "There will be consequences of this, my son."

Snorri waved his mother's words away. "Nobody will know it was us."

"They never learn," Ingibjorg said to the thrall, who handed her a drink. The girl smiled, quickly glancing at Snorri before going back to her chores. "You found nothing new then?"

"We know Griml travelled north, for what reason we cannot say." Snorri sat down on a bench and filled a cup with ale. He took a sip and smiled.

"Thorvald?" Ingibjorg asked.

Snorri looked up from his ale, his smile disappearing.

"I understand how you feel about him, Snorri, but he is—." She stopped when she saw Snorri's face darken. Lady Ingibjorg looked around to make sure that none of the thralls were in the hall. They had all left, following some cue which Ulf had not noticed. "Your father has been broken since the battle, but he still hopes Thorvald will come back and make amends."

"He cannot make amends for what he has done." Snorri put his cup down, his face turning red.

"Perhaps, but he is still –"

"He is nothing!" Snorri jumped to his feet and slammed the table with his fist. No one responded to this. "Thorvald betrayed us all! Sacrificed Vidar for his own gain!" Snorri jabbed a finger towards Ulf.

Ulf closed his eyes, bowing his head at the memory. He could still see them walking out of their line, Griml with Thorvald behind him and dragging Vidar along with a rope tied around his neck. He still remembered the smile on Vidar's face before Griml took his head.

"That is not why you are angry with him." Ingibjorg said, not reacting to her son's outburst.

"The coward ran with his tail between his legs," Snorri growled before storming out of the hall.

Ingibjorg took a deep breath as if she was settling her thoughts before she looked at Oddi, who was sitting next to where Snorri had been.

"Jarl Arnfinni gave him shelter after the battle, but he would not tell us anything else."

Ingibjorg took a sip of her drink as she considered Oddi's words before she nodded at him.

Snorri stood outside the hall, eyes screwed shut and fists clenched as he took deep breaths. Around him mothers were shouting at children for getting in the way, while men greeted those they knew. Birds were singing as they flew overhead and he could even hear the sounds of sword play as warriors trained in the field outside the village. But there was one sound missing, a sound he had not heard for many weeks. Laughter. Thorgilsstad had always been a place of joy, warriors laughing and singing, children play fighting, women chirping away to each other. Not anymore, and he was worried that it might never be again. Not with their jarl hiding away in his bed. Snorri opened his eyes and looked at his father's longhouse. Gritting his teeth, he was about to take a step forward.

"That won't do you any good, my son."

Snorri turned to his mother, surprised he had not noticed her, but then she had the ability to move as quiet as a mouse. Snorri always thought that was how she knew so much. Or perhaps she belonged to the gods, and they whispered things into her ear. "Father needs to come and lead his people."

His mother stared at him. She looked older than he remembered, the new lines around her eyes a testament to the battle that must have been raging on inside of her. There was also a sadness in her piercing eyes he had never seen before. "He will come out when he is ready, but until then, my son, you must lead these people and keep them safe."

"But you are doing a great job, mother. And besides, I'm too busy at the moment." His attention was drawn to the statues of the gods in the square in front of the hall. Three large stone statues, the tallest one in the middle being Odin, standing tall and wise with his ravens on his shoulders. On either side of him were Thor, brandishing the mighty Mjöllnir, and Tyr, proudly displaying his missing hand, sacrificed to Fenrir so they could tie the giant wolf into his unbreakable chains. Snorri felt their stony eyes judging him, deciding whether he was worthy of their attention. As a child, he was terrified of those statues, but the constant weight of their stares drove him to become the man he was today. Now, though, he wondered if it was enough.

"I am not your father's successor." Lady Ingibjorg followed her son's stare and saw him looking at the statues. "I know you don't think you are ready for this responsibility, but these people trust you and they are now looking to you for leadership." She placed a comforting hand on his shoulder.

"But father..." Snorri wasn't sure what he wanted to say so left the sentence unfinished.

"Your father is fighting the hardest battle of his life. One, I pray to the gods, you never have to fight. Like you, he is angry and ashamed of what Thorvald did, but there is also pain like no other."

"Father has always been so strong, it's hard seeing him so..." Again, he could not find the words.

"Human?" She smiled a sad smile. "It's easy for a child to lift their parents to the top of the mountains, to see them as unbreakable. But in the end, we are as human as you, and sometimes the fate which the Norns give us is hard for us to deal with as well."

"You seem to be dealing with it pretty well." Snorri took his eyes away from the statues and looked at his mother, again surprised by the sadness in her usually strong eyes.

"Am I?" Snorri shrugged, not knowing what else to say. "Never underestimate the strength of a woman, my son. Not even Odin makes that mistake."

Snorri nodded. "Does Gunnhildr know?" Snorri had enough of this conversation.

"She does. Choose your words carefully when you speak to her, Snorri. You might not have any feelings for her, but she is still the mother of your boys."

Snorri took a deep breath. He was more nervous now than if he were standing in a shield wall on a ship in the middle of a storm. Steeling himself, Snorri walked to his house.

Inside it was dark. The hearth fire had died down and the only light came from the smoke hole in the roof. Even with the heat outside, inside felt cold. The hairs on his neck stood up and Snorri had to fight the urge to draw Tyr's Fury from her scabbard. His instincts, honed after years of fighting, told him there was danger, but he could not understand what it was. Before he could take a breath to calm himself, she flew out of the shadows, screaming like an outraged eagle and swinging an axe at him. Snorri just had time to dodge the axe, at the same time trying not to punch her. Gunnhildr's face, red and contorted in anger, was unrecognisable, and Snorri wondered if demons had possessed his wife. Again, she swung the axe at him and this time he batted it away. He tried to grab hold of her, but she moved too fast. Gunnhildr aimed another swing at his head and, as Snorri moved backwards to dodge it, he tripped over a bucket. His hand went to the hilt of his sword as he fell, but he resisted the urge to draw his blade. His mother's words echoing in his head. *She is the mother of your boys.* Snorri rolled out of the way as soon as he hit the ground, and not a moment too soon as the axe bit into the dirt where his chest had been.

"Gunnhildr, stop!" he shouted, jumping back to his feet.

Gunnhildr responded with a screech as she charged after him with the axe. Snorri grabbed a cup from the table next to him and threw it at her, but she swatted it away with the axe before coming at him again. "You killed my father!" she shrieked, her red face wet with tears and snot.

Snorri had no time to respond. He ducked under another swing that would have taken his head off. Moving backwards, he stayed out of the reach of the axe. But Snorri only had so much space to move around inside his house. He kept trying to calm her, but his words had no effect. If anything, they only seemed to make her more determined to kill him. Snorri had never known his wife was so handy with a weapon. His back hit the wall, and Snorri saw Gunnhildr lift the axe above her head to split his skull in two. Snorri moved his head at the last moment and heard the axe bite into the wood. Instinctively, he lifted his fist to punch her, but stopped himself. Instead, Snorri ran for the door before she could free the axe.

Outside Snorri's longhouse a group had gathered, drawn there like a bear to honey by the noise inside.

"What do you think is happening?" Drumbr asked, scratching his head.

"They're making babies," Thorbjorn mocked.

"Really?" Drumbr raised an eyebrow.

"Of course not, you idiot. Gunnhildr is probably flaying Snorri for roasting her father." Thorbjorn tried to smack Drumbr on the back of the head, but Drumbr was too tall.

"Should we go in and help him?" Ulf asked. They all winced at the sound of a loud crashing noise, followed by a skin-crawling shriek. All around them, people were whispering to each other. They all knew what the fight was about. Ulf was just glad that young Thorgils was being kept busy somewhere else.

"No, I'd rather kick Thor in the balls than go in there." Thorbjorn looked at those around him as they nodded their agreements. Ulf only shrugged.

"Where can I find Snorri Thorgilsson?" A strong voice came from behind them. They all turned, some looking annoyed at the interruption. Behind them stood a tall warrior, shorter than Ulf, but with wide shoulders. He was wearing a fine brynja, its metal links glistening in the sunlight, while holding a gold-rimmed silver bowl helmet with a golden nose guard. He had a beautiful sword at his side, accompanied by an ivory handled sax-knife.

"Tormod Torleifson," Oddi said by way of greeting. "It's been a while since you've been in these parts."

"Who's he?" Ulf took in the man's long hair and the beard braided into two forks, with finger rings attached to each one. From his armour and the gold arm rings he wore, Ulf could tell this was an important warrior.

"Hirdman of King Halfdan, one of the finest warriors in all of Norway," Brak responded.

"Aye, and usually when he shows up here, it means the king wants something from us," Asbjorn said.

"A welcoming party for me?" Tormod asked with an amiable smile.

"No, just enjoying some late afternoon entertainment." Thorbjorn thumbed over his shoulder towards Snorri's house. Just then, another loud scream was followed by a thumping noise.

Tormod looked at the house, his face showing his confusion. "Where's Snorri?"

The door to Snorri's house burst open, and Snorri came flying out. He tripped over something and went crashing to the ground before quickly rolling to his feet and backing away from his house. "Gunnhildr, calm down!" He held his hand out, trying to placate his wife.

Gunnhildr came stalking out of the house, her hair dishevelled and face red. She gripped her axe in both hands as she scowled at her husband. "You killed my father," she growled the words.

"I had no choice. He was going to attack Thorgilsstad." Snorri tried to explain, still backing away from his wife. Neither of them seemed to notice the crowd watching them.

"You had no choice!" Gunnhildr shrieked before launching herself at Snorri, axe held high in the air.

Snorri stepped to the side and tripped her up as the axe sliced through empty air. As soon as she hit the ground, he was on top of her. He ripped the axe from her grip and threw it away before screaming at her, "He was a treacherous bastard who was about to attack my home!"

"Snorri." The calm but strong voice of Lady Ingibjorg made Snorri look up. He saw the crowd for the first time, his face flushed with embarrassment. Gunnhildr still hadn't noticed and was kicking and screaming under him.

"We were just talking," Snorri explained as he got off his wife.

"If that was them talking, then I don't want to see them fighting," Drumbr said, unable to keep the smile from his face. Gunnhildr stopped trashing about and got to her feet. She ignored the crowd as she dusted the dirt from her dress and stormed back into her house without a word.

Snorri looked conflicted. He knew he should go after her, but didn't want to. He also seemed embarrassed with everyone looking at him. Lady Ingibjorg walked up to him. "I'll talk to her. You have a guest to see to." She nodded towards Tormod. Snorri looked at Tormod and a slow smile spread on his face.

"Tormod, you bastard. What brings you here?" He walked to Tormod and the two men gripped forearms.

"King Halfdan sent me to—"

Thorbjorn interrupted him before he could finish his sentence "Told you." Thorbjorn crossed his arms, almost as if it helped prove his point.

Tormod gave him a quizzical look, before Snorri waved him away. "Come, Tormod. First a drink, then you can tell me what the king wants." Snorri led him towards the hall.

"They know each other well?" Ulf asked Oddi, noticing the jealousy in his own voice and hoping the others didn't.

Oddi nodded. "Tormod was born here. The two of them grew up and learnt to fight together."

"But Tormod now fights for King Halfdan?"

"Aye, Tormod felt he would get more fame if he fought for the king."

"And all he does now is run errands and deliver messages," Thorbjorn said. "A waste for such a talented warrior."

"Is he that good?" Ulf watched as Snorri and Tormod walked side by side. The only difference between them was that Snorri was taller and his hair was lighter.

"Tormod could almost be a match for Snorri, but Snorri would get the better of him," Oddi responded. "Come, we could all use a drink after what we just witnessed."

"Aye, Odin knows it might be the last drink we get to enjoy," Thorbjorn said, smiling. Thorbjorn always relished danger. Ulf could only shake his head as he followed them to the hall.

"Here he is, the great Bear-Slayer and destroyer of Griml's army," Snorri called out when Ulf stepped into the hall. Tormod stared at him, judging him with his warrior's eye.

"This is the famous Ulf?" Tormod seemed unconvinced.

"Aye, killed a handful of Griml's men before they knew what was happening." Snorri took a sip from his cup. "Fought with the might of Tyr."

Tormod scrutinised Ulf, before shaking his head and taking a sip of his drink. Ulf was irritated by this. He was the same height as Snorri, although his shoulders were not as wide and his limbs not as thick.

"You were not there that day, Tormod." Oddi defended him. "Besides, Ulf is descended from Tyr, you should not underestimate him."

"If you say so." Tormod watched Ulf as he sat down and filled his cup with ale. "Where did you get those scars from?" He pointed to the three neat scars on Ulf's face.

"That is a story for another day," Snorri responded. "So, my old friend, what brings you here?" Snorri must have known, but Ulf guessed he still wanted Tormod to say it.

"The king wants to see you."

CHAPTER 3

"Welcome to Yngling Hall!" Tormod exclaimed as the Sae-Ulfr neared the city of Halfdan the Black. The King of Vestfold.

Ulf looked over his shoulder as he pulled on the oar, seeing the dark splodge surrounded by the green hills. As they rowed, the smudge turned into a city larger than Ulf had ever seen. Thick smog hung in the air, being fed by the many houses squeezed into the wooden palisade, and Ulf wondered how many people lived there. They passed other ships along the way, smaller ones busily pulling in nets filled with fish and larger ones filled with warriors who greeted them. Tormod and Snorri, both men standing by the prow near Ulf, waved back. The sounds of the large city bounced off the water, and Ulf heard men shouting over metal striking metal, which reminded him of the smithy back in Thorgilsstad. Dogs barked in the distance as the Sae-Ulfr altered course. Ulf saw they were aiming for an empty spot on the wharf as Snorri gave the order for the Sae-Ulfr to slow down. Half the crew pulled their oars in. Ulf handed his oar to one of men and stood by the prow, watching the city of King Halfdan the Black grow in front of him.

"Careful, you don't fall over," Thorbjorn warned him with a smile. Ulf didn't realise he had been leaning over the side of the ship and blushed as the men laughed at him. He caught Geir's eye, the young warrior giving him a sympathetic shrug. Like him, Geir was new to the crew and had also come from a small farm. Unlike him, Geir had managed not to make a fool of himself.

"This is very different to Thorgilsstad," Ulf commented, trying to forget about what just happened. His nose wrinkled at the stench of fish that had been left out in the sun for too long. The excited screams of sea birds drew his attention to the smaller boats docked near to where they were heading. Men were busy carrying barrels filled with fish off the ships while the sea birds circled above them, looking for a chance of an easy meal. As Ulf watched, one bird, braver than the rest, dived towards one barrel. Just as Ulf thought the bird would be rewarded for its bravery, a stone struck it. The bird screamed angrily at whoever had thrown the stone as it joined the safety of its flock. The men on the wharf laughed, and Ulf saw one man ruffle a boy's hair. He couldn't help but wonder if that was an omen of what was to come.

The Sae-Ulfr reached the wharf and Oddi threw a rope to a man who deftly caught it and tied the ship to a post. Snorri disembarked with his hirdmen and gave instructions for the rest of his crew to stay with the ship. Ulf almost gagged on the reek of rotten fish and, looking around, wondered how no one else was affected by it. Trying not to cover his nose, he followed Tormod, who led them to the King's hall. Away from the wharf, the smell of the fish was replaced by the stink of shit and piss, mixed in with stale food and the sweatiness of too many people living together. Ulf decided to breathe through his mouth, missing the open spaces he was used to. His ears were assaulted with noises so disorientating; it felt like he had spent the entire night drinking ale with Thorbjorn and Drumbr. Ulf had thought that Suðrikaupstefna was a busy place, but it had been nothing like this. People were everywhere, all of them walking around, shouting greetings at each other or just shouting. Women were going from house to house in groups, sharing gossip and collecting news. Children were running around, play fighting and chasing each other. Amongst all this chaos, there were also thralls, broken down people scurrying around and trying to stay out of the way while they saw to their chores. *Vidar would have hated this place.* Ulf felt the pain in his chest as he thought of his friend. He missed the comforting silence that had surrounded the mute boy. As they walked along the path, a scruffy dog ran up to Tormod and sniffed his leg. Tormod kicked at the dog, which yelped as it scurried away.

"My father never wanted to build a wall around Thorgilsstad. Said it was like caging up a wolf." Snorri said, looking at the wall that surrounded the town. Ulf wasn't sure if the scowl on his face was because of their impending meeting with the king, or because he felt the same way about this place as Ulf did. He guessed it was the former when Snorri's eyes fixed on their destination straight ahead of them. The hall of King Halfdan the Black. Ulf stared at the hall as it got bigger, his heart beating faster in his chest. He clenched his fists, so the others did not notice them shaking.

They stopped in front of the hall, and Ulf could not help but feel disappointed. It was bigger than Thorgils' hall, its roof almost twice the height and walls twice as long. Ulf had always thought that kings lived in grand halls with richly carved doors and posts and walls depicting tales of the king's exploits. He realised he had been expecting something similar to Valhalla and chided himself for being so childish. The hall in front of him was plain. That was the only way he could describe it. The only impressive thing about it was its size. Unlike the decorated door posts of Thorgils' hall, the door posts of Halfdan's hall were plain apart from a line of runes carved on each of them, one claiming the king was from the Yngling dynasty, which was said to come from Frey, and the other placing a curse on any man who would attack the king in his own hall. Two heavily armoured guards on either side of the door, almost the size of Drumbr, stood there, spears in hand, glowering at the new arrivals. One of them smiled as he recognised Snorri and his men.

"If you are here, then there must be trouble," the guard greeted them.

"No, it's just that if the king needs something done right, then he calls for us because you lot still don't know which end of the spear you kill with," Thorbjorn responded as he gripped the man's forearm.

"I never enjoy coming here," Snorri said to Ulf, scowling as the others greeted the guards and handed their weapons over.

Ulf nodded, not knowing what to say. He looked around, taking in the small square houses, smaller than the long houses he was used to, and again thought about how much Vidar would have hated this place. Vidar had spent most of his life in the forest and even Thorgilsstad, without a defensive wall, had depressed his friend. "What do you think will happen?" Ulf asked, to distract himself from thinking of Vidar.

Snorri shrugged while scratching his neck. "It's in the hands of the Norns now." He turned and walked into the hall before Ulf could respond.

Ulf rushed to catch up, but the two guards blocked his path. "Aren't you forgetting something, boy?" one of the guards said while indicating at Ulf's weapons.

"Careful, that's the Bear-Slayer you are talking to," Asbjorn mocked with a sneer. The two guards looked at each other and shrugged as if the name meant nothing to them.

Ulf handed his weapons to the guards, while glaring at Asbjorn, who only laughed at him. He did not like the way the guards' eyes lit up when they saw Ormstunga.

The inside of the hall wasn't much different from Thorgils' hall, only bigger. There was a large hearth in the middle, the fire almost roaring as it fought to keep the darkness at bay. Two rows of timber post lined the hall, supporting the roof and carrying torches to aid the hearth fire in its fight. Benches lined the walls, acting as both seats and beds for those who occupied the hall. On the walls was a collection of different weapons and shields. Ulf took a deep breath of the earthy and smoky aroma of the inside as his ears adjusted to the constant throng of voices, which sounded like a waterfall pounding on the rocks.

"Snorri Thorgilsson!" a loud voice boomed, silencing everyone as if Odin himself had appeared. Ulf looked towards the source of the voice and saw a large stout man sitting on a plain wooden throne. His thick black hair almost melted into the shadows and, with his black beard, neatly groomed in contrast to his wild hair, made his face seem paler than what it was. Stern eyes glared at them from under black eyebrows, and Ulf felt the warmth leaving his body.

"King Halfdan." Snorri inclined his head, but did no more. Ulf followed everyone else and bowed towards the king.

The king remained silent for a while, his gaze shifting over them before it landed on Ulf. He stared at Ulf with a raised eyebrow, but then shook his head and returned his attention to Snorri. "How is your father?"

"My father is well, thanks to Odin," Snorri responded. Ulf caught the glance between Thorbjorn and Oddi. Everybody seemed to be interested in Jarl Thorgils at the moment.

King Halfdan nodded. "That's good to hear." He leaned back in his chair, linking his fingers together on his lap. "Now tell me why a large army invaded my land?"

"It's a long and boring story, King Halfdan."

"Really?" Another raised eyebrow and a quick glance at others in the hall. "It wasn't because you kidnapped the bride of some sea king?"

Snorri looked shocked by the king's response.

"Shouldn't be surprised the king knows," Oddi whispered. Ulf wasn't sure how the king could know about this, but then Thorgils knew about everything that happened in his land.

"Don't look so surprised, Snorri. You really thought I wouldn't find out about it." The king smiled at Snorri as if he were a naïve child. Snorri didn't respond. "What I don't understand is why you kidnapped this woman. Don't you already have a wife?" Laughter rang out in the hall in response.

"It was because of me." Ulf stepped forward before Snorri could respond. Thorbjorn sighed audibly behind him.

The king looked at Ulf, his hardened eyes lingering on the scars on Ulf's face as his mouth tightened.

"Forgive my young friend, King. He is new to my crew. Sometimes he forgets his manners," Snorri interjected, pushing Ulf back with the others.

The king held up a hand to stop Snorri. "No, let him explain."

Ulf stepped forward again. He saw the disdain in the faces of the other men in the hall, but what surprised him more was the looks of curiosity mixed in. One man pointed at him while whispering to others, before shaking his head. He ignored the man and faced the king, whose steely gaze was still on him. "Griml slaughtered my family and burnt down my uncle's farm," he explained.

"Griml?" The king looked at the man standing beside his chair. An old man dressed only in a tunic and trousers, unlike the rest of the men in the hall, who were all warriors. On his head, he wore a felt cap.

"Griml Jotun, King. He is the sea king whose army Jarl Thorgils defeated," the old man explained in a frail voice.

"Griml Troll-face," Thorbjorn whispered a bit too loudly.

"So you kidnapped his woman and invited his army into my land?"

"That was my fault, King," Snorri explained. "I had promised Ulf I would help him avenge his family." Snorri spread his hands.

The king leaned forward in his seat, resting his chin on his fingertips. "While I agree that a man must avenge his family, as Vidar avenges Odin," Ulf felt the thump in his chest at the mention of Vidar's name, "I don't understand why the son of a jarl would help a boy he has never met before."

"He saved my life. Odin would have turned his back on me if I didn't offer my help."

The king thought about this for a while before leaning back in his chair again. "I can't argue with that, and besides, from what I heard, it was a victory worthy of the sagas." The warriors in the hall all nodded at this. "But that is not why I wanted to speak to you." Halfdan the Black leaned forward in his chair again and studied the men before him, like a predator sizing up its prey. After what felt like a long time, the king growled, "Jarl Arnfinni."

"Told you," Thorbjorn whispered again.

Snorri glanced at Thorbjorn with narrowed eyes. It looked like Snorri had misjudged the king's reach.

"I've been told that Jarl Arnfinni, one of my strongest jarls, has recently died in a hall burning." The king stood up. He was taller than Ulf had first thought, easily reaching the height of Snorri. "I have also been told that you were in his hall that day." He took a few steps towards Snorri. The hall went quiet.

"We were hunting the remnants of Griml's army and—" Snorri started.

"I don't care why you were on his land!" the king's voice thundered around the hall. "I want to know why you killed my jarl!" Ulf saw from the looks on the faces of the men in the hall that they all knew about this. Some even smiled at Snorri's discomfort. Ulf clenched his fists as he grit his teeth. Snorri did not deserve this.

Snorri looked the king in the eye, keeping his back straight and hands by his side. "He gave shelter to a traitor. He was planning an attack on my father's village," he responded, struggling to keep the steel out of his voice.

"And I would have let him!" The king's face went red as his neck bulged. He was of a similar height to Snorri, but at that moment he seemed a giant amongst men. Snorri took a step back, his eyes wide and face pale. Snorri's hirdmen all took a step back, glancing at each other with open mouths.

"W... why?" Snorri struggled to get the words out. His hands were shaking and Ulf could not tell whether it was because of shock or anger.

"Because since the battle, your father has been cowering in his house." The king turned and walked back to his chair, waving his arm dismissively. "By Odin's sake, Snorri. I need my jarls strong and ready to fight. Your father's army is now weak, and he seems incapable of doing anything."

"My father—"

"Your father froze at the battle. You had to give the command to attack," the old man interrupted Snorri.

Snorri could not respond. He just stared at the old man, his mouth agape. In the end Oddi took a step forward, "King Halfdan, if I may," he continued when he saw the king nod. "The jarl had just witnessed Thorvald's betrayal. Even Odin was saddened by the betrayal of Loki."

"Odin punished Loki for his betrayal," the king responded.

"As I'm sure the jarl will when we find Thorvald."

"That still does nothing about the fact that I lost my two most powerful jarls." He turned his hard eyes back to Snorri, who was glowering at him in return. King Halfdan smiled at that, before continuing, "While Thorgils might still find his steel again and return to us, Arnfinni is lost to Valhalla and he has no sons to take his place."

"Even if he did, they would be dead now as well," one of the warriors in the hall said. The king nodded his agreement.

"I can take his lands, be jarl in his place," Snorri offered.

"You're not fit to be a jarl," the king sneered back.

"Why?" Snorri's eyes widened.

"Because of the very reason you are standing in front of me!" King Halfdan shot to his feet, his shoulders bunched up and his fists clenched.

"Odin knows you are a fine warrior, one of the finest in Norway, Snorri, but you are too reckless to be a jarl." The old man explained to Snorri as he and the king glared at each other. Ulf wondered who this man was, but said nothing. The tension in the hall was too high. Even the king's men were on edge.

King Halfdan took a deep breath before sitting down again. "No, Snorri, you will not be the jarl of Arnfinni's land, but you will compensate me for the loss."

"Just tell me how, King Halfdan," Snorri responded, also breathing deep to calm himself.

"This will not be good for us," Thorbjorn whispered beside Ulf.

"Aye, the gods will see to that," Brak agreed.

"I am told that this Griml was planning a raid on Francia," the king continued, not paying attention to the whispering of Snorri's men.

"He was," Snorri agreed. "But I doubt the raid will happen now."

"That, Snorri, is where you are wrong." The king smiled when he saw the confusion on Snorri's face. Ulf knew where this was going and did not like it. "It seems the raid has found a new leader. Some Danish jarl, a young upstart, who wants to make a name for himself."

"I see." From the sound of his voice, Ulf could tell that Snorri also knew what was about to happen.

"Odin knows I would like to take part in this raid. The plunder from this would do much to fix the problems you have caused me, but I have business to take care of in the north. So, Snorri," the king leaned forward in his chair, a satisfied smile appearing on his face, "you will go for me. How many men you take will be up to you, but you will give me three-quarters of the plunder." The king watched Snorri, waiting to see if he would object, but Snorri kept quiet. "To make sure that you don't cheat me, not that I think even you would be that stupid, but then the gods do like their games, I am sending one of my ships, captained by Tormod, with you."

Snorri looked at Tormod, seeing the smile on his face. "When do we leave?"

"I am told the raid will start by the next full moon, so the sooner the better," the king responded.

"No!" Ulf said before he could stop himself. Everyone in the hall gasped in shock, as if the air left the room.

King Halfdan glowered at him, curling his lip into a sneer. "No?" he growled.

"We must find Griml, I must avenge my family." Ulf grit his teeth.

"Ulf, for Tyr's sake, shut up," Drumbr urged him, but Ulf paid him no attention.

"You destroyed his army. I think you've done enough," the king responded as he gripped the armrest of his chair.

"Griml still lives. He must die."

"Egil, teach this pup what happens if he disobeys me," Halfdan said to one of his men.

A warrior dressed in a brynja stepped forward. He was shorter than Ulf, but broader in the chest. The grey hair and lines on his face did nothing to make this man look less dangerous. The man walked up to Ulf and headbutted him before Ulf could do anything about it. As Ulf stumbled backwards, his lip bust open, Egil punched him in the stomach, shoving him to the ground before Ulf could regain his balance.

"Stay down," Snorri whispered, but Ulf ignored him and got back to his feet.

He charged at Egil and threw a punch, which Egil ducked underneath before punching Ulf hard in the side. Ulf grunted as the pain surged through his body, but this only ignited the flames in his chest. He blocked the next punch before retaliating with one of his own, catching Egil on the side of the head. Ulf grabbed hold of Egil's brynja, throwing him to the ground before jumping on top of him and punching him in the face. Egil's nose broke in an explosion of blood and snot. Ulf thought the fight was over then, but a broken nose would not stop Egil. He punched Ulf as he was about to get up, catching him on the chin. Ulf fell to the ground and before he could do anything, Egil was on top of him, raining down punches. Ulf brought his arms up to protect his face, not knowing what else to do. He tasted the blood from his lip as punches landed on his head, bouncing his skull off the ground floor. Ulf saw sparks and knew he had to do something. He tried to remember the lessons he had with Snorri, but his mind would not focus as another punch caught the side of his head.

"Stop," Halfdan commanded, his voice sounding amused. Egil stopped and climbed off Ulf. Snorri's men rushed to pick him up.

"You fucking idiot," Thorbjorn growled at him. Ulf glared at him as he wiped the blood from his lip with the back of his hand. He looked at Egil, who was smiling at him while using his tunic to clean his bloody nose.

King Halfdan laughed. "I'm disappointed. I expected more from Ulf Bear-Slayer." The warriors in the hall agreed with their king, some clapping Egil on his back. "Yes, we have heard of the young warrior who charged at the enemy alone, killing many single-handedly and almost killing their leader," King Halfdan explained when he saw the confusion from Snorri and his men. "Perhaps those tales were exaggerated."

"They were not," Snorri defended his friend. "Ulf has the blood of Tyr in him and that day it was like the god of war had possessed Ulf."

"Perhaps Tyr is taking a nap at the moment," one of Halfdan's men suggested, causing the others to laugh and the king to smile. Ulf glared at the man, who only shrugged at him. They were not afraid of him, not after Egil defeated him so easily.

"Who is his father?" the old man asked, suddenly taking a keen interest in Ulf.

"Bjørn Ulfson, my father's former champion." Snorri glanced at his friend, hoping Ulf would not react to that. In the past, Ulf had hated talking about his father, believing that he had abandoned him when he was still a small boy. But since the battle at The Giant's Toe, Ulf understood the sacrifice his father had made.

"Bjørn Ulfson?" the king asked the old man, who nodded. "I heard that the man had no equal."

"I fought beside him once," an old warrior said from where he sat on the bench. The man looked at Ulf, his eyes judging Ulf the way a man judges a prize ox. "It was like fighting with the gods on your side."

King Halfdan looked at Ulf again, but Ulf could not work out what the king was thinking. Not that it mattered anymore. His head was hurting, and Ulf was desperate to get out of the hall. "Snorri, get young Ulf cleaned up and go home. Be ready to meet Tormod in the fjord in three days' time. I suggest you take as many men as you can."

"But it will leave Thorgilsstad undefended if I take too many men," Snorri objected.

"We will protect Thorgilsstad, I swear by the All-father," Halfdan reassured him.

Snorri nodded before turning and walking out of the hall, his hirdmen behind him. Ulf stood for a short while, looking at the king who only stared back with a smile on his lips which Ulf did not understand, before going after Snorri.

Outside the hall, they collected their weapons from the guards while Ulf used a bucket of water to wash the blood off his face. The cold water stung his lip, but at least it cleared his head.

"I think one day we'll have to teach Ulf some manners," Asbjorn said, glaring at Ulf through crinkled eyes.

"Well, it wasn't a fair fight. Egil is the king's champion wrestler. Undefeated, they say." Thorbjorn defended Ulf.

"Next time we just get Drumbr to fight him, he could just sit on Egil," Brak laughed.

"Nah, Egil will probably bite his balls off." Thorbjorn winced at the thought. "He is crazy, that man. Even the gods are nervous of him."

"Asbjorn is right." Snorri turned to face them. "By Thor, Ulf, you need to learn to control yourself. Halfdan the Black is not a man to anger. Getting Egil to knock some sense into you was him in a good mood."

"Why would the king be in a good mood?" Brak asked, scratching under his beard.

"Because we are going to risk our lives in Francia and he is going to gain everything from it." Snorri spat to the side before walking away.

Oddi rushed after him with the others on his heels. "It is compensation for you killing Arnfinni."

"Halfdan doesn't care about Arnfinni. He's just using that as an excuse to send us to Francia."

"So what are we going to do?" Ulf asked, prodding his lip to see how bad it was.

"We are going to Francia," Snorri responded, his eyes fixed ahead of him.

"But what about Griml and Thorvald?" Ulf flung his arms into air.

Snorri stopped so suddenly, the others almost walked into him. "Griml and that shit will have to wait."

"But—"

"No, Ulf." Snorri turned to face him, his face creased. "If King Halfdan sends us to Francia, then we go to Francia. Because if we don't then the next time there is a hall burning, we'll be the ones inside the hall."

"Snorri is right, Ulf," Oddi added. "Griml will have to wait and if the gods are still on your side, then hopefully not for too long. But we must do as the king told us." He placed a hand on Ulf's shoulder, as if trying to show Ulf that he understood. But Ulf didn't care. That was not what he wanted to hear, but he needed his friends if he was going to kill Griml. Ulf looked to the sky and, not for the first time, wondered what game the gods were playing.

When Snorri saw Ulf wasn't going to say anything else, he clapped him on the shoulder and headed for their ship. Ulf spotted a woman leaning against the house and staring at them. She smiled at Ulf when she saw him looking, revealing a mouth of blackened teeth. Her black hair was loose and wild, with what looked like twigs and small bones tied into it. She wore a dress made of animal hide, and Ulf noticed she wasn't wearing any shoes. Something about her seemed familiar, but before Ulf could figure out why, a small boy ran out in front of him.

"Watch it, you shit," Thorbjorn growled as the small boy ran into him. The boy stuck his tongue out at Thorbjorn and sped off before Thorbjorn could smack him. Ulf looked back to where he had seen the woman, but she was gone.

CHAPTER 4

"Why is it that every time you go somewhere, Ulf comes back with a fresh injury?" Ingibjorg greeted them, her green eyes scrutinising the swelling on Ulf's lip. It was midday, and the hall was empty apart from the thralls, cleaning and keeping the fire in the hearth going. An old hound with a grey muzzle sat by Drumbr's feet, waiting for the big man to drop a morsel.

"He's learning the way of the warrior." Thorbjorn elbowed Ulf in the side. The old dog looked at Ulf, shaking its head, before staring at Drumbr again.

"Then he needs to learn it faster before he ends up looking like you, Thorbjorn," Ingibjorg responded, smiling to show the short warrior she was only teasing him.

Her face grew serious when she turned to her son. "The king knows about Arnfinni?" Snorri nodded. "He knows you did it." A statement, not a question. Snorri nodded again, not wanting to admit that he had been wrong. Not about killing Arnfinni. He would never admit to that. Ingibjorg studied Snorri for a while, almost like she was looking into his mind to find the truth. "And now you must go on a raid to repay the king for killing one of his favourite jarls." She looked at the rest of them, but no one responded.

"To Francia," Snorri eventually responded. His hirdmen almost sighed in relief when he did. They did not want to tell Lady Ingibjorg that they were leaving on a big raid.

"To Francia," Lady Ingibjorg repeated, before looking at Ulf, who was staring into the flames of the hearth fire, while rubbing the names of his family on his axe's handle.

"Something the matter, Ulf?" Snorri asked. Everyone was staring at him, even the thralls.

"He's probably remembering how Egil humiliated him. That would send a shiver down my spine as well," Thorbjorn joked. His friends laughed as they agreed with him.

But Lady Ingibjorg's eyes bored into Ulf, searching for the answer. "No." Her firm voice stopped the laughter. "There is something else bothering Ulf, something darker." Ulf felt his brow furrow, realising he would have to tell Lady Ingibjorg.

"I saw a woman," he said, knowing how dumb it sounded. Thorbjorn's response confirmed it.

"A woman?" He laughed, slapping his knee. "Ulf fears women now?"

"I'm not surprised," Drumbr added, "not after the last one almost killed him." Drumbr was talking about the woman they had kidnapped to force Griml to chase them. Eldrid. She had attacked Ulf on the ship with a knife, angry that Ulf had killed her father. Snorri's hirdmen laughed at the memory. Even Snorri had a smile on his face.

"Tell me about this woman." Lady Ingibjorg ignored the men. The old hound must have sensed the change in the mood as it gave a small whine before trotting away.

Ulf stared at a sea of curious faces. With a sigh, he explained to Lady Ingibjorg what he remembered.

"A dried snakeskin around her neck?" Oddi asked when Ulf finished. Ulf nodded.

"Some crazy woman from the forest." Asbjorn dismissed what Ulf had said with a wave of his hand.

"No, there was something about her. She..." Ulf thought about how to explain it to them. "She seemed familiar, like I had seen her before. But more than that. It felt like..." He glanced at Lady Ingibjorg, trying to think of the words. Her face was serious as she sat on Thorgils' chair, fingers locked under her chin.

"Like what?" Snorri asked.

"Maybe you saw her when we arrived at Yngling Hall?" Oddi asked. "It was very busy there."

Ulf shook his head. "No, I would have remembered that."

"What colour were her eyes?" Lady Ingibjorg asked, surprising all of them. Ulf didn't understand why this was so important, and neither did his friends, but he answered anyway.

"I don't remember." He noticed the disappointment on Ingibjorg's face. "But I remember there was something strange about them."

"Strange?" Brak scratched his head.

"There was something about them that didn't seem right." Ulf stared at Lady Ingibjorg, hoping that she would explain all this to him. She always had the answers before, and he was sure that she had them now. But Lady Ingibjorg explained nothing.

Instead, she stood up and walked out of the hall without saying a word to them.

"Nothing's ever simple with you around, is it, Ulf?" Snorri stared after his mother with an eyebrow raised.

"Makes life interesting," Thorbjorn said, but this time, no one laughed.

Ulf turned to his friends, who stared back with concern written on their faces. "None of you saw her?"

Ingibjorg walked into her house, a place that not so long ago was full of life. The fire in the hearth burning strong, thralls would be in and out, talking and laughing as they performed their tasks. Ingibjorg would normally sit by the loom in the corner, with Hulda by her side. They would talk about the gods and about the lives of people. It had been a place of warmth and laughter, a place where even the thralls could relax and be themselves. But not anymore. The only light came from the small embers and the smoke hole, the darkness as suffocating as her emotions. The loom sat neglected, since Ingibjorg had no time or want to give to it. Even the thralls were no longer allowed in, only Embla. But only because she had been with them for so long, she was practically family. Ingibjorg saw a slouching figure sat by the embers, poking them with a stick. His usually well-kept hair and beard a mess, his moustache long and untamed. His eyes, once so full of fire, now devoid of life.

Thorgils looked up at her while she stood there, his heavily lined face not showing a patch of smooth skin anywhere.

"Snorri has returned from the king."

Thorgils only stared, his face so empty she wondered if he had heard her, but then, "Surprised the king didn't hang him." His voice gruff and raw. This was the first time he had spoken in a while. She glanced at the empty jugs around him, reminding herself to tell the thralls to make more ale.

"The king would have done, but with Arnfinni dead and you hiding away, he can't afford to lose another leader."

"Snorri is no leader."

"His men will follow him into Muspelheim. The king knows this and understands Snorri's worth as a warrior."

"The boy's too rash. What was he thinking burning down Arnfinni's hall?" Thorgils' voice rose in frustration, causing him to cough. He cleared his throat and spat into the small fire.

"What he did was dumb, but he did it to protect Thorgilsstad." She tried to hide her own frustration. Snorri had achieved so much, yet it was never good enough for Thorgils. Ingibjorg suspected she knew why.

"Arnfinni would never attack Thorgilsstad, the king would not have allowed it." Thorgils turned his stare to her, and she glimpsed a spark in his eyes, but it quickly faded.

Ingibjorg took a deep breath to calm herself. Thorgils had always been as solid as the mountains, but now he was like driftwood lost in the sea. "Arnfinni would have marched his army into Thorgilsstad before the end of the summer and the king would have let him." Thorgils flinched, and Ingibjorg knew he saw the truth in that. "The gods know he had always been jealous of you. He had always wanted to take your place as King Halfdan's strongest jarl, but he could never attack you. Your army was always better than his."

"But the king…"

"The king needs strong jarls." That came out harsher than Ingibjorg intended, and Thorgils flinched again. "Thorgils," she softened her voice, "your people need you." He looked at her but did not respond. Through his eyes, she saw the struggle inside of him. The pain of a father who had lost a child and the responsibility of a leader who must lead his people. "The bændr are complaining. Many have lost sons fighting in the battle. They feel disrespected because you are hiding away. There are whispers about not paying the landskyld this summer."

"Ragnar will remind them of their duties," the jarl growled.

"And what of your duties?" Ingibjorg retorted, unable to stop herself. "You can't expect others to put their pain aside and do what must be done, if you yourself can't do the same." Thorgils looked at the fire again, unable to look her in the eye. "Besides," she continued, "how can Ragnar do that if he is out hunting Thorvald?"

"He'll be back soon." Thorgils poked at the small fire, dragging as much life out of the wood as he could.

"I don't understand why you had to send him when Snorri was already looking for Thorvald." Ingibjorg pulled a loose lint from her dress.

"Because Ragnar will bring him back alive." He stared at her again, his eyes judging her. "You know where Thorvald is." Not a question, but a statement.

Ingibjorg returned her husband's stare, making sure her face revealed nothing.

Thorgils grunted and turned his face to the fire again. "I thought you said that Ulf would not be a danger to us."

"Storms are unpredictable, and besides there is always collateral when storms hit."

"Should have killed him before any of this happened." Thorgils picked up a jug and peered inside, before putting it down and looking for another.

"You tried, remember? And Griml tried, twice." Ingibjorg walked to the table and took a full jug before handing it to her husband.

"Why do the gods protect him?" Thorgils asked after taking a big sip from the jug.

"They still need him."

"Have we not had enough chaos?" His complaining voice almost irritated her. This was not the man she had married, but like her, he was hurting. Unfortunately, one of them had to be strong to protect those around them.

Ingibjorg watched the light streaming in from the smoke hole as she collected her thoughts.

Thorgils studied his wife. "There's something else bothering you."

"She's back." Her voice a whisper as she remembered what Ulf had told her moments before.

"Who is back?"

"You know who." Ingibjorg struggled to keep the fear from her voice.

Thorgils remained silent for a while. They both knew this day would come. "What does she want?"

"What do you think?" Ingibjorg took the jug from her husband and drank from it.

"Can you stop her?" Thorgils asked, his voice sounding more timid than he intended.

Ingibjorg looked at him, irritated. She stood up and walked to the door, pausing just before she left. "Ulf might be the storm that brings chaos to our lives, but she will be the maelstrom that drowns us." Ingibjorg left before Thorgils could say anything.

Ulf was sitting outside the hall, enjoying the light breeze. He needed to get out of the hall as his friends started talking about the raid again. A lot had to be planned, but he didn't want to be part of it. The door swung open, and Lady Ingibjorg left her house, her face impassive, but fists clenched.

"Lady Ingibjorg?" He tried as she walked past, but got no response. She didn't hear him, so he followed her as she stormed towards the forest. Ulf kept his distance as Lady Ingibjorg walked past the hanging tree, the broken branch still lying on the ground from when they tried to hang him. The last time he was here, Hulda's body sat naked with her throat slashed and Loki's name carved into her forehead – Ulf's knife in her hand. *Had it been Thorvald who killed her?* His heart beat faster in his chest as he grit his teeth. When he reached the forest, Ulf looked back to see if they were being followed. But there was no one behind him. This forest was another place he had avoided. Taking a deep breath, he followed Lady Ingibjorg in, careful not to disturb her. Ulf savoured the smell of the damp forest air. A rich aroma of dirt and plants. Around him, he heard birds calling to each other, spreading word of the trespassers in their domain. His hand brushed the bark of an oak tree and he remembered the forest godi telling him that the trees could talk. Ulf wondered what stories these trees could tell him. Lady Ingibjorg moved through the part of the forest he did not recognise. She stepped into a clearing Ulf had never noticed before, and he was surprised by what he saw there. Carved into the trunk of an old oak tree was a wooden statue, no bigger than a small child. The statue showed a beautiful woman wearing a long dress, standing tall and proud. Hanging from her girdle was a bunch of keys. A symbol of housewives, showing that women were in charge of the household. Ulf understood who this shrine belonged to. Frigg, the wife of Odin, and the queen of the gods. Ulf wondered how he had never noticed it before.

"Mother, please forgive my absence, but much has happened these past days as I'm sure you already know," Lady Ingibjorg said to the mother goddess.

"My family is in danger and, for once, I do not know how to help them. All because of a promise I made a lifetime ago." Lady Ingibjorg took a deep breath as she composed herself. Something had frightened her.

"We did what we could to protect her, but, Frigg, life does not always go the way you plan for it." Another deep breath. "I will accept my punishment, as will Thorgils, but I beg you, Frigg, please protect my sons and keep them safe."

Ulf was so caught up listening to Lady Ingibjorg's prayer that the first time he noticed the falcon was when it squawked at him from the branches of the old oak tree.

"You can come out now, Ulf," Lady Ingibjorg said to him kindly.

"How did you know I was here?"

Lady Ingibjorg looked at the falcon as it stared at them. "Frigg often takes the form of the falcon when she travels." Ulf studied the bird, seeing the sharp eyes that pierced through him, the beautiful sleek feathers and the powerful wings. "I asked for her help, but in my haste, I did not bring a gift for her. I'm not sure if she will help me." Ingibjorg's voice sounded sad, and Ulf thought desperately of a way to help her. He looked at his arms and smiled.

"Perhaps this will satisfy her?" Ulf took off his golden arm ring, the one Snorri had given him after Ulf won the holmgang, a duel between two warriors, against a Swedish jarl.

Lady Ingibjorg took the arm ring from him, smiling her thanks. "I guess we will find out," she said as she placed it by the shrine. The falcon screeched, and spreading its magnificent wings, took to the sky.

"Did she accept it?" Ulf followed the falcon as it flew away.

"I believe so." Ingibjorg smiled.

"It's strange," Ulf said, looking back at the shrine. It was a hollow cut out of the tree trunk a long time ago, judging by the colour of the wood. There must have been statues like this one in many houses in Norway.

"What's strange, Ulf?" Lady Ingibjorg probed, raising an eyebrow at him.

Ulf did not realise that he had gone quiet. "Vidar and I had spent a lot of time in the forest, but we never came across this shrine."

Lady Ingibjorg smiled at him. "It's been here since the days of my mother's mother, but few know of its existence."

"But why hide it?" Ulf's eyes were still fixed on the statue. Frigg watched him as a mother would her child.

"It's not hidden, Ulf. The women in the village know about it, but the men are more interested in the gods that will fulfil their needs." Lady Ingibjorg put a hand on Ulf's shoulder and led him back to the village. "Now, why did you follow me?"

"I... I..." Ulf couldn't find the words, and his face started turning red.

"You wanted to ask me about the woman you saw before?" Lady Ingibjorg smiled at him as he nodded. "You don't need to worry about her."

"But who is she?"

Lady Ingibjorg gazed at the trees as they walked through them. "She is someone who needed our help a long time ago, and who we have let down." She looked at Ulf and saw the worry on his face. "You have nothing to fear from her, Ulf, of that I am certain."

"I heard what you asked Frigg." The smile on Lady Ingibjorg's face faltered. "I promise you, Lady Ingibjorg, I will do everything I can to keep him safe."

Lady Ingibjorg smiled at Ulf, but he saw the sadness behind it. "Thank you, Ulf. But I fear your path will be hard enough as it is, without you worrying about the life of my son."

"What do you mean?" Ulf stopped, staring at Lady Ingibjorg as she turned to look at him.

"Nothing, my mind is tired and I don't know what I'm saying right now." She smiled. "Now come, let's enjoy the silence of the forest while we can."

Ulf wasn't convinced, but decided not to argue.

"You know, Ulf," Lady Ingibjorg said as he walked beside her, "Frigg knows the fates of all men, but she keeps it all to herself." Ulf frowned as he tried to understand what she was telling him. Snorri's mother walked tall and proud in her long dress, keys jingling at her waist.

A raven flew overhead, unleashing a cry that made the hair on Ulf's arms stand on end.

CHAPTER 5

Snorri and Thorbjorn watched as the horsemen walked into the village. It was the following day, and they were sitting outside his house, Snorri cleaning his brynja and Thorbjorn sharpening his sword. Both men enjoying the quiet morning while the women were preparing dagmál, the first meal of the day. A brown cat lay near them, relaxing in the sun, its tail flicking from side to side. The cat was always near their house because Gunnhildr left food out for it. Snorri didn't mind though. It kept the mice out of his house and away from his children. Ragnar Nine-Finger, his father's champion and one of the most revered warriors in Norway, was at the head of the horsemen. Ragnar was taller than Snorri, but shorter than Oddi. His broad shoulders swayed as he sat awkwardly on the horse, his flame red hair blowing in the wind. They called him Nine-Finger because the little finger on his left hand was missing. Snorri heard a wolf had bitten it off, but he knew there were different stories around. He doubted anyone really knew how Ragnar had lost his finger.

"Think they found him?" Thorbjorn ran the whetstone down the edge of his sword as Snorri studied the group. Ten men had left and ten returned. He knew his father had sent other men to search for Thorvald, but it surprised him that Ragnar was one of them. Ragnar also had a reason to want to kill Thorvald, but then Ragnar was more loyal to his father than any man Snorri knew.

"Doesn't look like it."

The group stopped before the hall. Ragnar climbed off his horse, the animal looking almost relieved, and waved a greeting at Snorri and Thorbjorn. Ragnar looked towards the jarl's house, no doubt considering whether he should speak to the jarl first, but then turned and walked towards the hall. Snorri decided to join him. He wanted to find out what Ragnar had to say.

"Thorgils!" Snorri called. His son ran out of the house, greeting his father with a gap-toothed grin. At least he was still on Snorri's side, although Snorri knew the boy didn't understand why his mother was angry with him. "Take my brynja and put it in my chest. Be careful not to get any sand on it." The boy nodded as he took the chainmail vest from his father, grunting under its weight.

"Gunnhildr still not letting you in the house?" Thorbjorn asked as the boy went back inside.

"It's safer to slap a sleeping bear in the face at the moment." Thorbjorn laughed at the response while Snorri remembered the fight he and Gunnhildr had before the king summoned him. Snorri still couldn't believe that she had attacked him, even though Gunnhildr had always had a temper and Snorri knew she wasn't happy living in Thorgilsstad, or being married to him.

As soon as the boy went into the house, Snorri and Thorbjorn stood up and walked towards the hall. The cat glared at them, unhappy that they disturbed its rest before walking off to find a quieter spot.

Inside, Ragnar was whispering something to Snorri's mother sat in his father's seat. Snorri didn't mind her sitting there, although he had heard some of the older men complain. They expected him to take over while his father was ill. But Snorri didn't want to. Leading a ship was one thing, but a village was something else. Besides, Snorri had other things he needed to do first.

"A lot of men sleeping in the hall at the moment." Thorbjorn eyed up the men in the hall.

"Aye, there are a lot of unhappy wives in Thorgilsstad." Snorri shook his head as he thought of his own wife. "It seems they are not as happy about the raid as the men are."

Thorbjorn laughed. "That's why I never got married."

Snorri smiled, pretending that was the truth, before turning his attention to his mother and Ragnar. "They're talking about Thorvald."

"Aye." Thorbjorn caught the glance Lady Ingibjorg directed at her son, as he sat with the others in their usual spot, a bench left out near the end of the hall. That was where they could usually be found when they weren't training.

The smell of food caught Snorri's nose as he walked to his mother and Ragnar, and he felt his stomach rumble. He licked his lips as he glanced at the pot with the leftover stew from the previous night that a thrall was warming up.

"Snorri," Ragnar greeted him with a forearm grip. "I heard you've been up to your usual trouble." A wolf grin parted Ragnar's moustache from his beard.

"You know about that?" Snorri wasn't really surprised. He nodded his thanks to a thrall who handed him a cup of ale.

"You burn the hall of one of the king's favourites and people will find out about it. You know that." Ragnar's white teeth flashed through his red moustache and beard. "The man was a bastard anyway."

Snorri nodded. He still felt he had done the right thing and suspected his mother felt the same. He caught her looking towards the door of the hall and when Snorri turned, he saw his wife standing there, glowering at him. "Didn't expect you back so soon." Snorri turned back to Ragnar.

"Heard the king's sending you on a raid," Ragnar said with a shrug. Snorri raised his eyebrows. He had not realised that the news had spread. He glanced at his men where they sat, listening to the conversation. Even in the gloomy light, he saw the fire in Ulf's eyes and knew his young friend was still angry about it. "Where's Oddi?"

"He's gone to his father's to ask for some men. I need to make sure Thorgilsstad is protected while we are away."

"The king has promised to protect us in your absence, Snorri," Ingibjorg responded with a raised eyebrow, not believing it either.

"How many men are you taking?" Ragnar took a deep gulp of ale, smacking his lips with a smile.

"Two ships." Snorri saw the surprise on Ragnar's face. "We barely have enough men for three ships. We lost a lot of men that day."

"Should have lost a lot more than we did," Ingibjorg added.

"Aye, thanks to Odin, we didn't," Ragnar said.

"Or perhaps it is Tyr we should thank." Lady Ingibjorg glanced at Ulf.

"Which ships are you taking?" Ragnar asked. Snorri smiled as his father's champion avoided that conversation. He didn't like talking about that battle.

"Sae-Ulfr and War Bear."

"Not Thorgils Pride?"

"No, no man can touch her."

"My husband is more protective of that ship than he is of me." Ingibjorg smiled. They all smiled back, but Snorri knew it was true.

"I'm taking Ebbe as her captain," Snorri continued.

Ragnar shook his head. "I'll captain her. Ebbe can protect the village. He is one of your father's most experienced men."

"I'd rather have you stay," Snorri responded. "Thorgilsstad will be safer if the people know you are here."

"You expect me to miss a raid in Francia?" Ragnar pointed in the direction he thought Francia might be in.

Snorri stared at his father's champion, opening his mouth to protest, but thought better of it. Any warrior would want to raid the Frankish coast, but what was the real reason Ragnar wanted to go? *Thorvald?*

"Ragnar is right," Snorri's mother said, before he could voice his concern. "Ebbe is more than capable of looking after us here. Ragnar would be of more use on the raid."

Snorri glanced at his mother, unsure of what she meant. "I don't need protection, and even if I did, my hirdmen and crew are more than capable of doing so." He pointed to his men sat on the bench.

"Aye, and last time you didn't bring a massive army to our lands," Ragnar mocked.

Snorri snarled at him. "You were with us last time as well."

"I was there to look after your brother, not you."

"That turned out well, didn't it?" Snorri and Ragnar growled at each other like two wolves over a carcass.

"Enough." Ingibjorg rested her forehead on her fingertips. Both men stared at her, while at least trying to look embarrassed. "Snorri, take Ragnar and the crew of War Bear with you. Ebbe and the rest of your father's men will stay and protect us." When she looked up, her hard eyes showed she would not be argued with.

"I agree with your mother," Thorbjorn said before Snorri could respond. Snorri looked at the rest of his men. They all nodded, except for Ulf who was prodding his swollen lip.

"What happened to him now?" Ragnar asked, as if he had just noticed Ulf's bust lip.

"The king introduced him to Egil." Asbjorn smiled, enjoying every bit of Ulf's suffering.

"Ulf wasn't happy when the king ordered us on the raid," Snorri explained.

"The pup needs to learn his manners still," Ragnar sneered at Ulf.

Ragnar's words brought Ulf back to the present as he glared at Ragnar. "Are you going to teach me?"

Ragnar took a step towards Ulf who got to his feet, his fists clenched. Snorri shook his head. This is not what they needed now. "Perhaps I will. Thor knows it's about time," the jarl's champion growled. But before he could take another step towards Ulf, a new sound split through the air.

"What was that?" Brak asked, all eyes turning to Snorri, who looked towards the hall entrance.

"A horn?" Snorri frowned, not understanding what he was hearing. That horn meant only one thing, but that hadn't happened for as long as Snorri could remember. He turned to his mother and saw the same surprise on her face. Even she did not expect it. One of Snorri's men ran into the hall, pointing towards the path leading into the village, his eyes almost bulging out of his head.

"We're under attack!"

"Under attack?" Ragnar turned to Snorri. "We're under attack?"

Snorri realised the red-headed warrior was also struggling to understand. No one had ever attacked Thorgilsstad, or at least not in his lifetime. He looked at his mother, her face calm as she re-composed herself.

"Arnfinni's men," she said, but how she knew Snorri could not tell.

Snorri looked to where he had seen his wife, the smile on her face confirming what his mother had just said. "Fuck!" he shouted as he ran out of the hall, his hirdmen and Ragnar behind him. Drumbr looked longingly at the pot of stew while the thrall stood there, not knowing what to do. Outside, men were pulling on armour and grabbing shields as they ran towards the village entrance. Stopping in the square, Snorri looked along the path, and then back to his house where his brynja was. Young Thorgils ran out of the door, carrying Snorri's sword and helmet. His brynja would be too heavy for his young son. Still, Snorri felt proud that his son had understood the danger and knew what to do. All around him, the warriors of Thorgilsstad were getting ready, while women were ushering their children and the old into the hall. Some of the older warriors, those too old to stand in the shield wall, also made their way to the hall. They would be the last defence. Snorri's hirdmen came rushing out of the hall, brynjas on and weapons ready. Thorbjorn was carrying two shields, one for Snorri and the other for himself. Ragnar was still in his brynja, having worn it while he was on his hunt. Snorri was sure the warrior slept in it as well.

"Here, father!" His son reached him. The boy's face flushed.

Snorri ruffled his son's hair, before taking his helmet, its golden eye guard and cheek plated to look like fish scales, and placing it on his head. His view now focused only on what was in front of him, as he gripped Tyr's Fury, feeling the fire burning in his veins as it did every time he held the sword. The army of Thorgilsstad was forming a shield wall along the path, a well-practised routine his father had drilled into them. Snorri rubbed the tunic he was wearing, wishing he had his brynja, but had no time to get it. The enemy was approaching. He glanced towards his father's house and shook his head. His father wouldn't even come out to protect the village he had built from nothing.

"Snorri," Ragnar urged him. He had also seen the enemy.

"That's a lot of them," Thorbjorn said as Snorri took the shield from him.

"How many men did Arnfinni have?" Snorri asked, but no one responded. Snorri looked around him, picturing the layout of Thorgilsstad in his head. The village had no defensive wall, which meant an enemy could spread out and attack from different sides. That's how he would attack a place like this. "Ragnar, take as much men as you need and go towards the path leading to the wharves." Ragnar nodded and ran off, shouting at a group of men to follow him. Now all Snorri needed was for the enemy not to attack from anywhere else. "Let's go." He ran towards the entrance path, his men behind him. Others had already formed up, his father's captains mustering their men on either side of the path. Snorri placed himself in the gap left in the centre of the path, with Thorbjorn on his left. Ulf was on his right; his new helmet fierce — emblazoned on the eye guard were two snarling wolves facing each other. But the armour couldn't mask the fear underneath. Ulf's hand twitched, searching for the only thing that could really protect him, Ormstunga. The sky was ablaze, the sun beating down on the land. The worst conditions, as Ulf could not draw Ormstunga. If he did, then they would almost certainly lose this battle. *Thank Odin, I don't have to worry about that.* Snorri tightened the grip on his own sword as his men formed up behind him. The enemy stopped about ten paces in front of them and a warrior stepped forward. He took his helmet off and Snorri recognised him as Hallr, one of Arnfinni's men.

"Snorri Thorgilsson!"

Snorri stepped forward with a wolf grin on his face. "What do you want, Hallr?"

"You killed our jarl!" the warrior shouted, his face red. Behind him, his men were brandishing their weapons, their screams silencing the birds flying above them.

Snorri kept the smile on his face, determined to show no other emotion than absolute calm. This was easy for him though; these were the moments he lived for. "Go home, Hallr. King Halfdan has already demanded compensation for that. We have no quarrel."

"Aye, we heard what the king has asked from you." Hallr pointed his sword at Snorri. "You killed our jarl, and the king sends you on a raid. Thor's balls! Where is the punishment in that?" Tears ran down his face. Snorri understood their anger. These men owed everything they had to their jarl. He was their gold-giver, the one who made them rich and who honoured them during his feast. But more than that, he gave them a place to live and food to eat. Because of Snorri, these men had lost that and many of their families would struggle to survive. So, he understood, but he still had no regrets. Arnfinni had been a threat to his home, and Snorri did what he needed to protect the families of his men.

Snorri spread his arms out. "Join us. Here, you'll win more glory than you ever could with Arnfinni. Join us and even the gods will know your names." His men behind him cheered, their noise silencing Arnfinni's men. A raven croaked in the sky above them like it was agreeing with Snorri.

"I'd rather stick my hand in Fenrir's jaws than join you," Hallr retorted, holding up his sword hand. His men cheered behind him.

"You're not brave enough." Snorri's wolf grin stung the warrior even more. "Go home while you can. Your village has lost enough."

Hallr bristled at this, and so did the men behind him. "Not as much as you're going to lose now." Hallr glanced over

Snorri's head and smirked. Snorri had to trust that Ragnar could deal with the men Hallr had sent that way. "By Odin, we are going to burn this entire village down over your corpse. After I gouge your eyes out and cut your hands off."

"That was a dumb thing to say," Thorbjorn said as Snorri stepped back into his line, his wolf grin turning feral.

"Come then, Hallr. Show me what the men of Arnfinni can do." Hallr had many men with him, almost as many as Snorri had. But Thorgils' army was full of men who raided often and had fought many battles. They were better armed and never faltered. Unlike Arnfinni's men. "Skjaldborg!" Snorri roared and heard the thunk of shields overlapping and locking into place.

"Odin!" Thorbjorn shouted next to him, the rest of his hirdmen echoing his call.

"Tyr!" Ulf roared, surprising Snorri. He smiled when Snorri looked at him.

Snorri returned Ulf's smile, glad to see the confidence returning to his friend. Hallr's men had formed their own shield wall and were creeping towards Snorri's while banging their weapons on the back of their shields, which sent rolls of thunder over them and scared the birds out of Thorgilsstad. Dogs barked in the distance, and Snorri was sure he could hear a small child screaming from the hall. He saw the ravens circling overhead and, as always, wondered how they knew of the impending bloodshed. Perhaps Odin had sent them so he could enjoy the results of his interference. "Hold the line!" Snorri ordered as Hallr's force was coming towards them. They were about four paces away and moving too slow.

"Gonna die of old age before they get here," Brak said to his right, where he stood beside Ulf.

Snorri waited. They were now three paces away. Two paces. He waited until they lifted their feet to move the next pace. "Attack!"

The army of Thorgilsstad moved forward as one, a giant wave crashing onto the shore. Snorri punched out with his shield, sending Hallr into the man behind him. He stabbed the warrior beside Hallr through the neck as he lifted his axe to attack Ulf. A spear stabbed at Hallr from over Snorri's shoulder, but Hallr had recovered and brought his shield up to block the blow. Snorri pulled Tyr's Fury free, showering him and Ulf with blood. His heart thudded hard in his chest as the euphoria of battle ran through his veins, strengthening his muscles and slowing the world around. Hallr swung his sword down and Snorri blocked it with his shield. Beside him, Thorbjorn roared as he almost cleaved a man's head in two, his opponent's helmet no match for Thorbjorn's stocky arms. Snorri saw the doubt festering in Hallr's eyes. The man realised his mistake, but Snorri would not give him a chance to do anything about it. He stabbed at Hallr, who blocked with his shield, but the force of the blow sent him a step backwards. The man behind Hallr stabbed at Snorri with his spear, but Snorri twisted his head out of the way. Ulf chopped the spear in half with his axe. His opponent tried to use this distraction to bury his axe in Ulf's skull, but Ulf got his shield up in time. Seeing a gap between two shields, Snorri rammed his sword into the man's gut, as Ulf crushed his opponent's face with the head of his axe. The crunch of his skull shattering echoed over the sounds of swords and axes clashing against wooden shields.

"Come on, Hallr! Show me your steel!" Snorri punched Hallr with his shield again. Snorri was bigger and stronger than Hallr, and again, Hallr was forced into the man behind. This created some time and space for Snorri to see how his men were faring along the shield wall. All around, Hallr's men were being pushed back. They were no match for the warriors of Thorgilsstad.

"For Arnfinni!" Hallr tried to rally his men. He must have seen the same thing and wanted to turn the tide. The name of their dead jarl seemed to inspire them, but they were still no match for the men of Thorgilsstad. Hallr stabbed at Snorri's chest, putting a lot of force into the strike. Snorri took half a step forward and deflected the blow with his shield instead of blocking it. Before Hallr could react to this, Snorri rammed Tyr's Fury through his mouth, breaking teeth and severing his tongue. Snorri laughed as the sword ripped through the back of Hallr's head. The men around Hallr froze as their leader died and were dispatched by Thorbjorn and Ulf on either side. Snorri pressed his shield against Hallr's body, using it to free his sword from Hallr's mouth. The man behind Hallr stepped aside so the body wouldn't fall on him and this created space for Snorri, who laughed as he rushed through it. The warrior who had stepped aside screamed as he realised what was happening before Snorri opened him up from chest to pelvis. His corpse fell away as the rest of Snorri's hirdmen rushed through the gap and got behind the enemy's shield wall.

"Kill them all!" Snorri roared, his blood lust taking over. With his hirdmen beside him, he hacked and stabbed, killing anyone who came within reach of his deadly sword. This is what Snorri was made for. This was the role the Norns had given him. He would fill the benches of Valhalla with warriors and they would sing his name in glory.

"Snorri!" His mother's voice ripped through the air, silencing the battle song and bringing Snorri back to Midgard. Snorri glared at her as she stood on the path, surrounded by the other women of the village. He saw his wife, clutching their youngest to her breast and young Thorgils, holding onto his mother's leg. Snorri recognised the fear in his son's eyes and remembered his son had never seen a battle before. Snorri breathed deep, trying to calm himself as he surveyed the scene around him. Most of Arnfinni's men were dead, and the rest dropped their weapons or ran away, calling for mercy from the gods. Snorri recognised some men from Thorgilsstad amongst the fallen as the battle lust left him. He spotted Ulf on his knees and worried that his friend had been injured. The shock of that hit him harder than he thought it would. But Ulf looked up, his face pale under the blood of his enemies, and smiled at him. Snorri felt relieved that his friend was fine. There was still the strange connection between them he never understood. The rest of his hirdmen gathered around him, all of them breathing heavily.

Snorri looked at Tyr's Fury, seeing the rivulets of blood running down her blade. He wiped her clean on his tunic and saw his reflection in it. His face was covered in gore, his eyes as hard as the steel of his sword. *No wonder young Thorgils looked frightened.* Snorri's tunic stuck to his body, drenched in blood and sweat, and Snorri knew it would reek soon. Large ravens circled the sky above them, their cries filling the silence left after the battle. A few dived, trying to start their feast early.

Something needed to be done with the dead before they attracted scavengers more dangerous than the ravens.

"Collect our fallen and take them to the square. Dump Hallr's men in the forest. Give the wolves a feast," Snorri ordered as he walked to where the women stood, searching for their men. Some smiling when they found them, others looking more concerned as they couldn't. Gunnhildr stared at him, trying to remain impassive, but Snorri saw the fear in her eyes and the tremble of her bottom lip. He doubted she would dare to attack him now with that axe of hers. Taking his helmet off, Snorri knelt down and took his son by the shoulder.

"There's nothing to fear, Thorgils," he said when his son tried to hide behind his mother.

"Snorri, don't—" Gunnhildr started, but the glare she got from him killed the words in her throat. His mother placed a hand on his wife's shoulder, and Snorri nodded his thanks.

He turned his attention back to his son. "Don't worry, Thorgils. It's over, we're all safe now." He kept his voice calm, trying to make it sound as soothing as possible, but it was difficult. His voice was hoarse from the battle, and he needed a drink.

"Are you hurt?" his son asked, his voice sounding small and afraid, but the young boy squared his shoulders and did his best to look strong in front of his father.

Snorri smiled and shook his head. "I'm fine."

"Why did you kill those men?" young Thorgils asked. Like all boys, his son dreamt of being a warrior. The sagas encouraged them, with tales of mighty warriors defeating their foes and the gods slaying the giants. But the sagas left out the truth of battles, the very things his son was confronted with right now as he saw his father soaked in the blood of others and stinking of death.

"Because we had to protect our home." Snorri didn't know what else to say. He glanced at his mother and saw the reassuring smile on her face.

"But…" young Thorgils started, but stopped. He watched as Ulf walked past, the scarred warrior smiling at him. Snorri wondered what was going on in his son's mind as he saw the darker side of the otherwise cheerful men he was used to.

Snorri gripped his son's shoulder, making him look at his father again. "There are many things in this world you still need to learn, son. Sometimes we need to do ugly things to protect those we care about. Do you understand?" Young Thorgils nodded, but Snorri saw the boy didn't. Still, he felt proud at the brave face his son was putting on.

"Come, Thorgils," Ingibjorg took her grandson's hand. "Why don't we go clean your father's sword?" Snorri handed his sword to his son, who always loved cleaning it. But after seeing how deadly it was, seemed too scared to touch it. "I'll talk to him," Ingibjorg whispered to Snorri.

"Thank you, mother." He smiled at her as she led his son away. Ragnar walked up the path, covered in blood and with one man limping beside him from a cut in his leg. "How many?"

"Only a small number, slightly more than what I had, but they didn't expect us. We dealt with them quickly enough," Ragnar responded while surveying the surrounding scene. "Looks like you had more fun."

Snorri nodded. "Hallr led them."

"That goat-fucker," Ragnar sneered. "His mother should have drowned him as a baby. Never had any wits."

"Was a good fighter though." Snorri watched the men of Thorgilsstad comb through the dead, looking for friends and looting the enemy as he scratched his beard, feeling the blood drying and his beard becoming sticky. "How many men did Arnfinni have?"

Ragnar shrugged. "Less than your father."

"There was about a crew's worth in the hall," Snorri replied. As he looked up, Ebbe, one of his father's captains, was walking towards him. The ageing warrior had a cut to his arm, but otherwise looked unscathed. He was one of Thorgils' most trusted men, having grown up with the jarl. "Ebbe," Snorri greeted him with a nod.

"Snorri, Ragnar." The warrior greeted them. "That was some fight." He looked at Ragnar, seeing his jarl's champion covered in blood.

"Snorri sent me to the back path." He thumbed over his shoulder. "Thought they might send some men around there."

"Your father taught you well." Ebbe looked towards the jarl's house and Snorri knew what he was thinking.

"That's what I would have done," Snorri responded. He surveyed the forest around the village, frowning.

"What's wrong?" Ebbe asked.

"Snorri thinks there might be more men out there," Ragnar responded, also searching the trees for any signs of life.

"How many did we lose?" Snorri's tunic was drying in the spring sun, becoming hard and causing his skin to itch.

"Can't say for certain, and Odin knows it could have been worse. I think about seven men died, but a few have serious injuries."

Snorri grimaced. He could not afford to lose men, not now that he had to go on this raid.

"So much for the king protecting Thorgilsstad," Ragnar half growled.

"Can you blame them?" Ebbe picked at some dried blood around the cut on his arm. "Would we just sit idly by if someone killed our jarl, even if the king ordered it?"

Snorri and Ragnar looked at each other. The old warrior had a point. "Should have expected it, I guess."

"Well, it's a good thing you posted guards," Ragnar responded.

"More out of habit than any caution." Snorri spat. "I think we should send some men to scour the forest. I don't want any more surprises." He looked towards the green expanse.

"I'll send the group I had. Our fight was shorter, and they are fresher," Ragnar said.

Snorri nodded, patting Ragnar on the shoulder before he turned and walked away. He turned to Ebbe. "If I take two ships with me on this raid, will you have enough men to protect the village?"

The older warrior thought for a while, as he scratched an old scar above his right eye. "Hard to say. It depends on how many of the remaining men will be able to fight."

Snorri nodded. "Get your arm looked at. I'll get one of my men to take charge here." Ebbe smiled and walked off as Snorri watched him, wondering if the old man blamed him for this. He shook his head. He had more important things to worry about now. "Asbjorn!" he called his friend from where he had been standing with the rest of Snorri's hirdmen and some of his crew.

"Snorri?"

"Can you take care of this?"

Asbjorn nodded, knowing what he meant.

"I need to get cleaned up and talk to my son." Snorri looked around. "Where's Ulf?"

Asbjorn shrugged. "He just walked off after the fight. Perhaps gone to the hall. Think they'll come back?"

"Doubt it, they've lost too many men. But I've sent Ragnar to make sure no one is hiding in the forest."

Asbjorn nodded. "What about those who surrendered?" He pointed to a group of men huddled together, being watched by some of Snorri's crew.

"Shit, I forgot about them." Snorri thought for a while. "We should send them to the king, so he can deal with them, but I can't send a group large enough to guard them, and I don't want to risk sending a smaller group." Asbjorn waited patiently. Snorri took a deep breath. Being a good leader meant having to make hard choices. He looked at his father's house again, his stomach twisting in furious knots. "Cut off their right hands and set them loose. They can serve as a warning of what happens when you attack Thorgilsstad." Asbjorn nodded and walked off to carry out the task. Snorri shook his head and headed to the hall. He needed a drink.

CHAPTER 6

Ulf stared at his shaking hands, still covered in blood, as he sat in the hall. The women had gone to help the injured after sending the children back to their houses, while thralls were bringing buckets of water so the men could be cleaned and tended to. Ulf should have been outside helping, but he needed to get away. The sight of the bodies lying on the ground, blood and gore soaking into the soil, and the screaming of the injured were too much for him. Others felt the same. He saw it in the faces of other men who needed to get away from the battleground. Even for the experienced warriors, the stink of death was too close to home. But for Ulf, it was not about that. He still didn't think of Thorgilsstad as his home. Even after all this time, there was still a shadow hanging over this village. The reason Ulf had to get away from there was because the scene reminded him of the carnage left behind after the battle at The Giant's Toe. Staring at his hands, all Ulf could see was the body of Vidar lying in his arms, his throat slit wide open by Griml.

"There you are." Snorri's voice made Ulf look up, and he saw his friend walking towards him. Snorri had rinsed the blood off his face and hands, but still wore his blood-soaked tunic. Ulf clasped his hands together so that Snorri wouldn't notice them shaking. "It's not always easy to face the battlefield after the fight." Snorri sat next to Ulf, smiling when Ulf didn't respond. Snorri nodded at the men in the hall.

"They looked shocked," Ulf said after a while, if only to move the attention away from him.

Snorri nodded, his face clouding over. "Thorgilsstad had always felt like the safest place in Norway." Ulf raised an eyebrow at this. He had thought the same about his uncle's farm before.

"No place is safe."

"Aye," Snorri agreed, "but Thorgilsstad had never been attacked in my lifetime. For many of these men it would have been the same." Ulf looked around the hall again, seeing the pale faces of the men there. A thrall brought two cups of ale and placed them on the table. She had a clean tunic over her shoulder, which she handed to Snorri with a glint in her eye – the same way Hulda used to look at Ulf. Snorri took the tunic from her, his hand lingering on hers for a few heartbeats more than necessary.

"They blame me." Ulf saw how the men glared at him. Snorri continued eyeing up the thrall, who was now returning to her duties, as he took off his fouled tunic.

"For what?" Snorri wiped his body clean with the dirty tunic before putting the new one on.

"The attack." Ulf took a cup from the table and studied the ale inside before taking a sip.

"The attack wasn't your fault. It was my decision to burn Arnfinni's hall."

"But I'm the reason we were there. If I had never come here, then none of this would have happened." Ulf took another sip of his ale, but the drink did nothing to calm his thoughts.

To his surprise, Snorri laughed. "You didn't come here, remember. We carried you here."

"They still blame me."

Snorri looked at the men and nodded, confirming what Ulf thought. "Like I said, they are in shock." The two of them sat there for a while, drinking their ale in silence.

"How's your son?" Ulf had noticed the fear in young Thorgils' eyes after the battle.

Snorri smiled. "He'll be fine. The first time you see battle is always hard."

Ulf nodded. "It's nothing like they tell you in the sagas." Snorri laughed as Ulf remembered his first actual fight. It had been against a group of pirates who had been harassing the bændr the previous summer. Ulf almost shivered as he remembered the spear that would have gone through his eye if he had not raised his shield in time.

"I still remember my first battle," Snorri said with a glint in his eye after he took a sip of his ale. "It's like fucking your first woman, you never forget it." Snorri slapped Ulf on the shoulder, laughing. *Hulda*, Ulf thought as he fought down another wave of shame.

"You never told me." He tried to distract his mind.

"About my first fuck?" Snorri teased him and laughed when Ulf frowned. Ulf could only shake his head. Many men got like this after a battle. The joy of being alive takes over and they lose control of their senses. "I barely had whiskers on my face when my father took me on my first raid. 'It's time to find out whose blood flows through your veins,' he said." Snorri scratched his beard as he remembered. "Aye, I never understood what he meant either," he explained when he saw the frown on Ulf's face. "We were fighting Arnfinni's men that day, a border dispute, I think. I remember standing in the shield wall between my father and Ragnar, so proud of myself. This was where my saga was going to start." Snorri laughed at the memory. "The first warrior who came at me was a big man, I swear by Odin. The ground shook as he charged. He had this enormous axe, which he swung at my head. It struck my shield so hard, I flew backwards. My father didn't take many men, so our shield wall was only one man deep. As I hit the ground, I thought my saga would end there. Ragnar killed the giant before he could take advantage and he and my father closed the gap."

"Your fight was over?"

"No, I stood back up and rejoined the fight. The rest is a blur, but Ragnar told me I fought well. After the fight, my father gave me Tyr's Fury. She had belonged to the giant and I remember my father saying, 'Perhaps this blade by your side will teach you not to be so reckless.'" Both Ulf and Snorri laughed, knowing that he had never learnt that lesson.

"She has served you well." Ulf glanced at the sword on Snorri's hip.

"Aye, she had. Just like Ormstunga will serve you well."

Ulf looked at his sword resting in her new scabbard. Lady Ingibjorg had it made for him after the battle at The Giant's Toe. It was made of leather, carved with an image of a wolf fighting Jörmungandr. Above the wolf were the symbols of Tyr and Thor. Wool lined the inside of the scabbard to protect the blade from the elements. "Providing it's not sunny," he responded after a while, and the men started laughing again.

"How much longer do we have to row?" the whiny voice echoed off the water, waking Ulf from his trance. It had been two weeks since the attack on Thorgilsstad as Ulf sat on his chest on the Sae-Ulfr, rowing in time with those around him. They had spent much of that time training, with Ragnar pushing them hard. The men had complained at first, many of them still sore from defending Thorgilsstad. But they quickly got into the rhythm. These men were warriors and understood what needed to be done. Ulf winced at the tightness of his muscles as he pulled his oar back. When most men had rested after training with Ragnar, Snorri made Ulf spar with one of his hirdmen. Snorri still felt Ulf could improve, even after the battle at The Giant's Toe.

"It's barely been half a day of rowing," Rolf Tree-Foot responded to the tall man sitting near Ulf. "My grandmother once rowed three days without stopping, not complained once." Snorri's steersman was one of the oldest men Ulf knew. Rolf got his by-name, Tree-Foot, because of the wooden stump he had on his leg after losing it in a sea battle.

"Was that after she saw you?" one of Snorri's crew retorted, causing the others to laugh.

Ulf looked at the tall warrior as he sulked. He was half a head taller than Oddi, but not as wide at the shoulder. He reminded Ulf of a young tree stretching for the sunlight and standing tall and slim. Ulf had seen this man once before with his red hair and familiar features. It had been at Jól during Ulf's first winter in Thorgilsstad, and even then, Ulf did not like him much.

"Why, in Odin's name, did he have to come with?" Thorbjorn complained about Magni, Oddi's older brother.

Oddi shrugged before answering. "My father decided he needed more fighting experience, especially after the battle."

"Heard he fought well there." Brak plunged his oar into the calm water of the fjord. Ulf glanced at Brak. He did not remember seeing Magni at the battle.

"He survived, you mean," Thorbjorn retorted.

"Doesn't matter," Oddi said. "My father wanted him to come with. I could not refuse him." Ulf looked from Oddi to Magni. Despite their similar features, the two brothers were completely different. Oddi was calm and friendly, even if he believed himself to be wise. Magni was the opposite. He was an arrogant bully who liked to pick on those weaker than him, or so Ulf had been told.

"Aye, well let's just hope that the cockerel doesn't get himself killed." Thorbjorn spat. The Cockerel was Magni's by-name. He liked to dress in bright colours and walked around like a prize bird showing off its plumage.

"How come you are not rowing?" Magni complained to Rolf, distracting Ulf's friends from their conversation.

"If Rolf rows, then his arms will probably fall off. Who will steer the ship then?" Thorbjorn responded.

"Me, of course," Magni said.

"You ever steered a ship?" Drumbr looked like he was actually interested. Ulf only shook his head as he carried on rowing, his bruised shoulder hurting from where Asbjorn had struck him during the previous day's sparring session. Snorri was sitting across from him, scowling.

"No, but how hard can it be?" The crew laughed in response. "Rolf can do it, and only the gods know how old he is!" Magni's face went red as he tried to defend himself.

"Rolf was Ran's lover once, a long time ago," Thorbjorn added to annoy the old sailor, "and the old sea bitch still loves him. That's why he can still steer a ship."

"Don't call Ran a bitch, especially not when we are in her domain. You don't want to anger the bitch," Rolf said, causing the crew to laugh.

Snorri pulled his oar in and got up from his chest. He cleared his throat and spat into the water before making his way to Rolf.

"Snorri, tell your men they should respect me more!" Magni complained as Snorri walked past him.

Snorri stopped, his teeth bared as he glared at Magni. The crew went silent. The only noise now was the oars slapping the water and the sea birds crying above them. "Why should my men respect you, Magni?"

Magni stood up, letting go of his oar. The men around him cursed as it interfered with their oars. If he hoped that his height advantage over Snorri would make him look more imposing, then he was mistaken. "Because I am the son of a jarl," he crooned proudly, puffing out his chest.

"That might be true when you are sitting in your father's hall, but on my ship you are nothing until you prove otherwise. And, by Thor, if you ever command me to do anything again, I'll gut you and feed you to Jörmungandr," Snorri growled, his fists clenched by his side. Snorri was still angry about the attack on Thorgilsstad, but Ulf could not tell who he was angry at. Himself or his father.

"But... but..." Magni shrank under Snorri's glare. A small wave rolled under the keel of the Sae-Ulfr, causing the ship to wobble. Snorri stayed on his feet, his body barely reacting to it. But Magni, who had less experience on a ship, fell backwards, landing on his chest and almost losing his oar. It was like Ran had sent the wave to prove a point.

"If you want the respect of my men," Snorri looked down on the taller man, "then you need to earn it."

"How?" Magni asked, his voice sounding weak.

"Ask your brother," Snorri responded and walked away. Ulf looked at Oddi, who was sitting in his usual spot. His face showed no emotion as he rowed, unlike Magni, whose face matched his red hair. Even the men his father had sent with him looked the other way.

Rowing beside them was the War Bear, the men on her benches looking towards them. Ulf guessed they were wondering what was going on. Ragnar stood by the stern as he steered and called for his crew to concentrate on rowing.

"We should be near the mouth of the fjord soon." Ulf heard Snorri saying to Rolf.

"Aye," the old steersman responded. "Where do you think they'll be?"

Snorri shrugged. "We're a day late, so he's either camped somewhere or gone back to the king." Ulf looked over his shoulder as he rowed. He could not tell where they were, but Snorri and his men knew this fjord well. This was only Ulf's second time leaving the fjord. The first time had mixed results. Ulf caught sight of something that looked like a bird in the distance.

"I think I see a ship!" he called to the stern.

Snorri looked ahead, shielding his eyes from the sun. "Thorbjorn?"

Thorbjorn got up and stood on the prow, clinging onto it as he stared into the distance. The prow beast was still in its resting place. The chest by the mast. They were still in friendly waters and also they didn't want Tormod to think they were attacking him. "Aye, the Bear-Slayer is correct, there is a ship there."

"Tormod?" Snorri asked

"Hard to say. The mast is up, but there's no sail. Looks like she's anchored." Thorbjorn surveyed the surrounding land. They were getting closer now, and Thorbjorn could make out more details. "Must be them, we're nearing the mouth of the fjord."

"What's going on?" Ragnar shouted from the stern of the War Bear, his hand cupped around his mouth to help his voice carry over the water.

"Tormod." Snorri pointed in the ship's direction. "He's waiting for us." Snorri looked ahead again, the anger building up in him.

Not long after, Snorri called the order to pull the oars in and the two ships came to a rest on the stony beach. Ulf rolled his shoulders to loosen the muscles, again feeling the bruise given to him by Asbjorn. It always felt like Asbjorn was trying to hurt him, and Ulf guessed that was why Snorri had them sparring. While the others always enjoyed watching them, Ulf hated those sparring sessions. No matter how hard he tried, he still could not defeat any of Snorri's hirdmen. Ulf shook the thoughts away as he jumped off the ship, his knees almost buckling under him as he landed in the cold water. He saw the tents set up by Tormod's crew, with campfires spluttering amongst them. The smell of cooked fish hung in the air, attracting a swarm of sea birds looking for an easy meal. Snorri ordered his men to put up their tents and to get some fires going as he walked past Ulf.

"You're late," Tormod greeted them with a sour face. Snorri did not respond. Instead, he walked away, pointing to a spot where he wanted his tent. Tormod grabbed hold of Snorri's shoulder, turning him around so they faced each other. "You are late, Snorri. The king told you to be here yesterday." Tormod grit his teeth, the vein on his forehead bulging.

Snorri shoved Tormod, sending the big warrior back a few steps. All conversation stopped as everyone turned to see what was happening. "Why do you think we are late?"

"I don't care why you are late." Tormod squared up to Snorri. "You should not be late when the king orders you do to something."

Snorri was panting, with his fists clenched by his side. Tormod's men stood up from their fires, looking at each other. Snorri's men stopped what they were doing and watched Tormod's. Ulf glanced at Snorri's hirdmen, trying to understand what to do from their behaviour, but his friends seemed unconcerned. In the end, Ragnar pulled the two warriors apart. Tormod looked like he was about to react until he saw who it was.

"Thorgilsstad was attacked two weeks ago," Ragnar growled at Tormod.

"Attacked?" Tormod looked confused, his eyes darting from Ragnar to Snorri. "By who?"

"Hallr, one of Arnfinni's men. Had about fifty men with him." Snorri had not changed his stance.

Ulf noticed concern on Tormod's face and thought it was for Thorgilsstad, but then Tormod asked, "What about Heidrun?"

Snorri sneered at him, but responded anyway, "She's fine. They didn't attack the farms. Only the village."

"Heidrun's his sister," Brak explained, seeing the confusion on Ulf's face. "She's married to one of the bændr." Ulf nodded his thanks.

"You defeated them?" Tormod signalled for his men to calm down, and Ulf saw the relief on their faces. They might be men of King Halfdan, but Snorri's crew still outnumbered them.

"Killed more than half of them and captured twelve. The rest fled," Snorri responded.

Tormod scanned the men as they disembarked Snorri's ships. "You sent them to the king?" he asked when he couldn't spot any captives.

Snorri shook his head. "We cut their right hands off and sent them back where they came from."

Tormod went red and threw his arms up in the air. "You should have sent them to the king. He could have taken them into his army. The king needs men, you know that."

Snorri stepped right into Tormod's face, their noses touching as he growled, "Seven men died defending Thorgilsstad, another eleven seriously injured, two of which died that night from their injuries. I had to make sure that I left enough men to protect Thorgilsstad from further attacks."

"The king has promised to protect our village while you were on this raid."

"He's done a great job so far." Snorri turned and stomped off, leaving Tormod gaping.

Ragnar turned to follow, but with a quick glance at Tormod said, "It's not been your village for a long time, Tormod."

Tormod just stood there, watching them. His mouth opened to say something, but he closed it quickly again, as Snorri's men got back to setting up camp and starting fires. Ulf caught him looking his way, Tormod's eyes lingering on the hilt of Ormstunga. He saw the lust in Tormod's eyes and reminded himself to never leave his sword alone during this raid as he turned to follow Snorri, his wet boots slippery on the stony beach.

Later that night, with the sun low on the horizon, they all sat around a fire finishing a meal of venison and fresh bread they had brought from the village.

Magni, who had invited himself to sit with them, was picking at the blisters on his hands. "I think I got a splinter," he complained. Ulf smiled as he saw Thorbjorn roll his eyes. "You guys must have been lucky; your oars were probably smooth. Mine was very rough." He waited to get a response from them, but nobody spoke. They were still tense from Snorri's confrontation with Tormod. "Hope it doesn't get infected."

"Don't worry about it," Drumbr responded with a mouth full of meat. "If it does, then we'll just chop it off."

"Aye, we did with the last guy who used your oar. He had the same problem, but then we just chopped his hand off and the problem was gone," his brother added, unable to help himself. Magni's face paled, which caused the brothers to laugh. He looked towards Oddi, who only shrugged. But Ulf saw the small smile in the corner of his mouth.

"If you live long enough, Magni, then we'll turn your womanly hands into those of a real man." Thorbjorn held up his own hand to show his rough and calloused palm. The skin thickened over years of fighting and rowing.

Ulf couldn't help but look at his own hands. He rubbed his palms with his thumbs, feeling the roughness of his skin as he recalled the last conversation he had with Lady Ingibjorg while they were still in the forest.

"I remember the day my son carried you into our village," Lady Ingibjorg said, as her eyes took in the surrounding trees. *"You were so consumed by your anger, by your quest for vengeance."* She glanced at Ulf with her green eyes, reading him as she would the runes. *"You still are. But I wonder, Ulf, do you still hate your father as much as you did then?"*

The question caught Ulf by surprise. He paused briefly as he thought of the answer. "I could never understand why my father would go to battle when he had a young son to raise." Ulf took a deep breath as he remembered the early days of his *life. "My uncle had tried explaining it to me many times, but it still felt like my father had abandoned me."*

"You didn't understand what it was like to have something to fight for. To have someone you were willing to die for to protect."

Ulf scowled, glancing at Lady Ingibjorg before shaking his head. "When Griml attacked my uncle's farm, I ran into that fight without thought. I believed I could kill the large troll." Ulf rubbed the scar under his tunic where Griml had stabbed him. "Everything changed for me that day. Now I have friends, a new home..." He wasn't sure how to finish.

Lady Ingibjorg placed a tender hand on his shoulder. "You have changed much since the day you arrived. But Odin likes his games, and he's made sure your path has not been easy." She looked to the sky as if she was searching for the All-father. "Tell me, Ulf, what else are you prepared to lose to get your vengeance?"

Ulf looked at Snorri, sat across the fire. The shadows cast by the flames hid his eyes under his brooding eyebrows. He studied the men around the fire. All of them, apart from Ragnar and Magni, were men he called friends. Men he had fought and drunk beside. Ulf prayed he would not lose any more friends as he stroked the names of his family on his axe, joined by that of Vidar and Hulda. Thunder split the air and Ulf looked skyward, wondering what that meant.

"Rain?" Asbjorn also turned to the cloudless sky.

"Bad omen, I'd say," Oddi responded.

"Well, don't say it then," Thorbjorn complained, rubbing the Mjöllnir around his neck.

CHAPTER 7

"Told you not to call Ran a bitch. She's angry now."

Ulf followed Rolf's gaze and saw the dark clouds on the horizon speeding towards them like an attacking army. Distant thunder could be heard on the wind as the sea birds fled towards land. It was late afternoon, and the weather had been good. The sun was out as they sailed towards Suðrikaupstefna, with only a few clouds in the sky and a nice wind, which meant they did not have to row. But Ran was a fickle giantess and now her mood had turned.

"Can we outrun it?" Snorri peered at his old steersman. Rolf smiled and shook his head. "Shit."

"This is what happens when you start a raid with the wrong intentions." Drumbr frowned as he sat near Ulf on his own chest.

"Aye," his brother agreed, rubbing the Mjöllnir around his neck.

Ulf was nervous. He had never been in a sea storm before, but his uncle had told Ulf enough stories to make him clutch his axe. Snorri scanned the horizon. His face was calm, but Ulf saw the way he gripped the gunwale.

"That storm doesn't frighten me." Magni stood facing the approaching clouds with hands on his hips and chest puffed out. "Let the gods bring their worst, we can take it." Around him, men paled and moved away, as if expecting lighting to strike the arrogant cockerel. Thorbjorn whispered a prayer and threw one of his arm rings into the sea.

"What?" Thorbjorn noticed Ulf looking at him. "It's never good to anger the gods." Ulf nodded. His aunt had told him the same thing. Ulf looked at his own arm rings, but decided against it. So far, the gods had brought him nothing but misery. Besides, Ulf doubted he would die at sea, not until he had killed Griml. That was the oath Ulf had sworn to Odin.

"We'll see if you are still as brave when the storm hits us, brother," Oddi responded to Magni's boasting.

Magni turned to Oddi with flared nostrils. "You don't think that storm will actually hit, do you? It's too far away, isn't it, Snorri?"

Snorri stared at Magni with an eyebrow raised. Instead of answering, he looked landward again. "Rolf, can we make it to the shore before she hits us?" Ulf would have smiled at how Magni's face paled when he realised they were in trouble if he wasn't so nervous about the storm.

"We can try." Rolf turned the Sae-Ulfr towards land. Snorri signalled for the other two ships to do the same. The clouds were rolling in fast, the distant thunder warning of the gods' anger. "Wind's picking up," Rolf shouted. "The gods are coming for you, Magni." He laughed as the sail bulged and the Sae-Ulfr groaned at the extra strain.

"Me?" Magni turned to Rolf, his eyes wide.

"Aye, you challenged the gods, and they accepted." Thunder ripped through the sky, the men covering their heads with their cloaks as the rain lashed down. Rolf Treefoot laughed as the storm caught up with them.

"Hang on!" Snorri shouted. The crew hunkered down, grabbing hold of anything they could find as the sea came alive. The increasing swell rocked the Sae-Ulfr around as men clutched the Mjöllnir pendants around their necks. Some threw offerings into the sea, hoping this would calm Ran – the mother of the waves. But Ran was angry now. She demanded blood and had sent her nine daughters to collect it for her.

Asbjorn glared at Ulf as he held onto the ship. Ulf had never wanted to go on this raid — he wanted to go north to find Griml. In the darkening sky, the Black Eagle, Tormod's ship, was thrown into the air. For a heartbeat, it seemed like she would fly away like her namesake before she came crashing down into the sea. The rushing water swept men across the deck as their crewmates tried desperately to grab hold of them. Ulf had no more time to see what was happening on the other ship as a wave crashed over the side of the Sae-Ulfr, drenching him. Ulf's heart skipped a beat when he lost grip of his chest and started sliding away, but a powerful hand grabbed hold of him and pulled Ulf back. Ulf nodded his thanks to Drumbr, who was smiling back at him.

"Why are you not scared?" Ulf shouted over the roaring storm.

"As long as we have that old bastard, nothing will happen to us!" Drumbr pointed to Rolf. The old steersman gripped the tiller as he screamed into the wind. Ulf could not make out what

Rolf was saying, his voice lost in the strong winds that tore around the deck. Snorri was shouting something and pointing towards the sail. Drumbr must have understood as he and Brak crawled along the sides and started untying knots.

"What are they doing?" Ulf screamed to Oddi.

"We need to trim the sail, otherwise the wind will break the mast." Ulf nodded as he watched the brothers struggling. Other crew members had joined them and together they reduced the sail. Ulf tried to see how the other ships were doing, but could not find them in the swells, some the size of mountains. He began to wonder if they would survive this. Rolf was still laughing and screaming into the wind, while Snorri stood near him, his face still calm as he tried to peer into the dark sky. Magni, cowering between chests, had his eyes screwed shut as he hugged his knees and prayed to the gods.

Ulf craned his neck over the side, looking for the War Bear, but the Sae-Ulfr crashed through a giant swell, throwing her into the air. It was like the gods had plucked him from the ship, and just when Ulf thought Tyr would carry him to safety, he crashed back to the deck again. The wind was knocked out of him and as Ulf struggled to regain his breath; a man was grabbed by a wave and thrown overboard. Those around screamed as they tried to grab hold of their friend, but there was nothing they could do. Ran had her first victim, and seeing the dark sky above lit up by lightning, Ulf knew she was not done yet. Another wave crashed over the side, drenching Ulf with sea water and dragging him along the deck. Panic took hold of Ulf as he desperately tried to grab hold of anything to stop him from going to Ran's Hall.

"Odin! You promised!" Ulf roared before choking on seawater. As if Odin had heard him, a hand grabbed hold of Ulf and pulled him to safety. Ulf nodded his thanks to Geir, who had found a rope and tied it around his arm. Some men were pointing over the side, the lashing wind only allowing Ulf to catch some of their words.

"War... ear! Sh... cap... zed!" The blood froze inside him when Ulf understood what had happened. The War Bear had capsized. Snorri shouted orders and men threw ropes overboard. Ulf tried to crawl to the other side of the ship so he could help, but as soon as he moved, another wave sent him crashing into the mast. Ulf clung to it as he spat more seawater out of his mouth. All Ulf could do as the crew of the Sae-Ulfr tried to save the men of the War Bear, was hold onto the mast, his eyes shut as they burnt from the salty water. Images of his family came to him as the world around slowed down. *His uncle and aunt working in the fields beside their small farmhouse, his two cousins running around, their shrill laughter echoing as they were being chased by their large hound.* The wind screamed in his ears as the images changed. *His family slaughtered, all of them, even the hound in front of a burning house. Then Hulda sat on top of him under the hanging tree, the pleasure pulsating in his groin as she rode him.* Thunder crashed around him. *Hulda slumped against the base of the tree, with her throat slit, blood drenching her breasts.* Men cried out. *A large army in front of him. Vidar lay by his feet on the blood-soaked ground, his head almost sliced off.*

"I will avenge them!" Ulf screamed into the wind, shaking his head to dispel the images. Thunder crashed above him and then everything went quiet. The ship stopped rocking as the winds died down.

"It's over?" Magni whimpered. Ulf opened his eyes, feeling them sting from the salt water. The sun broke through the clouds, chasing the storm away as the men of the Sae-Ulfr looked around in stunned silence.

"Aye, Ran got what she wanted; she'll leave us alone now," Rolf responded, long straggly grey hair plastered all over his face as he turned the Sae-Ulfr around. Or Odin did. Ulf looked up to the sky, convinced that Odin had sent him a warning. The Brak brothers reefed the sail, while others were throwing ropes into the water.

Ulf wiped the snot from his burning nose and got to his feet. His legs were weak, forcing Ulf to support himself on the mast. Most of the chests had been dislodged, some knocked open and their contents spilled over the deck. Geir was still huddled by his chest, the rope still tied to his arm. His wide eyes and pale face echoed the way Ulf felt. Ulf brushed the hair from his face and took a deep breath to calm his nerves.

"Get those men in quickly!" Snorri ordered. Stumbling to the side, Ulf saw the nightmare of many warriors. The War Bear was upside down, her keel floating in the calm water. Men clung desperately to the ship while trying to help others. Ragnar was swimming towards the Sae-Ulfr, still wearing his brynja and holding his two-handed axe in one hand. Ulf shook his head, amazed the red-headed warrior had managed to stay afloat.

"Snorri! What's the damage?" Tormod shouted from the Black Eagle.

"The War Bear has capsized," Snorri responded. "Half her crew will be dining with Ran tonight. We're bringing the others aboard now, but we're running out of space." Snorri looked amongst his own men. "Oddi! Did we lose anybody?"

"Three that I know of, but some men are injured." Oddi pointed to Asbjorn, who was lying on the deck, his forehead bleeding. Ulf saw Asbjorn was still breathing and was surprised by the disappointment he felt.

Snorri nodded and looked to Tormod, "What's your damage?"

Tormod surveyed his own ship, glancing at the sail before responding, "We lost a few men, some injured as well. Our sail is ripped, but it should get us to Suðrikaupstefna."

Snorri nodded. "Bring your ship nearer, we don't have enough space for everyone."

Tormod nodded in return and called the order to his crew. They unloaded a few oars and rowed the Black Eagle to the Sae-Ulfr. Ulf helped pull the men out of the water, thanking the gods that he did not end up in the sea like them. When the last man was pulled on board, Ulf walked to his chest and slumped down, his head resting against the side. His whole body ached. Ulf rubbed his neck, wondering when he had hurt it.

"Thank the gods we survived that. Came out of nowhere that storm." Brak sat down next to Ulf.

"You think the gods saved us?" Oddi asked, eyebrow raised as he untangled his beard.

"You don't?" Brak gave his friend a sideways glance.

Oddi shook his head. "I think they were the ones who sent it. The gods are not happy about this raid."

"Why would they care about the raid?" Thorbjorn took his tunic off.

"We left Thorgilsstad in her time of need because of the king's greed. The gods must not have liked that." Oddi adopted the tone he liked to use when trying to be wise.

"We left Thorgilsstad because Snorri roasted an important jarl in his hall," Thorbjorn responded. Ulf looked towards his friend, standing by the stern with Ragnar. They were discussing something with Tormod and Rolf, while some survivors were climbing onto the Black Eagle.

"You think this storm was because of that?" Ulf asked, still rubbing his neck.

"Hard to say. You never really know what the gods want. It could be as Rolf said. Ran was angry because someone insulted her." Oddi scanned the sky, as if searching for a sign.

"I agree with Oddi." Drumbr wrung his beard dry. "I don't think the gods want us to go on this raid. We should turn back and go home."

"We go home and King Halfdan hangs us from a tree. I doubt we'll be as lucky as him if that happens," Thorbjorn retorted, thumbing at Ulf.

"Thorbjorn has a point," Oddi admitted. "It's a hard place we find ourselves in, my brothers. Do we go against the gods, or do we go against the king?"

Ulf jumped to his feet and vomited over the side. No food came up, only seawater. Sitting down again, Ulf saw the others staring at him as he wiped his mouth with the back of his hand.

"It's a bit late to be making an offering to Njörd, don't you think?" Thorbjorn commented.

Ulf leaned on the prow, watching Suðrikaupstefna grow bigger in the distance. The thick smoke which hung over the market town matched the way he felt. Not just him, Ulf mused as he glanced at the slumped crew over his shoulder. It had taken another day to reach the market in the north of Denmark, the remaining two ships overcrowded, since they had lost the War Bear in the storm. Asbjorn had finally come around after sunset, but he was still groggy. At least for Ulf, it meant the glares had stopped.

"That's one place I was hoping not to see for a while. Odin knows how you must feel," Brak said, standing beside Ulf. Brak stared at him, waiting for a response.

The memories of this place were still fresh in Ulf's mind. The Sae-Ulfr had come here at the beginning of the previous summer, following the scent of her prey. They had heard of a new sea king from the north gathering a huge army to go raiding deep into Francia. The sea king turned out to be the man who had killed Ulf's family, and had stolen Ormstunga. Ulf shuddered as he remembered seeing Griml for the first time since that day on the farm. The fear Ulf had felt was as fresh in his mind as the sea air around him. The gods had led them here before, and Ulf still wasn't sure what to make of the outcome of that. Now they were here because of King Halfdan, and Ulf wondered what the cost would be this time.

"The market looks smaller," Brak said when Ulf didn't respond. He was right. There weren't as many ships as the last time they had been here.

"It's still early in the season." Oddi appeared behind them.

Brak scratched his head as he took in the large camp which sat next to the market. "Wonder who sits in the hall Griml built."

Ulf stared in the hall's direction, in his mind seeing the image of Griml standing outside it like a giant troll guarding the entrance to its cave.

"Perhaps this new jarl," Oddi guessed.

"Do we know who he is?" Ulf wanted to distract himself. Sea birds hovered around the ships, calling to the men. Ulf watched as one came in close and tilted its head at him before turning away.

Oddi shook his head. "Tormod couldn't tell us much about him. Some say he is a Swede, others he is a Dane." Oddi looked at the ship sailing next to the Sae-Ulfr. Ulf followed his gaze, seeing the king's ship, the Black Eagle — named after the majestic predator often seen soaring high in the sky. The name suited her. She was similar in size to the Sae-Ulfr, her keel decorated with runes — a protection spell which meant she could never sink and survive Ran's worst temper. *Perhaps that was how she survived the storm.* Her prow beast was an eagle's head, its mouth open and tongue sticking out as if it was screaming at you. Ulf looked up and spotted Egil on board, the man he had fought in the king's hall. Egil smiled at him and waved, Ulf waved back, before turning his attention back to Suðrikaupstefna.

"Trim the sails! Brak, Drumbr, remove the beast head!" Snorri ordered, walking along the ship to the prow.

Brak knocked the pegs out as Drumbr lifted the wolf head off the prow.

"Why are we removing them?" Ulf watched the men untying knots and pulling on ropes until the sail was half its size.

"That's a big army there." Snorri nodded towards the camp. "We don't want them to think we are attacking."

"Aye," Drumbr agreed as he carried the wolf head to the chest where it slept. The orders echoed on the Black Eagle, and Ulf watched as men carried out their tasks. He was trying to learn as much as possible by observing these experienced sailors. Ulf loved being at sea and wanted to help instead of being in the way.

The ships started slowing down as they approached the beach. There were no wharves for them to aim for, so Rolf pointed the Sae-Ulfr towards a part of the beach that looked safe. The crew prayed to Njörd there were no rocks under the surface. Sea birds resting on the water took flight while screaming at the two ships. One of the birds aimed a shit at them, which landed on one man's head. Those who saw it laughed while the man waved a fist at the birds.

"Looks like we have a welcoming party." Snorri pointed to a group of men walking towards the beach they were heading for. The Sae-Ulfr was still too far away, but Ulf could tell these men were armed. Dolphins breached the surface near the prow on the Sae-Ulfr, the sea creatures keeping pace just in front of the ships and to Ulf, it seemed like the dolphins were guiding them to the beach.

"Good omen that," Brak commented as he watched the dolphins. Ulf hoped he was right.

"How many are there?" Snorri asked.

Brak scratched his head as he leaned over the side of the ship. "About twelve, but there could be more under the water." The men looked at him in surprise and Brak struggled to understand their confusion. "What?"

Thorbjorn cuffed Brak on the back of the head, the short man having to stretch to do so. "Not the dolphins!"

"Oh," was the only thing Brak could say.

"About half a crew, I think," Oddi responded eventually. Snorri nodded to show that he agreed. Tormod was standing by the prow of the Black Eagle, but he was not looking at the beach like Ulf was expecting him to be. Instead, Tormod was watching them.

The men put their armour on as the ships neared the beach. They might not be attacking, but the men still wanted to look like the formidable warriors they were. Ulf slipped his brynja on, watching as Magni and his men got ready. Magni's brynja sparkled in the sunlight, and Ulf couldn't help but feel irritated at the cocky bastard. Ulf had to earn his brynja, while Magni got his because of who his father was.

"This is his first ever raid." Oddi sat on his chest near Ulf. Ulf nodded. Snorri had told him the same. Magni was older than Oddi by a few winters and was the first son of a jarl. "He has always been more interested in looking like a warrior instead of being one. My father realised this quite early on. That's why he did all the raiding with Jarl Thorgils and Magni stayed behind to protect our village."

"And you joined Snorri's crew?" Ulf tightened his belt, so the brynja was more comfortable. When he first got it, Ulf thought he would never get used to its weight. But as the year had passed, Ulf became more comfortable wearing it.

"Jarl Thorgils thought it would be best. Magni and I were always fighting and my father struggled to deal with us without my mother. I learnt to fight beside Snorri as we grew up." Oddi gave a wistful smile. "I was the first person he asked to be part of his hirdmen."

It was common for a jarl's children to be fostered out — another way to ensure the loyalty of a neighbour, or those under your command. "Is that why you and Magni don't get along?" Ulf struggled to understand how there could be a conflict between brothers. He glanced at the Brak brothers, who were laughing at some joke only they understood.

Oddi looked over his shoulder at the fast approaching shoreline and smiled at Ulf. "We don't have enough time for that story." Ulf returned the smile, checking his weapons were where they should be, before stroking the names carved on his axe's haft. The visions Ulf had during the storm came to his mind again, and Ulf was sure he heard the cry of an eagle. Odin was watching.

The keel of the Sae-Ulfr ripped through the stony beach, bringing Ulf back to the present. Around him stood Snorri and his hirdmen, Geir close behind. Magni was also there, his hand on his beautiful virgin blade. Magni wore his helmet, which made him stand out as none of the others were wearing theirs. As the ship came to a sudden halt, Magni fell forward and had to be helped by his father's men, much to the amusement of Thorbjorn. The Black Eagle came to a stop beside the Sae-Ulfr, both ships being expertly steered into position. The sails were pulled in quickly and efficiently, and Ulf saw the appreciation on the faces of the group who had come to greet them. There were about fifteen men, all wearing brynjas and with swords and axes on their sides. None of the men had any helmets or shields. In the centre of the group, one warrior stood out. He was not the biggest of them, neither was he the fiercest. But he was the first one to catch Ulf's eye because of his hair, which was as white as fresh snow. Snorri jumped off the ship, with Ulf and his hirdmen close behind. As Ulf landed on the beach, his foot slipped on the wet stones, but he managed not to fall over. Magni did not have the same luck, causing their welcoming party to laugh as he spluttered in the surf. Snorri shook his head as Magni's men helped him up. Tormod disembarked from his ship, and Ulf watched as the blue eyes of the white-haired leader studied them. No one had said a word yet as both groups got the measure of each other. Magni took his helmet off, his red hair plastered to his face.

"Welcome!" The leader of the group took a step forward. "I am Ubba the White."

Snorri took a step forward, standing taller than the white-haired warrior. Magni wanted to do the same, but Ragnar held him back. He glared at Ragnar, who was not paying any attention. "I am Snorri Thorgilsson and this is Tormod, hirdman of King Halfdan of Vestfold." Tormod nodded at Ubba.

"King Halfdan?" Ubba looked back at his men and then at Tormod. "We have heard much of Halfdan the Black." The men behind him nodded. "And Odin knows we have heard a lot of Snorri Thorgilsson." Ubba turned his attention back to Snorri. "One of the finest warriors in all of Norway."

Ulf knew his friend would smile at that. "You honour me," Snorri responded.

"And why should I not?" Ubba spread his arms and smiled. "If it weren't for you, I'd not be leading this army now." He grinned when he saw the surprise on Snorri's face. "Yes, we know what you did. Every day I thank the gods that you came here." Ubba regarded Snorri's men and his grin got bigger when he saw Ragnar. "And you must be the one who charged at Griml's army like you were possessed by the gods." Ubba raised an eyebrow when Ragnar snarled and Snorri laughed.

"No, this is Ragnar Nine-Finger, my father's champion." Snorri turned and pointed towards Ulf. "This is Ulf Bear-Slayer, he was the one who charged at Griml's army."

Ubba looked at Ulf, but there was no admiration in his eyes, not the same as when Ubba first saw Snorri. "This young man?" He pointed towards Ulf. The men behind Ubba whispered to each other, some of them also pointing at Ulf. Ulf ground his teeth. It reminded him of the meeting they had with King Halfdan and the reason they were here.

"Don't let his youth fool you, friend. Ulf is a descendant of Tyr." Snorri beamed. Ulf felt uncomfortable with all the attention and wished they would move on. His boots were soaked, and since they were still standing on the wet beach, would not dry for a while yet.

"Why do they call him the Bear-Slayer?" one man behind Ubba asked, still frowning at Ulf.

"He killed a bear with nothing but an eating knife," Snorri responded, his chest puffed out as if he had been the one who had done that. Ulf sighed. He had killed the bear with a broken spear, but Snorri always enjoyed embellishing the story. Ulf resisted the temptation to touch the scars on his face as he remembered the day.

"A fine warrior indeed. Blessed by the gods, it seems," Ubba responded. *Cursed more like*, Ulf thought. Something was familiar about this warrior. Ubba looked back towards Snorri and Tormod. "It is always an honour to meet warriors of renown. Even Ragnar Nine-Finger is a name we have heard in many tales." Ragnar nodded, but said nothing. Magni, on the other hand, did.

"And I'm sure you have heard of Magni the Cockerel." Magni stepped forward before Oddi could stop him, hand on the hilt of his sword, his shoulders square and head tilted upwards.

Ubba looked at the men behind him and then back at Magni. "No, never heard of you."

Before Magni could say anything, Tormod stepped forward. "King Halfdan heard you have taken charge of the raid to Francia." He glared at Magni, who was pouting.

Ubba smiled. "Aye, this opportunity is like a gift from the gods. It would be crazy not to. The king wishes to take part?" He glanced at Ulf, so quick that Ulf barely caught it.

"The king has business elsewhere, but has asked me to take part on his behalf," Snorri responded.

"The gods know it will be an honour to have you fighting with us, and besides, Francia has enough gold to make all of us as rich as the gods." Ubba smiled, tucking his thumbs into his belt. "I will let you disembark. Your men look eager to get off the ship." He nodded towards Snorri's crew, still on board the Sae-Ulfr, waiting to unload the ship. "But come to the hall tonight, we'll have a feast in your honour."

"Thank you Ubba, my men and I will not miss it." There were smiles all around at the prospect of feasting and drinking, especially after the storm.

Ubba nodded and left with his men.

"Seems like a decent man… for a Dane." Drumbr watched the group walk back up the beach, his hand already patting his round stomach.

"Looked very surprised when he saw Ulf," Thorbjorn added.

Ulf shrugged. He had seen it as well and wasn't sure what to make of it.

"Maybe he thought Ulf would be older?" Brak suggested.

"Aye, that could be it." Thorbjorn scratched his cheek.

"Will you lot stop chatting like old wives and help us here?" Ragnar shouted at them, pointing to the ship where the men had started unloading their chests.

"Did he seem familiar to any of you?" Ulf asked, unable to keep it to himself.

"There's something about him, I'll admit," Oddi responded. "But wouldn't say he seemed familiar."

"One of his men did. I'm sure I saw him last time we were here," Brak added.

"Maybe he was here. I'm sure most of the men would have stayed, expecting Griml to come back and lead them to Francia." Oddi turned and walked to the Sae-Ulfr.

"I suppose. Odin knows I wouldn't pass up an opportunity like this." Thorbjorn smiled.

Ulf looked over his shoulder, watching as the group disappeared into the distance.

CHAPTER 8

Ulf sat outside his tent, fingers drumming away on his knee as he watched the men from Thorgilsstad. All of them were excited by the raid as they talked and laughed. Some were sitting together in groups, cleaning armour or sharpening blades as they shared stories of the past. Others were napping in the sun or just lying around. Ulf flinched as laughter rang near him. He recognised Thorbjorn's barking laugh. Snorri's hirdmen were also in high spirits. The ale provided by the young jarl the previous night still muddled their minds while the memories of the feast lifted their spirits. It had been a splendid feast. The jarl had gone far to impress his new guests, and the men of Thorgilsstad had time to honour those who had died in the storm. But Ulf had not enjoyed the night. His visions still plagued him. Thorbjorn was deep into a story of how a bóndi attacked him after the man caught Thorbjorn with his wife. Ulf jumped to his feet, feeling suffocated by the camp. He checked his weapons were tucked into his belt before walking off.

"Where you going?" Oddi asked, interrupting the story Thorbjorn was telling.

"Going for a walk." Ulf tried to keep the frustration out of his voice.

"Need some company?" Geir offered. He had joined the group, along with some of the older men from the War Bear for breakfast that morning. Ulf shook his head, seeing Geir's shoulders sag slightly, but not caring.

"Don't worry about it, Geir. Ulf sometimes prefers the conversation of the trees to ours. The gods only know why," Thorbjorn said.

"Because the trees are smarter than you," Ulf responded before he could stop himself. The others laughed, assuming that Ulf had made a joke.

"Aye, well, take a spear with you. They say there's plenty of game in the forest, could do with some more fresh meat." Thorbjorn waved Ulf away with a smile.

Ulf grabbed his spear and left, walking past the men of Thorgilsstad, many of them greeting him with a nod or a wave. The forest was on the other side of the Danish camp, their tents placed randomly all over the place. It was like a child had taken a handful of stones and had thrown them on the beach, leaving them where they fell. Because of this, he had to zigzag his way past their tents and campfires. The air was filled with the smells of fires and food, mixed in with the odours of men not having bathed for a few days. Ulf was desperate for the fresh air he would find amongst the trees, but forced himself to walk calmly. He did not want the Danes to think he was scared. The Danes were doing much the same as the Norsemen. They sat in groups, laughing and talking. Some cleaning their weapons and armour while a few took advantage of the lull and slept. They even ate the same breakfasts as the Norse. Porridge or leftovers from the night before. Out of the corner of his eye, Ulf glimpsed someone pointing at him, and when Ulf looked, he saw a group of warriors watching him. The hostility Ulf saw in their eyes did not surprise him. The Danes and Norse had been fighting each other for generations. But Ulf doubted they would attack him. Ubba had announced them as friends, and these men would not go against the man who promised to make them rich. Ulf hoped.

Ulf finally reached the forest, leaving the campsite and the noise behind him. He breathed in deep, savouring the earthy air as it filled his lungs. Already he felt the calming presence of Freya in the air, something that was lost in the forest around Thorgilsstad. Stroking the trunk of a tree as he walked, its rough bark grating on his fingertips, he listened to the birds sing. A young stag stepped out of the trees and stood rooted to the spot as it stared at him. Ulf felt the weight of the spear in his hand, but did not lift it. He was not here to hunt, despite the request from Thorbjorn. He just wanted to get away from the noise. Ignoring the stag, he picked his way through the forest. His mind drifted in and out of different thoughts, but as always, it went back to the old forest godi. The old man had believed that the forests in Vestfold belonged to the Vanir, and Ulf wondered if these trees also belonged to the fertility gods. If what the old godi had said was true, then the Æsir had invaded their lands. Perhaps that was why the Scandinavians enjoyed raiding so much. He came across a small clearing lit up by the sun. An old ash tree stood on the edge, its slanted growth looked like an ideal spot for him to rest. Ulf went to the tree and sat down, the sun warming his face. It was as if Freya was warming him with her smile. Ulf closed his eyes and listened to the forest. *My ears are open to your words, old wise ones of the forest.*

"Finally, you are alone." An unrecognisable voice startled Ulf. He opened his eyes and saw six men standing in the clearing, all of them wearing leather jerkins and helmets and armed with swords and axes. Ulf jumped to his feet, spear levelled at the men.

"What do you want?" The trees fell silent as the forest held its breath.

"To kill you and collect the gold we were promised," one of the group answered. He was older than the rest, his beard speckled with grey. The others grinned. They were relaxed, and Ulf understood why. These were experienced fighters, and they had him outnumbered.

"And now you are alone, we can do just that." The group spread out, so they could attack from different angles, like wolves preparing to take down a large prey.

But Ulf did not feel like being prey. He attacked, stabbing at the older man with his spear. The man batted the spear away while one of his companions sliced at Ulf with his sword. The blade cut through Ulf's tunic, but missed his flesh as Ulf jumped out of the way, using the spear to keep the third man back. Two of his attackers charged at the same time. The first man aiming to cut Ulf in half, while the other tried to stab Ulf in the side. Ulf blocked the first strike with his spear, breaking the shaft, before twisting away from the second, grateful for all the time Snorri had forced him to practice. Ulf's attackers smiled at the broken spear in Ulf's hands. He dropped the bottom part of his spear and took Olaf's axe from his belt, feeling the familiar weight of this uncle's old axe in his hand. Movement at the edge of the clearing caught their attention, and Ulf gulped as Egil walked into the clearing with a grin. Ulf glared at him, thinking that Egil had hired these men. But he realised his attackers were as surprised to see Egil as he was.

"Who are you?" one attacker asked, glancing at the others as they shrugged.

"A friend," Egil responded in a rough voice. Ulf gripped the broken spear and axe tightly as Egil stood there, still grinning.

"Whose friend?" a brown-bearded member of the group asked. Egil responded by walking to Ulf and standing beside him, sword and shield ready. He nodded at Ulf, still smiling, as if they were meeting up for a drink.

"What are you doing here?" Ulf hissed.

"Is that really so important now?"

Ulf's attackers glanced at each other, but still were confident of their chances. "No matter." The leader of the group smirked. "It's still six against two." They split into two groups, three men to face Ulf and three to face Egil.

Ulf's three attacked together, forcing him back. He counterattacked by stabbing at one man with his spear, surprising him with his speed and cutting the man's arm. The second was more prepared and dodged Ulf's axe, while the third caught Ulf with a kick to the stomach, bending him double. Ulf straightened up, ignoring the pain as his stomach protested. He ducked beneath the sword of one of his attackers, feeling some of his hair land on his face. If Ulf had known there was going to be a fight, he would have braided his hair. Dodging another strike, Ulf got behind the man, stabbing him through the back with his broken spear. The man screamed, arching backwards as the spear burst through his chest. Ulf had to let go of the spear or risk losing his hand, one of his attackers chopping at it with an axe. As Ulf jumped back, his other attacker punched him in the side of the head, dazing him briefly. The man tried to take advantage of this and stabbed at Ulf's chest. Egil appeared from behind Ulf and blocked the strike with his shield. But this left him exposed, and he was stabbed in the side. Egil's brynja softened the blow, but the sword still broke through and took him out of the fight. Their attackers backed off, giving Ulf time to catch his breath. He glanced at Egil, seeing the blood on his side as the warrior dragged himself to the tree. Ulf's head throbbed from the blow he took, but he resisted the urge to rub it. There were four attackers left. Egil had killed one man, but Ulf only had Olaf's axe to defend himself with.

"Why don't you use that fancy sword of yours?" Egil gasped, clutching his side to slow the bleeding.

"I can't." Ulf kept his eyes on his attackers.

"What do you mean you can't?"

"Because of that." Ulf pointed to the sun with Olaf's axe.

"The sun?" Egil sounded incredulous.

Ulf glanced at him, going against his instinct. "It's a long story."

"Look out!" Egil warned, pointing at their attackers.

Ulf turned and dodged the sword coming for his head. He stabbed with his axe, catching the man in the side with the axe head. As his attacker reeled backwards, another stabbed at Ulf. Ulf brought Olaf's axe around to deflect the sword, but the man caught Ulf in the face with a punch. Ulf staggered back, shaking his head to clear it when the other two attacked him from either side. He dropped to the ground and rolled away, blocking another strike as soon as he got to his feet. The four men attacked him relentlessly and Ulf did everything he could to avoid their blows. But he was unable to land any of his own. Forced to dodge another sword, Ulf tried to counterattack by swinging his axe and was rewarded by a cut to the arm. Ulf staggered backward, gasping for air. The cut on his arm was shallow and would not affect him, but Ulf knew he would not last much longer. He could not defeat four men with only his axe. Ulf needed help, and Egil could do nothing now. He glanced at the king's man, surprised to see him smile. Egil looked up and when Ulf followed his gaze, saw that a dark cloud had appeared from nowhere. Blocking the sun.

"Thank you, Tyr," Ulf whispered as he moved the axe to his left hand and drew Ormstunga from her scabbard. She seemed to sing as he held her, her song spreading fire through his veins and sharpening his senses.

His attackers looked at each other, confused by the sudden wolf grin on Ulf's face, but then shrugged and attacked. The first one reached Ulf, stabbing at him with his sword. To Ulf, he moved slower than before. Ulf deflected the blow with Olaf's axe and stabbed the man through the chest with Ormstunga. A shocked gasp escaped the man's lips as the second attacker reached Ulf before he had time to remove his sword. Ulf turned the man and used his body as a shield to block the strike. The dying man spat blood on Ulf's face as his friend's axe buried into his back. Before the second man could react, Ulf cleaved his head with Olaf's axe, roaring his defiance at the same time. The other two attackers stopped in their tracks, shocked by the sudden turn of things. They had the advantage not so long ago, and now two of them were dead and Ulf was laughing at them. Their hesitation gave Ulf time to free Ormstunga.

"What in the gods' names…" the man with the grey-speckled beard started.

"The gods are not on your side," Ulf growled, hearing the raven over the rush of blood in his ears. He attacked before they could respond, slicing Ormstunga at the first man who blocked it, but could do nothing as Olaf's axe chopped his head in half. Ulf turned to face the remaining attacker, expecting him to come from behind. But the man stood frozen to the spot, fear etched all over his face. Ulf glared at him, panting hard to fan the flames inside his stomach. He had become the wolf now and the man before him the prey. The warrior backed away as Ulf took a step forward. He levelled his sword at Ulf, his hand trembling so much Ulf almost felt the air being moved by it. The wind rustled through the leaves, whispering a command in Ulf's ear. Ulf nodded. He attacked with Ormstunga held high as she prepared to take the man's life. Ulf's attacker dropped his sword before fleeing through the trees, screaming for the gods' mercy. Ulf lowered his sword and took a deep breath. The fire in him disappeared as the wind cooled his skin.

"By Odin, why didn't you fight like that in the beginning?"

Ulf looked at Egil, seeing how his face had paled. Blood was still seeping through his fingers and Ulf realised he needed to get Egil back to the camp. He quickly tucked Olaf's axe into his belt, but kept Ormstunga in his hand. She needed to be cleaned before he put her away. Rushing to Egil, he helped the man up. Egil grunted from the pain, but said nothing as Ulf put the man's arm over his shoulder. He only stared at Ulf, his eyes scrutinising the young warrior.

"What?" Ulf asked as the two of them started walking back to the camp.

"Why did you let the bastard go? You could have killed him."

Ulf looked at the trees before answering, "They told me not to."

"Who told you not to?"

"The trees." Ulf smiled.

"Uh." Egil glanced at the surrounding trees. "It's a shame to leave these weapons behind." Egil nodded to the swords and axe that belonged to the dead men.

"The forest can have them," Ulf responded as he helped Egil through the trees. As they reached the Danish camp, Ulf searched the faces of the Danes, trying to find the man who had run away. The Danish warriors just watched as they struggled past, none of them offering to help.

"Fucking Danes." Egil spat, blood spraying from the old warrior's lips.

"Thor's arse! What happened?" Thorbjorn exclaimed when they reached their camp. Egil had lost a lot of blood from his wound and Ulf's head throbbed. Behind him, he heard the Danes get back to their conversations.

"I was attacked in the forest," Ulf responded as men took Egil from him, the old warrior grunting but not saying anything.

"By this bastard!" Drumbr appeared with axe in hand, pointing it at Egil.

"No, there were six of them. Egil was there to help me." Ulf saw Snorri rushing over, with Ragnar and Tormod behind him.

"Why was he there?" Snorri asked, glancing at Tormod, who only shrugged.

"He wouldn't tell me, but I'd be dead if it wasn't for him." Ulf saw Egil grimace as his friends removed his brynja.

"The wound's fairly deep, but I think the old bastard will be fine. He can thank Odin his brynja took most of the force out of the strike," one man said. Tormod nodded and then looked at Ulf.

"Where are these men now?"

"Five of them are feeding the forest animals. One got away." Ulf noticed the surprise on Tormod's face.

"Takes more than six men to kill the Bear-Slayer." Thorbjorn clapped Ulf on the back, a wide grin on his face.

Ulf said nothing. He was exhausted. All he wanted now was to get to his tent and sleep.

"Get some rest, Ulf," Snorri said, as if reading his mind. "You can tell us about it later. In the meantime, I'll send word to Ubba, let him know what happened."

"Why?" Ragnar asked.

"Don't really know, but this is his army, he should know about it."

Ulf walked away as Snorri responded to Ragnar. He crawled into his tent and sat down. Spitting on a cloth, he wiped the blood off Ormstunga's blade. When she was clean, he rubbed his thumb over the serpents engraved on the guard and whispered the words written on them.

I am from a place of darkness. Do not draw me in the light of the sun.

The fire crackled as the flames chewed through the logs, throwing sparks into the air like Thor venting his fury. It was evening, even though the late spring sun could still be seen in the sky, and the men were sitting around the fire eating venison brought to them by Ubba.

"Again, Snorri, I can only apologise for what happened to your man," Ubba offered, pointing the bone he had been gnawing on at Ulf. He had rushed to their camp after hearing about the attack, his face showing all the concern you would expect from a friend, and had been invited to stay for dinner.

Snorri shook his head. "It is not your fault, Jarl Ubba. You are not responsible for all the men in the camp."

"But this is my army." He hit his leg with his fist. "I might not have brought most of these men together, but I have taken responsibility for them."

"Could these men be some of Griml's men who stayed behind?" Tormod licked the grease from his fingers.

Snorri stared at Ulf and the rest of his hirdmen, all of them remembering the night they had crept into Griml's camp many months ago. "It's hard to say. I can't remember any of the faces we saw then." The others nodded their agreement.

Ulf stared at the flames. The only face he remembered from that night was Eldrid. He had tried very hard to forget the tall woman they had kidnapped. She had been about to marry Griml, and Snorri had thought it would draw Griml away from his large army.

"Might be men who had survived the battle?" Ubba suggested.

Snorri shrugged. "Suppose they could have come back. One ship was missing after the battle."

"Why would they come back here?" Ragnar asked, his mouth still full of meat.

"Ragnar has a point," Thorbjorn added. "They lost a battle they should have won. The men who stayed behind might not have accepted them back."

Ubba thought about that, while scratching the side of his face. His sincerity had surprised Ulf. But there was still something about him that Ulf did not like. "What about this jarl you mentioned before?" Ubba offered.

"Arnfinni?" Snorri asked.

"Aye, you said some of his men attacked your village before you left." Tormod looked away as Ubba said this.

"Why would Arnfinni's men come here?" Oddi asked.

"Some ships arrived this morning with new men," Ubba replied. "They could have come on those."

"Or arrived before we did," Ragnar added. "The gods know how fast news can travel."

"Then why attack Thorgilsstad?" Thorbjorn threw a bone into the flames.

"Might be two different groups."

Oddi thought about this before shaking his head. "If they were some of Arnfinni's men, then why attack Ulf? Would they not have gone for Snorri instead?"

"Snorri was never on his own, Ulf was. He was the easier target." Ragnar stared at Ulf through squinted eyes.

"Not so easy in the end." Thorbjorn smiled. "It's a pity they didn't know that Ulf can't be killed."

Ubba looked up at that, his eyes focused on Ulf. "What do you mean?"

"Ulf swore an oath to Odin, and Odin likes the chaos this oath is causing. So until Ulf has had his vengeance, he cannot die." Thorbjorn smiled proudly as if he had something to do with it.

Ubba looked at Snorri and Ragnar. Ragnar nodded. "Trust me, those idiots were not the only ones who tried to kill him. Jarl Thorgils even tried hanging Ulf, but Odin wasn't having it."

Everyone laughed at the memory while Ulf grimaced. He remembered the feel of the rope as it crushed his throat and still had a faint scar on his neck from it. After the hanging, his friends kept telling him how lucky he was to have Odin by his side. But Ulf knew Odin wasn't. He had sworn an oath to the All-Father, and Odin was making the most of this opportunity. Ulf caught Ubba staring at him and was surprised by the look he saw.

"How is your man, Tormod?" Ubba asked, glancing away as soon as he saw Ulf looking at him.

The question caught Tormod by surprise, and he had to clear his throat before he could answer. "Egil? He is fine. The cut was fairly deep, but he got lucky. The blade got nothing important. He'll miss the raid, but he'll live."

Ulf glanced at the tent where the warrior lay, probably sleeping. Ulf still didn't understand why Egil followed him into the forest. He was glad the man did, otherwise Ulf might have died, but he wanted to know why Egil had been there.

"Lucky for Ulf, he was there," Drumbr echoed his thoughts. "Strange though."

"Aye," Thorbjorn agreed, looking at Ulf. "Did he tell you why?"

Ulf shook his head. "After the fight, I was more focused on getting him back here. Didn't even think of asking him then."

"Well. Thank Odin you didn't stop to have a chat. The man would be dead otherwise." Ubba turned his attention back to Snorri. "You've had a lot of bad luck so far. First you lose a ship and now one of your men gets attacked."

"Aye, it's like the gods do not approve of this raid." Snorri's face darkened at the thought.

"Then why carry on?"

Snorri looked at Ubba for a while. The only noise was the distant sounds of conversations around other campfires and the flames consuming the wood between them. "You don't say no to a king." Ulf caught the glance he aimed at Tormod. Ulf couldn't imagine that these two had been friends once. Almost like brothers from what Oddi had told him. Yet now, they could barely stand each other. Ulf hoped the same did not happen to him. He valued Snorri's friendship and guidance.

Ubba nodded like he understood. "Then I suggest you and your men be more careful."

"I agree." Ragnar looked at Snorri. "Our men should stay in groups from now on."

Snorri nodded. "We'll set a guard as well for the night."

The next day, Ulf and his friends were walking around the small market, all of them wearing their brynjas and with their weapons at hand. Ulf felt foolish as they moved past the stalls dressed for battle, but after the day before, even he didn't want to take any more chances.

"Not as noisy as they used to be," Drumbr said as they walked past empty tables and quiet traders. Ulf looked around, his face squinting in the bright sunlight. Drumbr was right. The last time they had been here, the whole place was full of traders selling their wares. He remembered the noise as the traders competed for the attention of potential buyers. Ulf had never realised people could make so much noise.

"Well, it's the beginning of the season for them. Not all the traders are here yet," Asbjorn said, his head bruised from the storm and with a long cut across his forehead.

"No, this is something else." Oddi stopped and looked around the market. "It's like they are nervous."

"Why would they be nervous, Oddi Vis?" Thorbjorn asked.

"Might have something to do with the three thousand strong army camped next to the market." Oddi ignored the mocking tone of Thorbjorn.

"They've been here since last summer." Brak tugged at his beard. "It's something else, I think."

They moved on while debating the reasons for the market being so quiet, but Ulf stayed rooted to the spot. He was staring at the back of a boy who was drifting past the stalls. *It can't be*, he thought, while fighting the urge to follow the boy. It must have been his guilt, he tried to tell himself. As if to answer his thoughts, the boy gave a quick glance backwards, and it was like something had kicked Ulf in the chest. He rushed after the boy, breaking away from his friends, who were still busy discussing the atmosphere in the market. He followed the boy, but could not catch up to him. No matter how hard he tried. They moved past the stalls he remembered from his last visit. The weapons stall where he had seen the helmet he liked. The one he had asked Bard, Thorgilsstad's blacksmith, to make. Past the stall selling cloth and the one with the jewellery and glass beads. The stall where he had first seen Eldrid. Ulf paused, the image of Eldrid's thin frame swaying as she glided past the stall coming to him. He shook his head and looked for the boy again. Ulf knew he was being led somewhere, but he didn't care. He needed to catch that boy. He had to make sure. Ulf rushed after him again, but the boy seemed to sense his approach and sped up. They went past the makeshift tavern where the Swedish jarl, Eldrid's father, had challenged him to a holmgang. There was no smell of roasting meat or sounds of men laughing. The tavern stood abandoned. So was the thrall market beside the tavern. The pens where Orvar, the overweight thrall trader, had kept his merchandise, were empty and had been for a long time. Ulf did not understand why the boy was leading him here. The boy rounded a trader's tent and Ulf lost sight of him. He rushed to catch up, but stopped in his tracks as he got past the tent. The boy had disappeared like a draugr in the sunlight. Ulf stared at the empty square in front of him, his mouth open and hands twitching. *Why did he lead me here?* Ulf wondered as he stared at the spot where he had fought the Swedish jarl. He could hear the crowd cheering as the traders came to watch. He saw the old warrior standing in front of him, his sword and shield at his side, as he smiled at Ulf. His hands shook as he remembered standing there, Olaf's axe and his shield feeling heavy in his hands. His brynja, the same one he wore that day, suddenly heavier. Ulf's heart beat faster in his chest as he recalled that fight. It was another day he should have died, but the gods had spared him. He spotted movement in the corner of his eye. A shadow creeping slowly at the edge of the square. Ulf tensed, half expecting the Swedish jarl to appear, but what he saw left his mouth dry and caused his legs to tremble. The wild black hair, with bones and twigs tied into it. The dress made from animal skins, the dried snake skin around her neck, worn like a necklace. It was her. The woman from Yngling Hall. She smiled as she stared at him with her strange eyes. Ulf stammered as he tried to say something, but the words would not come out. It was as if she had stolen his tongue.

"There you are." A voice from behind him broke the spell, and with a jolt, Ulf turned to see his friends. He looked back to where the woman was, but she was gone.

"Not learnt your lesson from yesterday," Thorbjorn said before realising where they were. "Ah, this is where you had the holmgang with that girl's father."

"That was a good fight, was convinced Ulf was dead that day," Brak added.

"Aye, but somehow he won. Cracked the old man's head open like an egg." Thorbjorn laughed. He turned back to Ulf and noticed his friend's pale face. "What's wrong with you?"

"Looks like you've seen a draugr." Drumbr gave Ulf a worried glance.

"I... I..." Ulf struggled to find the words. He looked back to where the woman had been. "Did you see her?" he managed at last.

"See who?" Oddi followed Ulf's gaze, but saw nothing.

"The woman."

"What woman?" Thorbjorn scratched his ear while glancing at the others.

Ulf was still staring at where she had been. "She was there." He pointed to the now empty space. "I swear by Odin, I saw her. She was standing there, smiling at me."

"Smiling at you?" Thorbjorn gave his friend a sideways glance. "Maybe that knock you took during yesterday's fight has affected you more than we thought." Drumbr nodded, giving Ulf a worried glance.

Oddi walked to where Ulf was pointing and studied the ground. "No one was here, Ulf, there are no prints."

"What?"

"There are no prints, no footmarks. No one has been here for a while."

"Perhaps she was floating?" Brak suggested, and got smacked by Thorbjorn as a response.

"It's a shame that tavern is gone. Think Ulf could do with a drink." The others nodded and turned to walk away. "Come on Ulf, let's get you back to the camp, bound to be some ale there."

Ulf looked at his friends and then back to where he had seen the woman. Were they right? Was it just an effect from the punch he took to the head? He rubbed the bruise on his temple. But it felt so real. He was sure he had seen her, but Oddi said there were no footmarks. Ulf tried to make sense of what had happened as he followed his friends.

"Orvar's not here, I see," Drumbr remarked as they walked past the empty thrall market.

"Aye, I heard that after we kidnapped Eldrid, Griml had him questioned. They said he was so scared afterwards that he freed all the thralls and fled. No one knows where to. Even abandoned the house he built for himself."

"Thank Odin for that." Thorbjorn spat towards the thrall pens. "Never liked that guy."

Ulf was only half listening to his friends. He was still trying to understand what he had just seen when the hairs on the back of his neck stood up, like someone was blowing gently on his skin. A voice whispered in his head. *We'll meet again.*

CHAPTER 9

"Been a long time since I took part in a raid this big," Rolf mused, hand on the tiller as he eyed the surrounding ships.

"Aye, about twenty ships." Snorri's eyes flashed as he looked around. The Sae-Ulfr was sailing near the front of a large fleet, just behind Ubba's ship and with the Black Eagle to her right. All around them sails bulged in the wind, the men on the other ships talking and laughing. All the noise drowning out the sea birds soaring in the sky above them. "Larger than any raid I've been on." And that was true. Snorri had never been on a raid this huge. He doubted even his father had been, and Thorgils had told Snorri many stories of the large raiding parties of his youth.

"And yet, you're not as excited as you should be," the old man said. Snorri glanced at him, but did not respond. Rolf smiled. "Perhaps there are other things you'd rather be doing than go on one of the biggest raids in your lifetime."

"There's nowhere else I'd rather be," Snorri lied, scratching his nose.

Rolf snorted. "Snorri, I've known your father since he was a little boy and you your entire whore-filled life."

Snorri sighed. The old man was more perceptive than he realised. "You know as well as I do, Rolf, that I have other business to take care of." Snorri looked to the sky, searching for any signs that the gods were listening to him. "The Norns have decided that this is my path for now. There's nothing I can do about it." He stroked the Sae-Ulfr as he leaned against her, finding comfort in her presence.

"Your young friend doesn't agree with you." Rolf nodded towards Ulf, his expression rigid as he sat by the prow with the other hirdmen. Ulf still had a light bruise on his face from the fight in the forest a few days ago. They had barely spoken since then. Snorri had been too busy trying to find equipment for the men who had lost theirs when the War Bear went down. There wasn't much in the market, so he had to trade with the Danes. It wasn't ideal, but at least all the men had weapons and, most of them, armour. Snorri glanced at Ragnar having a nap nearby him, still wearing his brynja. Snorri did not know how his father's champion had managed to swim wearing it and carrying his weapons.

"Ulf refuses to accept that his fate is not his own. The gods decide our paths," Snorri said after a while.

"And we should follow them blindly?" Rolf raised a bushy eyebrow. Snorri didn't answer, so Rolf continued, "You just going to give up on your hunt?"

Snorri sighed. "I will find him when the gods decide it's time. Until then I follow the path they choose for me."

"And what if you don't agree with that path?" Rolf smiled to show that he did not mean to upset Snorri.

Snorri crossed his arms, looking at the sky. Nothing from the gods. "The gods have led me to great glory and riches. Why would I not agree with their path for me?"

"But do you?" Again, Snorri didn't answer, choosing instead to look out to the sea. "The gods don't always choose the paths best for us. They choose the path that amuses them the most and idiots like you just follow along."

"Ulf has been fighting the gods his entire life and look where that has got him. His entire family killed. His best friend killed. Him almost killed." Snorri looked his old steersman in the eyes. "Fighting the gods is never a good thing. In the end, we are nothing but pieces on their tafl board."

Rolf smiled wryly, looking at Ulf where he sat polishing his helmet. "Aye, but some pieces are more important than others."

Magni interrupted them before Snorri could ask what Rolf meant by that. "It's a fine day for sailing." He stood on the other side of Rolf, his chin raised while resting his hand on the gunwale. "So how long until we get to gut those spineless Frankish bastards? My sword is eager to pierce their flesh, and my other sword," he grabbed his crotch and winked at Snorri, "is also ready to do some piercing if its own."

Rolf glanced at Snorri, who spotted the small smile in the old man's beard. "If the wind holds, then we might get there tonight, but most likely it'll be tomorrow." Snorri studied the sail, only to avoid Magni. The tall man had been quiet, keeping mostly to himself and the men from his village. But like a cockerel in the morning, he liked to be heard.

"Ha! The gods know I am ready for a fight. I can feel it in my blood." Magni beamed, thumbing his chest. His face grew serious, and he looked at Snorri. "You and I, Snorri, are not so different." Snorri glanced at the smiling Rolf, but did not respond. "We are the sons of strong jarls. We have the blood of warriors flowing through our veins. I thank the gods that we can finally go on a raid together."

"Aye, we were just talking about the gods choosing a man's path." Rolf smirked, the old man trying hard not to laugh.

"Nothing stopped you from joining us before." Snorri knew the reason Magni had never joined them, and it wasn't because Snorri didn't want him to.

"The gods deemed it not to be. With my father raiding and my wayward brother run off, someone had to protect our village."

"Your wayward brother did not run off. He was fostered out to my father." Snorri tried hard to keep the edge from his voice.

Rolf responded before Magni could say anything, "You make it sound like you've had a hard life."

"A hard life indeed. The gods only know how hard it's been. Not being able to do anything I want."

"Oh, aye." Rolf winked at Snorri. "Must be hard being young and handsome, still have both your feet," Rolf tapped his wooden leg on the deck, "and those beautiful weapons of yours without having to kill for them."

"Plenty of thralls to warm your bed, not to mention women trying to gain favour," Snorri added.

Magni looked away from them, almost dramatically. "Yes, very hard indeed. All I've ever wanted was to go on a raid. Get out from under my father's shadow. That's another thing you and I have in common." He looked at Snorri again. "We both still live in the shadows of our fathers."

"Snorri hasn't been in his father's shadow for a long time." Ragnar's hard voice caught their attention. The red-headed warrior was still lying on his back, eyes closed. Snorri thought he had been sleeping and wondered if Ragnar had been listening to their conversation. "Even that miserable Ulf has outdone you, Magni, and the boy is a shit fighter."

"But he has the blood of Tyr in his veins. They say he is unbeatable," Magni protested, his face going red.

"He's been lucky so far. And don't make it sound like you've never had the chance to go raiding." Ragnar opened his eyes and pointed a finger at Magni. "Jarl Thorgils has invited you on many raids in the past."

"My father would not let me." Magni pouted.

"That's not what he said," Ragnar sneered, his eyes closing again.

Snorri almost felt sorry for Magni, but then remembered he didn't like the guy.

To his credit, Magni stood his ground. "Well, I will prove to all of you I'm just as good, no, even better than my brother."

"Those are big boots to fill, Magni," Snorri said with a smile. "Oddi is one of my best fighters."

"Gods! Look at that!" one of the crew exclaimed, leaning so far over the gunwale that Snorri was concerned the man would fall over. More of the crew jumped to their feet, while the men from the other ships cheered. Looking into the distance, Snorri understood why.

"How many ships are there?" Magni asked, eyes wide.

"I don't know." Snorri walked to the prow for a better view. The entire horizon was filled with warships.

"Did you know about this?" Oddi asked as Snorri got to the prow.

He nodded. "Ubba told me we'd be meeting another force with many more ships than his. But I didn't think there would be so many." He struggled to keep the awe out of his voice. Everywhere he looked, there were masts. There were so many ships that Snorri could not even see the water beneath them. Snorri rubbed the Mjöllnir on his neck. If he had ignored the gods and followed his own path, then he would not have lived long enough to experience this. Snorri glanced back over his shoulder and saw Rolf Treefoot smiling at him.

"How many ships are there?" Drumbr asked, hand on his forehead.

"Must be hundreds," Oddi responded. Snorri saw the awe on all their faces. Even Ulf was gaping at the sight.

Thorbjorn stood next to Snorri and shook his head. "By the gods, I never thought I'd see anything like this. But why have such a large gathering?"

"Francia," Snorri responded with a wolf grin.

"Why is Francia so important?" Thorbjorn scratched his head.

"Ubba said their king died last year,"

"King Louis the Pious," Oddi said. He saw the way the others looked at him and smiled proudly. "I speak to people."

Snorri nodded at Oddi. "And now his sons have started fighting each other."

"So?" Asbjorn asked, half his face still bruised.

Snorri smiled. He remembered Ubba telling him the story. At first he didn't get it either, but he understood now. "So, while they're busy with their family feud, the Frankish coastline is undefended." He didn't need to say any more. He saw the smiles on the faces of his friends. They all understood.

"Francia will make us rich, even after we give the king his cut." Thorbjorn grinned a toothy grin.

"Aye, that she will. More treasure than what Fafnir is guarding."

"Trust Ulf not to be excited by the riches of Francia," Thorbjorn said behind Snorri. He turned and saw the furrowed brow and tight lips that had replaced the look of awe on Ulf's face.

"I don't care about the riches of Francia." Ulf looked at Snorri, grimacing. "Griml is not in Francia."

Snorri sighed and shook his head. "I understand how you feel, Ulf. We all do," the men around all nodded, "but there's more to life than revenge."

"Aye, lad. You need to live a little," Thorbjorn agreed. Those who were not part of Snorri's inner circle had moved away.

"How can I live my life when the troll who killed my family and Vidar is still out there?" Ulf pointed in the general direction of Norway. "Probably building another large army."

"No one will follow him now, not after the disaster he had at The Giant's Toe," Oddi added, hoping it would calm Ulf. It did not.

"I never thought he'd get an army in the first place," Ulf protested.

"Aye, I admit, that's still strange. You think he knew about the trouble in Francia?" Thorbjorn looked at Snorri.

"Must have done. He was probably just waiting for the right moment before we came along." Snorri couldn't help but smile.

He liked the fact that not only had they defeated Griml, they also prevented him from raiding Francia. And now they were benefiting from it.

"So I just need to forget about my revenge so we can all get rich?" Ulf threw his arms up.

"Not forget, just be patient, Ulf. Remember, the gods —"

Ulf interrupted Snorri before he could finish. "The gods will decide when I can have my revenge. Is that what you are doing, Snorri? Forgetting about Thorvald, so you can get rich?"

Snorri reacted before he could stop himself. He launched at Ulf, grabbing him by the tunic. "Watch yourself, Ulf," he growled. "There's more to life than your revenge."

"And what about yours?" Ulf responded, his grey eyes as hard as the steel of Ormstunga.

Snorri roared and shoved Ulf back. If it wasn't for Drumbr standing behind him, Ulf would have fallen over. Ulf launched himself at Snorri with a roar of his own. His anger drove him on faster than Snorri expected, but Snorri was an experienced warrior. His instincts took over as he twisted out of the way of Ulf's punch. He heard the shocked gasps from the men on his ship, but Snorri didn't know if it was because Ulf had attacked him or because he had avoided the punch. Snorri brought his knee up and caught Ulf in the stomach, the force of the blow lifting Ulf to his feet and dropping him to the deck, gasping for air. Snorri stood ready, knowing that Ulf didn't know how to stay down, but his friend did not attack again. With a grunt, he turned and walked away.

"I cannot just stop, Snorri." The pain in Ulf's voice made him flinch. "Vidar died so I could retrieve Ormstunga. I can't just forget that and move on. Griml must pay for my family, for Vidar and for those who died at The Giant's Toe."

Snorri turned and saw his friend's face had changed. The anger replaced by anguish. "None of that was your fault, Ulf." Snorri tried to comfort his friend.

"Then whose fault was it? The gods?"

Snorri did not know how to respond to that. He just watched as his friend sat on his knees and clutched his stomach.

Oddi saved him by stepping forward. "I was told a story once. There was a man. His name was Einar. He had a younger brother who left home to fight for a jarl in another kingdom. One day, Einar got news that his brother was killed in a dispute over a woman."

"Nothing but trouble, women," Thorbjorn interrupted.

Oddi smiled and continued, "Of course, Einar was angry and swore revenge. He left home immediately and travelled to the village where his brother had been killed. The problem was that the man who had killed his brother was a hirdman of the jarl, and was never alone. So Einar came up with a plan. He joined this jarl's men, fought for him for a long time. One day, the jarl made Einar one of his hirdmen."

"And he killed the man who had killed his brother," Brak said with relish.

"No, he still could not get the man alone. Instead, he befriended the man. They fought many battles together and Einar even saved his life once." Oddi smiled when he saw the confusion on the faces of those around him. "One day, more than ten winters after his brother had been killed, Einar and his new friend were hunting together. Just the two of them. When the man was distracted by a deer, Einar pulled his knife out and stabbed him in the gut. He killed the man who had killed his brother and left his body for the ravens. It took him over ten winters to get his revenge, Ulf. He trusted the gods would give him his opportunity, and they did."

Snorri had never heard this story before and wondered if Oddi had made it up. It didn't really matter, though, as it seemed to have worked. He saw Ulf thinking about it. "Ulf, you know I want nothing more than to kill that coward, but I trust the gods will give me the opportunity. And so must you. The gods are on your side. You might not feel that way, but we can all see that." His hirdmen agreed, even Asbjorn. "The gods will give you your vengeance." Ulf was about to protest, but then someone called Snorri's name.

It was Ubba, pointing at the large fleet as a ship broke away and rowed towards them.

"Who's that, I wonder?" Thorbjorn peered into the distance.

"The leader of the fleet?" Oddi suggested.

"We're about to find out." Snorri held a hand out for Ulf, who only looked at it. Just when Snorri thought Ulf would not take it, he did. Snorri pulled Ulf to his feet, and the two nodded at each other. Orders were called out on the other ships, and sails were pulled in and oars brought out as they neared the giant fleet. Snorri didn't need to call the order. He knew Rolf would take care of it. Instead, he just watched the approaching ship. It was bigger than the Sae-Ulfr, perhaps as big as his father's ship, Thorgils' Pride. As she neared, he saw her prow beast was the head of a dragon, its mouth open as if it was about to spew fire at them. Snorri stroked the wolf head on his ship, not comforting her, but telling her to stay calm. He knew his Sae-Ulfr feared no ship, no matter their size or which prow beast they had. Ubba's ship broke away from the fleet and rowed towards the approaching ship. Snorri gave Rolf a signal to do the same. This might not have been his fleet, but Snorri wanted to meet the man who commanded such a large force. Tormod had done the same and the three ships rowed together as the other one stopped and turned sideways. Snorri's men kept pace with the other ships and he couldn't help but feel proud of them as they manoeuvred the Sae-Ulfr into place.

The captain of the other ship was easy to spot. He stood in the middle of the deck, hands on his side. On his head, he wore a bowl helmet with no nose guard. Long brown hair flowed from under the helmet and matched the beard, which went down to the man's chest. "Have you come to attack me?" The men on his ship laughed.

"Aye," Snorri responded before Ubba could say anything. "Although the fight doesn't seem fair. You don't have enough ships to defeat us." His crew laughed behind him as he smiled.

The man made a show of looking behind him at his fleet that stretched the horizon. "You might be right." He turned back to them, an amiable smile on his face. Snorri liked this man already. "My name's Asgeir." He thumbed his own chest. "Whom do I have the honour of speaking to?" Asgeir scanned the three ships arrayed in front of him, no doubt assessing them.

"I'm Ubba the White. We sail from Suðrikaupstefna, north of Denmark."

"Suðrikaupstefna?" Asgeir sounded surprised. "I was waiting for a sea king to join me from there. You are not him."

"Griml Jotun," Ubba responded.

"Griml Troll-Face," Thorbjorn muttered behind him.

"He was the sea king that commanded this force, but ran off to fight a personal battle and lost. I took over his army."

Asgeir looked surprised by this. "I met the man once, looked like a giant troll. Who did he lose to?"

"To us," Snorri responded. His men behind him cheered and howled like wolves. Snorri held up a hand, silencing his crew, but he could feel the energy from them.

"The man who doesn't think I have enough ships to defeat him." Asgeir looked at his men with a grin and they laughed. "And who might you be?"

"Snorri Thorgilsson."

"Well, well, Snorri Thorgilsson." Asgeir leaned forward to get a better view of Snorri. "You've made a name for yourself fighting us Danes." There was no anger in Asgeir's voice as he scanned the rest of Snorri's crew. "And that ugly red-headed goat fucker must be Ragnar Nine-Finger, if I'm not mistaken." His eyes stopped on Jarl Thorgils' champion.

Snorri looked behind him. Ragnar was standing there, arms crossed and scowling. "Aye, that is Ragnar Nine-Finger."

"The gods do like their games," Asgeir responded. "You get tired of killing Danes, now you decide to fight alongside them?"

"No, we are here on behalf of King Halfdan the Black," Snorri said.

"Halfdan the Black? He too important to come himself?"

"The king has important business elsewhere and has sent his best warriors in his place," Tormod responded from the Black Eagle. Snorri heard the annoyance in his voice and smiled.

"Who are you?"

"Tormod Torleifson, hirdman of King Halfdan."

Asgeir grunted and looked back at Snorri. "What happened with Griml?"

"We kidnapped his bride, and he chased us," Snorri said, a wolf grin on his face. "Fought a battle at a place called The Giant's Toe."

"Why is it called The Giant's Toe?" one of Asgeir's crew asked.

"Because a giant's toe turned to stone there, and the giant left it behind."

"I'd like to see this giant's toe," the man said, his friends nodding in agreement.

"So you defeated Griml?" Asgeir brought the conversation back.

"Aye, he outnumbered us by more than a hundred men, but we had the gods on our side." Snorri couldn't help but glance at Ulf as he said that.

"Is that so?" Asgeir asked.

"I've heard tales of this battle," Ubba added. "I swear by the gods that even if half of them are true, it was a fight to see."

Asgeir smiled. "Well then, Odin knows, I'd be more than happy to have warriors with your renown join my fleet, even if you are Norse."

"And we're honoured to join you," Snorri responded. "This looks like a raid that will be sung about for hundreds of years."

Asgeir beamed at that. "So what are your plans?"

"We're headed to a place called Hammaburg. I've been told there is an important monastery there," Ubba responded. "We were hoping to raid along the coast, then perhaps join you on your attack."

"Aye, seems fair," Asgeir said. "Find yourselves a place, we leave at first light." He called an order and his men got back to their benches.

Trust the gods and they will lead you to glory, Snorri thought as he signalled for his crew to get back to their places.

CHAPTER 10

The sun was past its peak as Ubba's fleet reached the fork in the river. They had broken away from Asgeir's fleet at sunrise and used the morning tide to enter the wide river. As they rowed and sailed, Ulf's curiosity had got the better of his anger and he could not help but stare at the surrounding land. Thick forests covered the riverbanks, reminding Ulf of those back in Norway. They had passed small settlements; the villagers looking at the warships with a mixture of curiosity and fear. Children ran along the banks, trying to keep up with the ships, while waving and shouting at the Norse and Danish raiders. They had not yet realised the danger these ships brought with them. By midday, the winds had picked up, and the oars were put away. The men on the Sae-Ulfr used the time to check armour and weapons, laughing and joking as they sharpened blades. The coming raid was a welcome distraction. Even Snorri was in a good mood as he moved around the ship, talking to his men and clapping them on their shoulders.

Ulf watched as most of Ubba's ships broke away from the fleet and aimed for the northern river of the fork.

"He's going for the church." Snorri walked up to Ulf, their altercation from the previous day forgotten. He must have seen the confusion on Ulf's face and pointed towards a small group of buildings stood separately from the rest of the settlement.

"What's a church?" Ulf studied the buildings, his eye catching on the biggest of them. The building stood as tall as it was wide, but what surprised Ulf most was the material it was made of. Stone.

"It's where they worship their god," Snorri responded.

"It's also where they keep a lot of gold and silver." Thorbjorn stood beside them, glaring at Ubba's ships as they went up the river while the rest of the fleet aimed for the southern fork. "Unguarded gold and silver."

Snorri nodded. "Aye, but this is Ubba's fleet, and that's why he gets the easy target."

"Lazy fucking Danes." Thorbjorn spat into the river.

"So what do we do?" Magni ignored the glares of Snorri's hirdmen as he invited himself to the conversation.

Snorri pointed to a city in the distance, not far from the church. Ulf could not tell how big the city was. The wooden wall surrounding the city stood taller that the houses, blocking Ulf's view of the inside. But from the amount of smoke rising from within the walls, he guessed it was bigger than Yngling Hall. "We get to show them how the Norse do things by taking the city."

"And what about those?" Magni pointed to the unprotected farms near the fortified city. There weren't many people outside, but this didn't surprise anyone. It was late in the day and with the work finished, the farmers were preparing for their evening meal. Ulf glanced at Magni, his eyes gleaming as the Sae-Ulfr moved up the smaller river and headed towards their target. Behind them, the rest of the ships followed.

"We leave them for Ubba's other ships." Snorri thumbed over his shoulder. Ubba had taken most of his ships up the northern fork, but five had come with Snorri's ships to the southern fork.

"Lazy fucking Danes," Thorbjorn repeated.

The villagers spotted the raiding fleet as the ships sailed past the farms and towards the city. Warning bells started ringing from within the walls as farmers erupted from their houses and ran to the safety of the city walls. Women pulled up their skirts and dragged children behind them. Men, some armed with pitchforks and spears, ran beside the women, but Ulf doubted they could do much to protect their wives and children. All around him, Norse and Danish warriors cheered the villagers on as if they were watching a race. Some men on the Sae-Ulfr were making bets on whether the farmers would make the city.

"Aim for that beach!" Snorri pointed to the open space between the coastal plants. A path ran from this beach to the city. The people of Hammaburg used the path to trade by sea and fish in the wide river, but today it would bring their death.

A small child, running towards the city with his mother, tripped, letting go of his mother's hand as he fell. His mother stopped and turned, her bulging eyes darting from her child to them as she struggled with some thought in her head. In the end, she ran back to her son and lifted him off the ground. But instead of going towards the city, she ran back to the farms. The men near Ulf cheered, and he knew she had made a mistake.

"A bunch of farmers and women." Ulf grit his teeth.

"Aye," Drumbr said, having heard Ulf. "It'll be an easy fight." Snorri looked back and beamed as he put his helmet on. His hirdmen had their helmets on already, their eyes shining fiercely through the eye guards. Only Thorbjorn and Drumbr had helmets without eye guards, although Thorbjorn's had a golden nose guard. Perhaps that explained the unbroken nose and the many cuts on his face. Magni stood tall, showing off his armour with a wide grin, while Ragnar waited with his two-handed axe, Skull-Splitter, in his hands. Ulf glanced at the silver cheek guards of Ragnar's helmet, admiring the standing bears embossed on them. He shook his head at his own childishness as he put his own helmet on, his vision now focused on what was in front of him. Ulf braced himself as the Sae-Ulfr hit the beach.

Snorri punched Tyr's Fury into the air. "For Odin!"

"For Odin!" the warriors of the Sae-Ulfr echoed, soon joined by the other ships as they cried their own cries. The thunderous noise drowned out the sounds of the bells and left none in doubt of what was about to happen.

The Sae-Ulfr came to a stop and Ulf followed Snorri and Ragnar as they jumped over, both men eager to start the slaughter. He rushed after them, following Snorri's hirdmen as they raced after those who had not yet reached the safety of the wooden walls. Magni was soon running beside Ulf, a savage grin plastered on the tall man's face.

"They're closing the gates!" Tormod shouted from somewhere. Ulf looked towards the walls and saw Tormod was right. They were closing the gates, even though many of the farmers had not reached them yet. There were still many stragglers, old men who could not run fast enough, and young people carrying too many of their possessions. Ulf shook his head as the raiders caught up with them, slaughtering the villagers with impunity. Ubba's Danes peeled off and ran towards the farmhouses not protected by the walls, and Ulf hoped that the woman with the boy would escape. Forcing himself to forget about them, he ran on. They were not his concern.

Snorri's men reached the city and found their way barred as the bell carried on ringing. "Drumbr, Ragnar, break the gate down!" Snorri ordered them. Both men took their large two-handed axes and headed towards the wooden gate as defenders started shooting arrows at them. "Shields!"

Ulf lifted his shield just in time as the arrows came down, feeling their force as they struck. But the man beside him was not so lucky. An arrow struck his face before the man could get his shield up and, as he dropped to the ground, Ulf recognised him as one of the crew of the War Bear. The man had survived the storm only to be killed by an arrow. *The gods are bastards*, Ulf thought as he grit his teeth, determined not to show the fear he felt as the arrows continued to rain down on them.

Ahead of him, Ragnar and Drumbr had reached the gatehouse, where the archers couldn't get to them. They dropped their shields and started hacking at the wooden gates with their axes. The rest of the force waited in front of the path, which bridged a wide ditch, not wanting to cross it until the gates were open. A large man from Tormod's crew rushed forward without a shield and only his enormous axe to help

Ragnar and Drumbr. As he ran over the path, an arrow struck his leg and, with a scream, the man fell into the ditch. Before the warrior could get up, more arrows pierced his chest. The defenders roared, pumping their fists and bows into the air.

"For Odin's sake, hurry, you bastards!" Thorbjorn roared over the din. Both men grunted with effort as they continued to hack at the gates, splinters flying all around them. "Thor's balls! How many more arrows have they got!"

Odin, do not let me die here. Remember my oath to you, I've not had my vengeance yet, Ulf prayed as another man fell beside him. Thunder echoed around them, and Ulf saw the wolf grin on Snorri's face as the arrows stopped. Looking up, he saw Ragnar and Drumbr charging through the open gates, their axes thirsty after eating nothing but dry wood.

"Odin!" Snorri stormed through the open gate. Ulf followed as a growl escaped his throat. He felt the flames spread through his limbs. The defenders of Hammaburg were going to pay for making him cower under his shield like a frightened girl. Ulf deflected a spear, which came from his right, and punched the defender in the face with the boss of his shield. The man fell back, spitting out a mouthful of blood and broken teeth as Ulf kicked him in the face before moving on. Ulf looked around him, trying to find more defenders, but saw only villagers fighting to defend their homes. Children were crying as Ulf watched a skinny man stab his spear at Brak. Brak blocked it with his shield before stabbing the man through the throat.

"Fucking farmers and women." Ulf spat to the side. Tormod moved towards an unarmed man trying to get away from the fight, the feral grin on his face igniting the flames in Ulf's chest. Ulf ran before he even knew what he was doing, determined to stop Tormod from killing a defenceless man. Tormod lifted his sword and Ulf, only a few paces away, worried he wouldn't make it in time. The unarmed man's face paled, and he dropped to his knees, his arms covering his head as if they could stop a sword. Ulf knew he had to get there, not sure why he wanted to save this Frank. He reached Tormod a moment before the sword came down. Lifting his shield, Ulf blocked Tormod's blade and kicked the unarmed Frank out of the way.

"What in Thor's name are you doing?" Tormod barked as Ulf turned to face him. Ulf only glared at Tormod, who smiled back. "You think I'm afraid of you, Bear-Slayer?"

"What's going on?" Snorri's voice broke through the tension.

Tormod scowled at Snorri. "You still haven't taught your pup his manners."

Snorri shrugged. "You can't tame a wolf, but some dogs," he pointed his sword at Tormod, "will roll over for anyone who promises a reward."

Tormod glared at Snorri, while Ulf watched him, determined to defend Snorri if Tormod attacked him. Not that Snorri would need any help. After a few heartbeats, Tormod spat at Ulf's feet and stomped away.

"You never learn." Snorri smiled at Ulf before he walked off, looking for another fight.

As Ulf watched his friend walk away, a young boy wielding a homemade spear attacked him from the side. Ulf sensed the movement and stepped aside, the spear streaking past him. He struck the boy on the side of the head with the cheek of Olaf's axe. The boy dropped to the ground, eyes closed, but still breathing. "Geir, no!" Ulf shouted as the young warrior rushed in for the kill. Geir stopped, sword still in the air as he frowned at Ulf. "Farmers and fucking women."

"What's your problem?" Geir's eyes were bright under his bowl helmet. His sword, the one given to him by Snorri, was red and shaking with excitement.

"I should be chasing Griml, instead I'm here fighting farmers and women," Ulf growled.

"I don't understand you, Ulf." Geir tilted his head to one side. "The gods have given us a great opportunity and all you do is complain about Griml."

Ulf felt like punching Geir in the face, but only because he spoke the truth. The gods had given them a gift, but Ulf did not want this. Ulf had not spent months learning to fight, so he could kill farmers and women. He had not sacrificed so much for easy plunder. Ulf tightened his grip on his shield and Olaf's axe as he looked around him. Men were running wild, like wolves in a sheep pen. Blood lust all over their faces. Some houses were burning from torches thrown on their thatch roofs. A woman screamed as she was being dragged into a house by her hair. Two men Ulf knew well, followed her as they untied their pants. Asbjorn kicked in the door of one house and stormed in, only to walk out a moment later, a look of disappointment under his helmet. A large hound was barking at some raiders who were trying to get into a house until one man lost his patience and stabbed the dog with his spear. The hound yelped before dropping to the ground, whimpering as the laughing men stepped over it. "Where is the honour in this?" His nose crinkled at the smell of death surrounding them.

"Perhaps you should ask him." Geir pointed towards Magni, who, flanked by his men, was cutting down anyone in his path.

It didn't matter who they were, man, woman or child. Magni ended their lives while roaring his name.

"Bastard thinks he's fighting a mighty battle and writing his name in the sagas." Oddi's voice came from behind them. Ulf turned and saw his tall friend, helmet off and wiping the sweat from his brow.

"You done fighting as well?" Geir's eyebrows disappearing under his helmet.

"What fighting?" Oddi looked around, sweeping his sword, Death's Breath, across the market square. "This is a raid, not a fight. We come, we scare them away and take their stuff." Ulf agreed with Oddi. There was no honour in fighting farmers and children. They would take what they needed to get rich, whether it be possessions or people, and they would move on. But Ulf didn't want to be rich. He wanted his revenge. Ulf spat to the side again as Geir walked off, shaking his head. "He's young. He still wants to earn his fame." Oddi defended the young warrior.

"We are the same age, me and him."

Oddi laughed, which sounded strange while death surrounded them. "Aye, but the gods know you have lived more than he has." He clapped Ulf on the shoulder as both men turned to the gate and saw Ubba and his men approach.

"Search everywhere! We must find him, even if we have to burn this entire city down!" Ubba stormed through the gate, stabbing his finger towards the centre of Hammaburg.

"What's his problem?" Ulf took his helmet off and scratched his braided hair. His head was itching from all the sweat.

"Only the Norns will know, and I don't feel like asking," Oddi responded. "Come, let's see if we can find some ale. I'm sure the Franks also like a drink."

As the two of them walked towards the gate, Thorbjorn left one house with a satisfied grin, tying his trousers up. "What?" Thorbjorn asked when he noticed them looking at him.

Outside the walls, things weren't much better for the Franks. The small farms were burning, the flames leaping high into the air as if to get the attention of the gods. Ulf heard the ravens and when he looked skyward, saw many of the death-eating birds circling above them. The flames didn't need to try too hard. The gods were already watching. He looked back at the farms and saw the Danes walking away, some of them carrying goods in their arms, while others dragged captives behind them. The image of his uncle's farm burning, his family's bodies piled up in front of it, came to Ulf. He shook his head to get rid of it as he thought of the woman and the boy he had seen before, hoping they had got away. A raven croaked near him, as if answering his thoughts. Ulf turned and spotted the large black bird sitting on the wall, staring at him. *Are you Huginn or Muninn?* With a shake of his head, he turned to the building Snorri had called a church. "They build all their temples out of stone?"

Oddi shook his head. "Only the important ones."

"But they're all filled with gold and silver and protected by men wearing skirts who think that words can defeat sword and axes," Thorbjorn added.

"So that one is important?" Men were walking out of the church, their arms filled with golden crosses and chests. One man was dragging out what Ulf first thought was a woman, but realised it was a man when he heard him scream for mercy.

"One of their priests," Oddi said

"Priest? He is like a godi?" Ulf's uncle had told him once of this strange religion that only believed in one god, but Ulf had never believed him. *How could one god defend Midgard from the giants?*

"Something like that." Oddi scowled, watching Ubba's men kick the priest.

"Not as frightening though, they talk too much." Thorbjorn scratched his ear under his helmet.

"So why did we attack the city?" Ulf tucked Olaf's axe into his belt. "Ubba has more men than us."

"Because Ubba asked Snorri to take the city, and the idiot agreed," Ragnar responded. They all turned to see the large warrior checking the edge of his axe, thumbing at a nick in the blade. "Fucking nail in the gate. Thor knows it'll take me all day to get this out."

Ulf frowned as he looked back at the church, seeing the flames leap out of its windows. It made sense for Ubba to ask Snorri to take the city. The church was an easier option for them.

"He's doing it again," Thorbjorn said. Ulf looked at him and saw the smile on the short man's face.

"Doing what?"

"Thinking too much. You shouldn't, it's no good for you."

"Thorbjorn is right. Leave the mysteries of life to the gods," Ragnar agreed.

"We should find Snorri," Oddi said. "Need to make sure he didn't kill himself by tripping over a barrel." They turned and walked back into the city, apart from Ulf.

He stood for a while and watched the men torture the priest. He heard the raven again and wondered if Odin was watching them kill the servant of the rival god. Movement by one of the burning farmhouses caught his eye. Ulf blinked and held his breath. *Was that...?* It couldn't be. He scanned the houses with squinted eyes, but there was nothing. He shook his head. "Perhaps Thorbjorn is right. I think too much," Ulf muttered as he turned to follow the others.

Ulf found them all standing around Snorri and Ubba in the city's square. Snorri smiled, with his hands on his hips, while Ubba was scowling with his arms crossed. Warriors walked past, leading captives back to the ships. Men beaten bloody, women with torn dresses and tear-streaked faces. Ulf recognised the boy he had knocked out and felt a pang of guilt. The boy had only been trying to protect his home, much like Ulf had done once. And like Ulf, the boy was going to pay a heavy price for that.

"Ulf, you are still alive." Ulf heard the edge in Ubba's voice, but the smile on his face made Ulf think he had imagined it. "I was worried you had not survived when I didn't see you amongst your friends."

Snorri laughed and grabbed Ulf by the shoulder as soon as he was near enough. "It'll take a lot more than a few arrows to kill the Bear-Slayer."

"Aye, the young pup has more luck than he deserves." Ragnar cleared his nostrils.

Ubba frowned, giving Ulf a sideways glance. Ulf only shrugged, not wanting to be part of this conversation. He still felt uncomfortable around Ubba, even if the others thought him a friend.

"What a glorious battle!" The exclamation from Magni distracted them from the topic. Oddi's older brother walked towards them, his bloody sword still in hand and surrounded by his father's men. Magni was covered in blood, his red beard even redder than usual. He was still wearing his helmet as he spread his arms and laughed into the sky. "It's a slaughter that will go down in the sagas." He faced them with a crazed look in his eyes. "Even Odin has taken notice of us here." Oddi just lowered his head, shaking it as he walked away.

"I agree, the gods must be on your side," Ubba responded as Snorri scowled at Magni. The rest of his hirdmen looked at Magni as if he had knocked his head on a rock. "I did not expect you to take the gates so easily."

"This isn't our first raid." Ragnar scowled.

Ubba raised a hand in apology. "I meant no insult. You are all famed warriors. Odin knows I should not have expected less from you."

Snorri laughed. "Don't mind Ragnar. The gods did smile on us. This city was not defended by proper warriors. Once we got through the gate and killed the first few, the rest of them gave up." He glanced at Magni, who was too caught up in his own glory to get the meaning of the words. Most of the men barely had any blood on them and stood in stark contrast to Magni.

Ubba glanced at Ulf before turning back to Snorri. "Ulf here doesn't seem too happy about things."

Snorri smiled while he squeezed Ulf's shoulder. "Don't mind Ulf, he is always serious after a fight."

"Aye, doesn't yet understand how to enjoy the smaller things in life," Thorbjorn added.

"Our young friend does not see when the gods smile on us," Magni interjected, not noticing the others glaring at him. Ulf grit his teeth as he took deep breaths, trying to calm the flames that were threatening to erupt inside him.

"So what now?" Tormod asked, glowering at Ulf, still upset about Ulf not letting him kill an unarmed man.

Ubba shrugged and looked around the city. "We rest. As far as we know, there is no large army nearby, so our men can enjoy themselves for a day or two." Ulf saw some of his friends' eyes light up at that.

Snorri also couldn't keep the grin off his face. "Aye, Odin knows that sounds like a good plan." He turned and scanned the horizon. "Perhaps I can take my men and scour the lands around, see what else we can find." Ulf smiled when he saw Thorbjorn's jaw drop and Drumbr shake his head. They wanted to enjoy the spoils of the raid, not go wandering around.

"Not a bad idea." Ubba rubbed his chin and looked in the direction of the church where some of his men were probably still torturing the priests. "The priests told us of another church, not too far away."

"Another church?" Snorri purred. He eyed Ragnar, who wore a vicious wolf grin on his face. "How far is this church?"

Ubba was still rubbing his chin as he thought about it. "Not exactly sure, but I think about two days' march from here. Near a city called Bremen."

"Bremen? Perhaps I can take my men there, raid this church while you finish up here?" Snorri rubbed the back of his neck.

Ubba's face remained passive, but Ulf saw the smirks on the faces of the men behind him. "You don't want to stay here? Let your men get some rest."

Thorbjorn laughed at that. "Snorri is never one to sit around when there is fun to be had."

"If I was meant to sit around and wait for things, then the Norns would have made me a bóndi, not a warrior." Snorri patted the hilt of his sword. Ragnar shook his head, and Ulf saw the gleam in Magni's eyes. But Ulf wasn't sure if it was the prospect of more gold that appealed to him or killing more helpless people. He was beginning to understand why Oddi didn't like his brother. Ulf looked around to see if he could find his tall friend. He had walked off when Magni had appeared.

"Well then, I'm glad the Norns saw fit to bring you to me." Ubba turned to Snorri. "Should take you a day or so to get there if you walk east. If the gods keep smiling on us, then we can be there in three days' time with our ships full of coin." The two of them gripped forearms as they agreed on the deal.

Ulf guided his whetstone along the edge of Olaf's axe, savouring the sound of the stone grinding against the metal. It was late evening and even though the sun still sat low in the sky, they had a large fire going. His axe did not need sharpening. He had barely used her today, but Ulf needed a distraction. He was still trying to understand the day's events. With him sat Snorri and his hirdmen, Ragnar and a few others. They were enjoying the spoils of their attack on Hammaburg and were excited by the planned attack on the large church to the east. Magni was sitting opposite them, boasting about how many *warriors* he had killed today, but no one was listening to him. Even his father's men were ignoring him.

"That gate was a bastard." Drumbr chewed on some meat they had taken from the village. "Got a few nicks in Shield Breaker's blade from all the nails in the wood."

"Aye," Ragnar agreed. "But it felt good to kill some Franks again."

"You've been here before?" Geir asked, his head popping up like a seal's out of the water.

Ragnar stared at the young warrior, making Geir squirm and causing Snorri to laugh. "Many winters ago," Ragnar responded after a few heartbeats. "We used to raid these lands all the time when I first joined the jarl's crew." Geir's shoulders sagged in relief.

"Aye, my father told me many stories from his raids in these lands." Snorri lost himself in the flames as he remembered his childhood. "These lands were fat with gold, so fat that many towns paid you a ship full just to get you to go away or to attack their neighbours."

"And then we would take gold from the neighbours and go home happy." One of the older warriors around the fire laughed.

"Then why did you stop?" Geir asked.

"The king of the Franks got smart," Rolf answered, chewing on some bread soaked in ale. "Started building forts all around the coast and got himself lots of new ships and men to crew them. In the end, raiding in Francia became too risky." Ragnar and the men old enough to remember those days nodded their agreement.

"My father didn't mind, though. By that time he had already built his hall and had become one of the most powerful jarls in the region."

"By killing helpless men in skirts," Ulf retorted, still sharpening Olaf's axe.

Snorri smiled at Ulf with a raised eyebrow, while the rest of the men held their breaths. "Helpless men in skirts?" Snorri leaned forward. "When I was a young boy, I asked my father why our people had enjoyed fighting the Franks so much. I asked him if it was because of all the gold they had. My father gave me one of those stern glares of his and said no, it was not because of the gold."

"The gold helped though," Ragnar added to the smiles of those around him.

"Then why?" Geir asked, unable to help himself. He sat by the fire like a young child, enthralled by Snorri's words. Ulf just stared at Snorri, his face showing no emotion.

Snorri took his eyes off Ulf and surveyed the lands around him, like he was trying to see something in his mind. "Many winters ago, in the days when Rolf started going grey." Snorri couldn't help himself and the men laughed at Rolf's reaction. "These lands were filled with our kinsmen. People who lived the same way and followed the same gods as us. Then one day, the king of the Franks, a very Christian man, they say, marched his army here and told the people to get on their knees and grovel to his one and only god." Snorri paused as he stared at Ulf. "What would you do, Ulf, if you were told to grovel before a god you do not know?" Ulf didn't answer, but then he didn't need to.

"Ulf doesn't believe in the gods," Thorbjorn teased.

"Doesn't matter if he believes in them or not. The gods have taken an interest in him. He's stuck with them," Rolf responded, giving Ulf a knowing look.

"Ragnar, would you get on your knees for the Christian god?" Snorri asked his father's champion instead.

"Odin knows I'd rather take my own life." Everyone around him agreed with nods or grunts.

Snorri smiled. "That's what these people told the Frankish king. Do you know what this king did, Ulf?" Ulf shook his head, slightly cowed by Snorri's stern stare, made even sterner by the flames. "He brought his army in and slaughtered everyone. All the men were killed, the women and children sold into slavery. He used the coin he got from them to build his churches all over these lands once the smoke cleared from all the burnt villages. Entire tribes wiped out because they would not forsake their gods, our gods!" Snorri thumbed his chest. Everyone around the fire roared their support. Snorri pointed back towards the church. "Do not think these priests are helpless men, Ulf. In one hand, they offer you peace and in the other they carry the sword that will cut you down if you refuse their god."

Ulf stared at the church in the fading light as Snorri's words echoed in his head.

"For many winters we have waited for our chance to avenge our kinsmen, much like you want to avenge your family," Ragnar said, surprising Ulf. "And now the gods have given us a chance to do that."

"Is that why Ubba came here?" Geir asked, completely taken by what he had just heard.

"No," Oddi responded, surprising everyone. He had been quiet for most of the evening. Ulf thought he might have been ashamed by his brother's behaviour. "Ubba is not here because of something that happened in the days when our fathers were young men, but in the days when we were young boys." He was met with raised eyebrows as everyone stared at him.

"How do you know this, Oddi *Viss?*" Thorbjorn asked, saying Viss in his usual mocking tone.

Oddi smiled at him. "Because, Thorbjorn, while you were busy taking advantage of the captive women, I was busy learning more about our new friend."

"What did you learn?" Snorri asked him.

"Ubba is hunting a priest. That's the real reason he went for the church first."

"A priest?"

"What's so special about this priest?" Ragnar asked.

"From what one of Ubba's men told me, this priest was sent to Denmark about ten winters ago to convert them to Christianity. Needless to say, he was not very nice to the Danes and when King Harald died, the priest was forced to leave."

"So, Ubba wants him because of something that happened then?" Drumbr frowned.

"No, Ubba's man told me that the new Danish king, King Haarik, wants to invite this priest back to Denmark to continue his work." This was met with a shocked silence.

"The Danish king wants to be a Christian?" Ragnar asked in his growling voice.

Oddi shook his head. "No, he wants to strengthen ties with the Frankish empire. Unlike Norway, Denmark borders Francia and Haarik must be concerned that whoever wins this civil war might decide to force Denmark into Christianity." They all nodded as they contemplated this. Ulf understood nothing that was being said and not for the first time wondered why the gods had to interfere in their lives.

"So Ubba was sent to fetch this priest?" Thorbjorn scratched at his ear.

Again, Oddi shook his head. "Ubba wants to kill him before the priest can go to Denmark. That's why he looked so upset when the attack on the city was over. The priest had escaped."

"Why does he want to kill the priest? Doesn't matter what this priest does, Denmark will never bow to the Christian god," Brak said.

"And neither will Norway," his brother added.

"Only the gods will know that one, but from what this man told me, they did not love this priest in Denmark. His tactics were barbaric," Oddi responded.

"So, we came all this way for a fucking priest." Ulf spat.

"No, we came here because Snorri wanted to roast a jarl." Ragnar responded while eyeing Snorri. Snorri only smiled and shrugged.

"Doesn't matter why we are here. What does is that we are here and the gods have given us the opportunity to avenge our kinsmen and also go home with our ships full of gold." Snorri smiled his wolf grin. "And tomorrow at sunrise we will set off east and bleed this land dry until we find that church." He raised a cup to the cheers of his men.

But Ulf did not cheer with the rest of them. "Don't you think it's strange that Ubba sends us to this church if he's looking for some priest?"

"He didn't send us to the church, Snorri offered," Thorbjorn said, getting a smile from Snorri.

Snorri looked at his friend. "Ulf, I know you are desperate to find Griml and get revenge. We all want to find that troll and piss in his empty eye sockets. But before we can do that, we must do what the king has asked us." He stared at Ulf until he nodded.

"Aye, the gods smiled on us by letting Ubba take over this raid. The man will make us richer than Fafnir," Thorbjorn said.

"Aye, Ubba has been good to us," Snorri agreed. "A toast to our new friend!" He raised his cup, and the others followed his example, all of them cheering Ubba's name.

Ulf sat staring into the flames again, absorbed by their destructive nature while doubt ate at his mind. Everyone seemed to think that Ubba was their friend, but there was still something that Ulf did not like. There was also the strange sighting Ulf could not explain, but he felt a dark shadow creeping over him. *Tyr, give me the strength to face whatever dangers lie in my path.*

CHAPTER 11

"Odin's foot, how much further do we need to walk?" Magni whined. Ulf smiled as Oddi rolled his eyes. They'd been walking for half a day, enjoying the Frankish countryside as birds flew around, singing to each other. The men were in good spirits after the attack on Hammaburg, most of them still recovering from the Frankish ale they had found in a tavern.

"Don't know what you are complaining about," Oddi responded. "You're taller than everyone."

"What does that have to do with anything?" Magni gave Oddi a shocked glance.

"It means for every two steps we take, you only take one. So for you the distance is shorter." Oddi shook his head like it made all the sense in the world.

"I don't think it works that way, Oddi Viss." Thorbjorn raised an eyebrow.

"And how would you know?"

"Enough, all of you!" Ragnar shouted, causing some of them to laugh. "We've barely walked half a day." Ulf glanced at the sun as it reached its zenith. They had followed the sun east as soon as it lit the morning sky, the men like hungry wolves setting off on a hunt.

"I don't see why I couldn't stay with Rolf and the ship," Magni continued. Even his father's men had moved away from him.

Snorri looked over his shoulder at the tall man with a mocking smile on his face. "A mighty warrior like you would not want to stay with the ship."

Magni squinted, trying to work out if Snorri was mocking him. "And what of those other men who stayed with Rolf?"

"Old Treefoot can't steer the Sae-Ulfr all by himself. He needed some men to help bring her to this Bremen place with Ubba's fleet," Snorri explained, glancing at Oddi, who only shook his head.

"And Tormod?"

"It's better that Tormod stays with Ubba," Snorri responded as he gave Ulf a sideways glance. Ulf guessed Tormod was still angry with him. Tormod had spent the night drinking with Ubba's captains, leaving his men to join those from Thorgilsstad.

"I think Magni has gone soft while living his life of luxury." Thorbjorn was never one to be shy with his words.

"Magni has always been soft," Ragnar retorted with a growl. The entire crew stared at Magni, wanting to see how he would respond. Ulf hoped Magni would be smart enough just to let it go. He had learnt the hard way what happened when you challenged Ragnar Nine-finger. But like Ulf the previous summer, Magni was not that smart.

"I am not soft!" Magni's face went red.

"Then prove it, Cockerel," Ragnar sneered. Ulf watched Snorri, wondering if his friend was going to stop this. But Snorri just glared at Magni, like the rest of them, fed up with his constant whining.

Magni pulled his sword out of her scabbard and charged at Ragnar, who stepped aside and punched Magni in the face. The men around gasped as Magni fell to the ground, clutching his bloody mouth and dropping his sword.

"I see why Jarl Thorgils preferred Oddi." Ragnar walked away.

Magni lifted himself onto his elbow and shouted at Ragnar, his face red with blood and rage, "I am better than my brother!" The crew of the Sae-Ulfr responded with laughter. They all knew the value of Oddi, having fought beside him many times.

"For the love of Freya, enough!" Snorri stepped forward. "Magni, pick yourself up. You are the eldest son of a jarl, now act like one!" Magni looked like he was about to complain again, but the glare from Snorri killed the words in his throat. Instead, he nodded and got to his feet, wiping the blood from his lip. "We are here to fight the Franks, not each other." The men nodded their agreement. Snorri looked to the east. "From what Ubba told me, we should be near the church by nightfall."

"So, we attack in the morning?" Drumbr wiped the sweat from his brow as Snorri nodded. Magni glared at Ragnar and Oddi before lifting his head high and following Snorri.

Ulf stood and watched as the men of the Sae-Ulfr followed, scratching his beard. He felt a tingling sensation in his neck, which almost made him shiver. But when Ulf looked behind him, he saw nothing, not even a raven.

"You coming, Ulf?" Drumbr called after him. "What's wrong?" he asked when he noticed the frown on Ulf's face.

"Nothing, just feel like I'm being watched."

Drumbr chuckled. "We all know that Odin is watching you, there's no need to rub it in."

"But there are no ravens." Ulf scanned the skies, looking for large black birds who were Odin's messengers.

Drumbr searched the skies as well. "Perhaps Odin has other business to take care of." He scratched his nose as he glanced at Ragnar. "You know the story about how Ragnar lost his finger? They say he got lost in the forest once, disappeared for days," Drumbr continued before Ulf could respond. "He had no food and no water and to survive he cut off his little finger and ate it."

Ulf frowned at Drumbr. He had lost track of all the different stories about Ragnar's finger. "Why did he eat the smallest finger?"

Drumbr shrugged. "I don't know, but the bravery of the man to cut off his own finger and eat it!"

"You believe the story?"

"Aye, I'd eat my entire leg if I got lost in the forest without food."

"But why didn't he just hunt for something?"

Drumbr scratched his cheek as he thought about it. "Perhaps he had nothing to hunt with."

Ulf shook his head. This story made less sense than the others. Not that any of them made any sense. "Then how did Ragnar cut his finger off?"

Drumbr stopped and looked at Ulf. "By the gods, Ulf. You ask a lot of questions. That's the story I heard, and that's all I know." He walked off in a huff. Ulf could only shake his head and follow his friend.

Later that afternoon, they spotted a farmstead in the distance. A group of longhouses, unlike the ones in Norway. These did not have bowed roofs and their walls were coated in what looked like mud. The roofs were covered with straw, much like the ones in Norway, and their doors were on the narrow side. Small fields of wheat and corn were next to the houses, and all this was surrounded by a picket fence, about waist-high. Chickens wandered around, pecking at the dirt while a rooster stood on the fence as if guarding its territory.

"Doesn't look like much," Thorbjorn said as they studied the farmstead. Some men agreed with him.

"Should we have a look?" Asbjorn shielded his eyes from the sun.

"Where are the animals?" Oddi surveyed the land around the farm. He was right. Apart from the chickens, there were no cattle, sheep, or pigs. Only empty pens.

"They probably heard Magni complain and made a run for it. I swear, the gods probably left Asgard for a quieter place," Thorbjorn jibed, but this time Magni did not bite.

"Smoke's coming out of the roof, so there must be people around." Ragnar pointed to one of the houses. "Snorri?"

Snorri studied the houses and the surrounding land, taking his time before making a decision. But Ulf knew they would attack. Snorri never gave up an opportunity like this. The wolf grin parting his moustache from his beard confirmed what Ulf thought.

"Aye, let's go introduce ourselves." Snorri's men smiled as they prepared to raid the farm. The men placed their helmets on their heads and took the shields from their backs. Weapons were drawn as the men formed up, ready for the order from Snorri.

"It's too quiet," Oddi warned, still unsure as he studied the farm.

"Perhaps my little brother has gone soft." Magni couldn't help himself as the words came out slightly muffled because of his swollen lip.

"We'll see who's soft when the real fighting begins," Oddi said without looking at his brother. Thorbjorn gave Magni a smile, which suggested he kept quiet.

Ulf looked at the sun shining through the few clouds. Shaking his head, he took Olaf's axe from his belt.

"What is the use of that pretty sword if you never use it?" Magni asked.

"Ulf has his reasons," Snorri responded for him, "and after what we saw at The Giant's Toe, I'd rather he not unsheathe it now." Magni tilted his head, frowning.

"The sword is magic and, like all magic swords, she has rules," Oddi explained. Ulf knew he believed it more than anyone else. If Oddi had not become a warrior, then he might have been a godi. But Oddi was too good at killing not to be a warrior. Magni looked at the men from his village, who just shrugged. They had all been in that battle. They all knew they should have lost it.

"Are we going to stand here and talk like wives, or are we going to pillage that farm?" Ragnar asked, frustrated with them all.

"Aye, let's get going." Snorri walked to the farm. Ulf fell in to his right and Ragnar on his left. The men of Thorgilsstad spread out as they marched to the fence in silence. The men prepared for anything.

"I agree with Oddi, this doesn't feel right," Ragnar said as they stopped near the fence. His eyes darted everywhere as he looked for a hidden threat. Ulf also felt uncomfortable, but then, he had been for days.

"What's the matter, Ragnar? Have you gone soft as well?" Magni taunted the champion. Again, everyone stopped and looked at Ragnar.

"You're fucked now," Thorbjorn said to Magni, whose face slightly paled when he noticed the angry scowl on Ragnar's face.

But Snorri was not in the mood for this now. Grinding his teeth, he turned to Magni. "Magni, if you are so brave, then I give you the honour of going in first."

"Snorri, what are—" Ragnar started, but was stopped by Snorri's upheld hand.

"Magni is eager to show us what a strong warrior he is, so I give him the honour of going in first."

"I was never given that honour," Brak whispered.

"Because it's not real, you idiot," Thorbjorn responded.

"Oh," Brak said, looking at his feet.

Magni straightened his back and wore a proud smile. "Thank you, Snorri. It's about time you noticed my worth." He signalled for his father's men to form up behind him. But Ulf saw they felt uncomfortable. Unlike Magni, these experienced warriors, and knew when a situation seemed strange. But Magni, blinded by his own pride, marched confidently through the gate, his shield and sword carried low by his side. The men behind him were more cautious, their shields in front of them and their weapons ready. The rest of the crew held their breaths.

Snorri kissed the Mjöllnir around his neck — many of the men around him doing the same. Ulf stroked the names of his family on the haft of Olaf's axe, as he glanced at the sun again. The men following Magni held back, their shoulders tense. For these men, it must have been like creeping into Fafnir's cave to steal his gold. As they moved towards one house, Snorri signalled for his men to spread out along the fence, while he and Ragnar stood by the open gate, wide enough for just the two of them.

Magni stopped a few feet away from the first house as he scanned the farmstead. He spotted nothing amiss as he turned around and exclaimed, "Nothing to worry about." Magni adopted a wise look, similar to the one Oddi liked to use. "That is your problem, Snorri. You see a fight —"

The door behind him burst open as a large, fair-haired warrior stormed out, roaring as if to wake the gods. Chickens scattered in an explosion of feathers. The warrior launched his spear at Magni, who had turned to see what the noise was, his face as white as fresh milk. Magni dropped to his knees, and the spear flew over his head, but one of his father's men behind him was not so lucky. He did not see the spear because Magni was in his way and it struck him in the chest, bursting out of his back.

"Skjaldborg!" Snorri roared as more men burst out of the other houses and charged at them. The rooster on the fence squawked and fled, abandoning its duties.

"Run, you bastards!" Thorbjorn shouted at the men in the farmstead. Magni quickly overcame his shock as he fled after his father's men, all of them desperate to get to the safety of the shield wall. Ulf locked his shield into place beside Snorri and took Olaf's axe in hand as Magni barged his men out of the way, his long legs taking him past them. Ulf realised they were outnumbered as more and more men poured out of the houses. He realised something else as well. They had been expected.

"Take a step back!" Snorri ordered. He must have seen the same and wanted to use the fence to their advantage. Ulf glanced at the well-maintained fence, hoping it was strong enough to stop this horde. The three-man deep shield wall moved back as Snorri and Ragnar opened their shields to let Magni and his men through with the enemy hot on their heels. As soon as the last man ran past them, Snorri and Ragnar locked shields again. They had no fence in front of them, so the enemy focused their attack on the two warriors. "Odin! Tyr!" Snorri punched Tyr's Fury into the air as he tried to get the gods' attention. The men around him echoed his call.

"Tyr, guide me," Ulf whispered, tightening his grip on his axe's haft. His stomach clenched and Ulf had enough time to cast a resentful glance at the sun before the first enemy was on him.

The first man to reach Ulf had a bushy beard sticking out from under his helmet and violent eyes glaring at him through the eye guard. He roared as he stabbed at Ulf with his sword. Ulf lifted his shield and felt the force of the blow run up his arm. He turned his shield before the man could free his sword, giving himself space to strike with Olaf's axe. His opponent blocked the axe with his own shield, but could do nothing about the spear which came over Ulf's shoulder and stabbed him through the throat. The man's eyes went wide as he choked on spear and blood. Ulf freed his axe from the dead man's shield before he collapsed and another took his place. As this man pushed his dead comrade out of the way, Ulf buried his axe in his skull, its sharp edge breaking iron and bone with a spray of blood, his eyes protesting at the unfairness of his death. The spear streaked over Ulf's shoulder again, causing the next man to lift his shield, exposing his stomach. Ulf cursed at the missed opportunity. If he was fighting with Ormstunga, he could have stabbed the man in the gut. But he was not. While Ulf rued the missed chance, his new opponent stabbed at his face. Ulf deflected the sword point with Olaf's axe and punched the man with his shield. There was a satisfying crunch as Ulf's shield boss broke the man's nose. His opponent stumbled backwards, bumping into the man behind him, who shoved him straight into Oddi's sword. The man twisted in pain as Oddi's sword slipped in under his ribs. Ulf cleaved his chest open, spraying both him and Oddi in blood. Over the battle din, Ulf heard his constant companions. The large black birds which seemed to follow his every step, reporting all they see to the All-Father. Odin was watching.

"They're trying to break the fence!" Ulf looked down and saw hands trying to break the fence apart. They could not allow that to happen. The ambushing force was much larger, and the fence was the only thing which gave the Norsemen a chance. Ulf turned Olaf's axe around and smashed the fingers using the butt of his axe. He heard a shout of agony as the hand pulled back. But before Ulf could relish that, he had to block a sword coming for his head. Ulf reacted by striking with his axe, but forgot to turn the head around. The man's skull crunched as Ulf struck him and the body fell over the fence. Another man stepped forward, his two-handed axe high in the air as he prepared to split Ulf's skull. Ulf lifted his shield and was almost brought to his knees by the force of the blow. The man behind Ulf stabbed with his spear, causing Ulf's opponent to duck. At the same time, Ulf struck upward with Olaf's axe, catching the man under the chin and splitting his face in two. Ulf roared his defiance, the next man wavering before coming at Ulf. Snorri was being pushed backwards, but Ulf could do nothing as he blocked the axe of his opponent.

"Snorri! We need to do something!" Ragnar yelled over the battle music. The two of them had been dealing with the brunt of the attack and were slowly being pushed backwards.

Snorri dispatched his opponent and sucked in deep breaths of air. "Ragnar, Drumbr, get ready. The rest of you, when I give the order, punch out with your shields." Snorri waited three heartbeats. "Now!"

The men around Snorri, including Ulf, punched out as one. This forced the enemy back a step and gave Ragnar and Drumbr space to free their large two-handed axes. With grunts, they swung hard and showered Ulf with wood splinters and blood as they cleaved through the men of the enemy's front line. Snorri rushed through the gap this created before the enemy could recover. Ulf followed without thought, determined to protect his friend. He felt Ragnar's presence to his left as he blocked an axe aimed at Snorri. Ulf swung his axe at the man, but missed as he rushed past. The warriors of Thorgilsstad were flooding through the breach, catching the enemy by surprise. They cried in anguish, realising they now had to fight on two fronts. Snorri danced around his opponents, his skill too much for them as Tyr's Fury stole the life of any who dared to get in her reach.

Thorbjorn used his short, stocky frame to barge men out of the way and get underneath sword swings before ruthlessly slaughtering his opponents. Oddi killed men with his long arms before they could even dream of getting close to him as Drumbr and Ragnar swung their mighty axes in giant arcs, hewing all those around them. The enemy were stunned and could not deal with Snorri and his men, who spent years perfecting their skills in battle and on the training field. They had come to kill the men of Thorgilsstad, and now they were fighting for their lives.

The flames spread through Ulf's limbs as the voices of his ancestors whispered in his ears. *I will not die here today.* A man charged at him, wearing no helmet or vest, only trousers, as he swung his sword above his head. Ulf stepped forward and headbutted him, the man's skull no match for Ulf's iron helmet. He roared as he hacked at the shield of another before someone else killed the man. Someone stabbed at him with a spear, but Ulf twisted out of the way before chopping through wrist and wood and punching the man in the face with his shield. There were still too many of them as two men attacked Ulf at the same time. Ulf did everything he could to block their blows, his battle rage driving him on faster than his opponents until he tripped over a body and landed on his back. His heart skipped a beat when he saw the smiles on the faces of his attackers, one of them missing his two front teeth. As one, they lifted their weapons and were about to kill Ulf when a sword burst through the chest of one of them. The man with the missing teeth looked surprised, but quickly gathered his wits and swung his sword at Snorri, who stepped aside, his face calm as he dodged the blow and sliced through the man's neck with Tyr's Fury. A fountain of blood erupted as the gap-toothed man dropped to the ground next to Ulf, his body twitching as the blood poured out of his wound.

"My hirdmen are supposed to protect me, not the other way around." Snorri smiled as he helped Ulf up. Ulf nodded his thanks as he got to his feet. But Snorri did not see it. He was already fighting another man. All around Ulf, there was only chaos as the two armies fought each other. One for gold, the other for their lives. He could hear the gods laughing in the cries of the ravens who flew above them. The gods loved chaos. But Ulf had no more time to think about it as he jumped back into the fight, splitting a skull in two and blocking a spear with his shield.

It was a desperate fight, and Ulf had lost track of how long it had been going on for. The only thing that kept him going was the flames of his anger burning inside of him and refusing to let go. Voices of his ancestors screaming in his ears, demanding blood. Above this was the battle song. Metal on metal, metal on wood. Men roaring their defiance or crying in agony. Some praying to the gods for strength, while others begged for death. And then, a new noise. A noise Ulf did not understand until the enemy backed away. A horn. The horn kept blowing, urging the ambushing army back. Ulf looked around him, searching for another opponent to send to Valhalla. But there were none around. They were all backing off.

"On me!" Snorri ordered, his voice raw from the fight. His men obeyed, resisting the urge to storm at the retreating army. "Skjaldborg!" Ulf locked his shield in with Snorri on his left and Drumbr on his right. He watched the enemy over its splintered edge, seeing the apprehension in their faces. The cries of ravens filled the silence as if they were mocking the now wary ambushing force. They had expected a slaughter of lambs, but now faced snarling wolves. No amount of gold was worth the price they were paying, and as one, they turned and fled.

Thorbjorn stepped out of the shield wall. "Run, you cowards! Run before I chop you into pieces and feed you to my swine!" He stood there, glaring into the empty space with his nostrils flared.

"Thorbjorn has pigs?" someone asked.

The men of Thorgilsstad stayed in the shield wall for a few heartbeats, waiting for the ambushing force to return. Others checked their backs in case this was another trap. But nothing happened and soon it became clear the fight was over. The entire group exhaled as one. Ulf dropped his shield as his legs collapsed, too weary to support him. He stuck Olaf's axe in the ground, sucking in deep breaths to still his shaking hands. Beside him, Drumbr dropped his axe and lay down on his back, a laugh escaping from his lips.

"By Odin's Spear, that was a bastard of a fight." Thorbjorn bent over, spitting blood from his mouth. "Thought I'd be feasting in Valhalla tonight."

"Aye, those Franks put up a hard fight," Asbjorn responded, picking at some broken links in his brynja. Ulf saw no blood, so it looked like the brynja did its job well.

"These aren't Franks." Ragnar toed one of the bodies. Those in earshot looked up, surprised by Ragnar's comment. Ulf had not thought about who they had been fighting. He had been too busy trying not to die. He shuddered as he remembered tripping over the body and seeing the two men standing over him.

"What do you mean they aren't Franks?" Thorbjorn stood straight and walked towards Ragnar. "Who else would they be?"

"Danes." Snorri knelt down by one body. He tucked at the man's neck and held up a Mjöllnir pendant.

"I don't like this." Oddi took the pendant from Snorri and studied it.

"Aye, doesn't smell right," Brak agreed.

"Some Loki-shit going on here," Ragnar said, his eyes scanning the horizon. Ulf wondered if he was trying to spot the men who had attacked them.

"You think they meant to ambush us?" Magni appeared, covered in blood. His helmet as red as the others, even his sword showed signs of fighting.

Snorri did not respond straight away, instead he surveyed the farmhouses. "Hard to say."

"Could be another raiding party?" Drumbr suggested. Everyone looked at him while they thought about what he had said.

"Then why attack us?" Ulf asked. He had taken his helmet off and was scratching at the blood drying on it. It would take a lot of rubbing to get this clean.

Snorri only shrugged, but Oddi responded, "Perhaps they thought we were Franks, wouldn't be the first time an army mistook friends for foes."

Ragnar shook his head. "They'd have heard Magni talking to us in a language they understood."

"And Snorri shout to the All-father," Brak added. Everyone remained silent as they pondered this. The rest of the men, those not taking part in this conversation, started picking their way through the dead. Ulf watched as they searched for loot and friends, his helmet still in his hands.

"Perhaps they were nervous. Perhaps they had heard none of that," Oddi said.

"Aye, and I got to fuck Freya," Thorbjorn muttered, but quickly grabbed hold of his own Mjöllnir hanging around his neck as not to anger the gods with his words.

"Where would the other raiding party come from? No one left before we did," Asbjorn said.

"Could be some of Asgeir's men." Drumbr looked at Snorri. "They could have reached this place we're headed to and come further inland." Again, Snorri only shrugged as he looked around the farm. No one else seemed to have a response to this.

"But if it was an ambush, then who sent these men?" Ulf got to his feet and put his dirty helmet back on his head.

"Good question." Oddi scratched at his beard, which must have been itchy with the dried blood on it. Ulf's was. Itchy and sticky. Every time he licked his lips, all he could taste was the sweet iron of the blood caked over his face. "Who knew we were heading this way?"

"Ubba," Ulf suggested, feeling that familiar uneasiness he got every time he thought of the man.

Snorri shook his head, and the others looked surprised that he would think so. "Not Ubba. Odin knows we can trust him."

Ulf's lips tightened, but he did not respond. He did not understand why his friends trusted a man they only met recently, even Ragnar had nothing bad to say about him.

"Could be Arnfinni's men. Some of them did attack Ulf," Thorbjorn said, sounding confident.

"We don't know if they were Arnfinni's men," Ulf said. More ravens had gathered, some of them brave enough to land and start picking at the dead, while others screamed at the men for not leaving. As one raven took flight again, Ulf thought of the Valkyries and wondered if any had come to collect the souls of the bravest warriors for Odin's Hall. He hoped so. Many good men had died today.

Snorri stood up and looked at Ulf, who noticed the concern in his friend's eyes. "Doesn't really matter who they were. We live to fight another day." Snorri took his helmet off and wiped the sweat from his brow. "The sun will set soon. We must find our friends amongst the dead and give them a proper burial." Snorri scanned the farmstead. "Search the house, see if they left anything useful behind."

Ulf walked to one house, and with axe in hand, he slowly pushed the door open. In the dim light, he saw the family of the house dead on the floor. The man was coated in blood, his whole body covered in wounds, and his face contorted in pain. But it was much worse for the women. There were three of them, although one looked like she wasn't much older than fourteen winters. All of them were stripped naked, their thighs covered in blood. The air smelt of shit and blood, mingled with the sickening smell of sex. An image flashed in Ulf's mind before he could stop himself. Instead of the Frankish farmers, he saw Olaf and Brynhild. His uncle and aunt who had raised him after the deaths of his parents. His mother from disease when he was only a baby and his father in battle soon after his sixth winter. Beside his aunt's body were the bodies of his two cousins, younger than the girl in the house. The laughter of the man who had killed them the previous summer rang deep in his mind. The very man he was supposed to be hunting instead of risking his life for a king he barely knew. The sight and smells was too much for Ulf to bear as he doubled over and vomited. Ulf wiped his mouth with the back of his hand.

"You OK?" Snorri appeared from behind him. Ulf nodded, not trusting himself to speak. Snorri looked past Ulf and saw the family inside the house. "It looks like they've been here a while. The other houses are the same." He looked at Ulf, his eyes full of concern.

"Was this how you found my family?" Ulf asked. He remembered Snorri telling him they had been the ones who had found his family slaughtered on their farm and Ulf missing. That had been the reason everyone first thought that Ulf had killed them. Those old enough remembered the angry young boy who had forced his family to leave Thorgilsstad. An angry young boy who had blamed his father for abandoning him and took it out on everyone else.

Snorri did not answer, but his eyes misted over as he stared at the bodies of the Frankish family.

"What would have happened if we had got here first?" Again, Snorri did not answer, but he didn't need to. Ulf already knew. The same thing. They would have raped the women and killed the men, leaving their bodies behind as they left with anything valuable.

Snorri looked at Ulf, his eyes hardening. "It's a hard world we live in, Ulf. The gods know most people don't deserve the fates they get." He took a deep breath. "The Norns decided the fates of these people, not us."

"So we are no better than Griml," Ulf growled. He hated it when Snorri used that line. It felt like Snorri was shifting the responsibility of his actions onto the Norns. Perhaps that's how he lived with what he had done in the past.

Snorri smiled at Ulf. "We might not be, but you, my friend, are." With that, he clapped Ulf on the shoulder and walked away.

Ulf looked at the bodies of the family in the house. He ran his fingers over the haft of his axe, feeling the names of the loved ones he had lost. *Frigg, please don't let me become the monster I have sworn to kill.*

CHAPTER 12

Ulf realised something wasn't right as soon as he woke up. The last thing Ulf remembered was sitting around a large fire with his friends, their moods as dark as a moonless sky. But the fire was gone, and so were his friends. Ulf rubbed the sleep from his eyes while surveying his surroundings. It felt familiar, but Ulf didn't know where he was. All Ulf knew was that it was not in the field with the men of Thorgilsstad.

"Snorri? Oddi? Thorbjorn?" His voice echoed through the air. Ulf waited for their responses, but none came. "Brak? Drumbr?" Nothing.

The world around him was dark, but not the darkness you would expect from the night. A different darkness, one that weighed you down. It pressed on your body until your legs could not take it anymore and buckled. Ulf had been here before and had hoped never to see this place again. He looked for the hill that was as familiar to him as the boots he wore, but could not find it. Neither was Ulf standing in the marsh filled with blood and bone. The ground he stood on was dry. But Ulf still got the sense that he had been here before. Wind blew over his skin, causing him to shiver. He waited to hear his name whispered in it. That's what happened in the dreams before the battle at The Giant's Toe. But the wind did not whisper his name, or the name of his father. Instead, it carried a scent on it. A scent familiar to Ulf and one he had hoped never to smell again.

Ulf followed the breeze, hoping it would guide him to a place where he could get some answers. It took him to a farmstead, just like the one they had been ambushed at earlier in the day. The hairs on his arms stood on end as Ulf walked through the gate. His hand went to his side, where Ormstunga would normally be. But she was not there, neither was Olaf's axe. *Why can't I ever have weapons in these dreams?* The scent drew him further into the farmstead, towards the house he had looked in during the day. Ulf stared at the house, his hands shaking as a bead of sweat ran down his face. He would not like what was in there. But Ulf had no choice. The dream would not let him go until he saw what it wanted to show him. He looked around, swallowing hard as he half expected the troll from his previous dreams to jump out and attack him. But the farmstead was eerily quiet. There was no sound at all. Cautiously, he moved towards the house, the familiar fear growing inside him. Ulf stopped in front of the closed door. Whatever the dream wanted to show him was behind that door. Taking a deep breath, he pushed the door, but it wouldn't open.

"Come on," Ulf groaned as he pushed harder, but the door was as unyielding as the winter's cold. His heart beat faster and Ulf did not know if it was from fear or frustration. He wanted to know what was inside the house. He wanted to know why the scent had drawn him here. But Ulf feared what he might find. Dreams were messages from the gods. His aunt had always told him that, but Ulf had learnt that they only talked to you when they wanted to give you bad news. In his frustration, Ulf started banging on the door, hoping that whatever was inside might open it. But nothing happened. The door refused to move. This made Ulf even more desperate to find out what was inside. He looked around the farmstead, trying to find anything that might help him open the door. The other houses had disappeared, even the fence they fought by was gone. It was only Ulf and the house. Ulf tried to take a step back, but his feet were stuck to the ground. Hands gripped his ankles, refusing to let go. But when Ulf looked down, there was nothing. No hands, no roots. Nothing but his boots on the ground, yet he could still feel something gripping him.

"Argh!" Ulf shoved the door. Again, it did not move. "Why am I here?" he screamed into the nothingness.

The rumbling laugh from behind froze him in place. His breath clouded as if winter had crept up on him, but this was much worse. The ground beneath his feet shook as the laugh got louder. Ulf recognised that laugh. It had haunted him most nights since his family had been slaughtered. But Ulf did not expect to hear it again, not in his dreams. Even in the dream's darkness, Ulf saw the shadow loom over him, larger than any mountain. Ulf shut his eyes and hoped it was the cloaked figure who had spoken to him in his dreams before. The one he believed to be Odin. The laughter got louder. It unnerved him as it ripped through his core.

"What's behind the door?" the gravelly voice boomed in Ulf's head.

Ulf was trembling. This time it was fear. "I... I don't kn... know," he whispered, unable to speak any louder.

The voice laughed again, rattling his head. "Yes, you do."

"How could I?" Ulf tried to summon his anger, taking deep breaths to stoke the fire, but nothing happened.

He sensed the smile behind him. "Open it," the voice commanded.

"I can't." Ulf placed his shaking hands on the door and pushed, as if to prove himself to the creature he loathed and feared. Ulf did not understand why he was so scared. *Did I not defeat him?*

"Did you?" the voice read his thoughts. Ulf heard the smile on it. He recalled the battle at The Giant's Toe.

Griml's warrior stepped out of the shield wall with a confident smile on his face. Ulf launched his spear at the man, who was too slow to lift his shield. The spear struck him in the chest before his shield was halfway up, driving through the man and sending him flying back. The next man died while still trying to understand what had happened to his friend, his face still wearing a half smile as Ulf's axe bit into his neck. At the same time, Ulf unsheathed his sax-knife and stabbed another in the neck, feeling the warmth of their blood as it sprayed over him. Three men dead in a single heartbeat. But Ulf did not stop. The voices in his head wouldn't let him. One of Griml's men swung his axe at Ulf. Ulf dropped to his knees, sliding underneath the axe and past the man on the wet grass, hamstringing the man with his knife before jumping back to his feet. Ulf had never felt so alive before, never so free. The men around him moved so slowly that Ulf felt like he could kill all of them before they even knew he was there. Ulf saw the giant back of Griml, still walking away from him. "Griml!"

Ulf charged at Griml, cutting his way through his men, none of them able to deal with his speed and ferocity. But just as he turned to where Griml was, a mountain struck him. Lying on the blood-soaked ground, Ulf looked up at the smiling Griml, who was holding a shield in his left hand.

"Looks like I'll have to kill you for the second time." Griml drew Ormstunga from her scabbard, her blade reflecting the sunlight. Ulf watched the point of the sword as it came to end his life, Griml's laughter echoing in his head.

"Did you defeat me?" The voice smiled again, but this time there was an edge to it.

Ulf didn't know anymore. The last thing he remembered from the battle was Ormstunga coming for his throat, ready to steal his life away. "I... I...," he stammered, unable to find the words.

"You can never defeat me." The voice laughed, the shadow shaking as it did so. "You can never defeat me, because you are me." The door swung open, and Ulf dropped to his knees when he saw what was inside.

"No..." The bodies of his aunt, uncle and cousins piled on top of each other as if someone had dumped them there. Hulda, Lady Ingibjorg's unusual thrall, who had used her body to temper his anger, her throat slit open like when they found her under the tree. Vidar, his head half hanging off his body. But they were not the only ones there. The men who fought and died in the battle at The Giant's Toe, those who drowned when the War Bear capsized on their way to Suðrikaupstefna. Even the men who died earlier in the day when they had been ambushed. But most surprising of all, he saw Jarl Arnfinni, his body charred from the flames that had burnt his hall. All of them staring at Ulf, their eyes accusing him. Even Vidar's eyes showed a hatred that Ulf did not understand, but knew it was directed at him. "I am not you." Ulf tried to make sense of what he was seeing.

"No?" the voice asked, amused. The shadow extended an arm and pointed to the inside of the house. "You killed all these people."

Ulf shook his head. "I did not kill them."

"They died for your vengeance. Vengeance, which you have failed to carry out."

"I will," Ulf growled, trying to summon his anger. But the sight in front of him quelled his fire like a wave over a burning ship.

Again, the shadow shook as it laughed. The booming noise almost splitting Ulf's skull. The bodies of those who had died for his vengeance laughed at him. "You will never defeat me," it boomed. "She told me so."

She, the thought split through the fog of Ulf's fear. He turned and faced the shadow behind him for the first time. Ulf saw the large body of the troll, like a mountain with tree trunks for limbs. The small head with its beady eyes. As always, there was nothing but emptiness in them. This time, though, there was something different, something he had never seen before. *You are me.* The words echoed in his head as Ulf saw the three scar lines running down the face of the troll, matching his own scars. With the fog clearing in his head, the embers inside him finally burst into flames and the heat spread through his body. "No!" He charged at the troll.

194

The troll laughed as it grabbed Ulf by the tunic and lifted him up. Face to face, the troll's eyes changed from the black empty pits to the steel grey of his own. The words he had spoken to Snorri earlier in the day came to him. *We are no better than Griml.* The troll tightened his grip on Ulf's tunic as Ulf hung in the air. Its face changed, becoming more like Ulf's with every heartbeat. The troll lifted him higher, pulling him in closer as it roared all its anger at Ulf.

Ulf woke with a start, the troll's face still burnt into his vision. Only it wasn't the troll anymore. He shook his head, trying to clear the image, but he could not. All he saw was his own face, roaring its anger at him.

"Another dream?" Oddi was sitting by the fire, poking at it with a stick, his face more thoughtful than ever. He smiled when he saw the confused expression on Ulf's face. "We all know about your dreams, Ulf. Although, you've not been having them recently."

Ulf lay back down again, staring at the stars as he willed his heart to slow down. The troll's face was still on his mind as he tried to understand what the dream was telling him. *Am I turning into Griml?*

"Want to talk about it?" Oddi interrupted his thoughts. Ulf looked at him, but did not answer straight away. Instead, he sat up and looked at the fire as Oddi poked it with his stick. From behind Oddi, Ulf saw a line on the horizon like dawn was approaching. But it was not the sun rising. It was the farmstead. After the fight, they had moved all their dead into the houses, laying them next to the bodies of the Frankish farmers. Some men wanted to throw them out, but Snorri refused. Ulf wondered if it was because of the conversation they had before. It took them the rest of the day to complete their grizzly task and burn the houses. They left the dead of the enemy to feed the ravens and the wolves. After they were looted, of course.

"A lot of men are feasting in Valhalla tonight."

"Aye, and half a crew's worth of women and children will never see their men or fathers again." Oddi nodded. "They died, so we could live. They would not want us to be sad about it."

"It's the way of the warrior, Thorbjorn keeps telling me." Ulf looked at his short friend lying on his back and snoring the night away.

Oddi smiled. "Rare words of wisdom from the bastard." The fire sparked as Oddi gave it a poke with his stick.

Ulf thought back to his dream again, remembering how the troll's face morphed into his own. "You ever wonder if you are a bad person?" Oddi looked up from the fire and frowned. "Griml killed my family for no reason that I can think of." Ulf stared at the glow on the horizon again. "Those farmers would have died even if we got there first."

"You are wondering what makes us better than Troll-Face?" Ulf nodded. Oddi scratched his beard before answering. "Odin knows I can't deny that we would have killed those farmers. Most likely, the women would still have been raped. But we are a raiding force. It's what we do." He noticed the disappointment on Ulf's face. "It's an ugly world, and to survive, we need to be ugly men. If you gave that farmer a chance, he would have killed you faster than you could fart."

"But the women?"

"Men turn into beasts when our blood is up." Oddi gave a weak response.

"So we are no better than Griml?"

Oddi smiled, which Ulf found strange. "Ask yourself this. If you were travelling on your own and came across a farm, would you kill the people who lived there and steal their valuables?" Ulf stared at the fire as he thought about it. "Do not confuse raiding an enemy and randomly killing one of your own, Ulf. Yes, we would have done the same to those farmers, but if they raided our lands, then they would have done the same. Their priests love to tell you how theirs is a peace-loving god, but in the end they are just as ugly as us."

Ulf had no answer to that. Men like Oddi and Thorbjorn had been part of this world a lot longer than him. "My uncle used to tell me about the raids he had been on." Ulf's eyes glossed over as he stared into the dancing flames. "He told me of the warriors he had slain, of the fear he felt in those battles. But he said nothing about killing and raping innocent farmers." He realised now how sheltered he had been on his uncle's little farm.

"Perhaps he was just trying to protect you." Oddi poked at the logs in the flames again.

"Perhaps." Ulf stared at the glow on the horizon. "I still don't understand why we were ambushed today."

"Only the gods and the Norns will really know, Ulf. But it is strange at what lengths Arnfinni's men will go to avenge him." Oddi scratched the side of his beard.

"This had nothing to do with Arnfinni." Snorri's voice surprised them both. Ulf thought Snorri was sleeping, and from Oddi's raised eyebrow so did he.

"How can you be sure?" Oddi asked.

Snorri sat up and rubbed his face, making Ulf wonder if he had been asleep and their conversation woke him. "Why would Arnfinni's men use the Danes?" Ulf couldn't answer that, and neither could the all-wise Oddi. "Been thinking about it all day. Like us, they have been attacking the Danes for a long time, so it makes no sense that they would turn to the Danes to get their vengeance."

"Perhaps they didn't have enough men and needed help?" Oddi ventured.

"No." Snorri shook his head. "There were no Norsemen amongst the dead. That was a Danish force. I'll give Odin my right eye if I'm wrong, but that ambush had nothing to do with Arnfinni."

Ulf and Oddi remained silent as they thought about Snorri's words. A wolf howled in the distance and was soon answered by others. The three of them looked towards the burning farmstead.

"If not Arnfinni, then who?" Oddi asked at last, his eyebrow raised as he stared at the glow of the flames in the distance.

Snorri shrugged. "Arnfinni's men are the best candidates, but most of them would have heeded Halfdan the Black. The ones that attacked Thorgilsstad were a few rebels, nothing more. This is different."

"And the ones that attacked Ulf?" Oddi looked at him.

"Might have been part of the same force that attacked us today," Snorri responded. "And it's thanks to Ulf's oath to Odin that he is still with us."

"Odin is not the reason I am still here, Egil is."

"But who sent Egil?" Oddi asked, his tone almost conspiratorial. Ulf only shrugged. There was no point in having this argument. He believed Odin held him to his word and was keeping him alive until Griml was dead, but other times it was as if Odin himself was trying to kill Ulf. Words spoken by Lady Ingibjorg not so long ago sprang into his head like a frog leaps into a pond. *The gods give us obstacles to test us, so we may learn who we are and what we can do.* Ulf wished he had never made that oath. The flames leaped into the air as a sudden strong breeze blew over them. Ulf shivered, hoping he had not angered Odin. "So, if they have nothing to do with Arnfinni, then who?" Oddi continued when Ulf did not answer.

"Frigg knows I wish I knew, but I can't figure it out." Snorri lay back down and stared at the stars as if they had the answers.

"Some of Griml's forces?" Oddi asked. Ulf looked at him in surprise. He had not thought that any of those who were loyal to Griml might still be around. "Some of them might have found a way back after the battle." The fire crackled, almost as if in response to Oddi. Ulf remembered his strange encounter in the market before they had left. The boy who reminded him of Vidar, leading him to the square where he had fought the Swedish jarl. The woman from Yngling Hall standing there, smiling at him with malice-filled eyes. He shook his head, trying to get the image out of his mind.

"You okay, Ulf?" Snorri asked with a frown.

"I'm fine," Ulf lied. Snorri looked at him for a while before shrugging.

"You have been acting strange recently, Ulf," Oddi added, "and now you even had a dream again." Ulf saw the surprise on Snorri's face.

"What dream?" he asked.

"I'm guessing the same ones as before, but as always, our friend does not want to tell us about them." Ulf did not look at either of them, instead focusing on the fire.

"There is something strange going on," Snorri said.

"So what do we do?" Oddi asked.

Snorri shrugged. "Tomorrow, when we get back to the fleet, I'll talk to Ubba. Find out if any men were missing. Perhaps we can find some answers then. In the meantime, we should be careful. The men of Thorgilsstad are being hunted."

They all sat in silence, thinking about what Snorri had just said. The only sound was the fire crackling and men snoring. Ulf thought of the woman from the market again and tried to forget about her, but could not. The harder he tried to get her out of his head, the more she resisted. She still seemed familiar to him, but Ulf couldn't understand why. He stared into the fire, trying to make sense of everything. The flames danced away, twisting and turning to some music only the fire could hear. Ulf thought back to his dream. Its message was obvious, even if it was one he did not want to hear. Even so, he could not stop the question as it came to him.

How many more must die so I can kill Griml?

CHAPTER 13

Dawn arrived with an overcast sky, as if the gods were acknowledging their mood. Ulf yawned as he stood with Snorri and his hirdmen looking at the remains of the farmstead in the distance. He had not slept after his conversation with Oddi and Snorri. Every time Ulf closed his eyes, all he saw was the troll's face changing into his.

"Not much left of the place." Thorbjorn brushed the knots out of his bushy beard. Ulf rubbed his own beard, wondering if he should do the same. He took out the fine bone comb from his pouch and ran it through his beard. The comb had belonged to Thorbjorn's father, but it was Ulf's now after he took it from the corpse of the pirate who had stolen it. Birds were flying around them, their songs echoing over the warriors. Nature did not care about the affairs of men.

"Aye, the wood was good and dry," Snorri said. "There must not have been much rain recently." They all stared at the charred remains of the farmstead, wooden skeletons sticking out of the blackened ground. The half-eaten bodies of their attackers told of visitors during the night. At least their friends who had died in the ambush were saved from that fate. Only their ash remained amongst the skeletons of the farmhouses.

"We stick to the plan?" Ragnar asked in his rough voice, while Ulf tugged at the knots and tangles in his beard.

"Could be dangerous." Oddi crossed his arms and stared into the distance, trying to determine their path ahead. "This might not have been the only ambush planned."

"Aye, and Odin knows those bastards will be even more pissed off after being chased away yesterday." Asbjorn's face was as sour as always.

Snorri scratched his beard while he thought. He looked at his fingertips, seeing the dirt his nails had trapped. With a deep sigh, he responded, "We don't have a choice. The ships will be there, so going back to Hammaburg is pointless." And cowardly, Ulf knew his friend was thinking. Snorri hated running from a fight.

"So what do we do?" Drumbr asked, his mouth full of dried meat.

Snorri looked to the sky and spotted some geese flying eastwards. He smiled. "We trust in the gods."

"The Norns will have decided our fate already." Oddi grinned. Ulf ground his teeth while the rest of the men smiled. He had stopped blaming the gods for the deaths of his family, but Ulf still did not like the idea that they controlled his fate.

"Fucking Norns." Ragnar spat as he turned and walked away. "They'll fucking kill us just to amuse themselves."

Ulf wasn't sure how far they had walked, but through the clouds, it looked like the sun had climbed to midday when they spotted the stone church in the distance. The men sat down, some drinking from their water skins and others chewing on dried meat.

Snorri scratched his beard as he stared at the small church, his hirdmen patiently waiting. "We should send a scout," he said at last, more to himself. "Can't afford to lose more men to another ambush."

Before anyone could respond, Geir piped up, "I'll do it." The fair-haired warrior puffed his chest out and tucked his thumbs into his belt. "I can run there and back faster than Sleipnir crosses the Bifröst." Snorri raised an eyebrow. That was a bold statement to make, but it didn't surprise Ulf. Geir was always trying to show how useful he could be.

Snorri looked at the young warrior before nodding. "Stay out of sight." Geir sprinted towards the church before Snorri finished his sentence. His hirdmen laughed at Geir's eagerness while Ulf shook his head and studied the church in the distance.

It was smaller than the one they had seen by Hammaburg, but looked big enough to hide a small army of men. Ulf caught himself stroking the haft of Olaf's axe, feeling the names of his family and friends getting worn out.

"You okay, Ulf?" Drumbr noticed the frown on Ulf's face.

"Probably lost in his dreams again," Asbjorn mocked.

"I'm fine." Ulf glared at Asbjorn, who only smiled back.

"What do you think?" Ragnar asked Snorri, both men studying the stone building.

"Looks quiet enough," Snorri responded, shielding his eyes even though there was no sun. *At least if there is a fight, I can use Ormstunga*, Ulf thought.

"Aye, so did the farm," Thorbjorn retorted, scowling at Magni, who just looked away. The church doors flew open and they all tensed, half expecting a warrior to walk out, sword in hand. But instead, it was a man wearing a long brown dress and carrying a stick. The priest marched his way to a young man working in the field next to the church. "He's got a good arm," Thorbjorn joked as the priest viciously beat the youth, now cowering on the ground, and trying to protect himself with his arms. Even from this distance, they heard him scream as the stick struck his flesh. Ulf glanced at Oddi, remembering what he had said the night before about how ugly the Christians could get.

"We might have to go in with a shield wall if all the priests can swing like that," Brak said. Most of them smiled at that, but Snorri and Ragnar stood with puckered foreheads, their eyes scanning the horizon.

"I doubt the priest would do that if there was a Danish army inside his church," Drumbr said.

"Perhaps he is doing that because there is a Danish army in his church?" his brother responded.

"He'd be dead if there was." Ulf saw the surprised looks on the faces around him. "Why would they kill the farmers but leave a priest alive? From what you told me, they hate the Christians as much as the Norse do."

"Ulf's right," Snorri said, "but we'll wait for Geir to return. The Danes can be crafty, so they might have left one alive to trick us." Ulf shrugged as he accepted Snorri's point.

"Where is the bastard, anyway?" Thorbjorn scratched his neck as he searched for the young warrior.

"Perhaps found himself a lovely priest," Brak responded with a mischievous smile. Even Ulf couldn't help but smile at that one.

"Well, he better hurry with his priest," Ragnar growled, as if he didn't know it was a joke. "The men are getting too relaxed." He thumbed over his shoulder. Some men had dozed off while a few others had removed their armour. A few men were sharpening their weapons, but most of them did not look like a force expecting a fight.

Snorri also looked at his men, but only shrugged. "They'll be ready when they need to be. The men of the Sae-Ulfr have never let me down." Snorri raised his voice, so the men could hear him. They smiled at the compliment and once again, Ulf admired Snorri's leadership.

"Thank Thor's little toe, here comes the priest fucker." Ulf turned at the sound of Thorbjorn's voice and saw Geir running towards them, a grin covering most of his face.

"Well?" Snorri asked as soon as Geir got close enough. Behind them, the men were getting ready. They knew they'd be moving on soon. Either to fight or to plunder a church.

"No sign of any Danes or warriors." Geir sucked in a deep breath as he answered. "Only a few priests and slaves."

"You sure?" Ragnar growled at the young warrior.

"Aye, got as close as I could, but found nothing troubling."

"Unlike the young priest," Brak joked again, causing them to laugh and even Snorri to smile. Geir scowled but saw that no one was going to explain it to him.

"Warriors of Thorgilsstad!" Snorri turned to his men. "The gods have rewarded us for the courage you showed yesterday." The men cheered, many still sore from the previous day.

"Aye, but don't forget the gods love playing tricks." Oddi kept his voice low, not wanting to dampen the spirits of the men.

"They'll be wary," Snorri responded. Ulf watched the warriors of Thorgilsstad get ready. Even with their smaller number, they still looked like a formidable fighting force. And Ulf had been with them long enough to know that these were some of the best warriors in Norway.

As one, they marched towards the church with their weapons at hand. Even Magni had learnt his lesson as he walked close behind Snorri's hirdmen with his sword drawn. No longer was he trying to show off. Bells started ringing from the church, sending birds scattering in all directions as dogs barked from somewhere behind the church, but none came rushing out at them.

"We've been spotted." Oddi scanned the horizon. Just because there were no men in the church, did not mean there was no army around. But there was nowhere for an army to hide. The land around the church was flat with no forest nearby. Beside the church was a fenced area with plenty of wooden crosses sticking out of the ground. Ulf wondered if these were offerings to their god. The priest who had been thrashing the young man looked up and, as soon as he saw them approaching, darted towards the back of the church.

"There'll be a back door," Thorbjorn commented, his eyes following the priest. The young man the priest had been beating raised his head, staring at them as if trying to work out who these warriors were. He got to his feet and ran away from the church, deciding the newcomers were a threat.

Snorri nodded and signalled to Oddi with a flick of his sword. Oddi selected a group of men and loped towards the rear of the church. The rest of the Norse warriors lifted their shields and held them in front as they walked towards the front door — Ulf copied what the rest of the hirdmen were doing. As they neared the church, the locking bar fell into place with a loud thud, the priests now secure. Or so they believed.

"Drumbr," Snorri said.

Drumbr smirked as he walked up to the plain church doors, almost twice his height. He took Shield-Breaker, his large two-handed axe, from his back. Ulf had seen at Hammaburg how it was used for more than breaking shields and cutting men in half. He doubted the doors would last long. Drumbr leaned his axe against his leg, spitting into his hands and rubbing them together for a better grip.

"You going to take all day, brother?" Brak feigned a yawn.

"Aye, we want to get in there before Ragnarök comes," Thorbjorn added.

Drumbr ignored them as he picked up his axe and gave it a huge swing. Dust jumped off the rattling doors as Shield-Breaker bit deep into the wood, but the door held. Planting his foot on the door, Drumbr freed his axe and swung it again. The dogs were barking more frantically now. Ulf guessed they were up somewhere around the back.

"It'll go a lot faster if I help," Ragnar said, taking his axe from his back.

"Not necessary," Snorri responded. "Drumbr will be through in no time." Ragnar shrugged and picked at something in his teeth.

"You ever raided a church before?" Geir asked Ulf while they waited, his eyes bright from under his bowl helmet. Ulf shook his head as he studied the church up close. He had never seen a building made of stone and was fascinated by who might have built it. It must have been their god, because Ulf didn't understand how men could shape stone like this. It was very different from the stone statues they had in Thorgilsstad. Ulf looked up and realised the windows had some coloured material, which he thought might have been ice. But ice would have melted by now. They all had images of people on them. There was a woman cradling a small baby. Another showed a man with long hair and beard, much like their own. But this man was not a warrior. He was wearing what looked like a dress, similar to their priests. His hands were in front of him, one held in a fist and the other with two fingers held straight. Ulf wondered what that meant. "Strange, isn't it?" Geir asked and Ulf realised he was still next to him. Before Ulf could respond, there was a loud crash, and the men cheered. The priests wailed as the door gave way, which only caused the men to laugh even more. The bell was ringing desperately now.

They walked past Drumbr, who was leaning on his axe and wiping the sweat from his brow. Inside was a lot brighter than Ulf had expected. He had thought it would be dark, like the long houses they had back in Norway.

"Ulf, deal with that bastard." Snorri pointed with Tyr's Fury towards the back of the church where a priest was pulling on a rope. Ulf nodded and walked towards the terrified old man. As he passed the wooden benches, Ulf couldn't help but look around. He had never been inside a church before. There were more holes along the walls, all of them filled with the strange ice, which was why the inside was so bright. Stone pillars ran the length of the church, much like the wooden posts inside a hall which helped to support the roof. Ulf glanced at the wooden beam supporting the stone-like roof. Everywhere he looked, there were gold crosses, silver candle holders, gold and silver bowls and cups. Even a large chest-like object, decorated with gold and with an elaborate cross on it. But despite all its beauty, Ulf felt nothing. Perhaps that was why all the priests he had seen so far looked so miserable – and why they collected so much gold and silver.

Ulf stood admiring the treasure on display when something struck the side of his face. His head snapped to the side as the blow bounced off his helmet, his vision blurring instantly. He turned and saw a blurry figure standing in front of him, its raised arm holding something long and thin. Ulf still had Ormstunga in his hand, and before the blurred figure could strike again, he twisted and stabbed up with his sword. Ulf felt a brief resistance, but then the sharp blade sliced through his attacker. He heard a grunt as warm liquid leaked onto his hand. The church plunged into silence as Ulf's vision cleared. Instead of seeing a warrior with armour and a helmet, Ulf found himself looking at the shocked face of a priest. The one who had been thrashing the young man outside. Ulf saw the long stick the priest held as his head throbbed. He felt the flames inside of him threaten to erupt as he glared at the priest, who had been dumb enough to attack him. The same priest, whose eyes turned to fear as both men realised he would die. That surprised Ulf.

He had been told that when Christians die, they go to a place called heaven, which was like Valhalla. Perhaps this priest did not want to spend eternity drinking and fighting with other warriors. Ulf pulled Ormstunga from the man and let him fall to the ground. He stood glaring at the priest as his life left him, his blood flowing over the stone floor. Without looking at his friends, Ulf walked towards the old priest who had been ringing the bell. The old man was cowering on his knees, the sudden violence too much for him. He looked up when Ulf stopped in front of him, his face as white as the sheets covering their altar. Glaring at the man, Ulf cut the rope of the bell with his bloody sword and let it fall on top of the priest. He turned and walked back to his companions.

"By Odin, Ulf is finally a real raider," Ragnar mocked. Ulf looked at the body of the priest as he walked past it. He had expected to feel some guilt for killing a defenceless man, but all he felt was annoyance. Ulf did not want to kill one of their priests, but the man left him no choice.

"The dumb bastard attacked you. All of us would have done the same. Sometimes it's needed to get them to understand," Thorbjorn said, reading Ulf's mind.

"Understand what?" Ulf frowned.

"They like to say that their god will protect them from harm," Snorri responded. "Makes them arrogant. But we've yet to see their god come to protect them from us."

"Well, he is only one," Brak added to the annoyance of Thorbjorn.

"What does that have to do with anything?" Thorbjorn threw his arms up in the air.

Brak shrugged. "He can't save everyone, can he?"

"That's why we have more than one god." Drumbr stroked his beard.

"Our gods wouldn't waste their time with you idiots." Ragnar scowled at them as if they were annoying children.

Ulf stared at the body — as the priest's blood spooled over the stone floor, slowly creeping towards them. He looked at the sword, her blade still covered in his blood. *Am I turning into Griml? Is she turning me into him?* He twisted the blade, seeing the candle lights reflected back.

"You better clean her before the blood dries. Priest blood is a bastard to get off once it does," Brak said to him. Ulf looked at his friend and nodded. He found a cloth hanging on a bench. It was beautifully made and decorated with a woman who had wings. Ulf wondered if she was a Valkyrie as he wiped the blood off his sword.

"At least we won't leave empty-handed." Ulf heard the joy in Thorbjorn's voice. The men cheered as if the gods had rewarded them for the previous day's valour.

"Aye, but there'll be more hidden away." Ragnar's eyes scanned the entire building. He reminded Ulf of an eagle as it searched for its prey from the clouds. And just as the eagle's sharp eyes never failed it, neither did Ragnar's. "There." He pointed to the altar. Ulf looked at it, trying to understand what Ragnar had seen as some of the crew walked to the altar and pushed it over. At first, Ulf saw nothing, but then one of Snorri's men used his axe to lift a flagstone.

"By the gods!" the warrior exclaimed. They all saw the hidden compartment filled with golden crosses, cups, candle holders. There were gold-plated chests filled with gold and silver coins. Ulf looked around the church, half expecting Fafnir to appear and defend his treasure. But there was no dragon.

"Take as much as you can carry!" Snorri shouted at his men. "And hurry, we might not have come across those Danish bastards, but there might still be a Frankish force nearby. That bell would have warned somebody." The men cheered as they ran around the church, filling their arms with everything they could. Some went looking for bags to carry their plunder.

"I wish I could sniff out gold like Ragnar," one of the younger men said as they walked past Ulf and Snorri. Snorri smiled at the frowning Ulf.

"Aye, he must be blessed by the gods," another responded. "I heard he sacrificed his little finger to them for that gift."

The young warrior who had spoken first looked at his own hand. "Perhaps I will do the same."

Snorri almost laughed and explained when he saw Ulf's tilted head. "They always hide their treasure in the same spot. Not a very imaginative bunch, these Christian priests." Ulf looked at the hole in the ground under the altar. "Every church we've ever raided had a hole under the altar where they hide their most valuable treasures. All raiders know that by now, but these priests still seem to think it is a safe place to hide things." Ulf shook his head.

"So what was all that before then?"

Snorri smiled. "Simple brother, so that young pups like those boys," he pointed to the two young warriors who had just passed them, "talk about him like that."

Ulf looked at the two young men. He knew they weren't much younger than him, perhaps only a winter or so. They had joined the crew after the battle at The Giant's Toe, their heads still filled with tales from the sagas.

"Snorri!" Ulf and Snorri turned as Andor, one of Snorri's crew, walked towards them. Behind him, some other men were dragging three priests who they threw at Snorri's feet. Everyone stopped what they were doing to see what was going on. Some of the older men's eyes lit up in anticipation of getting to torture them. One of the priests, the youngest by the looks of it, glanced at the body of the man Ulf had killed. He jumped to his feet and thrust a golden gilded cross in Ulf's face. It took all of Ulf's strength not to flinch in front of the surrounding men. The young priest's face turned red, and he almost foamed at the mouth as he spewed words at Ulf that he did not understand. Those around rubbed on their Mjöllnir pendants or the metal of their weapons. None understood what the young priest was saying, but a curse always sounded the same. Didn't matter what language it came in. Ulf grit his teeth as the words fuelled the flames inside him, his hands trembling as they coursed through his limbs. The young priest was blind to all this. His eyes looked like they were about to jump from his skull. Spit was flying all over Ulf's face. The priest's words laced with enough venom to drop a giant. Ulf took deep breaths to control himself, not wanting to kill another one. The first priest might have been by mistake, but this would not be. Thorbjorn saved him from making that decision as he punched the hate-spewing priest in the side of the head. The words died mid-sentence as the priest's head snapped sideways and his legs gave way like seaweed. He dropped to the floor, his eyes rolling in his head, and the church was filled with a moment's silence. It felt like the stones themselves were honouring the priest for his bravery until the silence was broken by the men laughing.

"Cocky fucking bastard." Thorbjorn spat at the young priest he had punched.

"Surprised you didn't kill him." Asbjorn eyed up the other two priests like he was choosing which pig to slaughter for the roast. The priest, who was aged in the middle of the three, shrank away, but the oldest one only smiled back.

"Didn't want to get Bloodthirst dirty," Thorbjorn responded. He was still staring at the unconscious priest. "What was the bastard saying, anyway?" Everyone around just shrugged. In all their years of raiding churches, they had been more interested in learning where the priests stashed their treasures instead of the language.

"He was condemning you all to an eternity in hell," an old voice responded in Norse. They all looked at the old priest, who was still on the ground, smiling at them. His companion had crawled towards the young priest and was trying to wake him up.

Snorri laughed. "You speak our tongue, old man."

"My father was one of you," the old priest responded. "Do you mind if I stand? My old bones don't respond well to the cold floor." Snorri nodded and signalled to Andor to help him up. Ulf guessed the priest must have seen about fifty winters. His head was bald, and not from shaving like the other priests, and his face heavily lined. Sharp eyes sat on top of a thin red nose, which showed there was still plenty of intelligence left in him. Around his neck, he wore a simple wooden cross instead of the elaborate ones his brethren were wearing. In a way, the priest reminded Ulf of the old forest godi he had met before.

The one who had kept him alive after Griml attacked his family. That was also when Ulf had met Vidar, his silent friend, who had suffered under the old godi. Vidar had killed the godi in the end, and that was when their journey together had started. Ulf looked at the old man again and wondered if he hid a dark side like the old godi had done. The old priest looked at Ulf and smiled. It felt like the priest saw inside of him, seeing all his fears and his worries. *Is this the magic of his god?*

"If your father was a Norseman, then how did you end up being one of their priests?" Ragnar growled at the old man like his presence offended him.

The younger priest said something to the old priest and violently shook his head, but the old man only smiled and shrugged. "He got injured during a raid and was left behind by his crew. Perhaps they thought him dead. My mother's family found him and healed him."

"Did he worship the Christian god?" Oddi cocked his head to the side. He had been with Andor when they brought the priests in. His sword was red with blood and Ulf realised the dogs weren't barking anymore.

"No. My mother's family implored him to do so. The king does not like for his subjects not to follow Christ. But he was a stubborn man and refused to give up his gods."

"A king has no right to decide which gods a man must follow." Asbjorn spat. "It's a man's own choice." Those around nodded, but Ulf just watched as the old priest smiled.

"Your leaders don't force you to choose a god?"

"No, we are free to choose ourselves," Snorri responded.

"So which gods do you worship?"

"What do you know of our gods?" Ragnar sneered, his hand twisting on the handle of his sword.

"My father told me many stories of your gods when I was a child."

"And you still followed their god?" Ragnar took a menacing step forward, but the old priest did not seem concerned.

With the smile still on his face, the priest responded, "After I was born, my father found work as a mercenary fighting for the local noblemen. I was about nine winters when he didn't come home from a battle. My mother was distraught, but I don't think it was because of love. My father provided for us and with him dead, my mother couldn't feed us. So in the end, she sold me to the church. They raised me and showed me the light of the one veritable God. I have been with the church ever since."

"What happened to your mother?" Ulf asked.

The priest stared at him with a raised eyebrow. "I don't really know. Last I heard, and this was from a nasty old drunk, was that she was selling her body and soul for money."

"But you still chose their god over those of your father's," Ragnar pressed again. Ulf got the impression that he found that very upsetting, but couldn't understand why. He glanced at Snorri, but Snorri was no longer paying attention to the conversation. Instead, he was marshalling his men as they collected all the treasure they could find.

"He is my God and my father's were his. How many of your men follow Christ?" A bushy eyebrow went up as he asked the question.

"None, because we don't follow a weak god. And if any did, then I would crucify them myself."

The old priest smiled again, which only irritated Ragnar more. Ulf wondered if that was the old man's plan. He hoped not. The large nine-fingered warrior was not a man to upset. Ulf was one of the few to survive such stupidity. "So you Norsemen can choose to follow whichever god you like, as long as it is not Christ or any other than Odin, Thor and Tyr?"

"My uncle and aunt worshipped Freya and her brother Frey," Ulf interjected before Ragnar skewered the old priest with his sword. He saw the curiosity in the priest's face. "They were farmers and relied on the Vanir for their crops and for healthy calves. Although, they also sacrificed to Thor, the protector, to keep our family safe."

"And did your Thor keep your family safe?" the old priest asked. Ulf tried to find the mockery in his voice, but there was none. He appeared genuinely interested.

Ulf shook his head, not wanting to say the words.

"But you survived?"

"The gods have other plans for me, it seems." Ulf tried not to remember the day Griml showed up on their farm, but the words he had spoken summoned the memories. He rubbed the names of his family on the hilt of Olaf's axe as he repeated the oath he had made to Odin two summers ago.

The old priest watched him with interest before responding, "Even we don't always understand the mind of the Almighty. But His might is clear for all to see. Your family asked Thor to protect them, but when they needed him, he was not there." Ulf felt his anger ignite as he looked at the priest, but again saw no mockery, only an old man interested in what he had to say.

"Your god did little to protect your priest from Ulf's sword." Thorbjorn pointed to the corpse, surrounded by a pool of blood. Ulf clenched his fists as he willed himself to calm down.

The old priest sighed heavily and, for the first time, looked sad. "As I said, even we do not understand the mind of God. Father Willelm was a good priest, but I cannot say that he was a good man." They all glanced at each other, unsure of what the old priest meant by that.

"Are the two not the same?" Drumbr asked.

Again, the younger priest hissed something at the old priest. Ulf guessed he must have recognised the name of the dead priest because of the glare directed towards him. Ulf sneered back, causing the priest to look away.

The old priest smiled again. "Not always. For some, being a priest is their life, it is their destiny, I guess."

"Like you?" Oddi asked.

The priest only shrugged. "For others, it is merely a profession. The same as for you. Most of you here, I can see, are born to be warriors, but there are some who look more like farmers. Even your young friend here with the scars," he pointed to Ulf, "looks very conflicted about having killed one of us. Something which I feel would bother none of you."

"Got that right." Thorbjorn grinned savagely. "I like the way you beg." He patted his sword for good measure, but the old priest only smiled at him again.

"Father Willelm was the fifth son of a not very rich nobleman, and so only had two choices. Become a warrior or a priest."

"Looked like he dreamt of being a warrior the way he attacked Ulf," Drumbr interrupted the old priest. He got a few laughs from those around.

"No, he didn't have the stomach for a fair fight, but he had problems with his temper. I think he resented those of us who truly felt a calling."

"What is your point, old man?" Ulf was getting frustrated with this conversation.

"Perhaps God has punished Father Willelm for his lack of faith."

"And the rest of you?" Ragnar wore a dangerous smile.

"Are you saying the gods had my family killed because they were being punished?" Ulf grit his teeth.

The old priest gave him one of those piercing looks again. "Or perhaps they needed something to push you into this journey of yours."

"The gods did not kill my family. Griml did."

"And who do you think sent this Griml?" The priest smiled, but Ulf saw the seriousness in his eyes.

"That's like saying your god sent us to punish you," Oddi responded in his wise voice.

The old priest glanced at his dead comrade, the smile on his face faltering. "Perhaps He did."

"Is that why your friend did not look happy to be going to your heaven?" Ulf remembered the fear he saw in the priest's eyes as he died.

"Perhaps he didn't want to go to Hel. It'll be like spending a never-ending winter stuck in the hall with your wife and her family," Thorbjorn said to the amusement of others.

"Our hell is not like yours. There is no feast with a god or goddess. It is an eternity of suffering."

"You haven't met Snorri's wife," Thorbjorn added again, causing the men to laugh. Snorri looked over from where he was at the sound of his name, confused. Even Ragnar was smiling.

"And unlike your Hel," the priest continued, "our hell isn't cold, but a burning furnace where the devil lives. But I don't think Father Willelm went there. For all his faults, he was a good priest. He'll be in heaven now, probably judging me for talking to you."

"You'd think then he'd be happy to go to heaven," Ulf mused, scratching his ear. He couldn't explain it, but he enjoyed talking to the old priest. His friends looked like they were waiting for an excuse to skewer him. Even Oddi, who could normally talk all night, did not enjoy the priest's words. Perhaps he had heard it all before, but to Ulf, this was all new. The only thing he knew about the Christians were the few stories his uncle had told him, but then, Olaf did not know that much about them either. Ulf saw the priest raise an eyebrow. "Our warriors look forward to going to Valhalla. It's what drives them on in battle, but your friend, his eyes were full of fear."

The old priest fingered the wooden cross around his neck as he pondered over Ulf's words. "There is a big difference between heaven and your Valhalla."

"Aye, Valhalla is full of warriors drinking and fighting, and heaven is full of priest drawing pictures," Thorbjorn mocked.

The old priest smiled. "Basically, yes. Heaven is a place of peace where we get to spend eternity in the warm embrace of our Saviour." He glanced warily at the Norse warriors around him. "And your Valhalla isn't real." He waited for a reaction, but got none. They had all heard this before.

"What makes you say it is not real?" Ulf asked, confused.

"How can it be?" The priest shrugged.

"And your heaven is real?" Oddi asked while Ulf tried to understand.

"Very real."

"How do you know?"

"Our Bible tells us so." The priest lifted his chin as he responded. Ulf took his helmet off and rubbed the side of his head where he had been hit. He looked at his helmet, expecting to see a dent where the dead priest had struck. But there was none. Only the ringing in his ears and the throbbing pain in his head told of the attack.

"Our sagas tell us that Valhalla is real," Oddi countered.

Again, the old priest smiled. "Your sagas are merely stories to entertain children."

"And what is your bible then?" Ulf squinted.

"Our Bible is the true word of our God and therefore is as true as it can be." The priest puffed his chest out and boomed his words around the church, as if trying to convince everyone there. The men around looked up from their looting and glanced at the priest before carrying on.

"Your bible is good for making fires," Ragnar growled.

"And wiping my arse," Thorbjorn added.

"But what makes your bible truer than our sagas?" Ulf's head was starting to spin with all the words from the priest.

"Because we are told it is." The priest smiled. His younger companion asked him something, but the priest only shook his head.

"By who?" asked Brak.

The priest looked at him like it was a strange question. "By other priests, of course."

The Norse men burst out laughing, which only confused the old priest. Ulf saw Snorri walking towards them with a satisfied look on his face.

"When you women are done talking, we can leave. We've got as much as we can carry." Snorri looked towards the church door. "Besides, we don't know how long it'll take before somebody answers the bell."

"There are no soldiers to answer it," the old priest responded with a sigh. "They have all gone west to fight."

"The war between the brothers?" Oddi asked. The priest nodded.

"So, why ring the bell?" Ulf looked towards the bell tower where he had cut the rope.

"To warn the farms of your presence. It gives them time to hide."

"Well, we still don't want to hang around, so get ready. We leave as soon as we can," Snorri said.

"What about these priests?" Ulf asked. The one Thorbjorn had punched was still out cold, and his friend's eyes were darting nervously between them as he tried to understand what was going on. He kept asking questions to the old priest, but as before, the old man only smiled and shook his head. Ulf saw the smirks on the faces of the hirdmen and heard the whimper of the younger priest.

"The younger two we can take with us, they can be sold as thralls. The old priest, we'll leave that up to his god." Snorri turned and walked away, his hirdmen following him.

"And the church?" the old priest asked, his eyes pleading with Snorri.

Snorri looked around, as if admiring the stonework decorated with murals, the high ceiling with the darkened wood beams and the beautifully made windows, before he looked back at the priest. "We burn it."

"You can't!" the old priest protested. The younger priest saw his agitation and started babbling in his language. Ulf could not tell if he was praying or asking the old priest questions. "This is the house of God!" the old priest thundered, standing tall as he showed his Norse heritage.

Snorri gave his wolf grin to the priest. "Then let him come to defend it."

CHAPTER 14

The priests wailed as the flames consumed the church. They had thrown themselves at the feet of the men as they set it on fire and were now on their knees, imploring their God to send rain and douse the flames. But the clouds did not darken or release any water. There was no thunder or lightning to show the anger of the Christian god at the destruction of one of his temples. *Would our gods be this silent?* Ulf wondered as he stood with his friends. All of them relaxed as they enjoyed the scene. Ulf chewed on his bottom lip, his hand on the hilt of Ormstunga, as he waited for the Christian god to rush down and crush them all. Much like he would expect Odin or Thor to do. But nothing happened. The only noise was the flames feasting on the wooden support beams and the priests' cries. Ulf flinched when the strange material in the windows exploded and looked around to make sure that no one noticed. All their attention was on the church. The Norse warriors enjoyed burning the Christian churches.

"There goes the glass. Ah, they were so beautiful," the old priest lamented beside Ulf.

"Glass?" Ulf was still watching the windows.

"Yes, young man. Glass. I still remember the day they put them in." The old priest smiled as his mind drifted to the distant past.

"I've never seen it before," Ulf responded.

"No, I doubt you have anything as beautiful where you are from." The old priest sighed. "Perhaps that is why you insist on coming here and destroying our beauty."

Ulf gave the old priest a sideways glance. There were plenty of beautiful things in Norway and most of them not made by man. His mind flashed back to Eldrid, the daughter of the Swedish jarl he had fought the summer before. Ulf wondered where she was and what she was doing. A loud roar from the fire drew his attention back to the burning church and with it, Hulda came to his mind. Ulf could almost sense her anger in the heat of the flames. She had died because of him and he was standing here thinking of another woman. Ulf rubbed her name on the hilt of Olaf's axe.

"You have a darkness hanging over you. I saw it the moment you walked into the church." Ulf turned to the old priest and caught him staring at the haft of his axe, his lips moving as he read the names.

"You can read our runes?" Ulf was getting annoyed at the old man for the first time.

"My father taught me as a young boy and the knowledge has stayed with me since. The names of your family?" Ulf nodded, grinding his teeth. "*Do not seek revenge or bear a grudge against anyone among your people, but love your neighbour as yourself. I am the LORD.*"

Ulf frowned at the old priest.

"It's what God tells us in the Bible, one of many things He says about revenge, actually. It's quite a popular topic."

"And what does that have to do with me?" Ulf felt his annoyance turn into anger. He did not like the way the priest was talking to him, as if he understood what Ulf was going through.

"I understand you Norsemen believe revenge is a noble thing. Even your Odin is considered to be the god of revenge, amongst many other things, but you are still young. Do not let your quest for vengeance consume you like that fire is consuming our church."

Ulf looked at the burning church, feeling the heat of the flames from where he stood. Or perhaps it was just the heat of the flames inside him. "Too late for that," he said to the priest and walked away. Ulf left the old priest with his companions as they mourned their church, and looked for his friends, who wandered away. At least they did not pry into his family. Ulf found them standing to one side, discussing their next step. All around Ulf, the men of Thorgilsstad seemed cheered. They had found a cart and a horse, which meant they could take more of the church's treasure with them, but it also meant that they'd be moving slower. But no one was thinking about that right now. The church soothed their anger over the ambush and the friends they had lost. Stealing from churches and burning them lifted a person's spirit. But Ulf could not share in their joy. His mind was in conflict, a constant battle between his guilt for Hulda's death and the unexplained attraction he felt for the daughter of a Swedish jarl he might have killed.

"That's why you should never talk to those Christians for too long," Thorbjorn's rough voice greeted Ulf as he got to his friends. Thorbjorn smiled at Ulf's glare. "Aye, those dress-wearing bastards do that to you. They can blot out the brightest sun with their words."

"Depressing they are," Asbjorn agreed. "You should fit in nicely with them, Ulf." Ulf glared at Asbjorn. But like the rest of Snorri's hirdmen, he was not concerned.

"Perhaps Ulf wants to join them, seeing as how he enjoyed the old man's words." Ragnar spat. Ulf ground his teeth as Ragnar sneered at him, almost daring Ulf to respond.

"Enough." Snorri broke in, diffusing the situation before anyone did anything dumb. "Thorbjorn is right, though. You shouldn't spend too much time listening to them. Nothing but bags of air, repeating the same words everywhere you go." Ulf nodded at his friend and saw the small smile in his beard. "Get the men ready. If we leave now, we should get to Bremen before the sun disappears. Runar said it's not too far from us." Snorri was talking about the scout he had sent after they attacked the church to discover how far they were from Bremen and if the fleet was there. The scout had returned with word that the fleet was waiting for them.

"I think we should camp here and go to the fleet in the morning." Magni stood with his hands on his hips as if he believed they would listen to him. Thorbjorn raised an eyebrow, while Oddi rolled his eyes. But neither man said anything.

Snorri shook his head. "We don't know if what the priest said was true. There might an enemy force nearby. Not to mention the Danes who attacked us."

"They'll be licking their wounds in a hole somewhere," Ragnar said.

"Aye, but what happens when they finish licking their wounds and realise they still outnumber us?" Oddi asked. Ragnar looked at him but had no response.

"I agree with Oddi," Snorri said. "The quicker we get to the ships, the better." Magni was about to protest, but then spotted the sneer on Ragnar's face and closed his mouth. Much to the amusement of Thorbjorn.

The sun was descending when they finally reached Bremen. The march had been tense, the men on the constant lookout for any threats. No one wanted to be caught out in an ambush again, especially not now when they were dragging a cart full of plunder with them. Snorri had sent scouts out ahead of them, deciding to trust the eyes of men over the goodwill of the Norns. The captured priests had not helped, either. They were tied to the cart and dragged along, apart from the old priest who sat beside the plunder the Norse took from his church. The youngest of the priests, the one Thorbjorn punched, refused to move in the beginning. He had stood his ground and glared at them through his one eye, the other swollen shut. In the end, it took a reprimand from the old priest to get him going, but throughout the march, he and the other priests struggled to keep up. They kept tripping over, forcing the group to stop, and would only get up after a few kicks from the Norsemen. Snorri avoided any farmsteads they came across, not wanting to risk another fight.

Ulf spent the march studying the surrounding countryside, if only to distract himself from his thoughts. Francia was flatter than Norway, but other than that, it looked the same. The forests had oak, birch, and beech trees, just like at home, with the same birds flying around, and the ever-present ravens following them. Foxes darted out from underneath the trees, watching them march past, before disappearing again.

"Looks like we missed all the fun," Thorbjorn said as they stood on a hill and watched the black smoke rising from the town below them. Ulf glanced at the priests and saw the tears in their eyes and the hunched shoulders.

"I think I've had enough fun for now. All I want is some hot food and ale." Drumbr rubbed his belly. Some men mocked him, but Drumbr didn't care. Ulf, though, agreed with his round friend. The last few days had been difficult for all of them, and Ulf's dream still haunted him. That, mixed with his conflicting emotions, left him exhausted.

"Anyone see the Sae-Ulfr?" Brak shielded his eyes as he looked at the large fleet of longships in the river. But from this distance, they all looked the same.

"She'll be there," Snorri responded before he turned to the old priest sitting on the cart. Ulf had not spoken to him since they burnt the church, but sensed the priest watching him during the march. "Well, old man. This is where we leave you. As you can see," Snorri pointed to the town, "there is nothing left there for you now."

The old priest watched him for a few heartbeats. "And what of my brothers? Will you let them go as well?" His fellow priests' eyes darted between Snorri and the old man, trying to follow a conversation they didn't understand. "The Lord says you should treat your enemy as your friend."

Snorri smiled. "These men are not my enemy. They are my captives and I will sell them as thralls."

The old priest nodded, rubbing his wrinkled cheek. "Honour and loyalty are very important to you Norse warriors, I believe?" Snorri nodded. "And they are to us Christians as well, so I thank you for your offer, but I will stay with my brothers and share their fate."

"Your fate will be very different from theirs," Ragnar retorted.

"Be as it may. The Lord will protect me and keep me safe. As He will for my brothers. I will go with you to Bremen."

"As you wish." Snorri shrugged and turned away from the priests. "Tell the men to be careful. We don't want to fall into another ambush so close to our destination." Oddi nodded and did as Snorri ordered. The younger priests asked the old priest something in Frankish. As soon as the old priest responded, the two older ones wailed and dropped to the floor while the youngest one pulled at his restraints to get to Ulf, all the while shouting and spitting at him. This time, Ulf had enough. He grabbed the priest by his habit and pulled him in close so the young priest could see the roaring flames in Ulf's eyes as his face creased in anger. The young priest paled, his legs weak underneath him. The old priest barked something at the young one who nodded so hard, Ulf was sure he heard something rattling inside his head. He let go and the young priest dropped to the ground. Some men laughed, while others looked disappointed that Ulf had not done more. They all knew what could happen when Ulf lost his temper. Many were there when

Thorvald had pushed him too far. Even Ulf still remembered the singing sound of Olaf's axe as she flew through the air.

"Thank you for not killing him. The young ones sell for more," Snorri said as Ulf walked past him. Ulf stopped and stared at his friend. He hated the idea of selling people like that, ever since he had seen the thrall market at Suðrikaupstefna. Snorri smiled at the look on Ulf's face.

"Looks like we have a welcoming party." Thorbjorn pointed to a group of horsemen coming their way from the town. Snorri's face tightened as the horsemen got closer, but then he smiled.

"Ubba," Snorri said. All around them, the men of Thorgilsstad relaxed and let go of their weapons. Snorri turned to the old priest, "Last chance, old man!" But the priest only smiled and shook his head, before glancing at Ulf. But Ulf turned away. He was not in the mood for any more of the priest's words. He did not need some old man who had spent his whole life kneeling in front of a book to tell him about the way the wind blew.

"You sure we can trust him?" Oddi asked Snorri, surprising him. "You said it yourself. The ambush had nothing to do with Arnfinni. Those were Danish men. And Ubba is Danish, even if he looks Swedish."

"Bullocks to you!" Thorbjorn jabbed a finger at Oddi. "Odin knows Ubba is a good man."

"Has Odin told you this?" Ulf asked.

Thorbjorn only smiled. "This I expect from Ulf, he is a sour bastard, but not you Oddi."

"Ulf is just jealous of Ubba." Asbjorn sneered.

"Jealous?" Ulf glared at Asbjorn.

"Aye, you don't like the fact that he is Snorri's new friend and you are not."

Ulf was about to take a step towards Asbjorn, but then saw Snorri shake his head. With a deep breath, he ignored the smiling Asbjorn.

"We can trust Ubba, he has been a good friend to us so far." Snorri looked at Oddi and Ulf. "I know what I said last night, but my gut tells me Ubba is a friend." Oddi nodded, looking convinced, but Ulf knew he would never go against Snorri.

"I agree with Snorri," Magni added, wanting to be part of the conversation. "My gut also tells me Ubba can be trusted."

"Well, if Magni is convinced, then the gods know it must be true," Ragnar mocked. Magni opened his mouth to respond, but wisely decided against it. "Now let's get going. I'd like to find some ale and a woman before those bastards waste everything." Ragnar walked down the hill, not waiting for a response.

Snorri laughed. "You heard old Nine-Finger!" The men cheered, causing the horsemen to pause before they all marched towards Bremen.

"Greetings, Snorri and men of Thorgilsstad!" Ubba said as they got close, his white hair blowing in the breeze. Tormod rode at his side, but remained silent. "We were worried that something happened to you, but thank the gods, we find you all well."

"Not all," Ragnar responded. Ubba frowned and ran his eyes over the men, as if judging their number. His eyes lingered over the cart loaded with chests, the hunger in them obvious to everyone.

"You do seem lower in number." Ubba stroked his beard.

"We were ambushed, not far from Hammaburg," Snorri said.

"Ambushed! By who?" Ubba asked, his eyes wide. Ulf saw the strange glances the rest of Ubba's entourage gave each other, but didn't have the energy to work out what they meant. Perhaps the news was also concerning to them.

"That's what we'd like to know," Thorbjorn responded.

"They were Danes, that's all we know. But we don't know who sent them or why they were there," Snorri answered.

"Where was this?" Tormod asked, scowling as he waited for an answer. Perhaps it was because Halfdan the Black would hang him if he went back without the plunder owed by Snorri.

"A farmstead, about half a day's walk from Hammaburg." Snorri looked at Ubba. Ulf rubbed his eyes, feeling the lack of sleep. He wanted to sit down and rest his head against the cart, but knew he couldn't. All Ulf needed was for the men to finish their conversation so he could get to the Sae-Ulfr and rest. Perhaps the ship's spirit would allow him to sleep properly.

"I will send men immediately. See what they can find out." Ubba seemed furious. He turned to his men, about to give the order, when Snorri stopped him.

"There's no need. We burnt the farmstead. You'll only find charred bones and burnt fields." Snorri smiled. "All we want now is to get to our ship, unload our cargo and find a place for our captives."

"They from the farmstead?" one of Ubba's men asked.

"No, we found a church not far back. Not sure if that was the church you mentioned, but they had enough to ease our pains." Snorri smiled. Tormod was the only one who was not smiling. Ulf wasn't sure why. Of everyone, he should have been pleased. Most of those chests filled with gold and silver would go to his king.

Ubba shrugged, smiling as he did so. "I don't really know myself. I was only told there was a church between Hammaburg and Bremen. Odin knows I wasn't even sure if you'd find it, but I guess I should never underestimate you or your men." The men of Thorgilsstad cheered, causing the priests to flinch. All but the old one who had been watching Ulf the entire time. "Now come, you all look like you need a rest." Ubba turned his horse and went back to the burning Bremen, the men of Thorgilsstad following him.

"Why do you keep looking at me, old man?" Ulf asked as the cart drew level with him.

The old priest studied the surrounding men before responding, "My father once told me you Norsemen believe that your fate has already been decided by the three sisters of fate."

"The Norns."

"The Norns," the priest continued. "We believe our Lord has also chosen our paths."

"And this is the path your god has chosen for you? You accept that?"

The old priest shrugged. "Our Lord is far more intelligent than any mere man, so we can never really understand His true motives." Ulf didn't know if he agreed with that. He hated the idea of someone or something deciding his path for him, especially as so far they had given him nothing but pain and grief, with only a few stars shining through the storm. "But I sense you have a long journey ahead of you, young Ulf."

"Aye, people keep telling me that," Ulf growled.

"I'm sure they do, but I fear you will not get the outcome you seek."

Ulf stopped, struck by the words as if lighting had melted his feet to the ground. He watched as the cart pulled away, the old priest looking at him from over his shoulder. Ulf saw the sadness in his eyes as he tried to understand what the priest had meant by that.

"Any problems taking the place?" Snorri walked with Ubba and Tormod towards Bremen. The town had a large wall, bigger than Hammaburg. A moat surrounded the wall with four bridges spread out across it. It would have been a hard wall to breach, even harder than Hammaburg, but Snorri saw no signs they had attacked from the land.

"Not as hard as you'd think. The land defences are strong, but from the river's side there was nothing. We just simply sailed up the river and landed in the middle of their town." Ubba confirmed what Snorri was thinking.

"It was a simple slaughter after that," Tormod said, smiling. "You would have enjoyed it."

Snorri glanced at Tormod, but could not get himself to smile back. They had grown up together in Thorgilsstad. Tormod's father had been one of Thorgils' best warriors, a barrel-chested man with a powerful arm. As children, they spent all their time together, running through the fields and playing in the forest. But all that changed when Oddi arrived. Snorri never thought he could be closer to anyone than Tormod, but when his distant cousin came to live with them, they became instant friends. It had always been easy for Snorri to make friends. He just liked being around people and welcomed anyone. For Tormod, though, it was not so easy. He had the same humour as Snorri, but wasn't as accepting of new people. Tormod didn't want Oddi to spend time with them, always finding reasons not to like Snorri's cousin. It had caused friction amongst them, which Snorri had not liked. As a young boy, Snorri wanted to be a mighty warrior with his best friends by his side. They were going to be his first hirdmen. Snorri had even made them swear an oath when they were only nine winters. As they grew older, Oddi showed his natural talent as a warrior. Tormod was a great fighter, but he had still felt jealous of Oddi's abilities. Just before they reached manhood, Tormod's father died during a raid. After that, Tormod decided there was no reason for him to stay in Thorgilsstad. They had argued. Snorri had wanted him to stay. They were to be the future of Thorgilsstad and conquer Norway. But those had been the silly dreams of boys high on sagas. Tormod left soon after and Snorri had been furious with him. He had broken the oath they had made and to Snorri it didn't matter that they were only children. You didn't break an oath. But that had been many winters ago, and both men had moved on. Snorri accepted that their friendship was over, but still respected the man as a warrior. He knew the attack on Thorgilsstad had nothing to do with Tormod, but he could not help blaming him for it. Tormod was the king's man and Halfdan had promised to protect Thorgilsstad.

"Tell me more of this ambush," Ubba said as they walked through the town. All around, Snorri saw the familiar sights after raiding a town. Men pillaging and raping. Some passed out drunk on the ground, while others lounged about, singing tales of distant warriors. Bodies of the dead still lay where they fell, the Frankish soil soaked in the blood of her people. The air was filled with smoke from the burning houses, mixed in with the scent of death. Snorri took a deep breath. Tormod had been right. He would have enjoyed this attack. But memories of the ambush still darkened his mood.

"We lost a lot of good men," he growled as he relived the desperate fight in his mind. Snorri loved being in the shield wall. The sounds and smells of it ran through his blood and he never felt more alive than when he was face to face with his enemy, separated only by their shields. When he could see in their eyes, it almost felt like he saw into their minds and knew what they were going to do. His heart always seemed to beat in time with weapons striking shields. But this fight had been different. It had been desperate. There had been no joy in it for Snorri, only the growing need to get his men out of there alive. They had been caught off guard, and Snorri blamed himself for it.

"How many men attacked you?" one of Ubba's men asked.

Snorri looked at the man. "They outnumbered us by almost two or three to one, I'd guess, but the Norns didn't exactly give me time to count them."

"They might not have," the man responded, nodding to show that he understood. "But the gods were clearly on your side."

"The gods and a wooden fence." Snorri saw the surprise on their faces and told them what had happened during the fight. The group had stopped as Snorri told his story, and he saw the admiration in their eyes. All but Tormod, who had a look that Snorri did not understand. But he didn't want to worry about Tormod. Like his men, he was tired and on edge. He hated not knowing who to trust. But at least now he was amongst friends. His men could rest and recover and hopefully, with Ubba's help, they could find out who had sent the ambush.

"Well, Odin knows I am happy you are safe, my friends. It seems we should not underestimate the men from Thorgilsstad." Ubba smiled. "We'll spend the night here, so your men can rest. And besides, you look like you can do with a drink."

Snorri laughed, the relief rushing through him. "Not even Thor could outdrink me tonight!"

CHAPTER 15

For three days, the fleet travelled along the Frankish coast. The weather had been good, the constant breeze allowing them to travel by sail, so the men didn't have to row. On Snorri's ship, the men were grateful for this. They were exhausted after their trek between the two rivers and many were still injured from the ambush. Ulf almost believed the gods were with them on this raid, but only if he forgot about the attack at the farmstead. He looked towards the priests huddled together by the mast where they were tied up. Apart from the old one. They tried leaving him behind, but the old man refused to abandon his fellow priests. Not that they looked grateful for it. The youngest one kept glaring at everyone, constantly muttering things in his strange language. Latin, the old priest had told Ulf. It was a language from the greatest empire to have existed, the priest had said. Ulf had never heard of this empire and doubted it was real. If they had been so great, then why did they not rule the world anymore? Snorri felt that the old man did not need to be tied up, and so far he had been correct. Many times, the younger priests urged him to do something, most likely to free them, judging by the way they always held their hands up. The old priest would just shake his head and go back to watching everyone around him. Ulf wondered if the old priest felt the Norse blood pumping through his veins.

All along the Frankish coast there was evidence that Asgeir's large fleet had passed this way already. Nothing remained of coastal villages other than smoke and misery. Often they saw people standing on the shore, watching in despair as the fleet sailed past. Children would point their way, while some women collapsed and cried. Men brandished weapons at them, but they would run as soon as the ships turned towards the beach. The Danes on the other ships complained that there was nothing to raid, but those on the Sae-Ulfr didn't care. They already had filled her hull with plunder from the church and they had their captives to sell.

"What's that place?" Geir pointed at the white cliffs in the distance.

"Britain," one of the older men responded. He was one of the War Bear's crew.

"Britain?" Geir repeated the name, scowling at the same time. The other young men joined Geir as they all looked at the faraway land. Ulf was curious as well, but did not want to join them. Instead, he stretched his neck and looked over the side of the Sae-Ulfr.

"A land almost as rich as Francia," Ragnar responded, his voice sounding nostalgic.

"You been there?" one of the younger men asked the jarl's champion, his voice a whisper. Many of the young warriors feared Ragnar, and most of them never dared to speak to the red-haired warrior.

"Aye, many times." Ragnar scratched his beard. "We started raiding there when Francia became too difficult." Ragnar turned and walked away, leaving the young men gaping at him like needy children. They wanted to know more, but Ragnar would not tell them anything else.

Snorri walked towards the new members of his crew, smiling. He clapped them on the shoulders as he stood with them. "Like Francia, they have many churches filled with treasure."

"Aye, and that's where the similarities end," Oddi said. The young men looked at him with raised eyebrows. Ulf shook his head and saw the old priest smile.

"Oddi is right," Snorri continued. "Where Francia is one large kingdom with a king, Britain is an island made up of different kingdoms constantly fighting each other. It makes them less organised and easier to raid."

"Also means that they'll sometimes pay you to attack their enemies." Thorbjorn laughed. This time, Ulf did raise an eyebrow.

"But they are the same people?"

"Aye. Anglo-Saxon bastards." Thorbjorn nodded.

"It doesn't matter that they are the same people," Oddi said. "We are the same people as the Danes and Swedes." Thorbjorn spat over the side in contempt as Oddi said this, but Oddi ignored him. "We still raid them and fight against them."

"Aye. Nothing better than making them beg for their mothers," Magni cheered, hoping others would join him. No one did. They all knew he had never raided those lands.

"The Anglo-Saxons in Britain have different kingdoms, and then you have the Britons on the west of the island and the Scots on the north. It's an island constantly at war with itself and that's what makes it weak." Oddi lifted his chin and stroked his beard as he always did when he thought he was being wise.

"And they happily pay us to raid their neighbours." Asbjorn smiled.

"Twice the plunder for us." Drumbr nodded.

"So it's a good thing that they are not one kingdom," Geir said. The young crew around him nodded to show they understood as well.

"Aye, if they ever unite under one king, then they'll be a force to reckon with." Snorri scowled at the white cliffs.

"So why not raid them now if they are easier to attack than the Franks?" a young warrior asked, scratching his head.

Snorri smiled at the boy the way a father smiles at his child for asking a dumb question. "Because right now Francia is in the middle of a civil war, which means they are distracted. This is an opportunity too great to miss. This country has been at peace for a long time and has become very rich." Snorri's eyes lit up, no doubt picturing his hull full of Frankish treasure.

"Your leader is right," the old priest said, surprising everyone. "The winds are changing and I fear the peace we have known for so long because of Charlemagne has ended." The old priest sighed, sadness written on his face. Ulf lowered his head, remembering the dream he had before. *You are me,* the troll's voice said in his mind, its face turning into his. He looked up and caught the old priest staring at him. Ulf shook his head, clearing his mind. His thoughts were his own, and he did not want others to see them. He didn't know if the Christian priests could read minds, but he did not want to take a chance.

They sailed for another day before they reached the river that would take them to Rouen, the large city Asgeir had told Snorri about. Ulf did not understand why Asgeir was so interested in attacking that city. There were plenty of other places in Francia, many of them closer to home. As they sailed up the river, Ulf saw the same destruction they had seen along the coast. Asgeir's fleet was efficient. But this time, Ulf noticed the dark eyes and sallow faces of the people as they watched this new fleet sailing by. Even the children looked afraid, a stark contrast from when they were travelling up the river towards Hammaburg. Then the children had not understood the danger these strange new ships brought with them. Perhaps Olaf had been right in becoming a bóndi. Ulf tried to distract himself by looking at the Frankish countryside. All along the river, the land was covered in forests, thick with trees and life. Where the forests stopped, fertile lands started. Ulf had been raised on a farm, so he knew good soil when he saw it. And even though most of the farms had been burnt to the ground, they were still larger than those in Norway.

"This is good land," Drumbr said as he gazed around.

"Aye," his brother said. "Father would be happy tilling these fields."

"Many bændr in Norway would be." Thorbjorn scratched his beard. His father was also a bóndi. But Thorbjorn had an older brother who would take over the farm when his father died, and Thorbjorn preferred violence over the quiet life.

"You never know what the future will bring," the old priest said behind them. They all turned in surprise and saw him standing there. It was the first time he had left his companions and they looked frightened without him by their side. Even the young one was trembling.

"What are you talking about, old man?" Thorbjorn snarled. "We are here to raid your land, not settle on it."

The old priest smiled as he eyed the land with moist eyes. "True, but who is to say that your children, or perhaps their children, won't come to settle on this land instead of just stealing from it."

They all looked at each other, unsure of how to respond.

"Rubbish!" Thorbjorn spat. "Why would our children want to settle here?"

The old priest smiled. "You said yourself, it's good farming land. So I think the question is why wouldn't they." The priest rubbed the wooden cross hanging around his neck. "They might even decide to abandon your gods and follow Christ." Ulf heard an eagle cry somewhere in the trees. He felt the shiver run down his spine and wondered if Odin was telling him that the priest spoke the truth.

Thorbjorn jumped to his feet and grabbed the old priest by his habit, pulling him down, so the two were eye to eye. The priest looked surprised by this, but Ulf didn't think he was frightened. "Say that again, priest, and Odin knows, I'll gut you!" Thorbjorn growled. The old priest paled, but he did not respond.

"Relax, Thorbjorn," Oddi said, putting a hand on his friend's shoulder. "The old man does not know what he is talking about." Ulf thought he spotted a smile in the corner of the old priest's mouth, but it disappeared before he could tell for sure.

Thorbjorn released the priest and spat overboard.

"Why could we not follow your god and our gods?" This was something Ulf could not get his head around. "We already have many gods, one more would not hurt."

"Because the Christians are greedy bastards," Thorbjorn growled. "They believe their god is more important than our gods, even Odin."

"There is only one God," the old priest responded. "Your gods are not real."

"So you keep saying," Thorbjorn said before walking away.

The priest watched as Thorbjorn went to the stern and stood by Snorri and Rolf. "Your friend is not an easy man to like."

Drumbr laughed before he could stop himself, and Ulf caught Thorbjorn glaring back at them. "Aye, well, you Christians don't make it easy to like you." The old priest stroked his long beard as he thought over what Drumbr had said and then nodded with a smile. Without a word, the priest turned and walked back to his companions.

"He's a strange one," Brak said, as they all settled down again.

"Aye, normally those bastards just glare at us and curse us in their silly language." Asbjorn pointed towards the youngest priest. Ulf had to admit there was something unusual about the old priest. He did not behave the same way as his companions and even though Ulf had never come across a Christian priest before, he was surprised at how friendly the old man was towards them.

"Perhaps it's because he has Norse blood." Ulf thought out loud.

"Could be," Oddi said before laying back and closing his eyes. "Doesn't matter, we'll be rid of them soon."

"We're here," Rolf's gruff voice called out, waking Ulf from his trance. Much of what they had seen in the early afternoon as they rowed up the river was the same, so Ulf had stopped paying attention to it. But what he saw now stole his breath. On either side of the river, there were hundreds of camps dotted all over the place, as if Odin had sprinkled them on the land. More warriors than Ulf could count were milling around, some relaxing, while others were returning from raids. Smoke hovered over the tents from the many campfires, giving the air a greyness the sun could not pierce. A few times, Ulf glanced over his shoulder at the old priest, curious to see how the old man would react. But the priest sat with his eyes shut, his mouth constantly moving as he muttered to himself. The other priests tried to do the same, but they could not stop themselves from looking at the devastation caused by the invading Danes. At one point, Ulf saw a side of the youngest priest he had not seen before. Gone were the angry scowl and the venom in his words. For the first time since they had captured the priests, the youngest one looked like the boy he was as the tears ran down his cheeks. The old priest had been right. The life they knew was over and if the surrounding camps were a sign of things to come, then Ulf wondered how this land could ever be peacefully occupied by Norse and Danish bændr.

"By the gods! Would you look at that!" one man sitting near Ulf exclaimed. Ulf looked over his shoulder and almost let go of his oar as he saw a manmade mountain.

"It's like the story my aunt told me," Ulf said, unable to stop himself.

"What story?" Brak asked, glancing between Ulf and the enormous stone wall.

Oddi smiled his wise smile. "I think I know the story, but please tell us, Ulf."

Ulf looked at his friends, seeing the eager smiles on their faces. He gulped, and with a trembling voice, started. "One day, a smith arrived in Asgard and offered to build a high wall to protect the gods from danger when Thor was away. He promised he could do it in three seasons and all he wanted in return was Freya's hand in marriage and the sun and moon."

"Is that all?" Thorbjorn interrupted, but then signalled for Ulf to continue when Ulf glared at him.

"The gods were not sure, and Freya was against this. Loki, however, convinced the gods that they should let the smith build the wall, but that he had to do it in one winter and could only use his stallion for help. The gods believed it would be impossible for the smith to do this and agreed. The smith got to work, and throughout the winter, he and his stallion built the wall faster than the gods had thought possible. Even more puzzling was that the smith's stallion, Svadilfari, was doing almost twice as much work as the smith, hauling enormous boulders over considerable distances. With only three days left before the end of the winter, all the smith and his stallion had to do was add a few more stones and the wall would be complete. The gods were furious with Loki and demanded he do something. That night, while the smith and Svadilfari were on their way to the mountains to collect the last stones, they came across a beautiful mare. Svadilfari got so excited by the sight of this mare that he broke from his reins and chased after her."

"This is my favourite part." Oddi's smile grew wider. Ulf continued with his story, feeling a bit more confident.

"The following morning, the smith's stallion was still nowhere to be seen. The smith knew he had been tricked and revealed himself to be a giant. But before he could attack the gods, Thor returned from his travels and smashed the giant's head in with Mjöllnir."

"What happened to the giant's horse?" one of the crew members asked. Ulf had not realised that they were also listening to the story.

"If I may?" Oddi offered. Ulf nodded and sighed with relief that he did not have to finish the story. "Well," Oddi stared at the wall as he paused, "Svadilfari caught up to the mare, who was actually Loki in disguise." He smiled at the raised eyebrows in front of him. "And soon after, Loki gave birth to an eight-legged horse which he presented to Odin."

"Sleipnir?" Asbjorn asked, scratching his head.

"Aye, Sleipnir."

"Thor's balls! That can't be true, can it?" Thorbjorn looked at the men, who all shrugged.

"More like Svadilfari's balls," Drumbr said, causing everyone to laugh.

"This wall must have been built by giants," Geir muttered, still gaping at the fortification.

The old priest opened his eyes and without looking over his shoulder responded, "No, no giants built the walls of Rouen. It was men, with the help of God."

"Shut up, you old fool!" Rolf responded, causing the men to laugh as Rolf looked older than the priest. The priest only smiled and closed his eyes again.

"Follow Ubba." Snorri pointed to Ubba's ship ahead of the Sae-Ulfr. Snorri had been quiet for most of the day and had spent all of it at the stern with Rolf.

Rolf turned the tiller and the Sae-Ulfr followed Ubba's ship as she found a place to dock. Ulf couldn't help but wonder what Vidar would have made of these walls. He knew his silent friend would have hated them. He smiled as he pictured Vidar screwing his face the way he had done when he didn't like something. But the warmth of the memory was replaced by a pain in his chest. Vidar would never get to see these walls. But perhaps that was a good thing. Vidar had been a child of the forest. That was where he had always felt more comfortable.

"Here they are! Our Norse friends come to steal our glory!" a voice thundered over them, the sound of it echoing off the water. Ulf turned and saw the bear-like man standing on the shore, his smile as wide as his outstretched arms. Asgeir reminded Ulf of the beast he had fought when he met Snorri, and Ulf hoped he would never have to fight that man.

"There'll be plenty to go round," Snorri laughed in return. "The gods have blessed us with this opportunity."

"Jarl Asgeir, a pleasure to meet you again," Ubba the White shouted his own greeting as he stepped off his ship. Ulf watched him greet the brown-haired leader of this giant force, the two men sharing a warm hug. Tormod walked to them and greeted

Asgeir with respect. Tormod was not here to make friends with the Danes. He was here to help his king get rich. Ulf had almost forgotten about the man since they got back to the fleet. Tormod had spent most of his time with Ubba while his men mingled with their fellow Norsemen from Thorgilsstad.

"Ah, our friend from King Halfdan." Asgeir clasped Tormod's arm in greeting.

"Bastard," Thorbjorn whispered towards Tormod. Ulf looked at him, but Thorbjorn only shook his head.

"Come, friends! You must be tired. My fire awaits. I would hear about your journey after we separated," Asgeir shouted. Snorri's face darkened, no doubt remembering the ambush. Ulf knew some men wondered if the Danes who had ambushed them were part of Asgeir's force.

"Oddi, you know what to do," Snorri called to his cousin before jumping off the Sae-Ulfr. His hirdmen followed without being asked, with Ragnar and Magni close behind as well. Many of the Danish men they walked past gave them wary glances, but Ulf saw no one that he recognised from the battle. Although he doubted he would.

CHAPTER 16

Snorri sat around Asgeir's fire, studying the men present as he nursed his cup of ale. Apart from Ubba, his captains, and Tormod, he knew none of the men here. But most of them claimed to have heard of him and his father. Snorri would normally be proud of that fact. Like most Norse warriors, he thrived on notoriety. But Snorri felt uneasy – maybe because he was sitting with men whose villages he had most likely raided. Snorri took a sip of ale as the men laughed at a tale being told by Asgeir. His host was smaller than Snorri thought he'd be, a little taller than Asbjorn and Brak, but still shorter than himself. Asgeir was quick to laugh and constantly wore a smile on his face. Snorri now understood how the man had brought such a large force together and thanked the gods for bringing him here. But the events of the last few days still wore heavily on his mind. Snorri always prided himself on the fact that he was a good leader to his men and never placed them in unnecessary danger. But somehow Snorri had walked them into a trap and now he would have to explain to their families why their husbands, fathers, and brothers would not be coming home. Snorri saw his father's scowl in his mind; the image making him take a deep gulp of his ale as he tried to wash it away. His father had no right to judge him, not anymore. But Snorri still let his men down, although he couldn't help the sense of pride at the how the ambush had turned out. They should have lost that battle. They had been caught off guard and were heavily outnumbered, but the men of his village fought like bastards and in the end broke the ambushing force and sent them running.

Everyone had gone quiet around the fire and Snorri realised they were all looking at him. *I'm turning into Ulf.* He took another sip of his ale and saw the cup was empty.

"Has Loki stolen your wits?" Asgeir laughed. Ubba, sitting next to Snorri, filled his cup with more ale and slapped him on the shoulder.

"Forgive me," Snorri smiled, "I'm tired I guess."

"Aye." Asgeir's face grew serious. "Ubba told me what happened to your men. Just like those bastard Franks to do something like that."

"They weren't Franks." Snorri grimaced.

"Not Franks?" one man asked.

"No, they were Danes."

"How can you be so sure?" The same man scowled at Snorri.

Snorri stared at the man, his upper lip curling into a snarl. "Because I have killed enough Danes to know what your shit smells like." The man shot to his feet, hand on his sword before the laughing Asgeir stopped him. Snorri wasn't concerned by the man's response. He knew he could take him and besides, his hirdmen were right behind him by their own fire.

"Relax," Asgeir waved at the man who stood glaring at Snorri, "Snorri meant no offence."

"Aye, but I took offence," the man growled, his hand still on the hilt of his sword. Snorri smiled at the man, if only to provoke him more. Perhaps a good fight would make him feel better.

"This is Snorri Thorgilsson, you idiot," Ubba pointed out. "He'll gut you before you get over that fire." The man raised an eyebrow, and Snorri saw him waver a bit before he let go of his sword.

"Perhaps we'll settle this another time, Snorri Thorgilsson." The Dane spat into the flames and sat down again. Snorri nodded his agreement and then paid no more attention to the man as Asgeir spoke again.

"Did you recognise any of these Danes?" Asgeir asked. Snorri saw him glance towards Ubba, who shook his head.

"No," Snorri responded, and told the men around the fire what had happened. Apart from the downward glances when Snorri told of how his men defeated a Danish force of greater number, he saw no reaction, which suggested these men had nothing to do with the ambush. Snorri was met with silence when he finished the tale. The Danish warriors weren't sure how to respond.

"Well, the men of Thorgilsstad should not be underestimated." Asgeir smiled at Snorri and raised his cup towards him. "And it seems that the gods do indeed fight by your side."

Snorri nodded at the compliment. "Jarl Asgeir, I wanted to ask if you sent men raiding that way, or know of any ships that did?"

Asgeir scratched his ear as he thought for a short while, "I didn't, but I can't be sure that none of the ships left to go raiding." He looked at a man sat to his left. "Have you heard of any incidents from the raiding parties?"

"None," the man rubbed on his earlobe, before looking at Snorri. "But I'll ask around." Snorri nodded his gratitude and relaxed a little.

"You are the same Snorri Thorgilsson who fought the giant sea king?" one man asked. Snorri looked at him, seeing the thinning red hair and a scar which ran the length of the man's scalp. That was another battle he wanted to forget about. They had won great glory there, but it had cost them all more than anyone wanted to pay.

"Your young friend made quite a name for himself there," Ubba said from beside Snorri.

"Ulf?" Snorri almost choked on his ale. Ubba had shown no real interest in Ulf before.

"What's so special about this... Ulf?" Asgeir scratched his chin.

"He's a great warrior, from what I've been told," Ubba said. "The best of all of Snorri's men."

Snorri laughed, spitting his ale over the flames. "Forgive me. Ulf is almost like a brother to me, but he is not my best fighter. Any of my hirdmen can beat him."

"Then the story of him charging at the sea king's army alone is not true?" the man with the thinning hair asked.

"Aye, it's true. The dumb bastard charged Griml's army alone. And what he did, I had never seen before. But he is not my best fighter." Snorri saw the looks on the faces around him and the raised eyebrow from Ubba. "Ulf is a great fighter, but he is not a naturally skilled warrior. His strength comes from his speed and luck."

"He's fast then?" one of Ubba's men asked.

"Aye, faster than any man I've seen." Snorri was enjoying himself now, something he had not expected. But he loved telling stories, and Ulf's was his favourite to tell. There was still much Snorri did not understand about his young friend, especially the strange connection he felt towards him.

"But speed alone does not make you a good fighter," Asgeir said.

Snorri nodded. "It does not. Ulf's father was the greatest warrior I've ever seen. The man lived and breathed battles. It was the blood that flowed through his veins." Snorri saw he had their attention, especially Ubba, who leaned in closer. "The sagas say that Ulf's ancestor is the bastard son of Tyr."

"Tyr! Impossible!" someone exclaimed.

"Aye, I would have thought so too, but that day, it was like Tyr himself had taken over Ulf. In the short time I have known Ulf, I have never seen him fight like that. Not even against the giant bear that attacked us." Snorri beamed at their reactions. Even Asgeir was hooked. Ulf would hate him for this, but Snorri didn't care right now. Ulf needed to learn how to relax.

"A giant bear!"

"Sent by Odin himself, but that's another story."

"That's why he is called Bear-Slayer?" Tormod asked. Snorri nodded.

"So how is he not a skilled fighter then?" Asgeir pointed in Ulf's direction, where he sat with Snorri's hirdmen.

Snorri shrugged, not really sure himself. They had spent many months training Ulf, and although Snorri saw the improvement, he always felt that something was holding Ulf back. "Ulf sees fighting different from how we do. For many of us, it's our lives. It is what we do to survive, to live and to make a name for ourselves." The men around the fire agreed with him, some raising their cups.

"To have our names written in the sagas," Asgeir said to cheers from his men.

Snorri raised his cup to show he agreed. "But Ulf doesn't care about any of that. He only cares about vengeance. It's his driving force, it's what he lives for. And it's the reason he will not be defeated."

"Will not?" Asgeir asked.

"Will not," Snorri repeated. "I've seen a bear claw half his face off. Ragnar pommelling him to the ground, a Swedish jarl almost caving his head in and a two thousand strong army standing in his way. And none of these kept Ulf down or stopped him. He made an oath to Odin, and he believes he cannot die until Griml is dead."

"And what do you think?" Ubba's eyes were wide with interest.

Snorri smiled. "I think I don't want to get in his way when he is pushed too far. You heard what happened to the men who attacked him in the forest." Ubba nodded, but said nothing.

"I still don't understand," one man said while scratching his chin. "What makes him so great then?"

"Determination," Asgeir answered. Silence surrounded their fire as everyone stared at Asgeir. "A man like that is driven by his determination and that's why he will not be defeated."

"He will not allow it," Snorri agreed.

"You have good men around you then," Asgeir smiled at Snorri. "I look forward to seeing what they can do when we take this city." Snorri nodded and raised his cup. The rest of the night, they spoke of how they would attack the city. Asgeir had arrived two days before and had just been raiding the countryside. The enormous walls caused a problem, as the Danes did not have the experience needed to attack a large city like this. And neither had Snorri. Most of his raids consisted of attacking simple places, like churches, farmsteads, or small cities like Hammaburg, where the wooden walls were less problematic than stone. The general opinion was to wait and starve the people out. Snorri did not have the patience for that, and neither did the rest of them. Scandinavians did not do sieges, they liked to attack quick and disappear. The old priest was right. Things were changing.

Snorri stared at his helmet. He liked the way the golden eye and cheek guards looked like scales and stood out from the silver bowl part. His friends joked they were fish scales, but for Snorri, they were the scales of a dragon. Snorri studied the camp as he polished his helmet. It'd been three days since they arrived in Asgeir's camp. Not much happened during those days, which gave Snorri's men a chance to recover. Snorri puffed out his cheeks as he exhaled. He did not like sitting around and doing nothing. Ubba took his men raiding, hoping that there might still be farmsteads or small villages not attacked by Asgeir's men. But Snorri had declined the offer to join Ubba. Snorri doubted they would find anything. Tormod joined Ubba though, trying hard to get favour with the Danish jarls. Snorri didn't know if it was for King Halfdan or himself. Not that Snorri really cared. He had bigger things to think about. The ambush wore on Snorri's mind and his men were getting tired of constantly looking over their shoulders. Snorri made sure they went nowhere in groups smaller than five men, and he himself didn't go anywhere without his hirdmen or Ragnar by his side. It was embarrassing, but they were in a camp filled with thousands of Danes, and Snorri didn't trust any of them.

"Wasting our fucking time here." Ulf's face was as dark as his mood. He was sitting nearby cleaning his brynja for the tenth time in three days.

Snorri took a deep sigh. Ulf had been getting more difficult since they arrived. "The reward will be worth it," Snorri responded but knew what Ulf was going to say. This was not the first time they had this conversation.

"I don't care about gold or silver." Ulf put his brynja to one side and stared at Snorri with his sword grey eyes. Snorri understood Ulf's past, but he never understood all the anger in his friend's eyes. A lot of Snorri's men were still uneasy around Ulf, afraid that he might lose control like the previous summer, nearly killing Thorv…. Snorri breathed deep. He did not want to think of that name or the person it was attached to. "I know,

Ulf, and you know I have my own reasons for wanting to find them. But this is where we must be."

"According to who? The gods or Halfdan?"

"Both," Snorri said with a confidence he didn't feel anymore. Snorri trusted the gods more than he trusted himself and always believed they had a reason for everything that happened to him. But recently, it had been harder to agree with what was happening.

"For once, I agree with the Bear-Slayer," Ragnar said. The way he used Ulf's by-name made it sound more of a joke than what it was. "Hunting that troll would be more interesting than sitting around here."

"Speaking of hunting, here they come." Brak pointed to a large group of men walking their way, with Asgeir in the lead, Ubba and Tormod amongst them.

"You sure this is a good idea?" Oddi eyed the group with a raised eyebrow.

"Aye, at least one of us should go with. We still don't know if we can trust most of those bastard Danes," Thorbjorn said.

Snorri smiled. "You lot are worse than my mother."

"Your mother is not responsible for keeping your dumb ass alive."

Drumbr nodded his agreement to Thorbjorn. "If we go back to Thorgilsstad with you dead, then your mother will hang us. I'm not sure if Odin will feel like saving us, like he did Ulf." Snorri thought back to that day. His father had decided that Ulf was guilty of killing his mother's thrall and ordered Ulf to be hanged. It was another day when it was hard to deny that the gods were with Ulf because just before he gave his last kick, the branch broke and Ulf survived.

"Snorri?" Oddi brought him back to the present.

"Turning into fucking Ulf now," Thorbjorn said as Snorri realised they were still talking to him.

"You lot worry too much. I'll be fine. Besides, Ubba and Tormod were also invited."

"I trust Tormod even less than the Danes," Asbjorn said, which the others agreed to.

Snorri glanced at his hirdmen. "Asgeir only invited about fifty captains out of the hundreds here, and I was one of them. You really want me to be the only one to take hirdmen with and have these Danes think we Norse fear them?" He looked at all of them. No one had anything to say, not that he expected them to respond. Norse pride was everything, and most would rather risk death than lose that. Snorri only hoped that he would not have to make that choice. Asgeir suggested a hunt before they attacked the city and invited his most senior captains. Snorri was honoured to have been invited, even though he knew it was a risk. But then you didn't get your name in the sagas if you didn't take risks.

"He didn't invite me," Magni complained, again.

"Why would he invite you?" Ragnar growled at him.

"I am the son of a jarl as well."

"Not a very smart one." Thorbjorn smiled, enjoying getting under Magni's skin.

"Asgeir only invited captains. You, my brother, are not a captain," Oddi explained. Again.

"Are you ready, Thorgilsson?" Asgeir asked as the group stopped in front of them. None of the men were wearing any armour, but all had swords or axes by their sides and spears in their hands. A few of the men even had bows and arrows.

"Aye." Snorri stood up, like the rest of the hunting party, not wearing his brynja. He handed his helmet to Ulf, knowing his friend would put it in his chest, and made sure that Tyr's Fury was by his side. Snorri suddenly had an urge to rub the Mjöllnir pendant around his neck and had to resist and scratched his beard instead.

"Bring us back a deer, could do with some meat," Ragnar called as they left.

"There'll be plenty of deer for your men." Asgeir laughed. "My scouts tell me that Frey has blessed this forest with more deer and boars than they've seen in a long time."

"Aye, and the hunt will be a good way to get your mind off recent events." Ubba clapped Snorri on the shoulder. Snorri laughed, hoping Ubba was right.

A while later, they were deep in the forest, not too far away from Rouen. It reminded Snorri of the forest by Thorgilsstad, with its thick oak and spruce trees. Much of the birds sounded the same as the ones at home. But there was something missing, something Snorri couldn't quite explain as he ambled through the trees with the hunting party. The forests in Norway always had a sense of fear about them. You could feel the gods and their magic when you walked amongst the trees. This forest, undoubtedly old, didn't have the same magic about it. *The gods are not here.* This time, his hand went to the Mjöllnir hanging around his neck.

"Not a fucking animal in sight," one man complained as he stabbed at some low-lying shrubs with his spear.

"Not surprised, with all the noise you are making, Alvar," the man next to him joked.

The one called Alvar was right. So far, they had seen nothing, but that did not stop the Danes from having a good time. As they walked through the forest, the men joked and made fun of each other. Asgeir was in the thick of it and seemed to know everyone by name. He even knew some of their sons. Asgeir was the type of leader Snorri tried hard to be. Snorri glanced to his side, where Ubba and Tormod had been. He stopped when he realised they weren't there anymore and scanned the group of men ahead of him. He couldn't see Ubba's white hair or Tormod's large shoulders. "Where in Odin's name did they go?" Snorri decided not to call out their names. That would only make him look weak and afraid. Snorri sensed movement amongst the trees not too far away from him. *Perhaps they had found the tracks of an animal and followed? But then why not let me know?* He wondered as he broke away from the group and walked towards the movement.

Snorri had not gone far when he saw evidence that someone had come this way. A broken branch about chest height. Snorri still didn't understand why they had left the group without telling him. *Probably that fucking Tormod trying to get more favour for himself.* Snorri pushed past the broken branch and followed the trail. He could still hear the large group in the distance. Hunting clearly was not something the Danes were good at.

Snorri was about to take a step forward when the hair on the back of his neck stood up. He ducked just in time to see an arrow fly past and bury itself in a tree. Snorri turned and held his spear in front of him, his eyes scanning the trees. He saw nothing but the branches, their leaves barely moving. But he noticed the birds had gone quiet. Snorri resisted the urge to call

out for his friends, realising he was not alone. Another arrow
flew from the trees and Snorri had to deflect it with his spear.
Two more arrows forced him to roll out of the way and then it
was like a signal had been given as more arrows came at him.
Snorri turned and ran for the cover of the trees as the arrows
flew past, one of them tearing through his tunic. He rounded a
tree and pressed his back against it. *Odin's arse*, he thought as
he looked at the hole in his tunic.

"Fucking idiots!" The shout came from the trees. Danes.
"Can't shoot a fucking bear while it sleeps."

"But he wasn't sleeping," another voice responded.

"Or a bear."

Snorri didn't recognise any of the voices. He glanced
around the tree, trying to see the men who were trying to kill
him, but was spotted as he did so.

"There he is!" a man wearing a leather jerkin and a bowl
helmet shouted.

Snorri sprang away from the tree as arrows and spears flew
past him. He dodged low-lying branches and jumped over
exposed roots as the men behind him gave chase. Snorri ran
past another tree, trying to remember where the large group
was, but he couldn't hear them, not with the rustle of the
branches he was sprinting past. He wished he had Ulf's speed or
his hirdmen. A quick glance over his shoulder told Snorri that
he had lost his pursuers, so he stopped by a large oak tree.
Snorri bent over as he caught his breath. He thought about the
men he had seen. They had come prepared. All of them were
wearing armour, though none had brynjas, only leather jerkins.
Only a few of them had any helmets. All his experience told
him that these were not elite fighting men, but there were a lot

of them. And they weren't part of the hunting party. This meant only one thing.

They had been waiting for him.

CHAPTER 17

"Fucking bastards," Snorri growled, trying to understand how this had happened. He had been led into a trap like a horse about to be sacrificed to the gods. *Could it have been Asgeir?* Asgeir was not a friend, but Snorri did not think the man would be this low. *Shows what you fucking know*, he chastised himself. Ubba? No, he wouldn't have done this. Tormod neither, but only because he would never go against King Halfdan. *And Halfdan wants me to come back alive with his treasure. But where did Ubba and Tormod disappear to?* Snorri heard a twig snap and someone being shushed. They were close. Snorri looked around him, trying to work out which way to go. But the thought of running caused the bile in his stomach to rise. Snorri never ran from a fight. That's why his men followed him and why he had made them rich. The gods were with him, and he knew Odin would be watching. Snorri had always felt the All-Father near him and knew he was also blessed by Tyr. So Snorri would not run. If these bastards wanted to hunt him like wolves hunt deer, then they were about to learn the last lesson of their lives. Snorri was no deer. He was the wolf.

Snorri looked at the tree he was hiding behind and smiled. *The gods are with me, after all.* From the side his pursuers would come from, the old oak had no low branches or any way up. But from this side, there was a crack in the trunk which would allow him to climb up to the low branches above covered in foliage. Snorri wondered if this was like the oak tree Odin had hung himself on for nine days to gain his wisdom, but quickly dismissed the thought as he started climbing. He got a good grip on the crack in the trunk and, planting his foot halfway up, Snorri pulled himself high enough to grab the branch above. With a silent grunt, he hauled himself up, leaving the spear behind as it would have hindered him. Once on the branch, Snorri pressed his back against the trunk, waiting for the men hunting him.

"Where did he go?" An uncertain voice soon reached him.

"I don't know, this way I think." Snorri pictured a man pointing in the direction he had been running.

"Here, I found his tracks. The big bastard isn't that clever after all." A voice laughed.

"Aye, but be careful. I was told he is a good fighter." Snorri guessed that must have been the leader of the group and wondered who had told him that. If he remembered not to kill the man, he would ask him.

"It's like he just vanished," another said, his voice quivering.

"Well, if you idiots could shoot straight, then he'd be dead and we would be collecting our gold by now," the same voice as the man Snorri thought was the leader said.

"My arrow was going straight for him."

"Still missed though." A different voice. The men passed the old oak tree without stopping to look around. Danes definitely didn't know how to hunt. Snorri was glad he hid his spear in the trunk's crack. There were about twelve of them and, like Snorri had seen, most of them were wearing jerkins, although there were a few with only tunics. They walked close to each other, with not a single one looking backwards. If these had been his men, then Snorri would have gutted the last one. But then, if these had been Snorri's men, he'd be dead by now. A large raven landed on the branch Snorri was sitting on and opened its mouth. Snorri held his breath, praying the raven did not call out and give away his position. But the raven closed its mouth, tilting its head like it was watching to see what Snorri would do. Snorri thought the raven winked at him, but whether it did was not important. What was, was that the raven meant Odin was watching. The raven god wanted blood, and Snorri was about to give him some. Snorri slowly lowered himself from the branch when his pursuers had gone far enough. He took his spear from its hiding place and quietly stalked the last two men. Again, Snorri was glad they weren't spread out. With a quick glance over his shoulder, he saw the raven was still there. Still watching him with its mouth half open. Snorri turned his attention back to the Danes in front of him. Their eyes were glued to the front and not a single one of them looked behind. If they had, they would have seen Snorri stalking closer in a half crouch, spear in his hands and a wolf grin on his face.

Snorri was only a few paces away from the back two when he attacked. He shifted the spear to his left hand and took hold of Tyr's Fury's hilt with his right hand. He did not want to draw her too early and alert the men in front of him. Darting forward, Snorri thrust his spear through the back of the man on the left. He had no jerking on, so the sharp point of the spear easily slid through his back, piercing his lungs and heart as it burst out of his chest. The man grunted in shock, alerting his companion next to him. But Snorri had already let go of the spear and was drawing Tyr's Fury from her scabbard, turning the movement into a backhanded cut and slicing the man open from his stomach to his neck. The raven hopped from one branch to the next, screaming as blood sprayed through the air. Snorri moved onto the next man, this one alerted by the raven. Snorri twisted out of the way as the man stabbed his spear at him, using his left hand to deflect the strike, and thrust his sword through the man's neck. The Dane's eyes went wide in shock as he choked on the sword in his throat. Snorri twisted the blade and pulled it free. Hearing the commotion behind them, the group turned and Snorri smiled at their gaping mouths and raised eyebrows. Snorri swung his sword at the man closest to him, who jumped back to avoid the sharp blade and gave Snorri time to get away. He sprinted through the trees, away from the group as they came barging after him.

"There!" someone shouted, and less than a heartbeat later, three arrows flew past Snorri. Two of them went wide, but the third one sliced through his arm. Snorri twisted and turned as he ran, not to avoid any more arrows, but hoping that his pursuers would lose track of him amongst the trees. When it sounded like they were far enough behind, he ducked into a thick bush and dropped to the ground. Snorri checked his arm while he caught his breath. The cut was bleeding freely, but it wasn't deep. He just hoped he hadn't left a blood trail.

"Where is the bastard?" He heard from not too far away. The voice tried to sound strong, but couldn't hide the tremble of fear.

"He ran this way, I'm sure of it." The men were panting as they walked towards the bush he was hiding under. Snorri fingered the Mjöllnir around his neck, praying they didn't spot him. He briefly wondered where the raven was, but dismissed the thought as the men came close to the bush and stopped in front of it.

"Which way did he go?" It was the voice of the group's leader. Snorri saw their worn leather shoes from his hiding spot and wanted to get a better look at the man, but decided against it.

"He killed Helge and Asketill," one of the group complained.

"Don't forget about Baldur."

"And you let him get away!"

Snorri pictured them turning on the one he had swung his Tyr's Fury at. The man was still young, probably not much older than Ulf and Geir. He had probably thought this would be easy, but must have regretted coming along now.

"He... he c... came out of n... nowhere. I... I thought it w... was a d... draugr," responded the quivering voice.

"I thought the bastard was in front of us. How did he get behind us?"

"Told you to be careful," their leader responded. "Said he was dangerous."

"You also said it'll be easy gold for us!" A second pair of shoes came close, these newer than the first pair. Snorri pictured the two men squaring up to each other. He knew he needed to act before they spotted him. With a roar, Snorri jumped up and saw eight shocked faces. Their leader was turning to the noise behind him. Snorri kicked him in the back, sending the man flying into two of his companions while he sliced through the other's neck with his sword. Blood sprayed through the air as Snorri launched himself at the rest of them. Their shock made them slow to react, and Snorri's crazed laughter rooted their feet to the ground. He punched one man in the face with the pommel of Tyr's Fury, the man's head snapping back as blood gushed from his nose. Snorri was about to cut down another one when he realised it was the young man from before. The fear on his face and the wet patch between his legs reminded Snorri of Thorvald. Snorri hesitated for a heartbeat, which allowed one of the Danes to free his axe and attack him from behind. Snorri sensed the movement and twisted out of the way. The man missed Snorri but buried his axe into the young man, who screamed as the blood erupted from his chest. Before anyone could react, Snorri darted into the trees again. He had killed four, knocked one out, and the young man was dead as well. The remaining six roared in anger as they chased after Snorri. It was like hounds chasing the wolf — they believed they had the upper hand, but the wolf was always more dangerous than the hound.

Snorri heard them thrashing through the trees behind him. They were too close to allow him to hide and ambush them again, but now their blood was hot and that made them reckless. A shadow crossed his face and when Snorri looked up, saw a raven flying above. With a smile, he turned and charged at the six behind him. They had not expected this and the leading warrior died before he could even shout in surprise, Snorri slicing his chest open while drawing his sax-knife from his belt. With this, he stabbed another in the stomach. Snorri let go of the knife as the man fell. The next man stabbed out with his spear, which Snorri deflected upwards with Tyr's Fury. He shoulder barged the man, causing both of them to fall over. Snorri rolled onto his knees and blocked the sword coming at his face. He had to roll out of the way as another man swung an axe at him. The movement gave Snorri space to jump to his feet. He knew he could not give the remaining four men time to react, otherwise he would never get out of there alive. But Snorri was in his element. Fighting and bloodshed were what he lived for, more so than any of the men in his crew. Snorri was still laughing as he dodged a sword jab, grabbing hold of the man's arm and pulling him closer and headbutting him. The man dropped, like his spirit had been stolen, and Snorri moved onto the next man. It was the leader of the group. He was older than all of them, even Snorri, and judging from his beat-up jerkin, had been around for a while. He blocked Snorri's cut, but had to jump back as Snorri kicked out. Snorri dodged the spear which came from the side and swung a vicious cut at the man's face. The Dane tried to dodge the sword, but was too slow. Tyr's Fury sliced through his nose, cutting it in half. Snorri just had time to think that was a good reason to wear a helmet with a nose guard before he heard the twang of a bowstring. He ducked and felt the arrow fly over his head. When he looked up, he saw the arrow in the chest of the man whose nose he had cut in half, both of them looking at each other in surprise. Snorri turned and spotted the archer, his mouth agape at the realisation that he had just killed his own companion. Before the man with the arrow in his chest could drop, Snorri grabbed the spear from his hands and threw it at the archer, who was busy trying to load another arrow. The spear went through the man and embedded itself in the tree behind, holding the archer up as he died. Snorri sensed movement behind him and remembered the leader of the group was still there. His heart stopped, realising he could not turn in time to block the attack as the shadow loomed over him.

Loud thunder suddenly ripped through the forest air, vibrating off the trees. Snorri felt the movement behind him stop and saw the shadow move back. When he turned, the leader of his pursuers was staring at the trees, his face pale and his mouth working like he was trying to talk. Snorri turned to where the man was looking and saw a figure amongst the shadows. It looked half man and half forest as it stood tall with its arms stretched out wide. Instead of hands, it had giant hooves. Its black body, covered with branches which looked like they grew out of it, blended with the surroundings, making it hard to understand what was forest and what was the creature. There was no head, only branches and what looked like antlers. The sight of the creature made the Mjöllnir pendant around his neck feel heavy, and Snorri worried that the weight of it might cause him to collapse. He had thought there was no magic in these forests. He had thought the old gods were no longer here. Snorri was wrong.

"Odin, save me!" Snorri heard behind him and turned in time to see the leader of his attackers run away like a pig escaping the spit. He turned back to the creature as it was walking out of the trees, strange noises coming from where the head should be. Snorri tried to raise his sword, so he could defend himself, but Tyr's Fury was too heavy and he wondered if the creature had put a spell on him. What else could the strange noises it made be?

The creature stopped in front of Snorri as the forest around went quiet. Snorri raised an eyebrow, unable to make sense of the sight in front of him. The giant hooves he had seen weren't hooves at all, but small blackened pots. The shadowy body was a black cloak with branches sewn into it. A wrinkled face hid under the hood, covered with twigs and antlers. It was no forest demon, but an old man with his eyes closed and still chanting in his strange tongue.

Ulf moved the whetstone down the edge of Olaf's axe, taking comfort from the scraping sound of the stone against the metal. He had lost count of how many times he had sat here and sharpened the axe, but there was nothing else to do. Every day had been the same since they had arrived. They would wake up, have breakfast, usually porridge with bread, fresh meat if they got some from the raiding parties. But not all the Danes were happy about the Norsemen amongst them, so that rarely happened. After breakfast, it was just sitting and waiting, and sitting and waiting. Ulf had cleaned his armour so many times that his brynja shined brighter than the stars, and Ormstunga and Olaf's axe had been sharpened enough to cut through stone. But Ulf needed to keep busy. Unlike the rest of the crew, who spent most of the day sleeping and talking or just watching the Danes move about, Ulf needed to be distracted from his thoughts. The dream still bothered him, even though he had not had it since that night. He tried to understand what it meant and the only conclusion he kept coming to made him feel sick. Then there was the woman.

In the distance was a strange sound he had not expected to hear. A wolf howling. He turned to the sound and saw a large forest, its dark trees sticking into the sky like the fangs of a gigantic beast. Ulf felt the familiar fear creeping up his spine. But Ulf was drawn to the forest and before he knew what he was doing, he started walking to the trees. He looked for Olaf's axe, wanting to take a weapon with him, but the axe he had been sharpening not moments ago was gone. Before Ulf could wonder about that, he was amongst the trees. Their dark presence chilled him to the core, but he could not stop. The wolf howled again and Ulf was drawn to it, although he did not understand why. *The wolf is an animal associated with Tyr*, the thought came to him. Was Tyr trying to tell him something? *A giant wolf also bit Tyr's hand off.* Another thought interrupted the first. Ulf shivered and hoped that he was not walking towards Fenrir, Loki's offspring, who Tyr sacrificed his right hand to, so the gods could bind him. As Ulf walked into a clearing, a large grey wolf bounded past him. Something about the wolf seemed familiar, but before Ulf could understand what it was, a group of hounds broke from the trees and chased after it. Ulf had an urge to help the wolf, but he could not move. His legs would not obey him. All he could do was watch as the wolf turned and charged at the hounds. The hounds had not expected this and there was nothing they could do as the wolf jumped amongst them, ripping the throat off one and then biting another. A shower of black blood sprayed through the air, soaking Ulf. The hounds were no match for the wolf as it ripped them apart, but there were too many of them, and while the wolf was fighting one hound, another came from behind. Ulf tried to shout a warning, but his voice was gone. He could do nothing as the hound prepared to kill the wolf. But then the hound stopped, its eyes darting to the trees, a whimper escaping its throat. Ulf followed the hound's gaze and saw the trees come to life. Their branches turned to long arms with claws and hooves as their roots ripped from the ground to form legs. The tree monster looked at Ulf as a mouth full of sharp teeth appeared on its trunk. Ulf turned to the wolf and the hound. The hound was gone, and the wolf had hunched its shoulders as it bared its teeth at the tree monster, a low growl coming from its throat. Ulf made to run to the wolf, knowing that he had to stand by it, but then he felt something grab him from behind and yank him backwards.

Ulf sat up and rubbed his eyes. Around him, the camp was as he remembered it. His friends were sitting around their fire, some of them checking their equipment, others just relaxing. The noise of thousands of men hummed in his ears, while the smell of too many camps fires to count filled his nostrils. Somewhere in the distance, men laughed, and Ulf knew he was really awake. The laughter sounded happy, unlike the evil laughter from his dreams. Ulf's friends stared at him, Ragnar with a raised eyebrow. "What?"

"Must have been an interesting dream you were having," Oddi said.

"Aye, you looked like a dog chasing a rabbit," Asbjorn mocked. But the mention of the dog made Ulf remember his dream. There was something about the wolf that he could not place. He only knew the wolf was not him, which was strange because he normally dreamt of things involving him.

"How long have I been sleeping?" Ulf asked as he tried to distract himself from the dream.

"Not long," Oddi responded. That was strange. The dream felt like it was going on forever. Even stranger was the fact that Ulf had fallen asleep. He was normally too worked up to sleep during the day, unlike the rest of his friends.

"They're back," Brak announced. They all turned and watched the hunting party return.

"So many men and that's all they bring back?" Thorbjorn scratched his head. He was right. There were only a few deer and a handful of boar and not much else. He would have expected a large hunting party to bring back more. But as Ulf watched the group, something kept bugging him as his mind kept going back to his dream.

"I'd give Freya my left testicle in a bet that we're not getting much of that," Asbjorn said.

"Freya wouldn't want any of your testicles. She only likes real men," Ragnar responded. With his rough voice, it was hard to know if he was joking.

"He's not there." Ulf realised what was bugging him about the group.

"What?" Thorbjorn jumped to his feet.

"Snorri, he's not there," Ulf repeated. He scanned the group and spotted Tormod and Ubba, his white hair unmissable, but there was no sign of Snorri. Ulf's mind kept going back to the dream he had, but he was still struggling to make sense of it.

"What do you mean he's not there?" Magni used his tall frame to get a better look.

"Ulf is right." Oddi did the same. "I can't see Snorri either."

Ulf saw the concern on the faces of the hirdmen and Ragnar.

"Perhaps he stayed behind to find some meat for us," Drumbr suggested, although the sound of his voice showed he didn't believe himself either. "We all know how seriously he takes hunting."

"Could be," Thorbjorn said, if only to make them feel better.

"No, I think he is in trouble." Ulf frowned.

The others were about to reject what he said, but Oddi held up a hand. "Your dream?"

Ulf looked at Oddi, unsure of how to respond. He wasn't certain, but Ulf now wondered if the wolf in his dream was Snorri. Perhaps that was why it seemed so familiar to him. Ulf nodded to Oddi.

"Are we trusting his dreams now?" Asbjorn objected with a wave of his arms.

"Snorri does," Oddi responded. The men were silent as they looked at each other.

"What are we fucking waiting for then?" Thorbjorn asked. "There's only one way to find out." Without waiting for a response, he stormed towards the large group. The others fell behind, and Ulf saw the confused looks on the faces of the Sae-Ulfr's crew.

"There's Ubba, and Tormod." Drumbr pointed them out, and the group headed straight for the two men. The Danes stood up and watched the procession of the Norse warriors. No one seemed to be sure what was going on, but Ulf was glad the Danes didn't try to stop them. They were about fifty Norse warriors compared to over a thousand Danes. A fight between them would not end well. Ubba and Tormod noticed Snorri's men marching towards them, glancing at each other and shrugging.

"Where's Snorri?" Ragnar demanded. He was the oldest and most experienced warrior amongst them and the jarl's champion. None of the men from Thorgilsstad were going to argue about him taking the lead.

"Snorri?" Tormod asked, his frown making him look like a hound struggling to understand why it was not being fed. Tormod looked around the hunting party, his eyes opening wide as he noticed Snorri was not amongst them. "I don't know. I thought he was with Asgeir." Ubba nodded his agreement, looking just as confused as Tormod.

"What's going on?" Asgeir called as he approached them.

Ragnar turned to him and snarled with clenched fists. "Where's Snorri?"

Like Tormod and Ubba, Asgeir scanned the hunting party and seemed surprised not to find Snorri. "I thought he was with them." Asgeir pointed to Ubba and Tormod. "He was with us at one point, and then separated from us, to follow these two, I assumed."

"You left the group?" Oddi asked. His face seemed calm, but Ulf noticed the tension in his eyes.

"We saw tracks of a deer and followed," Ubba tried to explain as Tormod only shrugged.

Ragnar launched himself at Tormod, grabbing hold of his tunic and pulling him in as he growled in his face. None of the Danes moved, not even Ubba, who was standing beside Tormod. This was a Norse matter, and the Danes didn't care enough to get involved. "You are supposed to be keeping an eye on him for Halfdan, are you not?"

Tormod clenched his jaw as he stared at Ragnar. Ragnar might have been bigger and the better fighter, but Tormod was still a warrior and didn't like to be manhandled in front of others. "Snorri can look after himself. Odin knows that and so should you."

Asgeir moved between the men and pulled them apart, but Ragnar continued to glare at Tormod. "Perhaps Snorri is still hunting. Odin knows he seemed eager for the hunt this morning and from what he has told me, the man probably just needed some space." Those around him nodded as they agreed with Asgeir.

Oddi shook his head while the rest of the hirdmen frowned. "Snorri is not the type of man who needs space." Ulf scanned the group that appeared around them. It was mainly the men of Thorgilsstad wanting to know where their leader was, but also some of Tormod's crew had arrived. Ulf guessed they didn't like the way Ragnar was handling Tormod. He doubted they would start a fight over it. The two groups of Norsemen knew each other well and had fought many battles together. The

Danes looked bored and started moving away when they realised there would be no fight.

Ubba stepped forward, his arms spread. "I'll gather my men and together we can go look for Snorri." Snorri's hirdmen considered this as they glanced at each other.

"It'll be dark soon," one of Asgeir's men said. "You sure you want to be roaming in the forest when the sun is down? We don't know what spirits they have here."

Ragnar glared at the man, who shrank a little. "We are not afraid of the dark." Without waiting for anyone, he marched towards the forest.

"Speak for yourself," Thorbjorn muttered as he rushed to keep up with the large warrior. Ubba signalled for his men to follow as he and Snorri's hirdmen joined. The rest of the crew walked back to their camp as Ulf rubbed Olaf's axe and hoped nothing had happened to Snorri.

CHAPTER 18

Snorri kept glancing at the old man as they walked through the forest, unable to keep the smile off his face. The old man wasn't tall, only coming to Snorri's chest. His heavily wrinkled face had a large, veiny nose and two mismatched eyes. One blue, the other green. But despite looking as old as the trees, the man seemed strong as he walked at a pace Snorri was struggling to keep up with.

"Stop looking at me." The old man scowled. The words came out sounding strange, but Snorri guessed it was more because the old man had not spoken Norse for a long time and less to do with him having no teeth.

"I'm not," Snorri lied, laughing as the old man glared at him.

"Should have let that bastard kill you," the old godi muttered.

"Why did you help me?" Snorri couldn't stop himself from asking. He had been fighting long enough to know he would have been dead if the old man had not appeared. For all his pride in his skill as a warrior, Snorri could have never blocked an attack from behind like that. By the time Snorri stopped laughing at finding out that it was an old man who scared the warrior away, the leader of his attackers had disappeared into the forest. Snorri wanted to chase after the man, but the old man stopped him, saying it would be dark soon. Snorri settled on searching amongst the fallen, sure that he knocked at least one of them out. But he could find no one who was not dead.

"I had a dream which told me to come to the aid of a great wolf," the old man said in a gruff voice similar to Rolf's.

"A great wolf?"

"Aye, a great wolf fighting many hounds." Snorri wondered if all old people sounded like that.

"How did you know I was the great wolf?"

"I watched the whole fight from the beginning. You are the great wolf I was supposed to save."

Snorri puffed his chest out with pride. He couldn't wait to tell his friends about this, even if Thorbjorn would only mock him for it. But then Snorri thought about something else and frowned. "Why?"

"The gods don't tell me everything, but I guess you still have a part to play in their scheme."

"And what is their scheme?"

The old man turned to him. "Do you ask the birds why they don't swim, or the fish why they don't fly? I didn't think so," he said when Snorri shook his head. "You never ask the gods what their plans are."

Snorri nodded, understanding what the old man meant. "You trust the gods, no matter what path they set out for you."

The old man stopped and studied Snorri with his mismatched eyes. "You don't seem so sure anymore."

"I…" Snorri wasn't sure how to respond as he scratched the back of his neck. "I used to be. The gods have given me great glory, good friends, and strong sons. But recently, things have been different."

"Times have been challenging for you." The godi nodded. Snorri nodded in return, not wanting to talk about it anymore. "So when things go well, you trust in the gods, but when things get difficult, you question them?"

Snorri opened his mouth to respond, but then stopped. The old man had a point. "I've been urging Ulf to trust the gods, but now I find myself doubting them as well." He smiled. *I'm spending too much time with Ulf.*

"That's usually the way," the old man said. "It's easier to believe when things are going well. But that is not what true faith is."

"I understand."

"Do you!" The old man stood tall, and Snorri thought he was going to strike him. But then the old godi smiled and carried on walking, leaving Snorri confused. "I see you do," he said as Snorri caught up with him.

"You are from Norway?" Snorri glanced at the old man again, who nodded and looked at the trees as if they were speaking to him. Snorri remembered the old godi Ulf had told him about. "Why are you in Francia?" *The boy I raised betrayed me,* Snorri expected him to say, but the old man didn't.

"Many winters ago, I came across a woman who, like me, spoke to the gods. I thought this woman was my lifemate. We even had a child. A beautiful girl." The old man sighed at the memory. "But then my woman turned. She became obsessed with magic older than the Aesir. I tried to stop her, but she was too strong." He stopped and looked at his feet. "I had no choice but to run. I came here, hoping to hide from her and the gods."

"Did it work?"

The old man smiled. "The gods found me, and I thank them every day that she hasn't."

"Strange, I don't feel the gods in these forests." Snorri scanned the trees around him like he was hoping to find the gods standing there. But there were only the leaves rustling in the wind and small birds hopping from branch to branch in search of food.

The old man studied the trees, his eyes stopping to follow a squirrel running along a branch. "They are here. You just need to know where to look. But their presence is weak and always challenged by the Christian god." The old man took a deep breath. "He does not like to share his power with the other gods."

"But our gods will defeat him." Snorri beat his chest.

The old man raised an eyebrow at him. "How can you be so sure?"

"Because we have Odin, the most intelligent of all gods. We have Thor, the mightiest of them all and slayer of giants. Even Loki, with all his cunning, will join the gods in this fight."

The old man laughed. "I wish I had your confidence, young man." His face grew sad. "But I have been here a long time and from what I have learnt, I fear Ragnarök is coming. And it will not be the Ragnarök our sagas tell us about. There will be no mighty battle with the giants and the offspring of Loki. The gods will simply just vanish one day."

Snorri struggled to understand what the godi was talking about. "Impossible."

The old man gave him a sad smile. "What do you think is the fundamental difference between our gods and their god?"

Snorri scratched his head, trying to think of an answer to what he was sure was a trick question. "Our gods are many, their god is only one."

"Spoken like a warrior." The old man smiled. "But wrong. Our gods are wild and unruly. They drink, they fuck and they play games. They are all about emotions and chaos. Happiness, sadness, lust, anger and hate. Odin himself is the bringer of chaos. The gods of Asgard thrive on our emotions and that's why they like to play games with us." Snorri nodded. "But the Christian god, he has many rules. Too many, I feel, but he has many, and expects his followers to obey them." Snorri frowned, again lost at what the old man was getting at. The old man sighed. "Which army is more effective? The one which attacks with no order or discipline or the one where the men stand strong behind their shields and listen to the commands of their leader?"

This time, Snorri knew the answer. "The second one. Nothing can defeat a strong shield wall, especially not warriors charging at you aimlessly."

"Exactly." The old man wagged a bony finger at him, and Snorri felt like he'd been tricked. "In the end, the disciplined will defeat the unruly, and that's why I fear the days of our gods are numbered."

Snorri scratched his head. He had never thought about it like that, but then, he never spent any time thinking about the Christians or their god. They were just another people to raid, much like the people in north of Norway they would raid if they didn't want to be away for a long time. Even so, he could not believe that the Norse would ever give up their gods for the Christian god. The very things the old man mentioned as weaknesses were the things they loved about the gods. He was about to say the same to the old man when he heard voices echoing through the trees. Both he and the old man froze and scanned the forest. Snorri spotted movement in the shadows and without thought he stepped forward, drawing Tyr's Fury from her scabbard.

"There you fucking are!" Thorbjorn stepped into the clearing. "Odin knows we've been searching everywhere for you. What?" he asked when he noticed Snorri's wide eyes and his sword drawn.

Snorri just stared at his hirdmen as they came out of the shadows, all of them looking relieved to see him. Even Ulf wasn't scowling as much as he normally did.

"By Thor's balls, Snorri, what shit did you get yourself into this time?" Ragnar glanced at Snorri's sword, which had dried blood on it. More men walked out of the shadows, and Snorri recognised them as Ubba's men. The appearance of the white-haired warrior with a broad grin on his face confirmed that.

"What are you doing here?" Were the only words he could think of saying, even though it was obvious.

"Needed to find your body to bring it back to your mother," Thorbjorn retorted, unable to keep the smile from his face.

"Aye, but instead we find you alive and well, and not only that, but you are having a pleasant stroll talking to yourself," Brak said.

"Perhaps he lost his mind amongst the trees." Drumbr searched the trees like he was looking for something. "Asgeir warned us of the dangers of this forest."

Snorri frowned at them, unable to understand what they were talking about. He turned to the old man behind him and saw nothing but trees and shrubs. The old man he had spoken to moments ago was gone. Not a single trace of him left behind.

"What's he looking at?" Ubba asked.

"Not sure, but then he has always been a strange child," Ragnar said. Snorri turned when men laughed. All of them but Ulf, who was squinting at him.

"Did you not see him?" Snorri asked when his friends stopped laughing. They all looked at him like he had been dropped on his head.

"See who?" Oddi asked.

"There was an old man. He..." Snorri stared at the spot where the old man had been.

"Snorri, I'm sorry. Tormod and I thought you were with Asgeir. If we knew you were in danger, we would have tried to find you, so we could help," Ubba explained. Tormod was there too, but Snorri's former friend was hanging back and glancing at Ragnar.

"It's not your fault. I should never have left the group." Snorri paused as he remembered something. "Where did you two disappear to? One moment you were with me, and then you were gone."

"We found some tracks and followed them." Ubba shrugged. "But it came to nothing. We only found the group on the way back."

Snorri thought about Ubba's answer. He trusted Ubba and didn't think that he had anything to do with it, and despite his feelings towards Tormod, he doubted the man would have done anything like this, unless Halfdan told him to.

"We should get back, it's getting dark." Thorbjorn scanned the trees. "We don't know what creatures lurk amongst these trees." Snorri thought of the old man and how he had scared away the leader of the men who attacked him. "What?" Thorbjorn asked when he noticed the smile on Snorri's face.

"Come, my friends. I've got a story to tell you," he said as they turned back to the camp.

Snorri told them what had happened as they walked back to the camp. His men enjoyed the story, and so did Ubba, who was listening intently. But when Snorri described the old man, Ulf stopped in his tracks and looked back in the direction they came from.

"You sure?" he asked Snorri.

"As Odin is my witness." Snorri noticed the concern on Ulf's face and understood it. He had wondered the same thing.

"What is the young pup so upset over now?" Ragnar rolled his eyes.

"The old man Snorri described reminds me of the one who had rescued me." Ulf's face was tight with anger.

"The one killed by Vidar." Snorri saw the shock on the faces of his hirdmen and the annoyance on Ragnar's face. Ubba and Tormod looked confused, but then, they didn't know that tale.

"That's a long story," Oddi told them.

"Impossible! The gods know you can't come back from the dead," Thorbjorn said, but his face looked uncertain.

"Unless Ulf lied to us about what had happened to that old bastard," Asbjorn sneered. Snorri rubbed his forehead. He did not want to deal with this again. Ulf clenched his fists and grit his teeth. The relationship between Ulf and Asbjorn had always been strained, and Snorri guessed it always would be.

"You really think that Ulf lied to us about Vidar killing the old man?" Brak asked, his high voice showing he could not believe it.

"That old man is dead," Ulf growled as he took a step towards Asbjorn. "I saw it with my own eyes."

"But did you see Vidar kill him?" Asbjorn took a menacing step towards Ulf.

"Enough!" Snorri ordered and stepped between the two of them. "This ends now! We have enough problems at the moment and don't need you two fighting over something that happened a long time ago." He stared at both of them as he would at his young son when he had done something wrong.

"Snorri is right, friends," Ubba said. "I don't know this story, but you have someone here trying to kill you, and by the sounds of it, if it wasn't for this old forest man then Snorri might have been in Valhalla now instead of here."

"Aye, Valhalla almost seems more tempting now." Snorri smiled. His men laughed at that, but Snorri saw the doubt in Ulf's face. What Asbjorn had said struck like an arrow in the chest. Snorri believed Ulf when he had told them the story of Vidar, but he had to admit he found it strange that the old man here looked so much like the one Ulf had described to them.

They walked back to the camp, the men forgetting the confrontation between Ulf and Asbjorn. Instead, they were asking Snorri more about the fight. As expected, Thorbjorn laughed when Snorri told them the old man had called him a great wolf, and Snorri knew his short friend would make fun of him about that for a while yet. But the smile on Snorri's face disappeared as they got to the camp and he saw Asgeir standing there waiting for them. At first Asgeir seemed relieved to see Snorri, but soon his face looked concerned when Snorri launched himself at the leader of this great raid. Snorri grabbed Asgeir by his tunic, almost pushing the man over as he snarled in his face. All around them, Danish warriors grabbed their weapons. The sounds of so many swords being pulled out of their scabbards sounded like a rock breaking away from the mountain. Snorri sensed his men draw their own weapons and stand around him, ready to protect him.

"Snorri! What, in Odin's name, are you doing?" Tormod shouted, his face pale. If a fight broke out now, the Danes would kill him and his men as well.

"Somebody sent men to kill me in the forest," Snorri growled. He searched Asgeir's face and saw the confusion.

Asgeir signalled for his men to calm down, and although they took a step back, they did not put their weapons away. "Snorri, I swear on my forefathers I had nothing to do with that. If I wanted you dead, I could have slaughtered you and your men in this camp. And you know it." Snorri was impressed at how calm Asgeir seemed. His steely eyes never wavered, and he even smiled as he spoke. It made Snorri like him even more. He let go of Asgeir and patted him on the chest.

"Then who sent twelve armed men into the forest to kill me?" He scanned the faces of the men around Asgeir. He knew they were Asgeir's closest friends, but none of them looked like they knew what he was talking about.

"They were unsuccessful then, I take it," one man near Asgeir said, scratching his beard. The comment earned him a smack from his companion, but that broke the tension as those around smiled.

"Came close enough." Snorri showed his arm, which had been cut by the arrow. It had stopped bleeding now, but the skin around the cut felt tight and his green sleeve was now brown.

"Any of the men still alive?" Asgeir asked. "We could question them, find out who had sent them."

Snorri shook his head. "I killed most of them, and two got away." He decided not to mention the old man. He did not want these Danes searching through the forest for him.

Asgeir looked disappointed, like he would have enjoyed torturing someone, but in the end he just shrugged. "Well, I'm glad they didn't kill you today, because soon we attack the city and it would have been a pity if you missed out on that." He smiled at Snorri, who couldn't help but smile back.

"Odin knows not even Valhalla can keep me from taking part in the raid." All around them, men cheered at the prospect of ending days of doing nothing. A thunderous sound that must have sent shivers down every spine behind the walls of Rouen.

The overcast morning began with a boom as the battering rams struck the gates of Rouen. For the last two days Asgeir's army had cut down trees to build them, as well as scaling ladders. It had taken time to find the best trees, but like the Norse, the

Danes were expert shipbuilders and knew how to find the right ones for their needs. After the trees were chopped down, they were cleaned and their ends hardened with fire. Ulf had never seen this done before and didn't believe that these battering rams could break through the gates of the city that had been taunting them for days. Now Ulf watched as the men, given the honour of breaking down the gates, swung the battering ram back and crashed it against the gates again. There were ten men on each side of the enormous tree trunk, and another twenty holding shields to protect them from the archers on the walls. Ulf ground his teeth as an arrow found its mark and one of the Danes, a big man with a shaved head, collapsed. The shield bearer beside him dropped his shield and replaced the man who had died. The battering ram struck the gate again, the blow vibrating through him, even though they were standing back, out of the reach of those arrows. Snorri's men would be first to go through the gate on this side of the city. They wanted to break down the gates, eager to show the Danes how it was done, but Asgeir had already given the honour to one of his captains. A small man with a tattoo covering the left half of his face and with a fierce reputation. Ulf watched as the captain sent another man with a shield to replace the one who had fallen. Asgeir was attacking one of the other gates to the city, the one by the river. The plan was to attack all the gates at the same time and spread the defenders thin across the city. Asgeir's captain spoke to a man next to him, who nodded and raised a horn to his lips, blowing three long notes. The Danes beside them roared as they charged at the walls. Five groups, each with scaling ladders. It would be up to them to deal with the archers on the walls.

"Don't envy those bastards." Thorbjorn surprised Ulf.

"Aye, don't want to be going to Valhalla with an arrow in the eye. You'll never hear the end of it." Drumbr leaned on his two-handed axe.

The first group reached the wall and pushed the long ladder into place as a Danish warrior started climbing up, holding his shield above his head with one hand. No arrows were aimed his way, which Ulf found strange. Instead, the defenders gathered by the ladder and Ulf could not understand what they were doing as another boom echoed through the air.

"That can't be good," Ragnar said when they lifted a large pot over the walls. Ulf watched with wide eyes as they poured steaming water down the ladder, the screams of the Danes rattling through his spine. The men rubbed or kissed the Mjöllnir pendants around their necks, and Ulf couldn't help but stroke the haft of Olaf's axe. The defenders pushed one of the other ladders over, the Danes screaming as they fell amongst their comrades to the cheers of the Franks.

"We'll never get into that city." More men fell off the ladders, this time because of the archers they were supposed to kill.

Snorri smiled at him, and Ulf knew what he was going to say. "Trust in the gods."

Ulf was about to retort when the battering ram struck the gate again, this time sounding different from before. He knew what it meant when he saw the wolf grin on Snorri's face. Snorri punched Tyr's Fury into the air.

"Men of Thorgilsstad! Men of Halfdan! Attack!" Around Ulf the Norsemen roared loud enough the wake the gods. Ulf pulled Ormstunga from her scabbard, feeling the sword come to life in his hand, and charged at the gate with his friends. The archers faltered at the sound, allowing the Danes on the ladders a chance to get on the walls as the battering ram swung once more and the gates exploded, spraying splinters all over the defenders of the city. The Danes dropped the ram and charged ahead of Snorri's men.

"Fucking bastards." Thorbjorn panted as he struggled to keep up with the taller men around him.

The flames coursed through Ulf's veins. He had not wanted to be on this raid. He did not care about the path the gods had laid out for him. Ulf's anger fed the flames as they spread through his limbs. His brynja felt lighter than ever and his helmet focused his vision on what was in front of him. He knew there would be farmers and women in the city. But there would also be warriors. And they were going to suffer from his fury.

Ulf roared with the men around him as they charged through the broken gates. He had never seen anything like this city in his short life and got distracted by the many stone houses, some of them built on top of each other. But he had no time to think about it as Frankish warriors charged at them from all directions, desperate to defend their homes. The defenders didn't look too different from the Scandinavian attackers. Some wore brynjas, just like the one Ulf was wearing, while others had leather jerkins or just tunics. Even their weapons were similar. Ulf saw men with swords like theirs, axes and spears. Some had clubs and there were a few with only sax-knives. Only their conical helmets with nose guards were different.

"Tyr!" Ulf roared, summoning his courage as the two forces stormed towards each other. There was no call for a shield wall from Snorri as Ulf lifted his shield to block a blow from a Frank. The man had a club, and Ulf felt the blow rattle down his arm. Brak appeared beside him, slicing through the man's neck with his sword, Bear Claw, and covering both men in a spray of blood as they rushed past. Another Frankish warrior charged at Ulf, spit flying from his mouth. Ulf stepped aside as the man cut down with his sword and stabbed him in the side with Ormstunga. He could almost hear the sword sing in joy as she got to slake her thirst for blood. Ulf twisted the blade and pulled her out, just in time to raise his shield to block an arrow fired at them from the rooftops.

"Archers!" Asbjorn warned, and everyone lifted their shields to block the rain of arrows. Ulf hated how the Franks used bows in battle. He hated how insecure they made him feel. All he could do was cower under his shield, flinching each time an arrow struck the wood and praying to the gods that one didn't find a way through. From the few screams, it seemed like the gods could not respond to everyone. Ulf glanced back along the wall and saw the Danes, who had climbed the ladders, fighting more defenders. There was nothing they could do about the archers on the rooftops. The Frankish warriors had backed off as the arrows came down, and Ulf sensed what would happen before it even did. As soon as the arrows stopped raining down, the defenders charged at them, catching the Norse warriors off guard. A large warrior with a blond beard barged into Ulf, almost knocking him off his feet. Before Ulf could regain his balance, the man turned on his heels and swung a large two-handed axe in a wide arc. Ulf dropped to the ground, hearing the axe slice through the air above his head before it buried itself into another man. Jumping to his feet, he stabbed the large Frankish warrior through the stomach. The Frank stared at him, eyes wide in shock as the blade carved through vital organs. Ulf pulled Ormstunga free, the man muttering something, before Ulf sliced his neck open. His heart started beating faster in his chest, feeding the flames deep inside him. The heat of it coursing through his limbs as the voices of his ancestors continued to whisper in his ears. The first time Ulf had heard them, he hated them. Feared them even as he did not understand what they were. But now he understood what these voices were. They were his ancestors fighting alongside him. Their blood, the blood of Tyr, coursed through his veins and with it came their experience, feeding the flames of his constant anger. It drove him onto move faster than those around him. To understand what they were going to do before they knew it themselves. It was what made him sense the spear behind him, aiming for the back of Snorri. Ulf turned, chopping the shaft in half with Ormstunga, and punched its wielder in the face with the rim of his shield. Even Snorri heard the man's skull crack as he crumbled to the ground, blood, snot and brains leaking out of his nose.

"We're even now." Ulf grinned at Snorri when he saw the surprise on his friend's face.

Snorri smiled back. "Not quite. There's still the bear and the battle at the Giant's Toe." He laughed as he plunged into the thick of the fight again. Ulf could only smile and shake his head.

The houses around the square started burning as men threw torches onto the thatch roofs, forcing the archers to run. Some jumped from the roofs straight into the battle raging below them as they fled the flames. Frankish defenders struggled to match the ferocity of the Norse warriors and were being pushed out of the square they were fighting in. The Danes outside the city charged through the gates, eager to join the fight, and soon the defenders of Rouen were outnumbered.

Ulf deflected another spear with his shield and stepped into the man, headbutting him. The young Frank was not wearing a helmet and came away with a bloody forehead as Ulf opened his chest with Ormstunga, before moving onto the next one. The defenders were thinning out as most of them died and others ran. Some of the Norse warriors stormed into the houses, looking for anyone who thought it would be safer to hide away. Ulf heard the screams from inside the houses, but the voices in his head took his attention away from the cries of the Frankish women and back to the fight, looking for another enemy to kill. What Ulf saw instead stilled them completely.

Through the smoke that drifted over the square, Ulf saw a young man with light-coloured hair and a dirty face smiling at him from one of the streets. He wanted to rub his eyes, just to make sure the smoke wasn't playing any tricks on him, but the eye guard on his helmet was in the way. Ulf looked around him, trying to find one of his friends, so he could ask them if they saw the same thing he did. Geir was fighting a Frankish defender, the young warrior doing well against a more experienced fighter. Ulf was about to help him, but when he looked back down the street, the boy was gone. Ulf stared at the spot, his mouth agape. This was just like in Suðrikaupstefna and, just like then, Ulf was convinced of what he had seen. Vidar.

Ulf knew Snorri would be furious if he ran off on his own. The last time Ulf had done that, a group of Danish warriors had attacked him. But he could not just stay here amongst the safety of his friends as the fight moved away from where he had seen

Vidar. After a quick glance around, Ulf ran down the alley. He had to make sure. Vidar had died at the hands of Griml, but this was the second time he had seen his friend. Halfway down the street, Ulf heard a scream. It was not a woman being raped or a warrior being killed, but a young man swinging a club at him. Ulf spotted it too late and couldn't turn out of the way in time. He felt the wooden club strike him, but instead of the dull pain he expected, he felt a sharp burn deep in his shoulder. He looked at it in surprise and saw some of the links of his brynja broken and blood leaking out of the cut. The dark-haired Frank laughed at him and Ulf realised what had caused the damage. A nail sticking out of the top of the club. The nail had gone in between the links and broken them as it ripped through his skin. The fire inside of Ulf exploded as he launched himself at his attacker, moving faster than the boy could react. Ulf punched him in the face with the pommel of Ormstunga and, as the young man's head snapped back, kicked him in the chest. Ulf stood there panting as he watched the young Frank flying through the air before collapsing to the ground. He wasn't sure if he had killed the boy, but with the heat of his anger bubbling through his veins, he didn't care. Ulf kicked the club away and rushed to the spot where he had seen Vidar. But just like in Suðrikaupstefna, there was no sign that the boy had ever been there. Nothing even to show where he might have gone. Still staring at the spot, he sensed movement near him. When Ulf looked up, his blood froze and his heart stopped.

"We meet again, Bear-Slayer."

CHAPTER 19

Ulf felt like he was caught in a sea storm again as he stared at the two people he had never expected to find here. The woman wore a deer hide dress, with twigs and small bones tied in her black hair. They should not be here. Especially not him. He towered over the woman and had shoulders broader than any Ulf had ever seen. His arms and legs were like tree trunks and his thick neck supported a small head which looked out of place on the massive body. Small beady eyes filled with hate stared at him over a large nose and mouth. The scar which Ulf had given him so long ago had not healed well and left an ugly mark on his already ugly face. He sported the same hairstyle as Thorbjorn, the sides of his head shaved and covered in tattoos, his long hair tied up. There was a large scar on his arm, a token from the battle at The Giant's Toe, which had healed better than his face. Ulf struggled to breathe as he stared at the man who had killed his family and sacrificed his best friend to Odin. Griml.

"I've been waiting for this." The rough voice, which sounded like a mountain collapsing, shook Ulf to his core. He stared at the pair with wide eyes as his mind tried to make sense of what he was seeing.

"I think he is surprised to see us here." The woman smiled. She stood tall and straight, but still only reached half the height of the man who could be described as a giant troll. Griml smiled at Ulf, his enormous mouth parting his thick beard from his moustache to reveal blackened teeth. Ulf took half a step back. Not because he was afraid. Ulf was too shocked to be afraid. He wanted to look down the street he had come from, hoping that his friends had seen him standing here and were on their way to him. But he could not take his eyes away from the unlikely pair. The two of them stared at Ulf in return. Two vastly different stares. The woman looked at him the way a fox looked at freshly hatched chicks, and Ulf could almost see her lick her lips the way the fox would. Griml's stare was as terrifying as always. Those soulless eyes of his always made you feel you were being sent to the afterlife. There was no life in them, no emotion other than pure hatred for the world and a constant want of destruction. Ulf wondered what the gods had done to Griml to make him hate life so much. The thought broke his trance and Ulf took a deep breath through clenched teeth as he stoked the fire inside him, which had gone cold at the sight of these two.

"Ah, there he is. There is the famous Bear-Slayer, the hero of The Giant's Toe," the woman mocked. Griml sneered at the mention of the place of his defeat.

"You have my sword, boy." The giant troll took a step forward.

Ulf gripped the hilt of Ormstunga tighter. "She was never yours." He took half a step forward, finding courage as his anger surged through his body. "You took her from my family."

"You still whining about that." Griml looked bored, which only fanned the flames already burning inside of Ulf.

The woman stroked Griml's thick arm, surprising Ulf with her tenderness. "The boy has suffered much, just like you, Griml." She smiled a blackened, toothy grin.

"I'm not like him," Ulf growled. Images from his dream on the farmstead came to his mind. The ugly troll turning into him. *You are me*, it had said.

"Are you so sure?" The woman raised an eyebrow.

"He will suffer much more before I finish with him," Griml said. The woman's only response was her fox-like smile.

Ulf took another step forward, his limbs trembling from the anger raging through them. Griml hefted his enormous axe, larger than the ones carried by Drumbr and Ragnar. He wore no brynja this time. Griml had nothing on but trousers and boots, his bulging chest muscles rippling as he tightened his grip on the axe.

"Ah, look Griml. The boy wants to play. Why don't you show him how much you have missed him," Griml sneered at Ulf as the woman said this. Lifting his axe above his head with a roar, Griml charged at Ulf.

The ground shook beneath his feet as Ulf willed his ancestors to come to his aid. But despite the heat of his anger rushing past his ears, they remained silent. Gripping his shield tighter, he charged at Griml, not wanting to wait for the monster to reach him. If this caught Griml by surprise, he didn't show it. The giant man brought his axe down at an angle, forcing Ulf to duck and lift his shield at the same time. He felt the searing pain in his shoulder from the cut as Griml's axe struck the top of his shield, the force of the blow almost ripping his arm away. Ulf turned, hoping to attack Griml's now unguarded side. But Griml moved faster than Ulf expected him to, and by the time Ulf faced him, Griml was ready to attack again. Ulf jumped back to avoid Griml's axe as the troll chopped down with it. He swung Ormstunga at Griml's face as soon as the axe struck the ground. But Griml dodged out of the way. Ulf took a step back, wanting to give himself some space as Griml grinned savagely. He looked at his shield, wincing at the pain in his shoulder, and saw the top half of it missing. Ulf thanked the gods the blow had not been lower. Griml's speed surprised him. Ulf was fast. It was his best weapon in fights, but in the opening exchange, Griml moved a lot faster.

"Don't look so surprised, boy. Many have thought the same and paid for it with their lives." Griml read Ulf's thoughts. Ulf could only stare. Blood was running down his arm, soaking his hand and making it hard to hold onto the shield. He was also aware of the woman now standing behind him, the hairs on his neck standing on edge as he worried what she might do. Griml charged at Ulf with another roar. Ulf threw his shield at him, grunting at the sharp pain in his shoulder, but the troll blocked it with his enormous arm, the blow not even slowing him down. He swung his axe at Ulf, who did everything he could to avoid it, while also trying to find a way past Griml's guard. But with each attack and each dodge, he could not get close to Griml. All the while, the woman just stood there, yawning as the two men fought each other.

After another brief exchange, they parted. Ulf was panting, trying to catch his breath. Griml only smiled menacingly. "Not bad, better than the old bastard on the farm that day."

Ulf grit his teeth at the mention of his uncle. Olaf had been a good warrior and had died defending his family. The family Ulf might have saved if he hadn't been so cocky. He took Olaf's axe from his belt, willing his uncle's spirit to come help him.

"I think the young wolf's upset now." The woman smiled.

Griml laughed and charged again. Ulf's head exploded as the voices of his ancestors screamed at him to kill the bastard troll. Griml had insulted their honour and for that, he had to pay. Before Griml was halfway to Ulf, he launched into his own attack. His vision became sharp enough to see the dirt trapped in Griml's pores and lice crawling in his beard. Griml swung his axe, and instead of dodging out of the way, Ulf ducked underneath. For the first time, he got past Griml's guard. Ulf sliced at Griml, feeling Ormstunga cut into his side. The cut was not deep as Griml was moving away from it, but for Ulf, it was a minor victory. As he rushed past Griml, he turned and launched himself into the air, hoping to bury Olaf's axe deep into Griml's back. But somehow Griml moved out of the way and deflected the blow with his axe. Ulf attacked again as soon as his feet hit the ground, swinging Olaf's axe at Griml's face and stabbing at his stomach with Ormstunga. Griml twisted out of the attack, but not before Ulf cut Griml again. Ulf stabbed out once more, but this time, Griml grabbed hold of his arm and threw Ulf through the air. Ulf bounced off the stone wall, the blow knocking the air out of him, before landing on the ground. *At least I kept hold of my weapons*, he thought as he struggled to catch his breath. His shoulder was numb, but the voices in his head, his ancestors, urged him to get up. Ulf pushed himself onto his elbows, half expecting Griml to come finish him. But the ugly troll only stood there, sneering at him, his side bleeding from where Ulf had cut him. Ulf saw other slight cuts, but none of them seemed to affect the beast as he waited for Ulf to get up.

"This is the famous warrior who defeated your army so easily?" the woman mocked, but Ulf saw the admiration in her different-coloured eyes. Griml grunted and swung his axe in a circle as if he was loosening his shoulder. Ulf struggled back to his feet, using the wall to support him. He wondered how he was going to defeat Griml. Ulf had given it everything he had, but had not managed to kill him. *Don't give up*, the voice in his head said. Ulf was not sure if it was his or his uncle's. He took a deep breath, trying to keep the flames of his anger alive. He would need them to get through this fight and did not want them to disappear because of his doubt. As Ulf caught his breath, he watched Griml swing his axe in giant loops, waiting for the right moment. As soon as the axe was in the air, Ulf attacked.

"Tyr!" he roared as he launched himself at Griml, forcing his limbs to move faster than before. The attack caught Griml off guard. His axe was already swinging down, which meant Griml could not bring it up in time to block Ulf's attack. Ulf swung Ormstunga in a wide arc, forcing Griml to take a step backwards. Ulf followed by punching Griml with the head of Olaf's axe. The blow caught Griml on the chin, his head snapping back as Ulf's shoulder protested in a burst of pain. Griml's nostrils flared as the blood from his cut chin seeped into his beard.

Griml bellowed in fury, swiping his axe at Ulf. Ulf dodged out of the way before attacking again, swinging Olaf's axe at Griml's neck. Again, Griml twisted out of the way and before Ulf could do anything, kneed him in the side. Ulf crashed to the ground again, using all his willpower not to drop his weapons. Gasping in pain, he rolled onto his back, so he could block any attack that might come, but again, Griml stepped back. Ulf wondered if Griml was just playing with him, wanting him to suffer before he killed him.

"Just stay down, young wolf," the woman said as Ulf struggled back to his feet. His shoulder screamed at him and his back protested, but Ulf ignored her. This time, Griml didn't wait for him to get to his feet. Ulf just avoided Griml's axe as it sliced through the air, his side protesting at being forced to move. He stabbed out with Ormstunga, but there was no real force behind it and Griml easily batted it away.

"Pathetic." Griml stepped back. Ulf smiled through the pain, forcing himself to stand straight. He was hurting everywhere, but Griml was bleeding all over from where Ulf had cut him. Ulf just wished he had landed a killing strike. It still surprised Ulf at how fast and agile Griml was. No matter what he tried, he could not land a strong enough blow to hurt Griml. It was like trying to break a mountain. The voices in his head disappeared at that thought. But Ulf refused to give in. He grit his teeth as Griml charged again, his face creased in fury. Ulf stepped aside from another downward swing, using Olaf's axe to steer Griml's axe away from him. He stabbed at Griml with Ormstunga, aiming for the man's chest. But Griml turned faster than Ulf expected and avoided the sword while bringing his axe around. There was nothing Ulf could do as the blade came for his head. At the last moment, Griml twisted the axe so the flat side struck Ulf on the side of his head. The blow rattled his mind as his helmet absorbed most of the hit. Through blurry vision, Ulf looked at the woman as she nodded at Griml. Suddenly, he knew exactly who she reminded him of, but before he could say anything, he saw Griml's boulder-like fist and then nothing.

Snorri watched from over the rim of his shield as the defenders of Rouen fled. Around him, his men held their ground with shields in front of them. The Franks had already retreated once to allow their archers to strike. But this time, there were no archers, so Snorri lowered his shield and looked around. His hirdmen and friends smiled at him with savage grins. Even Magni, for once, looked like a real Norse warrior. The sounds of battle still raged — somewhere a child was crying, likely with no parents around to calm it. Snorri took his helmet off and wiped the sweat from his forehead as Tormod walked towards him. The man was smiling for the first time in days, and Snorri understood why. There was nothing like a good fight to help a warrior relax.

"I think we've won this side of the city." Tormod also took his helmet off to wipe the sweat from his face. He looked in the direction where there were still sounds of fighting.

"Asgeir's not done yet," Snorri said.

"His men here have gone to help him," Ragnar said. "We going to let them have all the fun over there?" Ragnar's shoulders were hunched. The champion obviously had not done enough fighting.

Snorri studied his men, taking in their blood-covered faces and grim stares. They looked tired. The fight had been hard, but they had expected that. The worst thing had been the archers, their arrows catching many by surprise. Quick thinking by someone had solved that problem, and Snorri reminded himself to find out who that person was. They deserved an extra arm ring for that. But the fire was spreading fast, leaping from roof to roof, and Snorri wondered how much of the city would survive this day. His chief concern though, was whether to join Asgeir's men and fight the remaining defenders of the city. The idea sounded good, but Snorri was worried. There were many small streets and hiding places. He was still aware of the Danish group that was after them, even if he didn't know who the leader of the group was. The last thing Snorri wanted was to take his men into another ambush. And where better for an ambush than in a large city in the middle of a battle.

"Snorri?" Thorbjorn asked. The short warrior was eagerly looking at the houses. Snorri knew what his friend was thinking. Many of his men, in fact.

"You're concerned about another ambush?" Oddi's sharp eyes studied Snorri.

"Aye."

"By Odin, are we going to live the rest of our lives in fear?" Ragnar shook his head. Snorri ground his teeth as Ragnar glared at him. But Ragnar was not responsible for the lives of these men.

"Showing caution is not fear, Ragnar. Or would you call my father afraid?" Snorri's father was a cautious man and never went into any situation without being prepared. *The raven watches and learns*, was his father's favourite saying. Ragnar didn't respond, as Snorri knew he wouldn't. Jarl Thorgils was anything but afraid, even if he was a broken man now. His father would have loved to be part of this. He had always told Snorri about the days of his youth when they raided this land.

"My men and I will stick with you, no matter what you decide," Tormod offered, bringing Snorri back.

"Where's Ulf?" Drumbr scratched under his helmet as he searched for the young warrior. Snorri scanned the helmeted heads around him. Drumbr was right. Ulf's wolf helmet was nowhere to be seen.

"Tyr's arse!" Thorbjorn exclaimed. "He was right here. I was fighting beside him the whole time." Thorbjorn took his helmet off and Snorri saw his wrinkled brow.

"Perhaps he had fallen?" Magni suggested.

"No, Ulf is protected by Odin," Brak said, echoing the belief most of them had.

Tormod scratched his face, leaving a few white lines on his blood-covered cheek. "I doubt those arrows cared about that."

"Brak is right." The white lines left on Tormod's face were like those left on Ulf's after the bear fight. Odin had been watching then, just as Odin must be watching now. Snorri scanned the air, looking for one of Odin's ravens. There were many scavenging birds already circling above them. Any of them might be Huginn or Muninn.

"We should check the bodies anyway. He might not be dead, but could have been injured," Ragnar suggested.

"Aye," Snorri said, "and not just for Ulf." Snorri had lost more men than he wanted to. "Those archers were bastards." He thought about the cut to his arm, which was bleeding again.

"So we will not fight anymore today?" Magni asked, his shoulders dropping.

"The day is still young. There's plenty of time for more fighting," Ragnar said.

Snorri nodded. "But first, we take care of our men here."

"I can do that while you carry on fighting," Oddi offered. That was the way they would normally do things. Snorri would take most of his men and follow the fight, while Oddi stayed behind with a few men to deal with the wounded and dead. But this was not a normal raid. They faced risks they still didn't understand. The Danes who had attacked them before might be fighting with them now, just waiting for the right moment to attack them again. Snorri did not want to risk it.

"No, we stick together." Oddi nodded. Snorri knew his friend understood the situation. All of his hirdmen did.

It didn't take them long to go through the wounded and dead. Snorri had lost six men, two dead and four seriously wounded. Most of them by arrows. Tormod had four dead. Some men had to be dragged out of the houses, complaining at first, but quickly calming down when they saw the glare of Ragnar Nine-Finger.

"No Ulf," Drumbr said when they finished. Some men were looting the Frankish dead and injured. Snorri didn't stop them.

"Fuck," Snorri muttered, looking around the city. They were in what looked like a market square, with many streets going in different directions. It was one of the biggest cities Snorri had ever raided.

"The gods know it'll take us all day to search for that bastard and we still might not find him." Asbjorn scowled.

"Asbjorn is right," Ragnar said. "You know we can't search for him, even Odin's ravens will have a hard time finding him in this place."

Snorri scanned the sky again, wishing he could ask Odin's ravens to do just that. He sighed. "Did anyone see where the Bear-Slayer had gone?" Hopefully one if his men might have seen something.

Geir stepped forward. He was limping slightly from a cut to his leg, but it didn't look too serious. "I saw him looking down that street during the fight. Thought it was strange —"

"Why didn't you say something sooner!" Thorbjorn shook a fist at the young fighter.

Geir paled. "I only saw him looking down the street, then I was attacked. By the time I finished the bastard, Ulf was gone." He shrugged. "Just thought he had rejoined the fight."

Thorbjorn growled at Geir, but Snorri placed a hand on his shoulder. Geir was a good fighter and had a smart head on his shoulders. Snorri knew he would be a great warrior one day. "You sure it was that one?" Snorri pointed Tyr's Fury at the street. Geir nodded. "Oddi, pick some men, watch the wounded. We will check down there. If we find nothing, then we'll come back." Oddi nodded.

"Thought you said we stick together?" Tormod asked.

"I did, but we aren't going far." Snorri signalled to his men and they went down the street where Geir had last seen Ulf. "Stay together, and keep your eyes open!" Snorri ordered his men. Shields raised, they walked through the smoke-filled alley with Snorri in the lead, Ragnar and Thorbjorn on either side of him. The flames raged above their heads as they crept along. Snorri wondered if this was what it was like to enter Muspelheim, the home of the fire giants. Halfway through the alley, they found a young man lying on the ground, his face bloody and bruised, and a club with a bloody nail sticking out of the top near him. Snorri glanced at Thorbjorn, who only shrugged, and they moved on. They made it to the other side with no incident, but what they found there almost took Snorri's breath away.

"Is that..." Thorbjorn couldn't get the words out. Snorri had never seen his friend lost for words.

"What does it mean?" Drumbr's hand went to the Mjöllnir around his neck.

"It means the gods are laughing at us," Snorri growled as he looked at Ulf's axe embedded in the ground. Around it, smeared in blood, was the symbol for Freya.

"Thor's balls!" Ragnar spat. "This is the last time I go on a raid with you, Snorri."

"I told you to stay in Thorgilsstad," Snorri responded as he looked around. He was not sure what he was looking for, but was hoping there would be something which would tell him what had happened to Ulf. He saw the fresh blood on the haft, rivulets of it running down to the axe head, and feared the worst for his friend. No one wanted to go near the axe, but Snorri knew he could not leave it there. Ulf would not be happy if he did. *If Ulf is still alive,* the thought came before he could stop it. Snorri walked up to the axe, not wanting to ask any of his men to do it. He knew most of his hirdmen would. Ulf was like a brother to all of them, but if this was a curse, then he didn't want it placed on his men.

"Careful," Drumbr warned, still rubbing the Mjöllnir around his neck. Snorri saw all his men do the same. Snorri's own hand unconsciously grabbed his own Mjöllnir pendant. He felt the strange comfort that came from rubbing the symbol of Thor.

Squatting down, he spotted something carved on the handle of the axe. Snorri knew Ulf had carved the names of his family on it when he had sworn to kill Griml. Since then, he had added the names of Hulda and Vidar. But someone had carved a new name on the handle. Snorri looked at it, trying to understand what it meant. The blood still looked wet, so this had happened recently. He looked around, squinting as he surveyed the area. Whoever had done this could still be around.

"Argh!" the shout came from behind, and as Snorri turned, he saw one of his men go down to an arrow.

"Archers!" Ragnar roared, lifting his shield over his head. All the men did the same, grouping together at the same time. Without thinking, Snorri grabbed the axe and ran back to his men as the arrows hit the dirt where he had just been. It was the second time he ran from archers, and Snorri was getting sick of it. As soon as he reached his men, Asbjorn handed him his shield. Danish warriors streamed down one of the streets towards them.

"We're fucked," Thorbjorn muttered, but Snorri saw the smile on his face. Thorbjorn was right. There were more Danes this time. A lot more. Whoever had organised the last ambush had learnt their lesson.

"What do we do, Snorri?" Tormod asked. Snorri glanced at the man. There was no fear in his eyes, but Snorri understood the concern he saw instead. Tormod was responsible for his men, and like Snorri, he would not want to throw their lives away.

"Back to Oddi!" Snorri needed to get the rest of his men and find a way out of there. *Thor protect us*, he prayed as the Danes charged at them. "Spread out! Make sure there are no gaps." The street wasn't very wide, which meant his men could create a shield wall from wall to wall. The only danger was the fires burning above them as smoke filled the street. It made breathing harder, but Snorri hoped it would also blind the Danes.

"Skjaldborg!" Ragnar roared. Tormod echoed his call, and so did Thorbjorn. The shields linking together could just about be heard over the roar of the flames. Snorri pictured Odin sat in his high seat in Asgard, rubbing his hands in joy at the chaos. As they moved backwards down the street, Snorri heard an order for the Danes to back down. The voice sounded vaguely familiar, but it was hard to tell with his helmet on and all the other noises around them.

"Why aren't they attacking?" one of his men asked.

"Aye, they outnumber us," another said. Snorri was pleased not to hear any fear in their voices.

"Because they are afraid of a Norse shield wall!" Thorbjorn shouted. Men around him cheered and banged their weapons against their shields as they backed away.

"They are herding us." Snorri now understood what was happening.

"What?" Brak asked.

"Right now, we are in the stronger position," Snorri explained. "They want us somewhere where their numbers will make a difference." He wanted to send someone to find Ubba.

Ubba had enough men to help them, but this was a big city and none of his men knew where Ubba was.

Oddi shouted something from behind, his voice just reaching Snorri, but Snorri could not make the words out. He didn't bother responding. Oddi wouldn't be able to hear him, and Snorri was too busy looking for the archers.

"Stay together!" he ordered as they backed out of the alley and into the market square. His men lengthened the shield wall without him needing to give the order.

"Snorri?" He heard Oddi again.

"Oddi, get the injured! We have trouble." Snorri kept his eyes on the Danes, who were spilling out into the square after them. This would be where Snorri would have attacked, so it surprised him when the Danes didn't. Something didn't feel right, and Snorri was beginning to think things were going to get a lot worse. He glanced at the other streets leading into the square, expecting to see more Danes, but those streets were empty.

"How is it that since Ulf joined us, we always end up in shit situations?" Asbjorn complained.

"If you don't want difficult situations, then you should have been a bóndi," Thorbjorn retorted before the roof of the house near the Danes collapsed. Walls crumbled, the falling stones crushing the Danes. Snorri's men cheered as the Danes screamed, and Snorri felt them tense, ready to attack as soon as he gave the order. As the dust and smoke cleared, Snorri saw the street they had come from was blocked. Few of the Danes had made it through yet, meaning they were now outnumbered.

"We should attack them now!" Ragnar saw the same thing he did. But Snorri was concerned that the rest of the Danes might find another way through. The Norns had given them a chance to escape and, as much as Snorri hated running from a fight, he would not throw it away.

"To the gates!" Snorri saw the shocked expressions on the faces of his men. They had expected to attack the Danes, not to run away from them. "Now!" Snorri didn't wait for a response as he turned and fled the city. He felt his men run after him, some of them carrying the few injured who could not walk by themselves.

"Why aren't we attacking them?" Tormod shouted as they ran.

"Because I don't want to be caught from behind by those bastards when they find another way to that square." They passed through the gate they had entered not so long ago. "We get back to the camp, find Ubba and with his —" Snorri stopped in his tracks. In his mind, he heard the gods laughing at him. Men bumped into him from behind as they stopped, all of them shocked to find a large force of Danes waiting for them. The large shield wall, with weapons sticking out like sharp teeth, meant only one thing — Snorri had led his men into another trap.

CHAPTER 20

Cold water splashed over Ulf's face, dragging him from the darkness he was in. He did not know where he was or how long he had been out. The last thing Ulf remembered was being hit by a troll. But not a troll... Ulf shook his head, trying to clear the fog inside. He regretted it as the sharp pain made him see stars. With a groan, Ulf tried to sit up. His arms were behind him in an uncomfortable position, and he could not move them when he tried.

"Wake up, you bastard!"

Ulf heard the voice. It sounded familiar, but he could not understand the venom in it. Ulf wondered if he was dreaming again, but this was different. He didn't have the same fear which came with the dreams. Ulf tried to open his eyes. His left eye refused to open, and his right eye couldn't see clearly. A blurred figure knelt down in front of him. At first, Ulf didn't know who it was, but then, he could make out the white hair on the figure's head.

"Ubba?" His mouth struggled to work, and the name came out slurred. The blurred figure nodded. Ulf smiled in relief. If Ubba was here, then he must have been saved from the tro... Ulf frowned. But it wasn't the troll. His right eye focused on the world around him, and Ulf realised he was in a tent. There were two more blurred figures standing behind Ubba. One small and wearing something strange on its head, and the other big. Very big.

"The bastard of Tyr is finally awake." The soft, purring voice sent shivers down his spine. Like the sun breaking through the storm clouds, her voice broke through the fog in his mind. It wasn't the troll that hit him. It was Griml. Ulf gawked at the two figures behind Ubba. Frowning, he glanced at Ubba, trying to understand what was happening. "You know now." The woman smiled as she walked towards him. He knew. Ulf wasn't sure how he had not seen it before. *It's the dirt*, he thought. The woman looked like she had been attractive once. As she leaned forward, her dress opened, giving him a view of her breasts. Ulf tried not to look, but even in this situation, it was hard not to peek. The woman noticed and smiled a playful smile Ulf never thought he would see again. The years living in the forest had not been too harsh on her. From up close, Ulf could still see her beauty, but the dirt in her pores hid that from the world. Her rotten teeth also drew his attention before making him want to look away, while her insect-infested hair, covered in twigs and small bones, smelt repugnant.

"Should have let me kill the bastard." Griml stood beside Ubba, looming over Ulf like a mountain over a farmhouse. "He deserves to die after what he did to me."

"Wha…?" Ulf tried to get the words out, but his mouth was too dry. *What I did to him?*

Griml leaned in and grabbed him by his shoulder, pressing on the wound. Ulf screamed as the blinding pain burnt through his senses. "You ruined my face!" Griml pointed at the ugly scar on his cheek, sat above his bushy beard. "For that alone you should die." Ulf felt the spark ignite inside him. Griml had slaughtered his family, raped his aunt and stolen his father's sword. Griml had sliced Vidar's neck open before the battle. He had done all that to Ulf, but Ulf had to die because he cut Griml's face. Before Ulf could stop himself, the spark of his anger exploded and Ulf headbutted Griml. He heard the crunch of Griml's nose breaking as pain shot through his head. Griml roared in shock, dropping Ulf to the ground. Ulf landed awkwardly because his legs were tied and instantly regretted doing that. Not because now Griml would definitely kill him, but because of the blinding headache that throbbed behind his eyes. Griml was still roaring his anger and lifted his boot in the air. Ulf braced himself as he prepared to join his ancestors in Valhalla.

"Enough!" The commanding voice of Ubba stopped Griml's giant boot mid stomp. Griml glared at Ubba, but moved his boot away. Ubba was holding Ormstunga in his hand, his eyes bright as he admired the blade.

"But the bastard cut my face. Again!" Griml sounded more like a child than the monster he was.

"You should know better than to bring a young wolf near your face," the woman purred. She walked to Ubba and ran a finger along his arm. Ulf noticed the shiver which followed and understood Ubba's unease around her, but he did not understand why Ubba was there.

"She's right," Ubba agreed. "You caused that yourself." Griml was about to launch himself at Ubba, something Ubba also realised from the way he tensed. But the woman held a hand up and wagged her finger. Griml stopped and looked at her, not with anger in his dead eyes, but fear. Ulf had never seen Griml afraid and couldn't understand the hold the woman had over him. Without a word, Griml stormed out of the tent, leaving only Ulf and Ubba, and her. "Surprised?" Ubba asked. Ulf did not respond. It was hard for him to focus, with the headache pounding through his skull. Ubba came forward and knelt in front of Ulf, resting the tip of Ormstunga on the ground near Ulf's face, sneering. "I heard the stories about you, about how you killed that Swedish jarl in the holmgang, how you broke Griml's shield wall, all by yourself. Even all the different versions of your fight with that bear. Not sure which one I believe, but if it wasn't for those scars on your face, then I wouldn't have believed any of them."

Ulf glared at Ubba, trying to make sense of everything. He did not understand why he was still alive. Were the gods just toying with him, wanting him to suffer for failing his oath. But he had tried. Fought harder than he ever had done, but Griml was too good. And Ubba? What was his part in all this? "Why?"

"Why?" Ubba's face hardened as he leaned in. "You don't get it, do you?" Ulf shook his head, wincing at the pain it caused. "That jarl you fought in the holmgang, the one you killed. Yes, he died soon after," Ubba said when he saw the shock on Ulf's face. "That jarl was my father." Ulf's eyes went wide, which only made Ubba smile.

"All this because I killed your father?" Ulf hated saying the word. He never wanted to fight the old Swedish jarl, but the man had challenged him to a holmgang, and Ulf could not refuse.

Ubba smiled. "You'd think so, but no. Odin knows that man deserved the cruel death you gave him, and when I see him in Valhalla, I'll tell him the same. The man was a brute. He never wanted me, said my white hair was proof that I wasn't his. So he beat me for a few years and then sold me as a thrall to the Danes." Ulf now understood the many rumours about Ubba being Swedish. "The man he sold me to treated me more like a son than my bastard father ever did. He raised me like I was his own, taught me how to fight and when he died, gave me his ships and crew."

"Why then?" Ulf struggled to understand. Ubba had been a good friend to them, even if Ulf didn't like him at first. The others did. Snorri swore by the guy, even Asbjorn, who was the least trusting, thought Ubba was their friend. "The attacks... you sent those men."

Ubba sneered at Ulf. "Aye, that was me. And by Odin, you and your bastard friends are hard to kill. I lost many good men because of you." Ubba leaned in closer again. "But I will not make the same mistake today." Ulf frowned as he struggled to understand.

"But they didn't kill your father." Ulf's headache made it hard for him to focus.

Ubba slapped Ulf on the head, the sparks flashing in his eyes blinding him. "This has nothing to do with that man! Were you not listening!" Ubba stood up and walked away. As the headache subsided and Ulf's vision cleared a little, he saw the woman smiling at him.

"Then why?"

"My sister!"

Ulf remembered the tall, slim woman he had seen at the market that day. She was the reason for the holmgang, but that was not what Ubba meant. They had kidnapped her to force Griml to chase them with only half his men. "But we sent her home." Ulf remembered that after the battle men from her father had come for her. She had served her purpose, so Snorri let her go. He remembered telling Ubba the same when Ubba asked him about the story not so long ago. At the time, he did not understand why Ubba was so interested, but now he did.

"She never made it home." Ulf looked at Ubba, the confusion written all over his face. "As soon as I heard about my father and the battle, I rushed home, only to find my mother destroyed. My father dead, my sister missing. We waited all winter, but nothing. No ship appeared with my father's men or my sister. So, in the summer I took my men to Suðrikaupstefna, thinking that perhaps they were still there." He glared at Ulf. "What do you think I found?" Ulf didn't respond. "A large leaderless army with nowhere to go, but no sister. Some of my father's men there told me she was kidnapped and even though my father's hirdmen went with Griml to get her, none of them were seen again."

"But we sent Eldrid home," Ulf repeated, unable to think of anything else to say. Just saying her name lifted the headache briefly, and Ulf was about to just repeat it for more relief.

"Don't you say her name!" Ubba launched himself at Ulf, Ormstunga held high as if he was preparing to strike. But Ubba halted in front of Ulf, who tried his best not to flinch, and glanced towards the woman. She also had some power over him. "I swore an oath to kill all of you for my sister, but I wasn't sure how to find you." Ubba smiled. "But then Odin answered my prayers, and you just showed up one day to take part in a raid I had no intention of doing."

"But Snorri thought you were friends."

"Snorri is an arrogant fool!" Ubba barked. "Strutting around and believing all that hype about himself. He will die for his part in this." Ubba took a breath and calmed himself down. Ulf glanced at the woman, who had been watching the conversation. She reminded Ulf of one of Odin's ravens, just sitting there and taking it all in, so she could report it to the All-father. "But Odin knows, you Norsemen have been harder to kill than I thought. I was sure that the ambush near Hammaburg would work and then I get to take that pretty ship of his." He sighed. "But now I have to resort to extreme measures." Ulf didn't understand what Ubba meant by that, but he didn't like the smile on the woman's face. There was another thing he still didn't understand.

"What does she have to do with all of this?"

Before either of them could answer, one of Ubba's men came into the tent. He glanced at Ulf, not surprised to find him there all tied up, before turning to Ubba. "It's ready."

Ubba smiled at the man. "They are in place?" The man nodded, another glance at Ulf. "Good. Let's get this done. Today we avenge my sister." Ubba turned to Ulf. "Soon you will join your friends in Valhalla. Then you can explain to them what this is all about." Ubba turned Ormstunga in his hand and walked towards Ulf, his intentions as clear as the cloudless sky.

"No," the woman said. It was the first time she had spoken since Griml left the tent.

Ubba turned to her, his face red. "He killed my sister. He needs to die."

The woman nodded. "But not by your hands. He belongs to the gods." For the first time, a sliver of fear crawl up Ulf's spine, although he tried hard not to show it. The cruel smile on Ubba's face didn't help.

"Very well," Ubba said, as he stepped back. "That sounds more fitting anyway." He turned to leave the tent, still holding onto Ormstunga.

"The sword stays." The woman held out her slender hand with long dirty nails.

Ubba bared his teeth at the woman. "The sword is mine."

She only smiled at him, still holding her hand out. "You don't want that sword."

"Why?" Ubba looked at Ormstunga, admiring her beauty. Ulf imagined that was the same look he had when he first laid eyes on Eldrid.

"The sword is cursed. No one who has wielded that blade died a good death, and all were shamed before that." Ulf stared at her, his eyebrows raised in shock. What did she mean by that? Ubba gave her the same look. "If you don't believe me, then ask Griml. He had the bigger army. He made a human sacrifice to Odin, yet he still lost the battle and almost his arm." Her eyes flickered to Ulf. "The sword is cursed to all those who don't have the blood of the gods flowing in their veins." Her face hardened and for the first time, Ulf understood how frightening she could be. "Take that sword and you will spend the rest of your days regretting it." Ubba wavered. Ulf saw it in the way the sword quivered in his hand. With a quick flick of his wrist, he turned the sword and gave it to the woman before walking away without a word. The woman took the sword, and Ulf was surprised at how uncomfortable she looked holding it. Not like someone who had never held a sword before. The knife on her belt showed she knew how to handle a weapon. It was more like someone who feared its power. As she got to Ulf, she dropped the sword. The blade stuck into the ground only a few fingers away from Ulf's face, causing him to flinch. The woman smiled at that as she sat on her knees. From a small pouch on her belt, she took what looked to be small finger bones. Ulf flexed his hands tied behind his back, hoping that his fingers won't be part of that collection.

"What are you doing?" Ulf tried to keep the quiver out of his voice and was not sure if he succeeded. Ulf spent most of his life being angry at the gods and cursing them, despite his aunt telling him not to. Since the deaths of his family, he had feared their retribution.

The woman smiled at him. "Like I said, you belong to the gods." She shook the small finger bones in her hand. "Only they can decide your fate." With that, she threw them to the ground. Ulf watched in horror as they bounced around before landing in a random pattern. He realised that the small bones all had different runes on them. Some he recognised, others he didn't. He stared at the bones, trying to understand what they were telling the woman. Ulf's heart started beating faster when he saw the vicious smile on her face as she read them. *Please, mother of gods, don't let me die today. Not until I have had my revenge.* Ulf prayed to Frigg, even though he wasn't sure why. For some reason, he felt that she would have more influence here than Odin or Tyr. The woman looked up at him and tutted like she had heard his thoughts, which made his heart skip a beat. Ulf was trying hard not to show the fear he felt on his face, and from the woman's smile, he doubted he was succeeding. After what felt like ages, the woman said, "The gods have spoken."

"What did they say?" Ulf asked before he could stop himself. He swallowed the spit in his mouth and willed his bladder not to embarrass him now. It was suddenly very full and Ulf had to use all his self-will not to piss himself. Which he almost did when the woman pulled out her knife. The blade looked dull and Ulf caught himself wondering when it was last sharpened. The woman stood up and, without a word, walked behind him. Ulf wanted to see what she was doing, but when he tried to turn onto his back, she put a foot on his shoulder to stop him. The smell of rot from her toes almost made him gag. He sensed her kneel behind his back. The gods had spoken, and Ulf knew he was going to die. He was unable to kill Griml and so Odin had no more need of him. Ulf wondered if he would go to Valhalla. He hoped he would, which was another reason he could not piss himself. He knew that if Thorbjorn found out about it, then he would make fun of him until Ragnarök. Ulf held his breath as the woman put the tip of her knife at his throat. The blade was dull, so he knew that this would not be quick. The gods did not like quick deaths when you made a sacrifice to them. They wanted you to suffer, to endure.

"You know who I am?" the woman asked him, her mouth close to his ear. Ulf felt her warm breath and smelt the stink as he nodded. He was too afraid to speak. "Have they told you about me?" She started moving the blade along his neck, not cutting him, but teasing him instead. Ulf shook his head. Fear had chased away the headache, so Ulf did not feel the pain like before. More of her warm breath washed over him. Ulf tried to move his head to get away from the stink. "Tell them I'm coming for what is mine." With that, she moved the blade away from his neck and cut the bonds on his wrists, nicking his skin. Before Ulf could understand what was happening, she leaned over him and licked his blood off the blade before she moved away. He rolled onto his back and sat up, not taking his eyes off her as he untied his feet. Ulf turned to grab Ormstunga and when he turned back, she was gone, vanished as if she had never been there. He looked at the entrance of the tent, but there was no sign of her. Ulf realised she left the finger bones behind. That and the cut on his wrist were the only evidence that she had been here at all. He stared at the bones, trying to understand what she might have seen, but still could not make any sense of them.

"Thank you," he whispered, although he was not sure to which god. Perhaps Frigg. He had asked for her help, after all. *Your friends*, a voice seemed to whisper in his head. Ulf looked around, still trying to make sense of things. He was still wearing his brynja and spotted his helmet, one side of it dented from where Griml had hit him. Ulf prodded his forehead. The left side of his face was swollen, which explained why he could not see well from that eye. He picked up his helmet and forced it on, wincing at the sharp pain from the cut. "Forgive me, Uncle," Ulf said as he grabbed a shield lying in the tent and ran out. He had sworn his revenge on his uncle's axe, but it was gone and Ulf did not have the time to search for it. His friends were in danger, and Ulf needed to help them.

Snorri was in shock as he stared at the Danish shield wall in front of them, trying to understand what was happening.

"Is that Ubba?" someone asked, and Snorri saw his friend walking along the wall. For a moment, he felt relief. Ubba had come to save them. Perhaps he would know what had happened to Ulf.

"What is he doing?" Oddi frowned as Ubba stood with his back to the shield wall, staring at them. Snorri could not see Ubba's face because he was wearing his helmet. The only way he knew it was Ubba was because of the long, white hair. No one here had hair like that.

"Snorri Thorgilsson!" Ubba pointed his sword at Snorri. "Today you and your men die!" The Danes cheered, and Snorri sensed the confusion behind him. Ubba was their friend, so why was he now standing there threatening to kill them all? Snorri searched his memory, trying to find something he had missed which might explain this, but there was nothing. In his mind, he thought he could hear the gods laugh at him for his stupidity.

"In the name of the gods, what is going on?" Tormod asked. He was just as confused as Snorri.

"What do we do, Snorri?" Ragnar asked. Snorri sensed the unease in the nine-fingered warrior. Something he had never seen before. The priest had been right, things were changing.

Snorri looked to the sky, trying to find any sign that the gods were watching. But the cloudy sky remained clear of any birds. Even the large flock of ravens he had seen before had vanished. The old forest man had told him the gods were here, but if they were, then their attention was somewhere else. Or perhaps the Christian god had chased them away, and this was his way of punishing those who attacked his people. Snorri took a deep breath. They were going to die here today, of that he was certain. The Norns had decided so, and he had never argued with them before. He gripped Tyr's Fury tight. "Make sure we take as many of those bastards with us to Valhalla as we can. We teach them you don't fuck with the men of Norway." No one around him responded. They all must have seen the same thing. Even Magni was silent. Snorri glanced behind him to see if the tall warrior was still there and found him standing beside his brother, the two of them looking so alike. Snorri wondered if Oddi knew. "After the battle or in Valhalla," he repeated their customary saying before a battle. His father had told him it was something all of his ancestors had said before every battle. He hoped someone would teach it to his son because Snorri was sure he was going to be in Valhalla.

"Look!" one man called from behind.

"Ulf? What, in Odin's name, is he doing?" Drumbr asked before Snorri got irritated with the man who had spoken. He looked behind the Danish shield wall and frowned. Ulf, dressed in his war gear, shield in one hand and Ormstunga in the other, was running towards the Danes. More importantly, none of them knew he was there. Snorri smiled as he glanced at the sky again. *The gods are with us.* Punching Tyr's Fury into the air, he shouted, "Spearhead!"

CHAPTER 21

Ulf loped towards the Danish shield wall like a wolf sneaking up on a deer. He held Ormstunga in his right hand, his grip not too tight. She did not like that. In his left hand was the shield from Ubba's tent. It sported Ubba's colours, so if any of the Danes looked back, they would think Ulf was one of them. Not that any of them would. They were all too focused on the group of men standing by the gates of Rouen. Ulf did not need to look at them to know who they were. His friends led into a trap by the one man they thought they could trust. The one man who had shared his food and ale with them. The white-haired bastard who had pretended to be concerned when they told him of the ambush he had planned. Ulf saw the white hair of Ubba blowing in the breeze from under his helmet as he pointed his sword towards the men of Norway, shouting words Ulf could not make out. All he heard was his heartbeat pumping the flames of his anger through his body. His headache forgotten. The dent in his helmet pressing on the cut above his eye forgotten. The deep cut to his shoulder forgotten. But the names and faces of the men who had died from Ubba's treachery were not. Ulf saw all of them in his mind, gritting his teeth as he remembered the men he had called friends and shield brothers.

Ubba finished his speech, and the Danes cheered, none of them aware of the wolf coming up behind them. None of them saw the snarl on his lips or the steel in his eyes. Before Ulf reached the back of the shield wall, he heard a new cry. This one different from the Danes and he realised it was the Norse warriors. He glanced at them and saw them charging at their enemy. Ulf knew they had seen him. He knew what Snorri was planning. *Tyr, guide my sword*, Ulf prayed as he reached the Danes.

"Ubba!" He launched himself into the air. The white-haired warrior turned at the sound of his name. The men around him looked uncertain, all of them wavering. They must have thought there were more Norsemen behind them. Ulf crashed into the men at the back of the shield wall, Ormstunga stealing the life of a young warrior as she sliced through his neck. He punched another in the face with his borrowed shield. The Dane fell back, giving Ulf the space to swing Ormstunga in a wide arc. Her sharp blade cut one man's arm before burying herself into another's chest. "Ubba!" Ulf roared again, his face red and spit flying from his mouth. The Danes hesitated, all of them taken aback by his ferocity. But Ulf did not hesitate as the voices erupted in his head. He launched himself at the Danes, stabbing one through the chest. The Dane screamed as Ormstunga ripped through his lungs and came out of his back. Ulf turned to avoid the axe of a Dane who found the courage to attack him, before caving the man's skull in with the rim of his shield. Others tried to get out of the reach of Ormstunga, but had nowhere to go.

Ulf stabbed another in the chest, kicking the dying man back in order to free his sword as he fought his way to Ubba. He sensed movement near him and turned just in time to block an axe. The young man holding it looked surprised that Ulf had blocked it and then even more surprised when Ulf sliced his throat open with Ormstunga's sharp point, drenching himself in blood. Ulf ducked under another attack, stabbing the man through the side. Everything else was forgotten, the headache, the cut above his eye, his swollen face, even Snorri and his men. There was only chaos. The screams of the Danes, surprise, fear and anger all came at him in one loud crash, like a wave breaking against a cliff.

Ulf felt the vibration ripple through the Danes and remembered about Snorri and the rest of the Norsemen. "In Valhalla!" Ulf heard the cry over the battle din as he punched a Dane with the rim of his shield, the man crumbling to the ground. He deflected a sword jab with Ormstunga before kicking its wielder in the chest. The man flew into his comrades, giving Ulf more space to move around. Dancing to the side, he dodged a spear and sliced the warrior holding it across the face. The man dropped the spear, clutching his face as Ulf rushed past him, stabbing another, who had turned to face the new threat from behind. As the Dane fell, Ulf almost lost grip of Ormstunga. His hand and the hilt were slick with blood, and Ulf had to block an axe aimed at his head with his shield. The voices of his ancestors were screaming in his head, pushing him on and not letting him tire. He kicked at the axe wielder, but the man jumped back, avoiding the kick while trying to chop Ulf's leg off. Ulf got his leg out of the way and, with a roar, freed Ormstunga. The Dane hesitated as the blood-drenched Ulf came at him. He tried to block Ulf's stab with his axe, not having a shield. But at the last moment, Ulf turned the sword and sliced through the man's leg. The Dane dropped to his knees, and Ulf stabbed him through the face before he could bring his axe up. Sensing movement behind him, Ulf turned, Ormstunga held ready to slice down on his would-be attacker.

"Ulf!" The scream came with an edge of panic to it. Ormstunga stopped mid-air as Ulf looked at the man, his face familiar. *Steiner*, the name came to him as he recognised one of the Sae-Ulfr's crew. Ulf lowered his sword and took a step back. Steiner smiled as the two men nodded to each other, the quiet moment feeling strange amid the sea of violence. Then Ulf spotted a Dane aiming a sword thrust at Steiner. He pushed Steiner out of the way and blocked the sword with his shield. Steiner realised what was happening and killed the man with his axe. Ulf recognised more men as the Norse fought their way through the Danish army and soon found himself beside Oddi, the tall warrior nodding an acknowledgement to him.

"To the ship!" Snorri shouted and Ulf saw his friend at the front of the Norsemen, covered in Danish blood, as he pointed his sword towards the Sae-Ulfr. Rolf was hobbling around the ship, trying to get her ready as fast as he could. Ulf glanced at Ubba, who, surrounded by his hirdmen, was fighting a group of Tormod's warriors. He wanted to kill the bastard, but Snorri only cared about getting his men to safety. Ulf tightened his grip on Ormstunga as indecision raged through his mind. With a frustrated scream, he turned and followed the men of Thorgilsstad as they rushed to the Sae-Ulfr. He blocked a large two-handed axe, which caused him to stagger and split his shield in two as they broke through the last of the Danes. The

Dane thought he had the best of Ulf then, but Ulf ducked under the next strike and stabbed the large Dane in the stomach, Ormstunga breaking through his brynja and bursting out of his back. The man grunted as he fell, and Ulf just freed his sword before the large body dragged him down.

Ulf caught up with Snorri as he rushed past the tents, those who were not taking part in the battle looking at them with confused faces. His friend laughed. "Can't you ever wait for the rest of us, so we can attack a large army together?"

"Maybe next time." Ulf laughed back. Despite everything, he felt a strange sense of joy. Somehow they got through the Danes and were almost by the Sae-Ulfr. It looked like they would escape the trap.

But the gods were not done with them yet. They wanted more chaos. Odin wanted more men for his own army to face the giants at Ragnarök.

"Argh!" the scream came from behind.

"Fuck," Thorbjorn said as he ran beside Ulf. They all turned and saw Brak lying on the ground with a spear sticking out of his back.

"Brak!" Drumbr cried.

"To the ships!" Ragnar and Tormod screamed together. They were close to safety, and both sensed what was about to happen and wanted to avoid it. The Norsemen stopped as confusion spread amongst them. On the Sae-Ulfr, Rolf was waving at them and gesturing for them to hurry. He had done all he could, but still needed more men to get the ship going before the Danes gave chase.

"Brak!" Drumbr made to go after his brother, but Ragnar held him back, his face straining at the effort.

"He's dead!"

"He's my brother!" Tears were streaming down Drumbr's face, creating white lines in the blood covering him, before being soaked up by his beard. "I won't leave him here!"

"We are leaving many other bodies here!" Tormod argued. Many of their men had died in this last struggle, some too injured to carry on, and were lying there at the mercy of the Danes.

As if the gods were mocking them, Brak looked up and reached out, calling for their help. "Brak!" Drumbr roared and shoved Ragnar out of the way.

"Snorri, do something! Stop him!" Tormod yelled at Snorri.

"Fuck!" Snorri screamed. He took an axe from his belt and threw it at Ulf before running after Drumbr. Ulf caught the axe and was surprised to find it was his own. But he had no time to think about it as the rest of Snorri's men ran after their leader. Oddi had enough sense to grab a few men and run to the ship, while Tormod ordered all his men to their own. Ulf ran after his friends.

"Tyr!" he roared again as he outpaced the men of Thorgilsstad and was soon running beside Snorri and his hirdmen. Ragnar had also caught up and was running beside Drumbr, who was ahead of them with his enormous axe, Shield Breaker, swinging above his head.

"Get them!" A call came from the Danes. With a loud roar, they charged at the oncoming Norsemen.

They reached Brak before the Danes and without hesitation Snorri called, "Skjaldborg!" The Norsemen linked their shields together. They were still heavily outnumbered by the Danes, who were angry after being humiliated by the smaller force earlier on. Ulf wanted to join the front rank. That was his place, on the right-hand side of Snorri, but he had no shield. He knew he would be the weak link in the wall, so he stood behind Snorri instead, while Oddi took his place on Snorri's right. Drumbr was kneeling by his brother, his back jerking as he cried. If Brak had not been dead before, then judging from Drumbr's hunched body, he was now. "Stand strong! We are the men of Thorgilsstad! We will never give ground! After the battle or in Valhalla!" Snorri roared as the Danes came at them.

"In Valhalla!" the men of Thorgilsstad echoed. The people of Rouen stood on the wall and watched their confrontation. Ulf wondered if they were confused, as the very men who had earlier on been rampaging through their city were now fighting each other. A roar from the Danes brought Ulf's attention back to them, and Ulf saw Ubba leading the charge. The white-haired Swede had lost his helmet and had a cut to his face. Ulf grit his teeth, glaring at the man who had deceived them as the flames inside ignited again.

The larger Danish force struck with a thunderous echo as shields clashed and men grunted, the Danes forcing the Norsemen back. Ulf pushed against Snorri's back, straining with effort, but it was like trying to stop an iceberg with a small fishing boat.

"Drumbr, get your brother! We must get to the ship now!" Snorri yelled. Ulf looked at their large friend and knew Drumbr would not do that. The gods wanted chaos, and Drumbr was about to give it to them. He stood up from his brother's body, pain etched on his face as he lifted his axe and, with a bellow, charged.

"Brak!"

Not knowing what else to do, Ulf grabbed Snorri and pulled him out of the way, at the same time barging Oddi aside. Both men yelled in shock as the breach in the wall was formed. But before the Danes could take advantage of it, Drumbr struck. His enormous frame sent the Danes flying as he crashed into them. With a huge swing of his axe, he cleaved those still standing in half with a spray of blood and guts. His anger gave him extra strength as he wielded his large two-handed axe like it weighed nothing, swinging it in large circles. Any Danes who tried to get near him lost limb or life.

"Protect Drumbr!" Ragnar yelled and was soon beside him, copying Drumbr with his own two-handed axe.

"Kill them!" Ubba screamed. The Danes took a step back, not wanting to be in the way of those deadly axes.

Snorri recovered and nodded his thanks to Ulf. He grabbed one of his men before he was about to join the fight. "Get Brak's body back to the ship." The warrior nodded and called on someone to help. "The rest of you bastards!" he called to his men. "Form up around Drumbr. We need to get him back!" Those of his men not fighting moved towards Drumbr, but the Danes had recovered and were fighting back.

"You sure that's a good idea?" Thorbjorn asked, killing a Dane by slicing his stomach open. The Dane stared at his intestines as they slithered out of his body before collapsing. "Even Thor would be nervous going near him now."

"We have to try. I'm not losing another friend today." Snorri turned to Ulf and nodded, with his wolf grin in place.

Ulf smiled back before both men launched themselves at the Danes. With only his axe and sword, Ulf felt lighter as he charged at them. The familiar heat surged through his limbs, the voices of his ancestors shouting in his ears. They wanted blood and they would lend him their skill to quench their thirst. The first Dane to attack moved so slowly that Ulf wondered how the man thought he was ever going to kill him. Ulf twisted out of the way of the spear and hacked at the man's face with Olaf's axe. With a scream and a spray of blood, the Dane collapsed, and Ulf was already moving onto the next. He stabbed at another Dane with Ormstunga, but the warrior blocked it with his shield. Before the Dane could counter, Ulf chopped his arm off with his axe. Another Dane came from the side, swinging his axe in a wide arc. Ulf blocked the blow with Olaf's axe and stabbed the man in the face with Ormstunga. Ulf screamed at the Dane as the sword broke through teeth and jaw, before bursting out of the now dead Dane's neck. He turned and with a backhanded chop of his axe, killed another who was fighting Magni, while freeing his sword. Magni nodded at him before attacking another Dane.

"Ulf! Ulf Bear-Slayer!" Ulf heard his name. At first he thought it was Griml, come to finish their fight, but then he recognised Ubba's voice. Ulf turned and saw Ubba stalking him like a cat who spotted another in his territory.

"Ubba! What are you doing?" Snorri blocked a strike on his shield.

"You killed my sister!" Ubba screamed, launching himself at Ulf. Ulf just had time to notice the confusion in Snorri's eyes before Ubba was on him. Ulf dodged the cut from Ubba's sword before chopping at him with Olaf's axe. Ubba turned and took the blow on his shield, stabbing at Ulf, but Ulf deflected it with Ormstunga. Ulf took a step back and realised many of those fighting near them had stopped. The men were more interested in watching Ulf and Ubba than fighting the battle. Ubba glared at him, his creased eyes filled with hatred. "Unlike my father, I will kill you. Odin is my witness." At the mention of Odin, Ulf glanced up and, as always, there was a raven nearby. It sat on the tents near the battle, watching the fight. Ulf took deep breaths, trying to fan the flames in his stomach, but the voices in his head had gone quiet. This was his fight, not theirs.

Ubba roared as he attacked again, stabbing with his sword before punching with the rim of his shield. Ulf deflected the sword downward before ducking under the shield. The Norsemen cheered while the Danes encouraged their leader. Ulf stabbed at Ubba's exposed side, but Ubba turned away from it and Ormstunga sliced through thin air. Ulf did not pull his arm in fast enough and was rewarded with a cut from Ubba. It was not a deep cut, but it stung. The Danes cheered as Ulf grit his teeth. He took a step back, Ubba smiling at him. "To think you killed my father." Ulf's response was to launch his own attack. He swung his axe, expecting Ubba to block with his shield and leave his side exposed. But Ubba jumped back. Ulf stabbed with Ormstunga, taking a step forward so he could keep the pressure on Ubba. But Ubba was an experienced warrior and no matter what Ulf tried, he always found a way out of it. Ulf cut with Ormstunga, but Ubba blocked it with his shield before stabbing out with his own sword. Ulf tried to deflect it with Olaf's axe, but because of the cut on his shoulder, wasn't fast enough. The tip of Ubba's sword broke a few rings on Ulf's brynja before Ulf could move away. He felt the sting and knew Ubba had cut him. Ubba grinned as the Danes cheered for him. Behind Ulf, his friends were encouraging him. This was like the holmgang he had fought against Ubba's father. The same fear was now creeping into Ulf and, just like then, he was wondering if he was going to survive. The voices of his ancestors, the power that drove him through battle, was gone, and Ulf was now tiring. His brynja weighed him down, while his sword and axe were almost too heavy to lift. His left arm was numb as he struggled to hold onto Olaf's axe, and his trousers soaked in the blood from the cut to his stomach. Sweat stung his eyes as Ulf struggled to catch his breath.

Ubba attacked with a swing of his sword which Ulf just dodged, before swinging Olaf's axe at Ubba's head, his shoulder straining with the effort. The white-haired warrior ducked underneath the axe and smiled as he stepped back.

"How can you have the blood of Tyr running in your veins?" Ubba sneered. "Odin knows I expected more from you."

"Come on, Ulf! Stop fucking around!" Snorri shouted behind Ulf. The battle had stopped and Ulf realised he was fighting for the fate of the Norsemen. It was a pressure he did not want, because Ulf was not sure if he could defeat Ubba.

Ubba launched himself at Ulf again, stabbing with his sword before turning it into a backhanded cut. Ulf dodged the stab, but was forced to block the swing with his axe. Ubba's sword bit into the wood of the haft and held fast. Before Ubba could react, Ulf kicked him in the side. Ubba took a few steps back, the movement freeing his sword from Ulf's axe. Ulf tried to take advantage and stabbed Ormstunga at Ubba's exposed neck. But Ubba recovered fast enough to turn and block with his shield, deflecting the sword and bringing his own around to swing at Ulf. Ulf was forced to jump back and felt the tip of

Ubba's sword grazing his brynja. Both men stopped to catch their breaths while those around them cheered. But Ulf could not hear them over his heavy panting. His helmet was uncomfortable and Ulf desperately wanted to take it off, but he remembered what had happened to Ubba's father. Perhaps if they had worn helmets in that holmgang, the old jarl might still be alive. Ulf's swollen left eye wasn't helping either. *Tyr, help me*, he prayed.

Ubba attacked again while Ulf was struggling with his thoughts, stabbing at his stomach. Ulf took a step back to give himself more room, but as he planted his back foot, it slipped. Everything slowed down as Ulf fell to one knee. The men around him gasped in shock and Ubba's eyes lit up as his sword was now heading for Ulf's face. In that half of a heartbeat, Ulf thought he was on his way to Valhalla. But Odin did not want him yet as the sword struck the side of his helmet, slicing along it. The momentum of Ulf's fall moved his head to the side, just enough for the sword to miss. A storm of noise erupted in Ulf's head, the ringing of the blow almost blinding him. Ulf stabbed up with Ormstunga, not sure if he did it or if the sword did it herself. He felt her strike something, a brief resistance before she moved again, her sharp edge cutting through everything in her path. There was a grunt and Ulf felt warm liquid spraying over his hand. The world around him went quiet as his vision cleared. Standing in front of him was Ubba, his face creased in pain, his eyes wide with shock. When Ulf looked up, he saw Ormstunga's blade inside of Ubba. She had gone in under his ribs, breaking through his brynja, before stabbing up into Ubba's chest. The two men just stared at each other, surrounded by silence. Ubba's mouth was working, like he was trying to say something, but no sound came out. An eagle screamed in the distance — Odin wanted his warrior, and he wanted Ulf to give him Ubba. With a roar, Ulf pulled Ormstunga free and, as Ubba fell to his knees, buried Olaf's axe deep in his neck. Ubba was dead by the time he hit the ground. Shocked silence met the eruption of noise from the Norse as they realised Ulf had won.

"Skjaldborg!" Snorri roared. The shields came together behind Ulf as he stared at the body of Ubba. The Danes weren't sure what to do. They had lost their leader, and no one else seemed willing to take over. "Ulf! Get your arse here now!"

Ulf just stood there, staring at the Danes. They almost took a step back, just to get away from Ulf. But he was longer in the mood to fight.

"Ulf!" Snorri shouted again. But Ulf could not get himself to move. He was too drained from the fight. His shoulder was burning and his stomach stung from where Ubba had cut him, while his head felt like the gods had dropped a mountain on it. Rough hands grabbed him from behind and dragged him to the safety of the shield wall. None of his friends were paying any attention to him. They were all too focused on the Danes. Geir glanced at him, a look of awe showing from under his helmet. "Back to the ship!" Snorri ordered and his men moved backwards, keeping the shield wall in place for if the Danes attacked.

"Always have to make it difficult," Ragnar growled as they edged back to the Sae-Ulfr. Luckily for them, the camp was empty because most of the Danes were still in Rouen, looting and destroying the city after their victory. Ubba's Danes were still standing where Ubba had fallen. The slow walk back to the ship was more tense than the battle itself, the uncertainty of the moment eating away at the men. But with grim silence they made it to the ship, not a single man had turned and run. Drumbr was the first to board and just collapsed by the mast next to the body of his brother. As the other men boarded, Ulf watched as Drumbr cradled his brother's body, fresh tears streaming down his face. It was not so long ago when Ulf was in a similar situation, but what affected Ulf more was that this was another death because of his vengeance.

"Get her going now!" Snorri shouted. He and his hirdmen, with Ragnar, stood in a small shield wall on the side of the Sae-Ulfr as her crew got the oars ready and started rowing. Ulf knew he should be with the hirdmen, protecting the crew from any other attacks, but he was too tired. Instead, he grabbed an oar, so he was at least doing something.

"No, you rest, Ulf. You deserve it." One of the older crew blocked Ulf's path. Ulf saw the smile on the man's face and just nodded. He walked back to his chest and collapsed, groaning as the pain exploded through his core. As the Sae-Ulfr rowed to safety, he tried to take off his helmet, wincing at the pain this caused. After two attempts, it came off and when the nausea stopped, he saw the long groove cut into the side of the helmet. Tyr had heard his call and had come to his aid. That was the only reason Ulf was still alive. He was sure of it. Either that or Odin was still holding him to his oath.

"What in Odin's name happened?" Thorbjorn boomed as the hirdmen relaxed. They had rowed far enough away from the camp and it did not look like the Danes were chasing them. But when Ulf looked back at the camp, he spotted the giant frame of Griml standing there watching them. He wondered why Griml had not taken part in the battle. Perhaps the völva had told him not to. She had some strange grip on him, that was certain.

"Ulf!" Ragnar shouted. Ulf looked up and saw his friends standing over him. Asbjorn and Ragnar were glaring at him, while the rest looked tired.

"By Odin, what happened to your face?" Oddi asked when they saw the left side all bruised up, his eye shut.

"Griml."

"Griml? Here?" Asbjorn asked, not sounding convinced. Ulf nodded. "Impossible!"

"He's with Ubba?" At least Snorri seemed to believe Ulf.

"Yes... and no." It still made no sense to Ulf, so he didn't know how to respond. The men stared on, confused. Even those rowing were looking at him. Ulf took a deep breath before uttering. "Ubba wanted us dead for his own reasons."

"His sister?" Oddi asked. They all heard Ubba shouting about it during the fight.

"Who's his sister?" Ragnar scowled at Ulf.

"Eldrid. He thinks we killed her."

"Who's Eldrid?" Magni asked, washing his face clean with sea water.

"The woman we kidnapped to bring Griml to us," Snorri responded. Ulf nodded. "So he was behind all the attacks on us?"

"Impossible!" Thorbjorn threw his arms up in the air. "Ubba had been a friend to us the whole time. He had plenty of time just to kill us."

"Ubba played us from the beginning." Snorri glared back in the city's direction, finally understanding.

"That's some fucking Loki trickery that." Thorbjorn spat.

"But how is Griml involved? Surely Ubba would also have blamed him for what had happened to her?" The men around nodded.

"There's a bigger force at play. Someone more powerful pulling the strings. She used Ubba's anger against us for her purpose, and Griml is just another piece for her to use. She wants her own vengeance." Ulf explained, unsure where the words came from. He looked at Olaf's axe, lying next to Ormstunga on the deck of the Sae-Ulfr. Just below the groove cut by Ubba's sword, he saw something he had not spotted before.

"Who is she?" Snorri asked.

Ulf picked up the axe and looked at the new name carved on the hilt. His name. He looked at his friends and saw they were waiting for an answer.

"Hulda's mother."

THE END

Glossary of Terms

Asgard: the home of the Norse gods

Bifröst: the rainbow bridge that connects Asgard with Midgard

Bóndi (pl. Bændr): a farmer, a husband

Brynja: a coat of chainmail worn by warriors

Draugr: the ghosts of dead Viking warriors that rose from the dead

Drumbr: a byname meaning thick, fat or podgy

Fafnir: legendary dragon that guards a great treasure

Fenrir: giant wolf and offspring of Loki

Gjallarhorn: the horn of Heimdall which he sounds to warn the gods of the coming of Ragnarök

Gleipnir: the magical chain forged by the dwarves of Svartalfheim and used to bind Fenrir

Godi: a chieftain, a priest

Gunwale: the top edge of the hull of a ship or boat

Hel: the underworld where most of the dead dwell, also the name of the ruler of Hel and offspring of Loki

Hirdmen: a retinue of household warriors

Holmgang: a duel between two men

Huginn and Muninn: Odin's ravens, they inform him of events in Midgard

Jarl: an earl, a Norse or Danish chief

Jerkin: a thick leather vest worn by warriors

Jól: a winter solstice festival

Jörmungandr: giant serpent that encircles the world's oceans while biting its own tall and offspring of Loki

Midgard: the world inhabited by humans

Mjöllnir: Thor's hammer

Muspelheim: one of the nine worlds and home of the fire giants

Niflheim: the world of primordial darkness, cold, mist, and ice

Norns: the three sisters who control the fate of men and women

Ormstunga: means serpent's tongue, from *orm* (serpent) and *stunga* (tongue)

Prow: the front end of a ship or boat

Ragnarök: the final battle between the gods and giants which will bring an end to the gods of Asgard.

Sax-knife: a large single-edged knife

Skald: a poet, a storyteller

Skjaldborg: a shield wall

Sleipnir: Odin's eight-legged horse

Snekkja: a viking longship used for battle

Stern: the back end of a ship or boat

Suðrikaupstefna: Southern Market, from the words *suðr* (south) and *kaupstefna* (market)

Svartalfheim: the world inhabited by the dwarves

Tafl: a strategy board game

Thrall: a slave

Valhalla: Odin's hall where those who died in battle reside

Valknut: a symbol made of three interlocked triangles, also known as Odin's Knot. It is thought to represent the transition from life to death, Odin, and the power to bind and unbind

Valkyrie: Odin's female warriors, they choose who goes to Valhalla

Viss: wise

Völva: a woman who practices magic and can see the future

The Gods

Æsir: the most prominent of the two tribes of gods
Odin: chieftain of the gods, also the god of war, poetry, wisdom and magic
Frigg: Odin's wife
Thor: god of thunder and fertility
Tyr: god of war, law and justice
Vidar: god of vengeance, also known as the silent god, will avenge Odin at Ragnarök
Vali: god of vengeance, avenged his brother Baldr's death
Baldr: son of Odin and Frigg, god of the summer sun and light
Loki: the trickster god
Heimdall: the ever-vigilant guardian of Asgard
Ran: mother of waves, those who die at sea reside in her hall
Vanir: the second tribe of gods
Njörd: god of wealth, fertility and the sea
Frey: god of ecological fertility, wealth and peace, son of Njörd
Freya: goddess of love, fertility

Made in the USA
Monee, IL
29 November 2021

83337018R20199